W9-DAQ-979

SMALL WORLD

SMALL WORLD

JONATHAN EVISON

THORNDIKE PRESS
A part of Gale, a Cengage Company

Thorndike Press® Large Print Historical Fiction.
The text of this Large Print edition is unabridged.
Other aspects of the book may vary from the original edition.
Set in 16 pt. Plantin.

LIBRARY OF CONGRESS CIP DATA ON FILE.
CATALOGUING IN PUBLICATION FOR THIS BOOK
IS AVAILABLE FROM THE LIBRARY OF CONGRESS.

ISBN-13: 978-1-4328-9778-9 (hardcover alk. paper)

Published in 2022 by arrangement with Dutton, an imprint of Penguin Publishing Group, a division of Penguin Random House LLC.

Printed in Mexico
Print Number: 01   Print Year: 2022

*For Lauren: my wife,
and my best friend*

FULL SERVICE REDUCTION

Later, long after the debriefing, after the interviews, and the hearing, and the retirement party that never happened, the events of that late afternoon would come back to Walter in bits and pieces, shards of memory like shattered glass: the hideous screech of the brakes as the train shuddered and lurched, hurtling toward the unavoidable; the sudden and irreversible recognition of impending catastrophe; and finally, the deafening jolt of impact, and the way the whole world turned on end as Walter's consciousness seemed to funnel down a hole in the back of his brain.

How long was he out? He could not say. How long before Macy charged into the cab to roust him?

"Wally! Wally, you okay?"

Afterward, Walter dazedly navigated a world wrapped in gauze: a chaos of colored lights assaulting the darkness like some horrific disco, the squawk of radios punctuating the silence, as the dim but unsettling knowledge of his own negligence settled in. Even in his fog, Walter contemplated the passengers: Flowers, and Tully, and Chen and Murphy, more than just names on a manifest, but faces in the broken mirror of Walter's confusion, people from all over who had bought tickets in good faith, people who had had every expectation of arriving safely at their destination, only to see their lives rent suddenly and irrevocably from normalcy. Walter could not help but wonder what circumstances, what decisions, had delivered them all to that moment.

I
GOLDEN

WALTER BERGEN

Oregon, March 2019

Eight days after his sixty-third birthday, when Walter Bergen arrived at the yard office, where he had arrived so many mornings over the course of thirty-one years, he walked past the vending machines to the bulletin board and paused to read the notes out of habit, as though they had any bearing on his future — they did not. For today was Walter Bergen's last day at Amtrak, a milestone that had been steadily and inevitably approaching for months, and a reality he still could not quite allow himself to accept.

As a senior operator, Walter had been offered relocation before the cutbacks, but he took the buyout instead and decided to pull the pin. He'd been a stranger to his family for three decades, and he figured it was time to start making up for lost time. But what would he do with himself beyond write checks for Wendy's endless wedding arrangements?

His wife, Annie, had no shortage of plans for Walter, and truth be told Walter was none too excited about most of them. She'd been haranguing him for months to join her gym. She'd probably make him take art classes down at the co-op studio, or, God forbid, dance classes. Hell, she'd probably try to make a vegan out of him eventually. And he was 99 percent positive she had some kind of surprise retirement party planned for him that night after work, a possibility he dreaded.

With the clock creeping closer to seven A.M., the reality started to sink in a bit. This was it, the last trip through the office. No more track bulletins. No more wiseass repartee with Nate, or Bill, or Sharon, or Monty, or whoever happened to be on shift. No more tepid coffee, no more faxes, no more bowl of Almond Joys. All of these little rituals and habits that had become the window dressing of his life for the past three decades would be gone tomorrow. Walter still hadn't cleaned out his locker.

It was a point of pride to Walter that no less than four generations of Bergens had given themselves to the rails at some point, beginning with his great-great-grandfather Finnegan, one of those intrepid and criminally underpaid souls who drove spikes halfway across the prairie and blasted through the mountains all the way to Promontory Point for that historic joining of the Union and

Central Pacific lines. On his heels came Walter's grandfather Emmet, fifteen years a brakeman on the O & CRR. Then there was Walter's own father, Pete, first a brakeman, then a hostler, and finally an engineer for BNSF. Walter's love affair with trains had begun before he could even walk. According to his mother, his first utterance, even before "Mama," had been "Too-too."

Walter had stopped holding out hope for Wendy by the time she was out of high school. She had no interest in the railroad or diesel engines, which was sort of ironic, all things considered. Walter had taken Wendy on countless ride-alongs since the time she was a toddler. He'd dressed her in overalls and a striped conductor's cap; bought her wooden trains, electric trains; and, the summer after her junior year in high school, tried to bribe her to do an internship at Amtrak. All of these attempts had been fruitless.

For the Bergens it seemed that the railroad, more than anything else, had delivered on the promise of America. The railroad had meant freedom and opportunity and mobility. And there was no getting around the fact that Walter's retirement spelled the end of the railroad line for the Bergen name.

It had never been Walter's idea to retire at sixty-three. He'd figured he'd be running this line for another five years, at least. Walter loved the railroad life; it was practically all he knew. Of course, the job had its drawbacks. The hours could be brutal and the shifts unpredictable. Then there was the fact that management culture had not changed since the Civil War. Hell, most of his superiors didn't know a train from a horse's ass. But every job had its drawbacks. The satisfaction that came with a job well done, the tangible result of piloting a train safely and smoothly from point A to point B, far outweighed the shortcomings.

"Wally," came a familiar voice.

Walter spun his head around to see Nate, clutching a Garfield coffee mug, cap pulled low over his forehead.

"What are you doing here? I thought you were dead," Nate said, pleased with himself.

"Get out of here," said Walter.

But he couldn't help feeling a little pang of nostalgia watching Nate go. Good old Nate; affable, familiar, consistent as hell. Pretty serious case of halitosis, but Walter had learned over the years how to keep just enough distance between the two of them to avoid breathing it in. It was hard to fathom that he'd smelled Nate's breath for the last time. Walter leaned against a folding table in the rear of the office (for the last time) and checked his forms, sipping his tepid coffee.

No flags, no holdups, no obstacles. A little snow in the forecast, but surely not enough to foul up the schedule. Swilling the last of his coffee, Walter walked out the back door, tossing his paper cup in the garbage pail. Hopping off the platform and crossing the yard, Walter paused to watch the goat clatter slowly up and over the hump. God, the beautiful racket of it all: the sighing and hissing, the rattle and clack of the cars over the rails. These were the sounds that had made America the greatest country on earth. More than any other sound, Walter would miss the deafening but plaintive cry of the horns, which no matter their proximity always managed to sound far away. For this was the very sound that had captured Walter's imagination as a child, the sound of possibility, the sound of faraway places, the sound of American ingenuity.

Walter looked up at the sky just in time for the first wet snowflake to hit his face before he continued on across the yard.

Bill Boyce was waiting in the roundhouse, clipboard in hand.

"Wally," he said. "I heard you died."

"Eat me," said Walter.

They began their walk around, inspecting the running gear back to front, as Bill checked the boxes. There was a little water leakage under the engine, but nothing excessive. Bill had checked the seals and the head gasket as recently as last week and found everything in order.

"So, when's the big wedding?" said Bill.

15

"July," said Walter.

"Bet that's gonna clean you out."

"Pshh. You're not kidding. You have any idea what a caterer costs?" said Walter. "A dance floor? Twenty-five blown-glass votives? Damn flower arrangements?"

"I don't wanna know. Should have had a boy, Wally."

"Don't make much difference anymore," Walter said.

"Suppose not. Riggings look good," said Bill, checking the box.

"Hell, Wendy thinks she's a man, as far as I can tell. I guess I'm okay with that. You just figure she might have some interest in trains, considering."

"What's her partner's name again?"

"Kit."

"Like Kitty?"

"Just Kit."

"What kind of name is that?"

Walter sighed, "I dunno, Bill. There's a lot I don't know anymore."

Bill set a supportive hand on Walter's shoulder and gave him a clap on the back.

"Let's go ahead and check the cab," he said.

Before he mounted the cab, Walter took a deep breath and savored the familiar smell of the yard one more time. It had taken him a few years, but he'd grown to love the smell of diesel. It clung to every stitch of his clothing and even his skin, according to Annie. Wasn't a laundry detergent in the world that could get rid of the smell, but it meant a paycheck. And it meant a lot more: It meant speed, and power, and passenger satisfaction. It was a noble fuel, diesel; it burned slowly and efficiently.

"She still getting shaky at seventy-nine?" said Bill.

"Little bit," Walter said. "Not so bad as she used to. About threw me out of my seat a couple years back."

"How about acceleration?"

"Full of oats."

Bill paused in his box checking to scratch his neck and peer out the cab window as the snow began falling harder, splatting in fat drops against the windshield.

"So, what are you gonna do with yourself, Wally? You gonna start doing crosswords? Model trains?"

"Thinking about a second career," said Walter.

"Porno, huh?"

"Haven't got the necessary equipment, I'm afraid. Always did want to play center field for the Mariners, though."

"I'd say you're strictly DH material with that gut," said Bill.

"Look who's talking," said Walter.

After Bill checked the last box, he gave Walter another pat on the shoulder that nearly morphed into an awkward hug but came up

17

mercifully short.

"Well," said Bill.

"Get out of here," said Walter.

Once Bill was clear of the ladder, Walter turned on the wipers and began activating the switchboard with robotic precision. He ducked down the corridor to the engine room and primed the engine, then, returning to the cab, he set the brakes. He could have done it all in his sleep.

Wishing he had another cup of coffee, Walter walked the length of the corridor past the passengers, nodding to the occasional soul who looked up to engage him. Once he released the hand brake, he walked past them again in the other direction. If Walter did his job right, some of those folks would be napping by the time he delivered them. That was the real sign of a good engineer: sleeping passengers.

Once the train was prepped and ready to roll, Monty assigned Walter a clear track, and Walter eased the throttle forward a notch and began crawling out of the yard, right on schedule.

THE BERGENS

Atlantic Ocean, 1851

Alma and the twins huddled atop their tiny pallet in the darkness, all that was left of the Bergens of Cork. Their throats scorched, they cloaked their faces against the fetid air. It was the only way. Stomach clenched, head throbbing, blood running thick as sap, Alma was slow to apprehend her thoughts. But two words saved her, two words she kept upon her ravaged lips, two words that buoyed her against starvation and infirmity, and fear for her children's lives, two words she clung to amid the relentless chorus of crying infants and moaning women, as the chamber pots sloshed and the great hull creaked and tossed on the open sea. They were the same two words emblazoned upon the stern of that cruel maritime enterprise tasked with delivering the Bergens like flotsam upon the distant shore. They were a prayer for the future, these two words: Golden Door.

The New World; not like the Old World.

Not like the windowless, thatch-hoveled, mud-hutted torment they'd left behind in the festering, fallow remains of Magh Eala, Cork, no longer the rebel county, no longer sacred soil, but a diseased and forsaken shell of itself. The New World was a world of promise, a world of opportunity, a world where with any luck the Bergens, and the Callahans, and the Cullens would not starve. And for this promise Alma had left her dead behind: a husband who'd given all he had, and a child who'd never had a chance.

Even as her ragged breaths sawed at the putrid air, Alma was determined to thwart death. She would surrender no more. She would not allow Finnegan to give up.

"Why won't he eat?" she said to Nora in the darkness.

"He doesn't like the biscuits," said Nora.

"And how would you know? Did he say as much?"

"No, Mummy."

"Of course he didn't," said Alma.

The boy had not spoken since the baby had died last fall, just two weeks after his father had succumbed to the fever. The appearance of a single magpie that morning on the eave of the hut had portended the death of the baby. It was Finn who'd discovered the infant in her crib, eyes glassed over, mouth agape, tiny fists clutched to her chest. Her name had been Aileen, and she was neither the first nor the last to perish from starvation. But Aileen had been a Bergen, and she'd been a blue-eyed ray of hope, and her big brother had adored her. That God should take his father was bewilderment enough for the nine-year-old boy. That he should take his infant sister was apparently too much for him to bear. That was the day he retreated into himself. Strike his thumb with a hammer, and he would not cry out in pain. No matter how his mother had tried to coax him out as the weeks and the months progressed, he remained unreachable.

Were it not for his twin sister, Finn might have disappeared altogether. For it was Nora who spoke for Finn, and only Nora who seemed to understand his needs or comprehend his grief. Only Nora could read his thoughts. That they could be so intimately connected by thought and by birth, and yet look nothing alike, was difficult for Alma to comprehend. Nora was brown eyed, with her father's dark hair and features, his broad nose and thin lips. Finn, meanwhile, was fair and redheaded, with high cheekbones, full lips, and blue eyes.

"Child, nobody likes the biscuits," said Alma. "But he must eat them."

To label them biscuits at all was a misnomer. They were practically inedible, with their charred black crust and gooey middle. Their only flavor was that of smoke, pure and unadulterated. All the water in the world could not wash them down comfortably, though six pints was their daily ration between them.

But the Bergens were stuck with biscuits, for they had nothing more to cook, neither pork, nor mutton, nor so much as a mush of oats. When they were permitted to escape steerage for the open air of the deck, upon those rare occasions when fair weather allowed for it, it was not to prepare food, but only to draw a breath of fresh air. Stretching their limbs, they watched as the others bickered and squabbled around the cooking grates.

The last of the pigs had been slaughtered days ago. With a pang of bottomless longing, Alma had smelled the fatty meat as it was seared upon the grates, though the bounty did not stretch as far as steerage, but was consumed in the relative comfort of cabins by those who could afford such luxuries. Those down below, if they had any oats left, were not apt to distribute them freely. And possessing but a few sovereigns reserved for their transportation to Chicago, which Alma had sewn into the lining of Nora's skirt, the Bergens had little to bargain with.

"Make him eat," she said to Nora.

"Mummy, he won't do it."

"Nora!" she said.

"But, Mummy, I can't get him to. I've tried."

"You must."

And as Nora began to reason gently with her brother, Alma's eyes began to cloud, and she soon felt the sting of tears running down her cheeks beneath her dirty veil.

That afternoon Finn did not eat. Passengers were confined like human ballast to the dark stench of the hold all day, where frequent retching from all corners joined the chorus of moaning. As the vessel was tossed upon the turbulent sea, passengers were heaved and flung about below. Children were thrown from their berths. Pots were upended. Steerage was soon awash in human waste, and yet, somehow the unmistakable odor of vomit still managed to penetrate the noxious air.

It was night by the time the seas calmed. Now that the infants were mostly sleeping, and the retching had subsided, the chorus of woe seemed to play out in a slower, less urgent measure. Still, the air was only slightly less stultifying as Alma looked down at the sleeping twins, their shadowy forms entwined on the tiny berth. Their love for each other was fierce. Where biscuits and water and sunlight failed them, love would see them through to the New World. It had to.

And what would they find on the other side of the Golden Door? What did America have to offer the likes of the Bergens, conquered lo these eight centuries, penniless and un-skilled? What awaited them in America but more soil, soil that would only forsake them eventually? What awaited them but more bosses and middlemen and Protestant gentry? And what would sustain them in the absence of familiarity?

Coughing into her veil, Alma checked it for blood.

Covering the twins in a blanket not fit for a horse, Alma stole into the cramped darkness, her heart hammering in her chest. Once again desperate measures were required. For five years, Alma's life had been little more than a series of desperate measures, a sequence of sacrifices and humiliations. And so far, she'd always answered the call.

The ruffian was not hard to find, even in the dark. When Alma drew close enough to him in his cramped corner of the hold, his stinking breath was unmistakable.

"And what if I don't feel like bargaining this eve?" he said, clenching Alma's forearm.

"Then, I will go."

"Let's say I've got a small bag of oats," he said.

"I'll bet you have," she said, straining against his grip.

He forced a gruff kiss upon her lips. And so it began.

When it was over, and the ruffian grunted one final time, his weight pressing down on

24

her, Alma coughed in his face before he could turn away.

"Gah," he said, wiping the blood from his face.

Blindly he rose, swiping at his eyes as Alma gathered her skirt and her small bag of oats and scrambled to her feet.

In the morning the weather broke, and those in steerage were allowed on deck in shifts of twenty-five and thirty. The wind was wet and frigid, and still the boat rocked, and Alma's stomach rolled.

After much jostling for position at the grates, including a near skirmish with a child-less woman from Wexford, Alma proceeded to prepare a mush of oats and water, dressed with a precious dash of salt.

Much to everyone's relief, Finn inhaled the mush with such vigor that both Nora and Alma saved better than half of their portions for the boy so that he might eat them later.

"He goes after it like a hog," said Alma.

"It's disgusting," said Nora.

"Perhaps we should slow him down," said Alma. "He's likely to get sick."

"I'm likely to get sick watching him," said Nora.

In a week, if they could hold on, they would reach New York, and with the help of the Callahans, distant cousins of Cork, if all went as planned, they would charter transportation to the great state of Illinois. Whatever awaited them in Chicago, it was sure to be grander than a mud hut. For it was said that beyond the Golden Door, anything was possible. This was the promise of America.

Never in her twenty-nine years had Alma witnessed such a dizzying and disconcerting array of human endeavor as she did walking through the Bowery for the first time upon that chill afternoon in February of 1851, just hours released from five weeks in the insufferable prison of steerage.

Shouldering their humble burdens, Finn and Nora flanked their mother so close that Alma could feel their wonder and anxiety radiating from them. Wide-eyed, they trudged past tailors and grocers, cigar makers and alcohol dealers. For blocks on end they wandered, parched and bewildered, over streets of brick and cobblestone, narrow boulevards choked with horse carts and barrows loaded with all manner of staples, wares, and refuse. The noise of the street was cacophonous, the smells too various to catalog or even ponder. Stately structures of stone and brick, peaked and corniced and flagged, their sheer façades punctuated with awnings, were situated alongside humble row houses. They passed two great brick edifices with glassed windows, both of them taller than any poplar, squatting so close together that they were almost touching. And yet, squeezed between them, as though in the grip of a vise, huddled a little wooden shanty crossed with clotheslines strewn with rags. New York had the unmistakable look of a place that was growing too fast.

And yet, here they came — Germans, and Irish, and Italians, and nationalities Alma could not guess at — like lemmings to the shores of America: the poor, the tired, the homeless wayward masses. Within a mile the Bergens had encountered countless people, and of every conceivable variety, stature, and dress, speaking in tongues hitherto unimagined. Who knew that such variety even existed? No two people were the same. The only thing they all seemed to share in common was that they were all apparently in a hurry. And though Alma shared their urgency, she was too exhausted to hurry her pace.

Further on, the weary Bergens found their spirits uplifted, if only briefly, as they passed a stone cathedral grander than any they'd ever laid eyes on. Graceful in its sprawl, its spire reached halfway to the clouds. The lay of the great city was like nothing Alma had ever imagined. Street after street, it seemed to go on forever. And surely the Bergens could not last forever. They had to locate the Irish settlement at Five Points. They had to find these alleged Callahans to light their way on the next leg of their American journey. For the Callahans were expecting them, or so

Alma had been led to believe.

As hard as Alma tried to temper her expectations for life behind the Golden Door, nothing prepared her for the conditions that greeted her in Five Points, which comprised a bowl-like depression in the east side of Lower Manhattan, like a swamp that had been drained. There were no stately structures nor brick streets east of here, nothing so uplifting as a towering cathedral. No, there were domiciles no more decorous than sheds, windows broken and patched, beams rotting, and stairways caving. No two bore any resemblance beyond the haste with which they were constructed.

There was mud and sewage coursing down narrow streets, packed with the filth of unwashed humanity. And not just humanity, but pigs, and chickens, and mongrel dogs, all running loose and underfoot. The stench of the place was nearly as stultifying as the ship's hold, and the Bergens found themselves covering their noses out of habit.

"Mummy, it's ghastly," said Nora.

To which Alma did not reply, for she hadn't the wherewithal to defend the place.

As if in direct response, Finn paused in that instant to double over and retch in the middle of the street.

"He doesn't like the smell, Mummy."

"You should think he'd be used to it by now," she said.

Alma was close to retching herself, and not only from the smell, but from the unique dispiritedness of one who has run from a terrible situation only to arrive in one that is potentially worse.

"C'mon, boy," said Alma.

Finn straightened himself up, wiped his mouth upon his coat sleeve, and trudged onward through the swamp of mud and sewage.

God, but why had Alma listened? Why had she chosen to believe? Already it was clear that the Bergens were as likely to starve in America as anywhere else. Surely Five Points ran rampant with the same fever that plagued Ireland. They should never have undertaken this terrible voyage. Better to die at home, among the rest of the dying.

"At least they're Irish, Mummy," said Nora.

Indeed, that they were among the Irish was the only thing in which Alma could take comfort. Filthy and depraved as the denizens of Five Points might have appeared, they were Irish, and they were mostly Catholic, and they were familiar.

When they reached Orange Street, they veered left as they had been instructed so many months ago. Orange Street, alas, had nothing more to offer than the other streets: mud, and filth, and wooden shacks. But upon one of these dwellings they would surely locate a shingle with the name Callahan, and their prospects would improve immediately.

And yet, dwelling after dwelling, they did not come upon such a shingle.

Late in the afternoon, a desperate Alma began to make inquiries.

Callahan, eh? None I can think of hereabouts. Was a CallaHAM in the summer, I recollect. But he's gone to Albany. County Cork? Well, there's the O'Briens. And the Kellys. Swing a cat, and you're likely to hit a Murphy on Orange Street. But not any Callahans that I know of.

Shortly before dusk, hopeless and exhausted, Alma sat down upon an upturned cart and began to weep inconsolably into her hands.

"It's okay, Mummy," said Nora.

An instant later, Alma felt a gentle hand upon her shoulder.

"Are you okay, miss?"

Turning to greet the voice, Alma was confronted by a dark-haired woman, roughly her own age, with a familiar lilt to her speech.

"Are you from Cork?" said Alma hopefully.

"No, Waterford," said the woman. "Are you in need of help?"

Alma wiped the tears from her face and straightened the lap of her skirt.

"I suppose I am," she said. "We have only what we carry in these bags. We're searching for cousins by the name of Callahan. Perhaps you know of them?"

"Alas, I don't. But you and yours are welcome tonight under my roof. This is not a place to be outdoors at night."

"God bless you," said Alma.

Of all the names in the world, even just the Irish names — from Aibreann to Ina to Siobhan, from Deirdre to Fiona to Sian — the dark-haired woman whose kindness saved them was called Aileen, the very same as Alma's deceased daughter.

Aileen led them to a dwelling as dark and dreary as any mud hut back home. It comprised but a single room, furnished with one bed, currently occupied by an indistinct figure.

"Aileen? Is that you?"

"Aye, Father," she said. "I've brought some friends from Cork."

"Oh?" he said without shifting in his bed. "What friends have we from Cork? Who's that?"

"I've only just met them, Father," she said. "They're just off the boat, and nowhere to go. A mother and twins."

"Twins?" said the old man.

"Yes, Father."

"Bring them here," he said.

"They're not identical, Father."

"Oh?" said the old man.

Alma motioned to the twins, who approached the old man's bedside and presented their faces. The old man groped blindly at Nora's face, running his open hand over her forehead, then her nose, then down her cheeks to her chin, where he brought his thumb and fingertips to a point.

"Now the other," he said.

Leaning in, Finn closed his eyes against the old man's groping fingers as they ran over his forehead, around his nose, down his cheeks to his chin, where they made their point.

"Fascinating," he said. "What are your names?"

"I'm Nora," said Nora.

"And you?"

"He's Finn."

"Is that right, Finn?" said the old man.

"He is Finn, sir," confirmed Alma.

"Why doesn't he say it himself?" said the old man.

"He doesn't speak, sir," said Nora.

"Ah," said the old man. "An idiot, my apologies. Blessed in the eyes of God, no doubt."

"Not an idiot, sir," said Alma. "He is capable of speaking, he's done it before. It's just that, well, he has chosen not to speak."

"Has he?" said the old man. "And you're certain he's Irish? Who knew such a thing was possible? And he's not slow, you say?"

"Far from it," said Nora. "He notices things before I do."

"Fascinating," said the old man. "An Irishman who sees things and doesn't speak his mind."

Alma breathed a deep sigh of relief at the old man's playfulness.

For dinner they ate potatoes, an irony that was lost on no one, boiled over an open fire in the alley and consumed greedily in the candlelight of the little room.

The old man, though sightless, was nonetheless garrulous and seemed to enjoy the company.

When the twins finally fell asleep on the floor, Alma and Aileen sat in the darkness of the cold room and commiserated like old friends.

"You must be an angel to find me," said Alma.

"Just a girl from Waterford who once found herself crying on a street corner like you."

The shabby room seemed to grow warmer with each intimacy. Alma's persistent cough abated, if only temporarily. Against her better judgment, she allowed herself to believe that maybe the Golden Door was not a mirage. And Aileen was there to indulge this hope.

"Once you get away from the filth of the city, once you get out in the open country, it's beautiful," Aileen explained. "It's not like this in the West."

"No," said the old man, surprising them with his wakeful state. "In the West everybody gets to starve on their own terms."

"Oh, Father, stop."

"You've been west?" said Alma.

"No, she hasn't," said the old man. "Nor have I. But I know already that this New World is no better than the world we left behind."

"Oh, stop being so gloomy, Father," she said. "Not everybody is blind and lame."

"You're right, of course. I'm a dreary old man. What do I know of the West? I suppose I just long for the familiar."

"Well, here you have it," said Aileen.

"Aye, you've got me again," he said.

At some point, the fabric of their voices covered Alma like a blanket, and she succumbed to sleep, heavily and gratefully.

In the morning Aileen pulled back the burlap window shade, and a slant of sunlight flooded the room. Cold and achy, the Bergens and the Murphys stirred from their cramped resting places and shared a half loaf of bread, not too terribly stale, with a smear of chicken fat. The old man, shaking off his gloominess altogether, entertained the twins throughout the morning with a humor that managed to inspire mirth even in Finn, though the boy was never moved so far as speech.

"The Bergens will do fine out west," said the old man. "Assuming you have the money to get there," he said.

"Perhaps not," she said, casting her eyes

down. "But my aim is to come by it in the near future."

"Until such time, you are welcome to room with the Murphys," said the old man. "That is, if you can stand us."

"God bless you," said Alma.

And so, for nearly a fortnight the Bergens depended on the kindness of Aileen Murphy and her father. By day, Alma left the twins in the care of the old man as she scoured Manhattan for prospects, awaking early each day and not returning until dusk. Aileen, meanwhile, went to work six days a week in a garment factory on the West Side.

As spring approached, Alma had only managed to come by income sporadically, and she began to feel as though she was abusing the kindness of the Murphys. Her determination to announce their departure before they wore out their welcome was only reinforced by the return of her persistent cough. Soon her handkerchief was spotted with blood, and a weakness gradually took hold of her. For days she managed to put a hopeful face on her suffering, but soon it was beginning to show.

"Mummy, you're pale," said Nora.

"I'm fine," she said.

But nobody was convinced.

Alma would never know Aileen's motivations for certain, whether she was trying to cast out Alma's illness or trying to save their lives, but one night in the spring, as they squatted over a supper of scorched potatoes and wilted cabbage, Aileen made an announcement.

"I've made some inquiries, and I believe I've found a route to Chicago that is the most economical, if not the most timely."

"Does this mean you're coming with us?" said Alma.

"I'm afraid not," said Aileen. "But I'm going to help you get there."

"How?"

"By providing you the funds you lack," she said. "I've managed to stash a little away."

"Oh, Aileen, I could never —"

"You could," she said. "And you will. Just hear me out."

"But, Aileen, I simply —"

"Let her talk," said the old man.

"Alma, darling," she said. "My father is blind, he's infirm, he can barely walk. He'll never make it out of Five Points, let alone New York. Isn't that right, Father?"

"Why would I bother?" said the old man. "I can starve right here."

"But what about you?" said Alma.

"Darling, I could never leave him. He's all I've got."

"She's right, you know," said the old man. "I may not look like much, but it's true."

"I've got my job," said Aileen. "I've got my friends. We don't need much to get by."

"What about when . . . ?"

"Please!" said the old man.

"He's right. Don't be fooled," said Aileen. "He's hearty as an ox."

"Don't doubt for an instant that I'll outlive her," he said.

"It's likely true," said Aileen.

"She's stuck with me," said the old man. "And I'll no sooner go west than I'll fly in a hot-air balloon. So take the money."

"Take it," said Aileen. "Please."

And thus it was owing to the kindness of the Murphys, veritable strangers in a strange land, that the Bergens were granted the means by which to make their passage west to Chicago.

BRIANNA FLOWERS

Portland, Oregon, 2019

Expect the worst, because like as not, that's what's coming. This had been the Flowers family mantra when Brianna was growing up in Albina with her two sisters in a crowded one-room apartment not a quarter mile from her and Malik's current apartment. Adulthood had done little to dissuade Brianna from this truth. Thus it was no big surprise that the numbers didn't add up, no matter how many times she did the math.

Sitting at the little table in the kitchen, she figured the numbers one more time, knowing in advance her calculations were futile. After rent, utilities, the phones, the car insurance, the groceries, the credit card minimums, not to mention Malik's new ninety-dollar sneakers, there wasn't nearly enough money left to swing the hoops invitational in Seattle, not with the hotel, and the train tickets, and their meals. There wasn't even a hundred dollars left after all that accounting.

Brianna couldn't bring herself to ask Coach McCarthy for any more help, though she knew Coach M would walk to the ends of the earth for Malik — so long as he didn't transfer programs. Of course, Coach McCarthy's concerns were not unfounded. Jefferson and Grant high schools, and even Lake Oswego, had already courted Malik as early as freshman year, and again before sophomore year, dangling incentives that included superior athletic programs, better resources, a bigger stage, and the promise of a better recruiting status. Not to mention numerous allusions to other benefits in an "unofficial capacity."

But Malik wasn't going anywhere. His loyalty was to Coach McCarthy and Benjamin Franklin High. If nothing else, Brianna had taught Malik the value of loyalty. Since the day he was born, Brianna had given Malik the benefit of every single thing she had ever earned, learned, or experienced, and when that wasn't enough, she went out and secured him better resources, whether or not she could afford them: math tutors, career counselors, basketball camps. Everything Brianna did, she did for Malik, so that he might enjoy better opportunities in life than she had. The good Lord seemed to have had the same idea as Brianna when he made Malik a giant.

By freshman year, Malik had been pushing

six foot five. He started varsity, averaging fifteen points per game and eight rebounds. Brianna had to take a second job at Burgerville just to feed him. Now, following the end of a junior season that had seen Malik average a triple-double (23.5 points per game, 16 rebounds, 11 assists) for the Quakers, earning first-team all-state honors and second-team All-American, he was six foot nine and not finished growing, according to the doctors. Brianna did her best to keep the recruiters at bay, while the grocery bill was barely sustainable.

If Brianna had observed one thing in her thirty-three years, it was that getting ahead in this culture was all about having resources. In spite of Brianna's giving Malik the benefit of everything she had, Malik's greatest resources were beyond Brianna's sphere of influence: his God-given size and athleticism. It was up to Brianna and Malik to see that these gifts were not wasted, that these resources were leveraged most effectively, so that Malik didn't wind up selling appliances for a living. That meant discipline and commitment. It meant eating right and conditioning. It meant not having the most glamorous social life.

It wasn't enough to skate by on size and athleticism. A body couldn't depend solely on one's gifts. A body had to work harder than anybody else. Because America was a rigged competition. Because the playing field wasn't level and never had been, at least not for the Flowerses, not since her forebearers had dared to free themselves from bondage 170 years ago. And so, a body had to sacrifice certain comforts, squelch certain temptations, eschew certain pleasures in the name of gaining an edge, because that was the only advantage you could ever have over the guy who'd started on third base.

Thus Brianna insisted, in spite of the promises of recruiters, and the fanfare, and the eye-popping statistics, that Malik hold himself to a high standard academically, that he keep his nose clean, that he limit his gaming time, that he read outside of his school studies for his own betterment, and, finally, that he attend services at Mount Zion Baptist at least two Sundays a month. You couldn't count on anything in this life when you had no safety net. Gifted as he was, Malik was one injury away from square one, back to being disadvantaged, where he'd started. Malik couldn't afford to make the same mistakes some of the kids in this neighborhood made — drugs, gangs, the trap of premarital sex. There wasn't any get-out-of-jail-free card for Malik.

If Malik's gifts somehow forsook him and he couldn't get a free ride, he was going to need an academic scholarship. And even if the full ride to a Division I school that the

41

recruiters, and journalists, and even Coach McCarthy, treated as the inevitable conclusion came to pass, what then? Malik sure as hell wasn't gonna major in basketball. What if he got injured? What if he didn't thrive in the program? A college education was more important than hoops, though it wasn't always easy to convince Malik of as much. How might Brianna have improved her own prospects if she'd ever managed to get a college degree? She'd probably have six hundred bucks somewhere to take Malik to Seattle. Whatever the basketball yielded, Malik needed to go to a university and learn. Just in case he wasn't the second coming of LeBron James.

For all her preparedness and contingency plans, deep down Brianna was optimistic about Malik's future. Most game nights, as Brianna watched anxiously from the bleachers, number twenty-three looked like a man among boys. His dominance was not just a product of his size; it was an awareness of the game around him, an ability to anticipate, a facility for improvising. He was bigger, stronger, faster, and more agile than anyone else on the court. It was beautiful to behold. And playing the game, it gave him a pure focus, because there was nothing in the world but eighty-four feet of hardwood and a hoop on either end. His focus was singular on the basketball court. There was only the moment, and nothing — not the crowd, not the score, not a turned ankle — could distract him from the moment. Beneath the intensity, the disappointment, the frustration, the triumph, there was the pure joy. And nothing gave Brianna more satisfaction than her son's joy. She would continue to provide him every opportunity within reason to be joyful.

Thus the invitational in Seattle was a must. This left Brianna with two options: Take a six-hundred-dollar loan from Moneytree, which amounted to half her paycheck and would cost her an additional hundred and eight dollars on payday, or ask Don LoPriori for an advance, like she had before last Christmas, a prospect so loathsome that it made Brianna's skin crawl. It would be foolish to pay the interest at Moneytree. A hundred and eight dollars bought a lot of breakfast cereal, milk, pasta, potatoes, and Gatorade. There was no getting around it; Monday morning Brianna would have to ask Don for an advance.

Malik ducked into the kitchen in his boxer shorts, opened the fridge, and started drinking milk straight from the carton.

"Malik Flowers, use a glass," Brianna said.

He wiped his mouth with a bare forearm and smiled. His father's smile, which was alternately a source of gratitude and chagrin to Brianna. Darnell Woods was a good-for-nothing deadbeat, then and now, but he had a beautiful smile.

"Sorry, Ma," said Malik in his new deep voice Brianna swore she'd never get used to.

"You not gonna get ahead in this world with those kind of manners, young man. You go around acting slovenly like that, folks, they're gonna make assumptions about you, and they're not gonna be good ones."

"What's with all the numbers?" he said.

"Doing our finances."

"And?"

"And what do you think? We're still not rich," she said. "But we're gonna make it."

"Always do," he said.

For the remainder of the weekend, Brianna agonized over asking Don for an advance. She shouldn't have felt that way after all the years she'd given to Consolidated Appliances, but Don LoPriori held his money close, at least until he went to the horse track.

Monday morning, Brianna found Don hiding back in his cluttered office, which hadn't changed much in the twelve years Brianna had worked at Consolidated. His desk was awash in paperwork, as always: invoices, shipping forms, catalogs, promotional pamphlets. The family portrait, years outdated, featuring Don with hair, his wife before she put on thirty pounds, and his two boys, then about four and six, sat at the edge of the desk skewed sideways like an afterthought.

"What is it I can do for you, Brianna?"

Brianna explained her situation. She stressed what a great opportunity the invitational in Seattle would be for Malik, how there would be college and even pro scouts sniffing around.

"Don, I need to buy train tickets and book a hotel," she concluded.

"I see," said Don noncommittally. "Can't you just put that on a credit card?"

"My cards are maxed out."

"Did you talk to the boy's father?"

"I think you know the answer to that, Don. Not in eight years, I haven't."

Don rolled back in his chair and swung his legs up onto the desk. He almost seemed to be enjoying this.

"Well now, Brianna, the thing is, you know I don't handle payroll. The accountant takes care of that, and there's all the withholdings and whatnot to consider. So really, there are no advances. It just doesn't work that way."

"But, Don, last December you —"

"Are you asking for a loan, Brianna, is that it?"

Don leveled a meaningful gaze at her and left her to fill the silence. Twelve years of service to the man's business, and this was the level of respect he gave her. He was going to make her squirm.

"If this is a loan we're talking about, as a policy, Brianna, Consolidated isn't in the business of giving loans. We're not a bank.

45

We sell appliances. You know that."

Brianna was seething, but she didn't show it. She was afraid to look Don in the eye for fear he would see the hatred written there, sinking any chance of getting the money.

"Unless," said Don, clasping his hands behind his head and leaning back still further in his chair, "you want to make this personal."

"Excuse me?" said Brianna.

Don smiled.

Brianna looked straight at the family portrait, and Don's smile wilted a little as he leaned forward and set the portrait facedown on the desk, then stretched back out again, as though relaxing on a chaise lounge by a pool somewhere.

"Do you want to make this personal, Brianna?" he said. "We might be able to work something out in the way of a loan. Why don't we grab dinner tonight, maybe a drink?"

It took every ounce of self-control Brianna could muster not to spit in his face.

"Mr. LoPriori, I've been working at Consolidated for twelve years, did you know that?"

"Has it really been that many?"

"Yes. Yes, it has been," said Brianna emphatically. "And during that time, I've done everything you ever asked of me. I've worked weekends, I've worked late, I've worked for free, I've taken the heat from disgruntled customers, so you wouldn't have to. I've run errands for you. I've entertained your boys. For you to talk to me like this, there's a name for it: It's called harassment."

Don immediately swung his legs off the desk and sat upright.

"Now, just slow down a minute, here, Brianna, I —"

"That's exactly what it is, you suggesting we work out some kind of 'personal' arrangement, looking at me like that, inviting me to come have a drink with you. Supposing we had any kind of HR around here, wonder what they'd think of that, you making veiled propositions, turning your wife's picture facedown. Wonder how Tina would feel about that?"

Don's face darkened, and Brianna thought she saw his eyelid twitch. He looked Brianna right in the eye, long and hard.

"Are you trying to blackmail me, here?"

The thought had not occurred to Brianna until he said it, but it wasn't a thought she let herself entertain for more than a few seconds.

"I don't want your damn money, Don," she said. "Fact, I don't even want this damn job anymore."

Brianna turned on her heel, stormed out of the office, and slammed the door on her way out. She strode across the showroom, snatched her jacket and her purse from the customer service station, and marched out the double glass doors. By the time she was halfway to the Camry, she was ready to break down. But she couldn't even afford to do that.

OTHELLO

Illinois, 1851

The Southern Gentleman was the name of the carriage that conveyed Worthy Warnock and his servant Othello from Lexington, Kentucky, toward the great city of Chicago, where Warnock was scheduled to attend to a certain commercial railroad enterprise with a man named Abraham Seymour. The Southern Gentleman was a handsome coach with its red velvet interior and its sleek teakwood trimmings, its lavish gold lace curtains, and its gilded hardware.

It being their fourth morning of travel, Othello, having slept three nights in three different stables, was stiffer than a man his age had any right to be. They were somewhere around the Illinois state line when Othello kneeled and began the indignity of taping Master Worthy's toes. As a rule, business travel tended to arouse Master Worthy's garrulous temper.

"And so they move westward in droves,

Othello," Master Worthy observed.

"Mm," said Othello, splaying his master's toes.

"And what do you suppose awaits them there, Othello?" said Master Worthy.

Understanding this to be a rhetorical question, Othello tendered no reply.

"Opportunity, that's what awaits them there," said Worthy Warnock. "Opportunities never before encountered."

As Othello liberated the second toe from its moist wrap, careful not to breathe in the offending odor, Master Worthy inhaled deeply and held the breath in as though savoring the rarefied stuffiness of the coach.

"On a larger scale, the opportunities of the common men are my opportunities. For it is my intention to profit from this westward expansion."

If only Worthy Warnock would shut his mouth long enough that Othello might be alone with his own thoughts, instead of having to play his part in this relentless charade. Compared to being in close quarters with Warnock, Othello welcomed the task of hauling luggage or freeing a mired wagon wheel from the mud. Even the task of ministering to the man's odious feet was preferable to the sound of his voice.

"If I am to capitalize on this westward exodus, I must see that these common men, who wish to make their fortunes mucking about in the west, have a reasonable means to transport themselves there. And that, Othello, is the railroad."

Mercifully, after another twenty minutes of unbroken monologue, Master Worthy fell asleep in midsentence, his mouth open, and Othello reclined opposite, rubbing his aching knees, as he looked upon his master. Look at him, the idiot. That God ever created anyone so clueless and inept and granted him freedom was a wonder. Were Worthy Warnock superior to Othello in any single way, it might have been easier for Othello to resolve himself to a life of subservience. But the self-proclaimed "Southern gentleman" was not Othello's better in any way; the man was needy, and vain, and largely ineffectual. He was petty and unforgiving, and wholly oblivious to both his own good fortune and his arbitrary good standing in a world that inexplicably favored weakness. All this talk of American opportunity and mobility, these flimsy ideals of controlling one's destiny and blazing one's path to good fortune, were less than mirages to a man of Othello's standing. That he possessed the grit, and fortitude, and skill to make his way in America seemed a cruel state of affairs given his situation.

As the Southern Gentleman trundled along under a low sky, an idea took root in Othello's mind. What if he should run away in Chicago?

51

The opportunity was almost certain to present itself. But supposing he made a break, how would he proceed? He knew not a soul outside of Lexington. He had no means, no place to seek shelter from the elements. He had not so much as a winter coat. And though his skills were many and his acumen considerable, where could he turn for opportunity in the metropolis of Chicago? And supposing he did land on his feet, what would he do with his newfound freedom? To which trade, if given a choice, would he apply himself? Certainly not butler — he'd rather butcher hogs than continue to serve other men. Stableman, carpenter, wheelwright? Othello was proficient in all of these tasks and more. He could cook, he could sew, he could milk a cow. He could prune a rose, or dress a chicken, or fix a water pump. And wasn't that the bitter irony of his enslavement, that he was so self-sufficient, so capable, and yet freedom and the pursuit of happiness were forever held beyond his reach?

To hear Master Worthy tell it, the teeming metropolis of Chicago was soon to be the commercial and industrial center of the West, a transportation hub, a bustling crossroad between the Mississippi and the great western frontier. But on the surface, the city was not quite so grand as Othello had come to expect. Situated on the banks of the great gray lake, and straddling the river, the town appeared to be sinking into the mud. As they slogged through the muddy corridors, the carriage shimmying side to side, lurching forward and back, past the bustling wharf, past wooden warehouses four and five stories high, past squat two-story brick buildings and grubby storefronts, past sprawling mansions side by side with clapboard hovels, past stalled wagons and upturned drays mired in the mud, past taverns and grocery stalls heaping with mud-spattered merchandise, Othello watched the streets pass, the name of each forming silently on his lips: Lake Street, Water Street, and Wabash Avenue.

At last, the carriage lurched to an unceremonious halt in front of the Tremont House early in the afternoon. The grandeur and conceit of the edifice, projected in its wide portico, gabled roof, and frilly window dressings, was no match for the sludge. Elegance was impossible in such environs. As always, Othello was the first one to duck out of the carriage and step into the muddy street, just in time to watch the horse relieve himself not four feet in front of him.

Boots mired in the mushy street, Othello held out the customary arm to assist Master Worthy down the single step.

"Tend to the trunks," he said, as though Othello required such instruction.

After three trips up and down the stairs, back and forth through the soup of sinking earth, Othello completed the task of unpacking the carriage. No sooner had Othello offloaded the luggage than Master Worthy emerged once more from the lobby to meet him on the steps.

"I have a mind to stretch my legs," he said. "Let us take in a slice of this fair city."

The street was an open cesspool. But Master Worthy was undaunted by the conditions. He walked with his chin up as Othello trailed in his wake, holding his coattail aloft. The only relief from the bog comprising the boulevard was the brick crosswalk at the corner, where currently a pair of waifs, a boy and a girl from the looks of it (though admittedly it was difficult to tell), both dirty faced and badly in need of haircuts, were sweeping the brick path clear of mud, no doubt anticipating a handout. Knowing his master to be tightfisted, Othello held out little hope for the waifs.

"You there," Master Worthy said to the boy, pausing in his crossing. "What's your name?"

The boy stared out from beneath his greasy mop of ginger hair but said nothing.

"Shy, are we?" said Master Worthy. "And you've got the devil's red hair, though from the looks of it not much else. Well, at least you're an industrious lad. I'll tell you what, son: I shall give you a half dime if you can manage to overcome your shyness long enough to tell me your name. Go on, then."

But the boy just kept staring at Master Worthy impassively, without uttering a word.

"Well, out with it then," said Master Worthy, dangling the coin.

Hereupon, the boy cast his eyes down and resumed his sweeping.

"Me brother don't speak," interceded the girl.

"Oh?" said Master Worthy. "And why is that?"

"He just don't," she explained. "His name is Finn."

"And what is this accent you speak with?" said Master Worthy. "Surely not German?"

"Irish, sir."

"Ah," said Master Worthy with a slight distaste. "And what would be your name?"

"Nora, sir."

"Hmmph," said Master Worthy.

"Sir," said the girl, "by chance could you spare . . . ?"

But Master Worthy had already pocketed the half dime and resumed his progress over the brick walk, Othello in his wake tending the train of his coattail.

Looking back over his shoulder, Othello flashed the girl a sympathetic look, and she cast her eyes down at the muddy brick. What was to stop Othello from dropping his master's coattail then and there and making a run for it? Surely, Master Worthy would never find him in a place this size. The thought of it set Othello's chest to buzzing like a hornet's nest. Perhaps tonight, under cover of darkness, he would summon the nerve to make his break.

Master Worthy's business dinner was a grand affair at the home of Mr. Abraham Seymour, a man Master Worthy described as being of "means and substance," who lived on the lakefront in a sprawling manor that seemed at once outsized and tiny in comparison to the lake. Apparently Master Worthy was not the only one in love with his own voice, for all of the fine gentlemen assembled there, seven in all, were fluent in the art of allocution, professing, and proclaiming, and exhorting one another at great length to consider this, that, or the other. Each time the great kitchen door swung open, their voices flooded in from the dining room.

Othello sat on a stool in the kitchen all evening, while the help busied themselves around him. The dinner service was endless. One of the kitchen workers was a young woman named Cora, who could not hide her beauty beneath her plain white servant's garb, nor could she disguise it beneath her unchanging expression. This beauty could be seen in the grace of her movements, and in the light of intelligence that shone in her eyes. The way she navigated the crowded space, spinning, ducking, and juggling tasks, made it seem almost like she was dancing.

Ashamed of his weakness, Othello could not help but stare at Cora as she attended to her duties. His attentions were not lost on her. Though she said not one word to Othello, she regarded him kindly with her eyes, and upon several occasions bestowed upon him the slightest hint of a smile. Each time she pushed through the swinging door, arms loaded with plates, and serving dishes, and soup tureens, Othello's heart thrilled anew.

But it was with a heavy heart that Othello took his leave at the end of the evening. Master Worthy, rarely one to intuit anything going on inside Othello's head, was not oblivious to this change in Othello on the carriage ride back to the hotel.

"I say, what's gotten into you, Othello? When I call your name, you stare off into space. It's as though you've been hit on the head."

"S'pose I'm coming down with something," said Othello.

"Well, for heaven's sake don't give it to me. Rest yourself tonight, we've got a long day of travel ahead of us."

Rest himself — ha! Let Master Worthy huddle among the horses in a half foot of manure on a chill spring night such as this one, with not so much as a blanket to call his own. For hours that night, hunkered in the damp stable amid the horses, Othello worked up the nerve to take flight. Nobody was likely to see him in the dark, and not at such a late hour. Where would he go? In which direction should he flee? Where could he find food, or shelter, or any small kindness? He thought of Cora, asleep in her quarters, and his chest ached as he imagined himself stealing into her darkened quarters and awakening her with a whisper. How was it that he had never spoken a word to her, and yet he was certain Cora was his savior?

But such a plan was only delusion. Should Othello be caught prowling about Mr. Seymour's place, there was no telling what they'd do to him. And how would he even find his way there in the dark? How could he locate her when he knew nothing of the manor but the one corner of the kitchen he had been permitted to see?

Once during the long night, Othello left his paddock and crept down the corridor in the darkness, past the restless horses. He made it as far as the stable door. But as badly as he yearned to, he could not move himself to open the door.

Was it possible that after a lifetime of bondage and dependency, a lifetime that had granted him not one whit of agency, what Othello feared was freedom itself? The notion was very troubling.

In the morning, stiff and despondent, Othello loaded the trunks down the front steps of the hotel in three trips, while Master

Worthy took his breakfast. It still wasn't too late, he kept telling himself. He could duck into the stable once more and leave out the back. It would be half an hour at least before Master Worthy would register his absence. A half hour amid these crowded streets was sufficient time to get lost. And who was to say he couldn't pursue Cora at some later date? Why, he could get himself on his feet. Maybe he could find work on the wharf, or in a warehouse, or if he had to in a residence not unlike Mr. Seymour's. Surely with his many skills he could find gainful employment, and in a few months' time he might have something to show for himself.

Upon the final trip with the trunk, as Master Worthy was settling the bill, Othello put his head down and started walking briskly toward the corner, his thoughts racing, his heart beating furiously. He got as far as the brick crosswalk, where he confronted the waifs, the little mute boy eyeing him as though he might have some inkling as to Othello's intention, and that alone was enough to turn Othello back, hating himself every step of the way.

His discomposure was not lost on Master Worthy.

"I thought I told you to rest," he said upon the front steps, buttoning his coat.

"I tried," he said. "But those horses were restless."

Master Worthy tsked him and shook his head in disappointment, apparently at Othello's inability to care for himself.

On the ride out of Chicago, thwarted by his own cowardice, Othello wished like never before to strangle the life out of Worthy Warnock, who was quite pleased with himself.

"Understand, Othello, this railroad shall revolutionize mobility as we know it. Imagine! No more must we endure the drudgery of canal travel or these bone-jarring carriage rides. No more tossing about on a riverboat. Just imagine it, New York to Chicago in two days, Othello! And from there, someday, westward across the Great Plains, and through the Rocky Mountains, all the way to California in a week's time. A week, Othello! No wagon train, no starvation, no sickness, no death at the hand of savages. Ah, but what a small world it shall be, Othello, when we connect the East and the West."

WINSTON CHEN-MURPHY

Oregon, March 2019

Winston still couldn't see the point of the trip. Universal Studios for his birthday next week, yeah, that would have been epic. But why did they have to take this pointless train trip to Seattle, when they were just going to turn around and come right back on Sunday? If it was a bigger city than McMinnville that they wanted, Portland was three hours closer than Seattle. Besides, all they would do in Seattle was adult stuff — go to restaurants, and clothing stores, and galleries. That was how it was with his parents. Winston and Tyler always had to do what their parents wanted. Not that they were strict or anything; that wasn't it. They just weren't interested in doing kid stuff. Evan Barker's parents practically planned their whole lives around Evan and his little brother. On weekends they did fun stuff like go to Giants games, or the zoo, or Alcatraz, stuff Winston's mom said was touristy. Winston's parents never took them

61

to Six Flags, or the kids' museum like she'd promised, or any of the places Winston and Tyler wanted to go. They never watched what Winston and Tyler wanted to watch on TV. They never went to the restaurants Winston and Tyler wanted to go to — like Applebee's or Dairy Queen. They always went to fancy places where they never gave you enough food and the kid's menus had cheeseburgers that tried to be fancy, with kaiser or sourdough rolls, but they were never as good as regular cheeseburgers, and the fries were too thick, and not cooked in the middle.

Even though Winston's parents didn't make him follow a million rules like, say, Hunter Mathison's parents, who only let him play his device on weekends and didn't let him watch PG movies, even though Winston's parents let him and Tyler stay up until ten o'clock on school nights and let them play video games just about any time they wanted, it seemed like Winston and Tyler were mostly an afterthought to their parents.

The train trip was only the most recent example. Nobody had asked Winston and Tyler if they wanted to go to Seattle. Seven hours on a boring train, two nights in a hotel, and they wouldn't even let Winston bring his iPad? This was gonna be torture.

"This is gonna be epic," his dad said as they filed across the platform and onto the Coast Starlight.

The train might have seemed awesome if it were taking them somewhere epic. But as it was, the Coast Starlight was fake news. They were at least fifty miles from the coast, and it wasn't even nighttime, so it didn't take Stephen Hawking to figure out that starlight was not in the forecast — and even if it were nighttime, so much for seeing any stars through all the clouds. It was even starting to snow and sticking a little, a possibility that would have been semi-epic if not for the fact that they'd be stuck on the stupid train, unable to screw around in the snow.

"Guess how fast this thing goes," his dad said after they took their seats across from his mom and Tyler.

"A hundred," said Winston.

"Not quite," said his dad. "Guess again."

"Definitely not as fast as a bullet train," Winston said.

"No, not as fast as a bullet train, but fast — eighty miles per hour."

"Dad, we go eighty in the Prius."

His dad sighed and shook his head.

"Well, sorry, Dad," said Winston. "What do you expect? America's got like the slowest trains anywhere. They're like dinosaurs. China's are way faster."

"Is there anything you don't know?" said his dad.

"Yeah, I don't know why we gotta sit on a train all day just to go stay in a hotel."

His dad smiled. "It's about the journey, pal," he said, mussing Winston's hair.

JENNY CHEN

Chicago, December 2017

Six generations of toiling and saving, 170 years of planning.

That Jenny should wind up in her midthirties stranded in O'Hare, questioning her entire existence, seemed incongruous. Sipping her over-roasted Starbucks medium blend, Jenny Chen dreaded the announcement. No way she was making it back in time for her Pilates class in the morning. There went her weekend. It was cold comfort knowing that she was drawing a healthy six-figure income and had excellent benefits, decent stock options, a dynamite 401(k), and a strong, stable portfolio. At the moment none of it seemed worth all the hassle and absenteeism.

"Ech. Jesus, that's bad," Jenny muttered, dropping her half-drunk cup of coffee into the garbage with a clunk.

Sure enough, the dreaded announcement arrived only seconds later. All flights delayed until further notice. A collective groan ran through the terminal. Travelers slumped in their seats and ran hands over weary faces. Phones came out of pockets. Stomachs growled and headaches commenced. Some of the pros were already digging in for the long haul, monopolizing the electrical outlets to charge their devices, James Patterson audiobooks and headphones at the ready.

Jenny dug out her laptop to Skype home with the bad news.

Todd looked drained. With all Jenny's travel, he was practically a single dad these days, not what he'd signed up for when they got married eleven years ago. It was obvious at once that Winston and Tyler were either hopped up on Cap'n Crunch or just restless from being indoors, which was sure to be wearing on Todd's patience and no doubt contributing to his washed-out appearance. Behind him, the kitchen was a mess of cereal bowls and milk glasses. Somewhere in the background, she could hear Tyler's high-pitched squeal.

"Take it easy up there!" Todd shouted.

To Todd's credit, he hardly ever yelled at the kids. He was infinitely more patient with them than Jenny could ever manage. Not only that, Todd was usually forced to play the heavy, laying down the law, setting boundaries, and saying no, while Jenny was free to indulge the boys on weekends, bringing them gifts and letting them stay up late.

"How'd the layoffs go?" said Todd.

"Oh, you know, the usual: Ruined a few lives. Probably got the CFO a ginormous bonus."

Without warning, Winston thrust his face to the camera and mugged for a split second.

"Hi, Mom, bye, Mom!"

"Winston, I —"

But he was already gone.

"So, what time will you be home?" said Todd.

"Uh, that's why I'm calling," said Jenny sheepishly. "There's been a snag."

She watched what was left of the color drain from his face. God, she hated disappointing him.

"You miss another connector?"

"Don't get me started on Delta right now. Worse; there's weather in Chicago," she said. "O'Hare's out of commission until God knows when."

Todd heaved a sigh and ran a hand through his thinning hair. The poor guy. He probably would have killed for the opportunity to sit by himself in an airport, drinking burnt coffee, if only to have a break from the boys and enjoy a moment of inactivity.

"Aw, honey, I'm sorry," said Jenny.

"Not your fault," said Todd. "How soon do you think?"

"It's Chicago, baby, hard to tell. I haven't

looked at the forecast, but some of these people are digging in."

A disappointed silence settled in.

"We miss you," Todd said at last. "The kids are driving me nuts. Winston was home with a cold today, and now Tyler feels hot. They're running me ragged over here."

"I can only imagine," she said. "When I get home, we'll send you over to Rose's for a massage. Maybe you and Jarret could go out for a few beers."

"I want to be with you," he said.

Jenny could have just about cried from frustration. "Oh, me too, baby," she said.

Tyler loosed a bloodcurdling scream in the background.

"I gotta go, honey," said Todd. "Keep me posted. Love you!"

No sooner did Jenny sign off than her guilt about Todd and the kids gave way to guilt about her mom. She knew she ought to return her mom's call, that her mom was literally probably standing by the phone — yes, an actual landline — waiting for such a call. Jenny knew her mom would guilt-trip her about never visiting when they were just down the peninsula, and probably guilt her for never visiting her grandparents' graves after all they had done for her. But dealing with her mom would likely only sour Jenny's mood further. It didn't seem to matter how successful Jenny was, how well she provided for her family, how well her kids performed in school, how much her house had appreciated in the past eight years; her mom was constantly talking up her little brother, Kevin, as though he were the family success story.

Kevin's reading in Mandarin. Kevin's dating a Chinese girl. Kevin made us the nicest dinner last night.

Never mind that Kevin was twenty-six and living at home, where he spent his days playing online poker, and probably watching porn, and apparently his nights cooking for Mom and Dad, who no doubt provided the groceries. Had Kevin given them grandchildren? No. Had Kevin ever once considered, even for a moment, any plans about supporting their parents in their old age? Of course not. He didn't need to. He could do no wrong. Why? Because Kevin was born with a penis. Four thousand years of Chinese culture, and somehow for her parents a worthy life was still inexplicably defined by having a penis. One stupid appendage, which for all intents and purposes was pretty much useless in Kevin's case. Jenny doubted he'd ever have kids. He was a kid himself.

The sad part was, if Jenny were being honest, Winston and Tyler would probably grow up to be just like Kevin: pudgy, unmotivated, and ineffectual. And it would all be Jenny's fault for making their lives too easy, despite the long-held beliefs of her forebearers. Todd

69

was right. They needed to set some parameters for the boys, draw some boundaries and demand some accountability. The kids needed to start pitching in, making their own lunches, cleaning their own rooms, doing their own laundry, otherwise they'd still be living at home when they were twenty-six.

Where had she gone wrong? She'd sent them to good schools, she'd enriched their lives culturally, she'd made it easy for them. Wasn't that the point of all the forethought and planning and saving, to make life more comfortable for her children so that they needn't yearn for freedom or opportunity? To secure their futures by laying opportunity at their feet? Wasn't that what her forebearers had in mind when they came to San Francisco 170 years ago? Wasn't that the pinnacle of the Golden Mountain? So why did she feel like such a failure?

Ah, but she was being too hard on the boys. They were just kids. How could she expect so much from them when they were still discovering themselves? Jenny hadn't really found herself until college; before that she had pretty much been a rule follower, rarely ever straying outside the behavioral parameters set by her parents: good grades, good manners, respect for her elders.

Jenny had half a mind to skip work next week, if she ever got home, Amtrak corporate be damned. Let them figure out their own layoffs. What if she simply chose not to fly back to DC on Monday and check into another faceless Holiday Inn Express? What if she just stayed home with Todd and the kids? What if she made good on her promise to take the boys to the kids' museum down in San Jose, instead? The world would only be a better place. How on earth had she managed to endure so long at a vocation that by its very definition valued profit over human life? How many hearts had Jenny's nifty corporate streamlining broken in the name of eking out a little more profit, which invariably found its way into the pockets of executives? In aiding and abetting these human purges, how many lives had Jenny ruined? Was it any wonder she had trouble sleeping?

She ought to quit her job. Never mind the salary and benefits. Surely, she could be of better service to her family, and to the world at large, doing something other than firing people for a living. Even if it meant a substantial pay cut. God, even if she worked in a bakery or got her real estate license. Even if Todd had to go back to work, an opportunity he'd likely jump at. Wouldn't their lives be better on balance? But Jenny's resolve began to wane in the face of the financial realities. They couldn't afford to live in the city without her job. Their mortgage alone was six thousand dollars a month. Then there was the kids' tuition, and the car payments, and

71

the insurance, and the college funds, and the vacations.

Without Jenny's job, they'd have to move to Foster City or some god-awful place down the peninsula, or worse, the East Bay. As hard as she tried, she just couldn't put a positive spin on that one. The city offered them an enviable lifestyle — the restaurants, the parks, the museums, the galleries, the countless cultural and practical advantages. To live in San Francisco anymore was an achievement in itself. She just couldn't see herself living in San Bruno or Walnut Creek, going to the mega-whatever-plex cinema or the mall, eating at Red Lobster. Having lived her whole life in the city, Jenny had grown to abhor the suburbs.

Todd, on the other hand, would likely welcome such a move. He was tired of the city, tired of the expense of it, tired of forever circling the block to find parking. She could hear his argument clearly.

"So, who cares if there's good restaurants?" he would say. "We hardly go out anymore. The line to get in anywhere decent is an hour long. And when's the last time we went to a gallery, or a museum, or even to Chinatown?"

He was right, of course. They ate in front of the television most nights, the kids with their faces in their devices. It wasn't as though they were really taking advantage of the enriching cultural opportunities the city had on offer.

"We could do that anywhere," Todd would say. "And cheaper. Why even stay in California? It's expensive. It's overcrowded. It's on fire. Baby, we could buy a house on acreage in McMinnville for two hundred and fifty grand."

He would never sway her with the moving-to-the-country argument; he had to know after eleven years of marriage that Jenny was a city girl, through and through. What on earth would they do with themselves in rural Oregon? They weren't farmers. But McMinnville was where Todd had spent his childhood, and Jenny knew that in his heart of hearts, he yearned to live there again, free at last from the noise and hassle of the city.

"Not everybody who lives in the country is a farmer," he'd say. "We could do anything we wanted, Jen. Our overhead would be so low, heck, we could practically do nothing. The boys would have a place to run around. They could fish and hunt and —"

"Hunt?"

"Well, I don't know, hike then."

"And how would we support ourselves?"

"That's what I'm telling you: We could do anything we wanted. We could open a restaurant."

"A restaurant?"

"Oh, I don't know, a shop, a store, something."

The further Jenny pursued this imaginary conversation, the more something troubling dawned on her, something that ought to have been obvious: Todd was unhappy. He clearly did his best to appear happy, and it worked well enough for Jenny to reassure herself that her marriage and her family life were in order, but when forced to really consider the matter, it was obvious her husband was disillusioned with their lives.

Jenny tried to convince herself about Oregon for the twentieth time. What was so bad about the country, anyway — well, besides the people? The Willamette Valley was pretty, she had to give it that. And McMinnville wasn't a complete backwater. There was a university nearby in Salem. There were okay restaurants, and funky little shops, and plenty of youth to liven the place up. At least you could get a decent cup of coffee. And Portland was only an hour away.

Ugh, but the ceaseless rain. The gray, dreary hopelessness of the endless winters. The bad Chinese food. Nope.

Shortly after midnight, the snow let up. Outside, the tarmac came to life as workers began deicing the runways. Though an official announcement was still forthcoming, agents returned to their stations, and wary travelers began to stir. Jenny thought about texting Todd to let him know the good news, but he was likely asleep by then. Guilt from her recent deliberations still clung to Jenny when the announcement was made shortly before one A.M. According to the Delta app, Jenny's connector was scheduled to depart at two forty A.M., all the way over at B24.

Heaving a sigh, she rose to her feet, fastened her purse to her wheelie bag, and began making the long trek down the corridor toward the next concourse.

It was well past ten by the time Todd finally got the boys down. He drank a can of Guinness at the kitchen table, looking out over Ivy Street, mostly quiet and still dependably idyllic at this hour. It was somewhere around ten when he texted Jenny for the last time, only to find out there were no developments to report from O'Hare. Tossing his empty can into the recycling bin under the sink, Todd retired upstairs to the bedroom, where he turned on the bedside lamp, stripped down to his boxers, and lay in bed, pulling the covers about himself and looking up at the ceiling, pondering whether he should get up and brush his teeth.

Probably Jenny would sneak in with the dawn. Or maybe she wouldn't get back until tomorrow afternoon. So much for their weekend. Her internal clock would be so out of whack she'd probably sleep half the day, and Todd would be tasked with keeping the boys quiet or shepherding them out of the house altogether. And do what? Breakfast at Stacks? A matinee down at the plaza? Of course, it would have to be a family movie. Probably *Justice League* — oh, joy.

Where was his piece of the pie, damn it? Todd was tired of sacrificing his fulfillment to the larger cause of raising his family. What had become of his opportunity to be self-realized? And what would that even look like? Lately, Todd had become acutely aware of how much his life was contingent upon Jenny, willful, determined, industrious Jenny. Jenny with the plan. Jenny with the crack organizational skills. Decisive Jenny. Unwaveringly confident Jenny. Proud Jenny. Jenny, who had kept her maiden name when they got married and insisted on hyphenating the boys' names, something Todd did not begrudge her in the least, knowing how much her heritage meant to her (though her parents would never buy it since she hadn't bothered to find a Chinese husband).

Jenny was unquestionably the head of their household, and there was no shame in that. She was their breadwinner, and a damn good one. She made the bulk of the financial decisions — well, all of the decisions, really. Ostensibly there were dialogues involved, but somehow it always seemed to be Jenny's judgment that prevailed: the best schools for the boys, the best investments, the best places to vacation, the best gas range, or refrigerator, or juicer.

And it was working, it really was, at least on the surface. The boys were nothing if not well provided for and well educated, with access to wonderful opportunities and excellent dental health. They lived a very comfortable life in the city. But how meaningful was that at the end of the day? Comfort was overrated. Americans had become soft, at least the ones living in his zip code. America, as Todd had been taught to conceive of it, was predicated on rugged individualism and self-sufficiency, and personal freedom, and moxie, and wide-open spaces. All of that was missing from their lives. The Chen-Murphys were the softest of the soft at this point, nursing at the corporate nipple, accruing passive income, and profiting at the expense of the third world. Given the choice, Todd would've gladly chosen life on the western frontier over his modern urban existence. He'd have welcomed the opportunity to be a rancher or a dirt farmer, if only to feel like the architect of his own life. That was freedom, to have some actual skin in the game, to control one's own fate, or at least believe that such a thing was possible. To see the stars at night, to breathe fresh air, to huddle close to a fire. In Oregon they could achieve these things if nothing else.

But Todd had all but given up hope on the Oregon argument several years ago, knowing that Jenny couldn't be persuaded to leave the city. The fact that their lives were working collectively by some financial or material standard was no consolation. The underlying issue was, how had Todd — once reasonably ambitious and somewhat decisive Todd, with a master's in transportation technology, Todd, who had twice run a marathon — ended up on the sidelines of his own life? What had happened to his aspirations, his will, his dreams? It was as though he'd ended up with this life by default. Not that it was a terrible, or ignoble, or wholly unrewarding life. It was not that his role was undignified, though stay-at-home dad was a bit of a cliché. It just wasn't the life Todd had meant to choose for himself.

Finally Todd turned off the lamp, rolled over onto his side, and did his best to push these thoughts from his head.

Jenny snuck in shortly after dawn, quietly parking her wheelie bag at the foot of the bed and slipping off her flats. She crept to the bathroom, so as not to disturb his sleep, but Todd was already sitting up in bed.

"Hey," he said.

"Oh, hi," she said softly. "Sorry to wake you, hon. Go back to sleep."

"You must be wiped," he said. "Sorry about the hassle in Chicago."

Jenny couldn't quite suppress a sigh. "Ugh," she said. "Just glad the nightmare is over."

"You sleep?"

"On the plane, sort of."

"You eat?"

"No."

Todd slipped out of bed and climbed into his sweats and crossed the bedroom, just as the rising sun managed to penetrate Hayes Valley, angling in through the bedroom window.

The kitchen was already flooded with sunlight as Todd primed the coffeemaker and the toaster, then cracked four eggs in the skillet. Out the window, across the street, the colorful row of two-story Victorians, blue and yellow and pink and white, was awash in the golden light of a new day. It was hard to imagine a more beautiful city than San Francisco. And Todd found this reminder comforting in light of his recent misgivings.

The eggs and toast were plated and on the table and the coffeemaker was still gurgling when Jenny joined Todd in the kitchen, barefoot and wrapped in her white terry-cloth robe, her hair tied up in a towel, which always made her look tiny somehow.

"You're so good," she said, sitting down in front of one of the plates as Todd readied their mugs. "I really don't deserve you."

Pouring the coffee, Todd paused to watch Jenny attack her eggs and toast. God, but she worked hard. She pretty much deplored her job, and yet she never complained. Not about the travel, not about the unsavory task of corporate downsizing that was her charge, nor about the fact that cumulatively it left her very little else to call a life. Jenny deserved to get what she wanted; she'd earned it. If only she'd want something else, something more than this standard of living. Perhaps the tragedy of Jenny was that she was relentlessly pragmatic and hopelessly bound to the expectation of financial stability above all else.

"You don't understand," she'd once told him. "My people came here with no money, no life waiting for them, no safety net."

"Wait a minute, so did mine," he said.

"It's different," she said.

"How is it different?"

"It just is. The expectations are different. Chinese culture is older," she said. "It hardly changes over time. It didn't change when we came here, not like it changed for Europeans. Your people assimilated. Mine did not."

"Um, your people seem like they assimilated pretty well to me. The Chinese footprint is all over this city. You've got your own neighborhood. Where's Irishtown?"

"Exactly," she said.

Whatever the case, Todd could hardly fault Jenny for being so committed to stability and creating better opportunities for her children, just as her parents had done for Jenny and her brother, Kevin, even if the guy did fail to launch. Todd's parents, too, had done everything within their means to create opportunities for Todd. They had taken a second mortgage to put him through Davis. They'd even helped him through grad school, though Todd had still ended up assuming twenty grand in student loan debt. It was up to Jenny and Todd to provide the same or better for Winston and Tyler. And what did Todd have to show for his fancy degree, anyway, besides debt? After college he'd tried unsuccessfully to land a job with BART or Muni, anything transportation related. But he'd ended up settling for Chase. For four years he'd worked as a loan officer (like that had anything to do with transportation technology), a job barely sufficient to subsidize half of their rent in their one-bedroom apartment in the Mission, and a job that certainly wasn't going to put anybody through college.

The fact was, if Jenny had not made something happen with her career, they'd almost certainly have been renting somewhere in the East Bay by now, instead of owning a three-bedroom town house in Hayes Valley. But would that be so bad, really? Didn't Jenny's insistence on remaining in the city despite its disadvantages smack of the sort of elitism Todd had grown to despise in recent years, an affluence wrapped in shiny liberal virtues, an entitlement totally blind to its own condition? Todd knew that wasn't who Jenny was, but lately it seemed like who she was becoming.

"What do you say we go visit my folks and my brother today when the kids wake up?" Jenny said over the rim of her coffee mug.

"You think?"

"Yeah, we could stop in Daly City and visit my grandparents' graves. We could have a picnic or something."

"In the cemetery?" said Todd.

"Yeah, maybe not. But we could at least visit my folks, then come back to the city and eat."

"Don't you want to go back to sleep for a while?" said Todd.

"No," she said. "I'd rather have a weekend with my family."

Todd had to wonder where Jenny got the energy. She put in a fifty-hour workweek, to say nothing of the brutal travel. It was almost like Jenny had sensed Todd's doubts and taken upon herself one more task to be executed, one more responsibility within her purview: placate her pouty husband.

Standing there in the sunny kitchen, rinsing Jenny's plate in the sink, Todd couldn't help but feel a little guilty. What on earth was he whining about? Talk about entitlement, Todd scolded himself. Instead of bemoaning the state of his comfortable existence, rather than wishing he could live somewhere other than the most beautiful city in all of America, he ought to quit complaining and be grateful.

WU CHEN

Shasta City, California, 1851

Amid the afternoon squall, Wu Chen beat the muddy trail down the mountain and through the canyon to town, the low sky pressing down on him, the green, broad-shouldered hills crowding in from all sides. If Wu Chen had a certain spring in his step in spite of the deluge, if his humming conveyed a certain levity to anyone who might have heard it, the reasons for this were manifold: First, there was the greater happiness that attended the success of his American odyssey. To think that only last spring he had been hunkered feverishly in steerage for seven weeks, from Hong Kong to San Francisco, mostly in the dark, subsisting on black bread and moldy rice and only the bare minimum of fresh water. And all the while just two words upon his parched lips, two words whispered beneath his breath like an incantation, two words that haunted his very dreams: *Gum Shan.* Golden Mountain.

84

To think that only last year young Wu Chen had traded the grim tolls of flooding and civil unrest for such adventures as America had to offer him. He would forever be indebted to his uncle Li Jun in Guangdong for making his passage possible. How fortunate Wu Chen was to have made the acquaintance of Jimmy Huang and his brothers within a week of his arrival. True, it had been a most difficult week, hardly an improvement over the ship's suffocating hold. A week of wandering the filthy streets, hungry by day, his bamboo hat and narrow eyes eliciting the curiosity or contempt of nearly every man he passed. And still, the nights had been worse, squatting beneath the stinking wharf with the vermin, the noxious vapors of creosote filling his lungs, tobacco smoke marooned in the hollows of his belly. But all great things required hardship to achieve. These were the very words of his uncle Li Jun, who had also taught him the value of hard work. And that was just what Wu Chen had done with his fortuitous opportunity; he had worked tirelessly, from dawn until dusk in all manner of weather, crouching along the banks of the river, hypnotized by its babbling, as he shoveled and scooped and panned, shoveled and scooped and panned, until his back ached and his limbs were numb.

Who knew where Wu Chen might have washed up in this new frontier without Jimmy

Huang and his brothers to guide him, to create this opportunity for him? Jimmy Huang would never forsake him, for Jimmy Huang was like a brother.

Wu Chen's work with the Huangs had been largely fruitless the first weeks, yielding barely enough gold to warrant a trip to town. But soon, he and the Huang brothers had refined their methods and streamlined their execution as systematically they panned up and down the gravel bed on either side of the river, trying to locate the vein.

And just as his uncle had promised, their hard work had paid dividends.

Which brings us to the more immediate cause of Wu Chen's good spirits: the small bounty of gold nuggets he now conveyed on his person in a leather satchel buried deep in his rucksack. Slightly less conspicuous, concealed by his filthy shirttail, was the six-barrel Stocking Pepperbox fastened beneath his belt, a small but effective agent of defense, according to Jimmy Huang. And should the iron fail him, his knife was sheathed opposite it. For it was the prevailing wisdom in these parts that a Chinese was an easy mark.

The contents of Wu Chen's leather satchel amounted to some eighteen ounces of gold, his quarter share of the claim's five-month yield thus far, every flake and nugget of it panned from their legal claim, the long and narrow gravel bed on the bank of the upper

Shasta, wedged so tightly between the canyon walls, one nearly had to turn sideways to access it.

And with this modest fortune Wu Chen would, among other things, expand his enterprise with the Huang brothers. Soon they would invest in tools and methods to increase their productivity, in cradles and Long Toms, and eventually they would locate the vein and begin to excavate in earnest.

So yes, Wu Chen had much occasion to be cheerful in spite of the weather as he shuffled down the mountain toward town. He forded the small stream at the bottom of the basin, then proceeded westward along the trail. At the far edge of the meadow, a figure on horseback impeded Wu Chen's progress. It was a white man, a week unshaven, with narrow-set eyes, and a nose flat and wide like a spade.

"You one of them working that gravel bank up canyon?" said the man, who proceeded to spit on the ground.

Wu Chen declined to answer. When he attempted to step around him, the stranger edged forward on his mount, blocking the path. Wu Chen thought immediately of the iron strapped to his waist.

"Word is, you coolies having a bit of success up there. That a fact?"

Wu Chen looked up at the stranger, as though unable to comprehend.

"No speak," he said.

"Well now, I suspect you understand a lot more than you're letting on. What you got in that pack there?"

Wu Chen nearly reached for his iron but resisted the impulse, mostly out of fear that he wouldn't draw quickly enough.

The stranger smiled and spit on the ground once more.

"Well," he said. "Suppose it don't much matter at this point. You go ahead and run along."

The stranger fell back on his mount a few steps, clearing the trail for passage.

Wordlessly, Wu Chen stepped around him without looking back, though he could feel the stranger's eyes upon him as he continued on into the forest.

"That's right, little man, you just keep walkin'."

The final mile into town Wu Chen's heart beat faster than usual. This was the downside of his American adventure, this feeling of vulnerability, this knowledge that he was viewed as somehow less than a white man, though the road he had traveled to get here was likely steeper and more demanding than any white man's.

The lone boulevard that comprised Shasta City was currently a slough of mud, scarred with the deep furrows of mired wagon wheels and dimpled with hoof tracks, each forming a tiny mud puddle. The amenities, such as they were, included the mercantile, the druggist, the bank, two saloons, and the land office. Noticeably absent was the church, a Methodist affair set well out of town.

In spite of the weather, the boardwalks were bustling on either side of the muddy slough, and the saloons, one on each side of the street, were in full swing, even at midday. Wu Chen knew that a man of bigger appetites and a hotter temperament would surely seize this opportunity to consummate some manner of celebration, one likely to conclude in a considerable loss of capital, a splitting headache, and possibly a case of the clap. But saloons held no allure for Wu Chen. For temperance, too, had been a lesson from Uncle Li Jun.

Wu Chen was already accustomed to the attention his presence seemed to warrant in America. Never mind that he kept his braided tail tucked under his hat — not a bamboo hat like the one he'd left behind in San Francisco, but a sturdy felt hat, the brim of which he wore low on his forehead to hide his face. Wu Chen did not traipse about in silk robes. Wu Chen smelled like anyone else on the frontier, smoky, grimy, and gamy. That he still stood out in a crowd in spite of his efforts to assimilate was a source of frequent vexation.

Wu Chen kept his eyes to the ground three

feet in front of him as he proceeded past the saloon, past the mercantile, and past the druggist toward the bank on the far end of town. The bank was of basic wooden construction, not unlike the druggist's or the mercantile, its lone distinction being that its twin windows were barred, which did not inspire much in the way of confidence. What use were bars when Wu Chen could probably kick a hole in the clapboard wall?

As it turned out, the banker, a sallow middle-aged man in a frock coat and vest, inspired even less confidence. Regardless, Wu Chen unburdened himself of his rucksack and dug around inside until he produced the leather satchel, presenting it to the man at the counter.

"Ah," he said. "We've had a bit of good fortune, have we?"

"Eighteen ounces," said Wu Chen. "A little more."

"Well, we shall see," said the banker.

Wu Chen soon realized that he should have heeded Jimmy Huang's advice and brought his own scales, heavy though they were. For the banker's scale read just over fifteen ounces.

"No, there is eighteen ounces," protested Wu Chen. "I weighed it myself."

"That, good sir, is not the reading with which our scale has provided us," said the banker. "I can assure you that our assaying apparatus is of the finest manufacture."

"Eighteen ounces," said Wu Chen.

The thin man pursed his lips and shook his head grimly.

"I am prepared to offer you sixteen dollars per ounce at fifteen ounces, minus a twenty-five-dollar administration fee, for a grand total of two hundred and fifteen dollars. In draft, of course."

Wu Chen knew this to be an inferior exchange. Aside from the fact that he had weighed his share himself at over eighteen ounces, according to Jimmy Huang, the current exchange rate was nineteen dollars per ounce, and not a penny less.

"Eighteen ounces at nineteen dollars per ounce," said Wu Chen.

The banker smiled less than pleasantly.

"If you do not approve of our terms," he said, "might I recommend as an alternative that — for a small fee — you deposit your holdings in our safe? Being of thick iron construction, manufactured in the east by none other than the reputable — nay, the preeminent — American Bank Lock Company, and guarded round the clock —"

"Guarded by who?" Wu Chen interjected.

"Why, either myself, Mr. Higgins, or Mr. Humbert," said the banker. "We work in shifts. But rest assured, your holdings will be protected. You shall, of course, leave this establishment carrying a receipt for this transaction, against which you are free to borrow from the mercantile or the saloons, though I would caution against the latter."

But Wu Chen did not trust the arrangement. How could he when the thin man had offered him such an inadequate exchange? And so, Wu Chen left the bank and trudged back down the middle of the muddy slough past the relentless eyes of every man he passed. There was little spring left in his step as he made his way back up the mountain in the rain. But his fortune was destined to change for the better.

Tucking his wet shirttail beneath his denim trousers to expose his iron, Wu Chen began ascending the muddy trail and once again began to hum a tune. He did not cross the stranger along his path, and soon his steps were accompanied by birdsong as the rain clouds scurried north and the sun beat down on the mountainside, steam rising off the squelchy earth all around him. Already, it seemed that Wu Chen's faith was being rewarded.

Just before he arrived at the narrow passage in the canyon, the report of a pistol shot echoed through the hills, stopping Wu Chen in his tracks. Then came the nervous nicker of horses and the shouting of men, followed by another pistol report. Later, he would reason on many occasions that he ought to have charged headlong into the fray, brandishing his pistol, or at least fired a warning shot in the air. Perhaps that would have made a difference. Instead, Wu Chen crouched down low, slinking through the passage, then made his way along the right bank of the stream, among the scrubby brush, until the claim was almost in sight. Only then did he draw his iron and drop to his knees. The voices were louder now, though Wu Chen still could not make out the words. He heard the nervous clomping of hooves. Then he heard something that sent a chill through his whole body: laughter, crude and heartless.

Wu Chen lowered himself to his belly and began to inch his way toward the gravel bank beneath the cover of shrubs until the claim was in clear sight. What he saw there was not one but four strangers upon horseback. What he heard was the cry of a familiar voice, that of Tommy Huang, the youngest brother, abruptly silenced by another pistol report, a shot that might never have happened had Wu Chen acted sooner, had he scared them off when he'd had a chance.

Now he was forced to watch Jimmy Huang on his knees begging for mercy. Jimmy, who had saved him from destitution; Jimmy, who had given him a life. Still, Wu Chen did not dare move as he watched the stranger on horseback sidle up nearer to Jimmy until he loomed directly above him. Though Wu Chen's finger was on the trigger of his pistol, he did not squeeze it, or even level the barrel upon the stranger. For he was hopelessly outnumbered and inexperienced with a gun. What if the old Stocking didn't even work?

Gun or no gun, Wu Chen would later berate himself for not at least creating a distraction, for not doing anything at all. Instead, he remained on his belly in the dirt, watching as the stranger spit on the ground, smiling down at Jimmy. And that was when Wu Chen recognized the stranger as the man he'd met on the trail.

"You have claim," said Jimmy Huang.

The stranger chuckled and looked in turn to each of his companions.

"You hear that, boys?" said the stranger, sidling his horse around to the back side of Jimmy. "Coolie says we can have it. Well, I'll be damned. Don't mind if I do."

In a flash, the stranger leveled his pistol and shot Jimmy Huang in the back of the head. And as Jimmy Huang fell face-forward in the dirt, Wu Chen felt his heart harden into a fist, and a golden flame in his mind's eye went suddenly dark, even as he clutched his pistol tighter, finger pressed fast to the trigger, tears of outrage streaming down his face.

Wu Chen crawled on his stomach, his heart beating like it was trying to escape his chest, while the four strangers ransacked the claim, rifling through the shack, upturning pans, kicking over buckets, and flipping straw mattresses. Hidden in the brush, he watched as one by one they rolled the Huang brothers over, and emptied their pockets, and left them bleeding on the bank, an image that would haunt his dreams.

"They gotta be holding it somewhere," said the familiar one, spitting on the ground.

But they would never locate the Huang brothers' shares, which Wu Chen knew were stuffed in an old rabbit warren not twenty feet from where he now lay on his stomach.

Soon it was apparent that the strangers had designs on settling the claim. They began unpacking their saddles and setting up camp, stepping over the lifeless bodies of the Huang brothers like they were logs on the riverbank. The thought briefly occurred to Wu Chen to go after the law. If he left right then, he might make town and return with the sheriff before sunset. Instead he hunkered down among the shrubs, resolving to avenge the Huang brothers personally if it was the last thing he did. While he had no experience with a gun, he knew himself to be a quick and formidable adversary in close spaces; he had bested his bigger and older cousins many times in the cane fields and rice paddies of the delta. Pound for pound, Wu Chen was as strong as any man in his village. The one time he had scuffled with a Huang, it had been with Johnny, the middle brother and the fittest of the three, and Wu Chen had licked him handily. But if Wu Chen were to stand any chance at all, outmanned and outgunned, first he would have to even the numbers. As he lay in the dirt, his heart finally began to slow its beating, and Wu Chen resolved to formulate a plan.

Hours passed before the strangers, apparently tired of stepping over them, finally dragged the Huangs' lifeless bodies to the bank and rolled them into the river, where they immediately caught the current and began washing down-canyon. Surely they would be found eventually, tangled among the snag of fallen trees, or washed up bloated upon the bank. But likely nobody would care.

At dusk the strangers started a fire, and Wu Chen fell back further into the cover of the brush, where he lay in wait as the night air began to cool. Only under the full cover of darkness, distant enough not to betray his presence, but close enough to hear the drone of their voices and the pop of the fire, did Wu Chen begin to pursue his purpose.

The strangers huddled around the fire, sipping whiskey from tin cups and rolling cigarettes. Occasionally they discussed their prospects, but mostly they sat in silence under the stars, the crickets trilling in the brush.

"You hear that?" said the stranger with the eye patch.

"Hear what?" said the little man with the

droopy mustache.

"That," said Eye Patch.

Indeed, a disturbance in the brush had silenced the crickets all at once.

"Probably just a cay-ote."

"Didn't sound like no cay-ote to me."

"There it is again," said Eye Patch.

"Well, go on out there and find out," said the familiar one.

"You go out there, Winthrop," said Eye Patch.

"You scared or something?" countered Winthrop.

"Scared, my buttocks," said Eye Patch, rising to his feet.

And with that, the one with the eye patch rose from his place by the fire and stepped out into darkness.

Crouching in the brush, Wu Chen could hear the reluctant footfalls of the one-eyed man in the gravel as he left the fire and, creeping deeper into the darkness, began to whistle.

"Who's that?" he said.

Wu Chen stopped breathing then, and poised himself to strike.

Back at the fire, the remaining strangers waited. A good ten minutes had passed, and yet, Leopold had not returned.

"S'pose I better go check on him?" said the one called Clete.

"Suit yourself," said Winthrop.

And so, the one called Clete ventured out into the darkened perimeter.

"Now they're just messin' with us," said the one with the droopy mustache, feeding another log to the fire.

"That, or they're trying to lure us out there," said Winthrop.

"Ya think?"

"Oh, I don't know, I never did trust neither of them."

The one with the droopy mustache considered the possibility for a moment.

"If they was gonna turn on us, seems like a roundabout way of doing it. Why, they might have just shot us in the back at any point this afternoon."

"Ain't either of them none too smart, if you hadn't noticed," said Winthrop, spitting into the flames.

"Well, I'm not buying it," said the mustachioed one. "Gonna take more than two bodies to find that vein, anyways."

"Says who?"

"Says me."

"Why, Boyer, I could work this claim all by my lonesome, and probably find that vein inside a week."

"Is that right?" said Boyer.

"Yeah, that's right," said Winthrop. "Don't take any genius to dig holes. It's called working smart."

"Well, now," said Boyer. "If that's the case, then I really don't believe you."

"What exactly are you getting at, Boyer?"

"What I'm getting at is that maybe it's you I'm beginning not to trust, not them others."

"Pshaw," said Winthrop. "Relax, Boyer. I didn't say I wanted to work this claim by myself, I just said I could if it came right down to it. And I reckon you could, too."

"You're damn right I could."

"Okay, then, it's settled."

"Fine," said Boyer, satisfied with the concession. "So what about the others?"

"Hell if I know," said Winthrop. "Go find out, why don't you?"

"Why don't you?" said Boyer.

"On account of I'm none too worried about the others," said Winthrop. "Chances are, they both got cold feet about killing these yellow devils and skulked on back to town."

"Well, I've never known Leopold to get cold feet about killing nobody," Boyer observed. "Clete, neither."

"Well," said Winthrop, "first time for everything, I s'pose."

Unconvinced, Boyer shook his head and pursed his lips. "Nope. Not buyin' it," he said. "I'm tellin' you, somethin' feels wrong about all this, here."

"Well, then, go check it out."

"I believe I will," said Boyer.

"You know where to find me," said Winthrop, spitting once more into the fire.

Hot bile creeping up his throat, Wu Chen fought back the sickness as he hunkered in the brush, knife still slick with blood, while the one called Boyer crept toward him in the darkness.

"All right, Leopold, Clete," he said. "Enough with the fooling around. Come on out, now. I'm liable to turn an ankle bumbling around out here in the dark."

Once Boyer was two steps beyond him, Wu Chen sprung on him from behind, got him around the collar with one arm, and after a brief struggle, slit his neck in one swift movement, all before Boyer could cry out for help.

Quietly, Wu Chen eased Boyer's limp body to the ground. Standing beneath the stars as Boyer gargled his final, fitful breaths, Wu Chen felt acutely — almost painfully — alive, as though he were breathing through every pore of his body. The roar of the river in the near distance seemed to echo in his chest. Even the light of the stars seemed improbably bright.

Back at the fire, Winthrop was left alone with his thoughts, and growing a little uneasy with them. Things were starting to seem a little on the wrong side after all. Three men had walked out in the night, and not one of them had come back. Stranger still, Winthrop had never heard a sound. Surely it wasn't wolves or a bear. The only logical conclusion was that Boyer, like Leopold and Clete before him, had gotten cold feet and fled back to town on foot. It looked like Winthrop was now the owner of not one but four horses.

Soon, though, Winthrop's discomfiture edged toward anxiety. Supposing all three of them were out to frame him, blame the murders on him, and take the claim for themselves? Well, now, that wouldn't do at all. The longer Winthrop sat there by the fire, the more his suspicions hardened into certainty. Why, the dang nerve of them! It was Winthrop who'd hatched the idea. And here they were, planning to double-cross him.

So, what to do about it? Did he go out after them? He sure didn't like the numbers, or the fact that they were likely waiting to ambush him. The thing to do maybe was to hunker down right there and defend his claim. By now Winthrop's heart was picking up speed, moving along at a canter and headed toward a gallop. Pistol drawn, he scanned the perimeter and put his ear to the night air. When the trilling of the crickets stopped abruptly, his heart froze.

Now the horses suddenly grew restless.

Winthrop cleared his sweaty brow on his shirtsleeve and tightened his grip on his pistol. Maybe he ought to fetch the rifle?

Three against one was a troubling arithmetic. Best to have options.

"C'mon out now, boys," he said, fetching the rifle. "Let's talk about this. Ain't no use in doing something rash. This claim's liable to yield plenty for all of us. Hell, those coolies didn't even find the vein."

One of the horses nickered, and the hair on Winthrop's forearm stood on end.

"All right, then, damn it. I've had enough of this. If you boys have got it in for me, then come and get me, already."

But nobody came.

Out in the brush, Wu Chen squatted on the balls of his feet, waiting. Time as he had once known it had ceased to exist, even as the stars wheeled above. The amplification of his senses was inexplicable. He felt the world around him, the touch of the night air, the rush of the river, the gentle wind in the grass, in ways hitherto unknown to him. His whole being seemed to be the embodiment of some purpose beyond his control, for how else could he account for his calmness and poise and patience in the face of such savagery? Squatting there in the shadowy starlit night, Wu Chen heard the ghost of Jimmy Huang whispering in the reeds.

Meanwhile, the exhausting effects of not knowing were beginning to wear on Winthrop as he sat at attention by the fire, scanning the darkness all around him. Every time a horse shuffled its hooves or the crickets stopped their trilling, his nerves wore a little bit thinner. For the first time, he began to think killing those Chinese hadn't been such a great idea.

It wasn't long before Winthrop's eyelids began to grow heavy. Twice he woke himself with a start, and fed more sticks to the fire on each occasion. He talked to himself for a while and hummed an old tune his mama used to hum to him when he was still just a pup. He couldn't remember the words, but he could remember the melody. A bitter taste rose in his throat at the thought of his mother. This world was no damn good.

Winthrop didn't remember falling asleep; he couldn't recall what thoughts were rattling around in his head before the fatigue overcame him, but he sure as heck remembered waking up by the dead campfire, flat on his stiff back and half-frozen. His pistol was neither in his clutches nor in its holster, and the rifle was nowhere to be seen. A little Chinese was standing directly above him, a six iron leveled right between Winthrop's eyes.

Winthrop scrambled backward to his feet.

"Now, little fella, just you stay calm. We can work something out. Just put that pistol away. Ain't no need of more violence."

"Down," said Wu Chen.

"Let's think this through," said Winthrop.

"Knees!" said Wu Chen.

Winthrop reluctantly lowered himself to his knees.

"Hands," said Wu Chen.

Winthrop placed his hands on his head.

"Okay, now, you've got my attention," said Winthrop. "I'll just pack up and leave you to your claim. It's all yours. Tell you what, I'll let you have three of those there horses."

Wu Chen stepped up and set the cool barrel of his pistol right smack against Winthrop's forehead.

"Aw, you don't want to do this. This is all just a misunderstanding," said Winthrop. "Now, let's talk about this."

"No talk," said Wu Chen. "Pray."

LUYU TULLY

Shasta City, 1851

Elizabeth was the name the Methodists had given her when she was ten years old, but she had always thought of herself as Luyu, her Miwok name, meaning "wild dove." She was never told what *Elizabeth* meant, nor did she ever ask, but she answered to the name because it pleased the Younts, and the Younts had shown her kindness, even if she hadn't particularly taken to their way of life or worship. These Methodists were not a joyous bunch, rather a pious one. They preferred their life experience like they preferred their food, song, clothing, and décor, which was to say, bland.

Now that she was a woman of nearly sixteen years, her mind and body transformed, her blood seeming to run both warmer and faster, her curiosities reaching for new frontiers, Luyu felt the oppressive weight of this blandness more than ever. Some nights, when the Younts were sleeping, Luyu stole quietly out into the front yard and stood for an hour or more under the light of the moon, in the great, humped shadows of the hills squatting patiently in the near distance, and to the south, the glowing white dome of Mount Shasta. In the stillness and resplendence of the moonlight, with the treetops swishing gently in the warm breeze, Luyu remembered what it was to live freely — free of the endless cycle of domestic toil, free of emotional restraint, and free of the bell jar of Christian piety. She knew these thoughts were both impure and ungrateful, for the Younts had only ever had her best interest in mind, that being the salvation of her mortal soul.

The soul, Luyu reasoned, must be different from the spirit, for Luyu knew beyond any doubt that her spirit was neither bland nor mortal, but lived forever in the wild things. It lived in the burbling and babbling of the mountain stream, in the hush of the wind, in the certainty of the raven's call, and yes, in the hypnotic coo of the wild dove for whom she was named.

This particular clear night, in the spring of the year 1851, as Luyu stood in the front yard before the Younts' perfectly square abode, basking in the moonlight, she was sure her spirit was dying. She could hear for the first time the song of the wild dove in a different aspect, one of mourning.

Luyu had half a mind to walk out into the

night and never come back. Mortal soul be damned, if her spirit was not soon fed it would go the way of her people, and what good was her mortal soul then? The Great White God drove a hard bargain.

The next morning, at the little weather-beaten church a mile's walk from the Younts' homestead, as Elizabeth sat upon her hard bench with Mrs. Yount grim and stoic beside her, wrinkled hands folded in her lap, they listened to Reverend Yount disparage at length the evils of greed and excess rampant in their little part of the world, decrying the thieves, drunkards, and slanderers who had infested this beautiful place.

"Gold," he said derisively. "Gold, gold, gold. Gold, on the lips of every man in these parts. Gold, every bit a curse on those who find it. What people value highly is detestable in God's sight. For the deceitfulness of wealth and the desires for other things choke the word and bend it to their own needs, making it unfruitful and false. The Lord himself told us that it is hard for a wealthy man to enter the kingdom of God. For one cannot serve two masters. Riches and pleasure, they do not mature. He who trusts in his riches will fall, but the righteous shall flourish as the green leaf. For all that is in the world, the lust of the flesh, and the lust of the eyes, and the boastful pride of life, is not from the Father, but is from the world."

Here, Mrs. Yount, as though feeling the aching restlessness that stirred in Luyu's every fiber, set her hand upon Luyu's knee.

"The world is passing away," said Reverend Yount. "And with it, its lusts; but the one who does the will of God lives forever. And thus, moderation, and adherence to the word of God, these are the Christian values to which we must cling."

Nearly every Sunday as she sat on this very bench next to Mrs. Yount, Luyu reminded herself how Captain Sutter, whom she could only dimly remember, had also called himself a Christian. And Captain Sutter was a man who had kept her people locked in cages at night, a man who by day moved them about beneath the watchful eyes of his overseers and their shotguns. Luyu's people had built Sutter's Mill. They had tended his crops and overseen his livestock. They'd seen no profit themselves for their labor. In return for building Sutter's fortune, they'd only been stripped of their ways. And when they'd dared to try to take them back, the Sacramento and American rivers had run red with Indian blood.

This was the story of her people: Conquered first by the Spanish, then the Mexicans, and now the whites. Slaughtered, pillaged, raped, and forced to work. If the meek would inherit the earth, then by all rights it should one day belong to the Miwok.

Unlike her parents, Luyu had been lucky enough to escape the ranch alive and find her way north, where the Younts had taken her under their roof and begun their own, less violent, less exploitive, though no less strident, campaign to subvert her Indian nature.

Reverend Yount concluded his sermon with a reminder for his congregation to remain steadfast; keep a straight face; not fall prey to the temptations of happiness, fulfillment, or plenty; and for heaven's sake, not have too much fun celebrating the business of being in the world. For the Lord did not deal in the tender of mirth.

After church, Mrs. Yount was not prepared to linger, for there was much work to be done at home, and cleanliness being next to godliness, Luyu was expected to do her share of the laundering and cultivating. But this day she dared to seek relief from the monotony of domestic chores.

"I thought I might help Father tidy up the church," she said.

Mrs. Yount regarded Luyu with a mild expression.

"Very well," she said. "See to it that he doesn't trip and break his neck with those failing eyes of his."

As Reverend Yount lingered in front of the little church, shaking hands and bestowing blessings upon his small but steadfast congregation, Luyu stationed herself at his side, nodding at his wisdom, smiling cautiously, while touching his elbow lightly.

When at last she found an opening, she appealed to Reverend Yount.

"Father," she said, "I hear that the Ambroses are in need of a hand at their farm," she lied. "They were not present at today's service. I thought that perhaps I might check up on them."

It did not take Reverend Yount long to consider this proposition.

"Yes, Elizabeth," he said. "I think that's a fine idea."

And still the question remained: Was she telling the truth? Was charity her true motive? Until the instant Luyu waved goodbye, watching the reverend resume his parting exchanges, Luyu did not know the answer to this question. However, the minute the little church was out of sight, Luyu acknowledged what had been her true intention all along, and her heart thrilled at the prospect.

The hike was roughly the same distance as if she'd actually gone to the Ambroses', two miles at most down the rutted lane running north to south. Luyu's thoughts percolated each step of the way. What if it should come back to Reverend Yount that she had in fact not paid the Ambroses a visit? What excuse could she fabricate to account for her absence?

Though the rain had let up the previous

afternoon, the lone road through the center of Shasta City was still a swamp of churned-up sludge. But mud was not enough to discourage Luyu. For the boardwalks and alleys were brimming with activity, and Luyu's heart swelled to see such enterprise. Though she had no money and not so much as a basket of eggs to barter, nothing was to prevent Luyu from pretending to have business in town. She could browse and make inquiries. Perhaps she could even meet somebody outside of her tiny social sphere.

As she strode past the bank, she was not surprised to find it doing brisk business on this day of worship. Had not Reverend Yount lamented this very abomination in his morning sermon, proclaiming that commerce before God was the work of the devil?

Luyu hiked the hem of her cotton skirt to mid-ankle, lest she sully it in the mud. She could feel the eyes of grown men upon her, a sensation she found both thrilling and disquieting. Passing the saloon, Luyu could feel herself blushing.

She knew that she was not beautiful, yet walking among such hungry suitors as those who lined the boardwalk in front of the Shastina Saloon, Luyu felt at once formidable and vulnerable in her feminine aspect. Hats were doffed. Beards were smoothed over, lapels were dusted, and postures were straightened as she passed by.

"Howdy, ma'am," said one man, gnawing on a toothpick.

"Eureka," said a grimy, heavily bearded soul.

Though neither could be characterized as a gentleman, Luyu could not belie a certain pride that attended their scrutiny.

Lacking any real purpose, Luyu ducked into the mercantile and began strolling the aisles aimlessly.

"Help you, ma'am?" said the clerk, after several minutes of this.

"Have you any purses?" she said.

"Not for a lady, per se," said the clerk. "But I do have leather satchels, and pouches of various sizes."

"And what have you for perfumes?"

"Aye, none, I'm afraid," he said. "But we do stock soap powder."

"Well, thank you all the same," said Luyu.

A moment later she exited the mercantile, just in time to see a lone Chinese slogging down the center of the muddy street with his canvas pack, hat pulled low, eyes to the ground. To come all the way from China, a world away, only for this, seemed a waste. Perhaps Luyu's fate could be worse, though she doubted it. For where was her golden possibility, where was her hope of a better life? Unlike those who flocked to this place from all corners of the world, seeking their fortunes, Luyu and her people had been here always. And yet their land had been stripped from them and their numbers decimated by disease, privation, and violence. The sum total of their language, their culture, their thousands of years of accumulated knowledge, was not worth so much as an ounce of gold.

With no particular aim, Luyu stood on the corner of the boardwalk, gazing out into the street.

"You the preacher's girl, ain't you?" said a voice.

Luyu turned to face a tall Indian, smooth faced beneath his wide-brimmed hat, and not unattractive, though this observation shamed her.

"Yes," said Luyu, blushing anew. "Reverend Yount."

"Nothing here for a preacher's daughter," he observed. "Not in this town. That I can tell you."

"It seems there's nothing for me anywhere," she said, surprised by her own candor.

"I must say, I'm well acquainted with such a feeling," he said. "What's your name?"

"Elizabeth."

"Your real name."

"Luyu," she said.

"Ah, the dove," he said, extending a hand. "I go by John Tully. Sometimes they call me Long John. But Bearskins is my Washoe name."

"What should I call you, then?" she said.

"Whatever pleases you."

"Then I shall call you John," she said. "A strong name."

"I reckon so, if you believe in the Bible."

"Do you believe in the Bible, Mr. Tully?"

"Ha," he said. "Oh, I believe in it, all right. There's no denying its existence. Lot of wrong has been done in the name of that book. I do like a psalm, now and again, though," he added, almost as an afterthought. "I gotta ask," he said. "What possessed a lady of your standing to seek out this hellhole on such a fine morning?"

"Restlessness," she said. "And you?"

"Stocking up on supplies," he said.

"What manner of supplies?" she asked. "Are you a miner?"

"Hardly," he said.

"A rancher?"

"I've worked with cattle," he said. "But I'm no rancher."

"What is it that you do?"

"Whatever they pay me to do," he said. "But not anymore. I'm leaving this place."

"For where?"

"I dunno," he said. "South, I guess. Maybe east."

"To what purpose?"

"That I might find one, I suppose."

"I envy you," she said.

"Well, now, that's just sad," said John Tully.

"I suppose it is, John Tully. But the Lord seems to have no plan for me."

"Well," he said, "it's my observation that his plans aren't always the best, anyway, if that's any comfort."

"I wish it were," she said.

"Just what is it you want, Ms. Yount?"

"I'm afraid I couldn't even guess," she said.

"Birds of a feather, you and I. But there's something out there for me. Some kind of life better than this here."

"When will you leave?" she said.

"Today," said John Tully.

What came next caught Luyu even more off guard than it did John Tully.

"Take me with you," she said.

John Tully was none too sure about bringing the Miwok girl. In fact, his instincts were dead set against it. This was a journey he'd intended on making alone. Bringing the girl along on his aimless search for a new life would only create needless complications, not the least of which was transportation. The brown mare was a shadow of her old self, and they were liable to run her into the ground riding tandem. Not to mention the extra supplies such a pairing would require. Besides, her Methodists were likely to miss her, maybe even come after her. And none of this even considered the fact that he knew nothing of the girl, what she wanted, or where she was hoping to run to. Just about every which way John Tully worked his mind around it, bringing the girl was a bad idea.

She was no beauty, the wild dove, with those close-set eyes, and thin lips, and a bit of a hook nose, but then, neither was John Tully any beauty, he supposed. John had always thought his own nose too wide, and one of his eyes was a bit lazy, and there was no denying that he slouched, as he never did care for being tall.

"What about your people?" he said, standing astride the old mare.

"They're not my people," she said. "They're decent people, but they are not mine."

"And what about me?" he said. "You don't know the first thing about me."

"I know everything I need to know," she said.

"And what's that?"

"That you're leaving this place."

"Fair enough," he said. "But what have you got to offer me?"

"I'm useful," she said. "I'm a hard worker. Also, I'd like to think I'm decent company. And I'm decisive."

"That much we know," said John Tully.

"I can mend clothing, I can hunt, I can track, and I can judge a man's character."

"And what do you make of mine?" said John Tully.

"You're a good man, all in all," she said. "I

116

suspect you lack belief, but you —"

"Belief in what?"

"You tell me."

"I'll have to think on it," he said.

At the mercantile, John doubled up on oats and rice and bought an extra blanket, along with a second bladder for water.

The old mare eyed him with suspicion as he approached her with the additional load.

"What's her name?" said Luyu, stroking her muzzle.

"She doesn't have one."

"But you said she's old."

"She's old, all right," said John Tully. "Old and ornery."

"How long have you had her?"

"I stopped counting."

"And in all this time you never gave her a name?"

"What's the difference?" said John Tully. "She hasn't once called me by my name."

"She will be called Sugar."

"Why call her Sugar?" he said.

"Because she's sweet."

"Obviously you haven't spent any time with her. Turn your back on that old nag and she's likely to kick you in the head."

"In your case, that might be a good thing," she said.

John Tully guffawed. Who was this Wild Dove who spoke so freely? How did this light-spiritedness endure among those gloomy

Methodists?

Even as he loaded up the old nag, John Tully was almost beginning to believe in something.

Luyu and John Tully left town late in the afternoon, riding tandem on the old brown mare. Proceeding south, they skirted the foothills along the Siskiyou Trail with the monolith of Shasta towering above them, wrapped about the shoulders in a dense, green blanket of forest, its snow-capped dome glaring in the sunlight.

With each mile Luyu felt freer and more alive. Never again would she be called Elizabeth, never again would she stifle her true nature.

"It never gets old," she said, gazing up at the mountain.

"One day it will explode again and bury the world in ash."

When the heat of afternoon had subsided somewhat, they stopped to water the mare in a little stream a couple hundred feet east of the trail. Luyu stood on the bank beside the mare, stroking the horse's withers, as she gazed back at the mountains.

"Where will you take us, Sugar?" she said. "Will there be mountains? Will we be farmers? What awaits us there?"

"Don't get too friendly. That old nag is bound to quit on us sooner or later," said John.

They resumed their progress south for another three or four miles as the trail rose and fell through the rolling foothills, and the sun dipped toward the horizon. An hour before sunset, they made camp, again by a little stream, where John collected wood and started a fire.

They dined on a handful of oats and a hunk of jerked elk.

"I could sing you something," said Luyu.

"Please," said John.

Luyu sang a song Mrs. Yount sometimes sang while boiling the laundry, when she thought nobody was around. John Tully sat rapt. He had underestimated Luyu's beauty by looking in the wrong places. After only one day it was already impossible for John Tully to conceive of his journey without Luyu.

When night fell, they lay side by side upon cowhide under the stars, and John Tully's heart beat as never before.

LAILA TULLY

Red Bluff, California, 2019

God, Laila hated this place. Never mind the ghosts of her Miwok ancestors. Any real connection she felt to her heritage had died months ago along with Grandma Malilah. So what was left to hold her in this forsaken town, this valley, or even California, for that matter? The heat was oppressive, the people were stupid, and half the town smelled like cow shit. The other half smelled like fast food. Laila hated her job, she hated her house (okay, trailer), and she hated their stupid truck with the broken window Boaz had said he'd fix weeks ago. But then Boaz had also said he'd fix himself at least a dozen times, most recently Tuesday morning. And how was that working out?

She ought to make a break once and for all, like Maddie said. Boaz still let her go to meetings, but he could no longer abide Laila's drinking coffee alone with her sponsor. Talk about supportive. Unbeknownst to

Boaz, Laila had almost enough money squirreled away that she could give him up, run six hundred miles north for the rain forest, and stay with her cousin Genie up in Queets. Genie could probably get her a job cooking at the lodge up in Kalaloch, or even waitressing. Anything, anywhere, away from this godforsaken valley. But Boaz had threatened to track her down if she ever tried to run off, and so far, Laila hadn't had the fortitude to test him. He'd also threatened to get a job four months ago, and that had never happened, so maybe he was just bluffing after all.

The swelling had gone down on her eye enough that she didn't have to call in sick for her Thursday shift, and she could work a double on Friday to make up for yesterday. Sitting behind the wheel in the back corner of the lot, the radio on low, Laila angled the rearview mirror down to eye level and applied some green concealer to her left eye, then a little orange, and finally some yellow. The results were only so-so, but they'd have to do. Of course Tam would probably say something, but Tam maybe ought to look in the mirror. She ought to mind her own damn business. It wasn't like Duane was any saint.

Laila walked across the hot parking lot and in through the back entrance, where a wall of cool air mercifully greeted her, even if it did carry the stink of stale cigarette smoke. Looking straight ahead at her locker, Laila donned her white coat, white apron, and white hat. Sure enough, she could feel Tam's eyes on her.

"Lemme guess, doorknob?"

Laila set her chin, narrowed her eyes, and didn't tender a reply as she tied off her apron. Tam was about ten years older and had twice the road miles as Laila, and Laila knew that Tam meant well much of the time. But that didn't change the fact that she ought not to have her nose in everybody else's affairs.

Laila walked right past Tam into the kitchen without a word and immediately started bleaching towels and wiping down the cutting boards. Peyton always left the kitchen such a goddamn mess, and Dennis hardly lifted a finger when it came to cleaning, which he was quick to remind them all was outside his jurisdiction as a manager.

Tam sashayed into the kitchen four steps behind Laila and started stacking dirty pans in the basin and hosing them down.

"Girl, I don't know why you put up with him," she said after a minute. "You ought to leave his sorry ass."

"You don't know anything about it, Tam."

"I know a good deal more than you think," she said, scraping crusty ziti into the garbage.

Just then, Dennis burst through the double doors from the dining room, forehead glistening with sweat. Laila swore he was on something. Always running to the bathroom. Always clenching his jaw and checking his wristwatch. And every now and again his eyes would suddenly get really wide, like somebody had his balls in a vise.

"We need a full of chicken Alf, a half of backs, and a refill at the dressing station," he said. "What happened to your eye?"

"Doorknob," said Tam. "Ain't that right, Laila?"

"I got stung by a bee," said Laila. "It was swelled up the size of a golf ball yesterday. Allergic, I guess."

"Hmph," said Dennis. "Take care of that chicken Alf and the baby backs, will you? I gotta hit the can."

Alone again with Tam, Laila kept her eyes down on her work.

"Listen, girl, I know you don't much care for me," Tam said. "But I'm older than you, and you could stand to learn a few things from me. Particularly about men."

"Tam, please, not today," said Laila.

"You got to remove yourself from that man, Laila. He ain't ever gonna change, no matter how many times he swears up and down to it. It's a vicious cycle, sweetie. I know from experience."

Tam set a hand on her forearm and looked kindly into Laila's eyes.

"Honey, I know you're scared to leave him. That's the way he wants it. But you gotta

123

leave that man. Listen, you could stay with me and Duane until you find a place to land. Boaz would be crazy to come harassing you with Duane around. Duane's likely to shoot damn near anybody who shows up to our place uninvited. If you need a little money to get out of town, I can help you there, too. You can do this, honey."

Just like that, Laila broke down crying, and Tam pulled her close until Laila was crying into her apron.

"It's okay, honey," said Tam. "Everything's gonna be all right. You got this, girl. You let old Tam help you out of this mess. I got four hundred dollars laid aside. That and whatever you scare up ought to be enough to get you clear of Boaz for good."

Dennis returned from the bathroom, clenching his jaw.

"What's wrong with her?" he said.

"Nothing you need concern yourself with, Dennis."

"It is if she don't get that chicken Alf and those baby backs out there on the double. We about to get hit in a few minutes."

After she cried herself out, Laila felt calm and surprisingly grounded throughout the rest of her workday.

Tam was right. Laila could do this. Maybe not today, but soon. Tomorrow, between shifts, when Boaz wasn't around to hear, Laila could call Genie up in Washington and test the waters, and maybe start making arrangements. It might take her a week to get her ducks in line, but this time she was resolved to making the break. In the meantime, she'd just do her best to stay out of Boaz's way and act like everything was normal.

While the thought of escaping this miserable town was thrilling, it was also daunting on any number of levels. But Laila was determined not to let her resolve weaken, not this time. She wouldn't talk herself out of it. She wouldn't let Boaz bully, or intimidate, or guilt her into staying. In fact, Boaz wouldn't even know she was leaving. One day she just wouldn't come home from work. Laila wished it could be tonight.

After her shift Laila stopped at the Chevron for a half gallon of milk and a six-pack of Busch Ice for Boaz. Otherwise, he'd be in a foul mood and probably wouldn't even talk to her. It wasn't until after eight when he usually started getting mean. Best to just swim with the current until such time as she could make her break.

After the Chevron, she stopped at the Sonic drive-through, where, because of the damn window that wouldn't roll down, Laila was forced to open the door of the truck and squeeze her arm through in order to execute the transaction.

The food runner smiled sympathetically

through the glass. Hell, her window probably didn't open either.

Once she got to the interstate, Laila rolled down the passenger-side window for a little relief from the heat, but the trapped wind started reverberating through the cab like it was a damn helicopter, so Laila leaned over the seat and rolled it up again. She flipped through the FM stations and finally settled on Kid Rock, which reminded her of senior year of high school. Not that she'd ever liked high school much, but it was starting to look good from this remove.

Laila would have bet fifty bucks that Boaz would be slumped on the sofa, clutching the TV remote, when she arrived home, and sure enough, that was exactly how she found him. He wasn't even wearing a shirt. His bony chest was pale from being inside all the time, and his tattoos looked dull, all of them faded to gunmetal blue.

"You get beer?" he said the instant she crossed the threshold.

"Don't I always?"

"Good," he said. "Aw, why'd you get Sonic again? I hate that shit. Why don't you cook something for once?"

"Boaz, I been cookin' all day. Why don't you cook something?"

" 'Cause there ain't no food in this house," he said. "Well, shit then. Open one of those beers for me."

It was hard enough, Boaz drinking in front of her every damn day of the week. One of these nights she was likely to fall off the wagon. But it was downright cruel how Boaz made her open his beers when she was nearly two years sober, and he knew damn well the temptation. Every goddamn day she thought she'd give in, but somehow she kept going. She could still feel that slackening of concern and expectation, that relief that came with a two-beer buzz. Problem was she never had learned how to stop at two.

It was a cruel fate that she still cared for Boaz in spite of all his weaknesses, but God, how she despised him sometimes. Seven years she'd put up with this shit — seven! Grandma Malilah had warned her against him from the beginning, but Laila hadn't listened. Did Laila really still love Boaz, or was staying with him just a bad habit? What did she see in him anymore? She used to think he was so competent and self-assured. Boaz could fix just about anything he put his mind to. But now that Laila had committed to leaving him, any polish Boaz still had left on him wore off altogether. His steely blue eyes no longer held any coy charm or promise of mischief. His lean tattooed frame no longer struck her as sexy, just hard and mean. Laila wished she could see the look on his face the day she didn't come home from work with his beer and his dinner. The day was coming.

WALTER BERGEN

Oregon, 2020

Months after the collision, in bed at home, or in the shower, or driving to the grocery store, Walter would dimly recollect navigating the aftermath through the haze of shock. He would remember the vague but pervasive sensation of being an imposter as he acted out the motions. How could he possibly be any kind of authority? How could he provide any comfort to those unfortunate souls when he had been the source of the calamity?

The Black kid must have been seven feet tall, thin but broad shouldered, like he was still inconceivably growing. There was panic in the whites of his eyes.

"It's my ma, she's hurt bad, you gotta do something."

"Okay, now, stay calm," Walter said, his legs jelly, the world still wrapped in gauze. "Where is she?"

"Two cars back," said the kid.

Mechanically, Walter followed in the giant's

wake, hurrying to keep pace with his prodigious strides, as they passed the blur of inquiring faces, the groping, desperate mass of humanity vying for Walter's attention.

MALIK FLOWERS

Portland, Oregon, 2019

The closer recruiting season drew, the nearer Malik got to his mom's single-minded objective of Malik's escaping the only neighborhood he had ever known for higher ground, the more Malik felt nostalgic for the life he'd be leaving behind. Particularly his work with the kids at the rec center: Rudy and Earl, Desmond and Rashard and Terry, Michael and Steph and J.R., all boys between nine and eleven that he coached two days a week and once on Saturdays, kids just young enough to steer clear of trouble unless it was at home, but old enough to yearn for independence.

Malik's job was not just to teach them how to ball, but to teach them how to build themselves into responsible and accountable young men, just as Mr. Green and Mr. Dwyer and Mr. Thorpe had done for Malik when he was a boy. The only difference was that Malik let the boys call him by his first name.

130

"Yo, Malik," said Michael as they rounded up basketballs at the end of practice and stuffed them into the big net bag. "You think I could ever play varsity?"

"If you want it bad enough."

"Even if I'm short?"

"Look," said Malik. "You're like five years off from trying to make any varsity. Who knows how big you'll be in five years? It don't matter. Right now, you just gotta do the work, little man, ball every day, be mindful, stay out of trouble, and do good in school. Because it won't matter if you can ball out if you can't make your grades."

Malik knew it sounded cliché, probably even to ten-year-old Michael, but the message was tried and true. And the more Michael heard it, the stronger the likelihood that it would stick.

"But I hate school," he said.

"Aw, man, it's not as bad as all that," said Malik. "It gets better."

"My brother says it gets worse."

"Well it doesn't have to," said Malik. "You just gotta learn how to embrace it. You gotta see school as an opportunity. The more you know in this world, the more you can build yourself up, and the bigger the man you can build yourself into, the more opportunities you're going to be able to create for yourself going forward. The whole world ain't basketball, little man."

Though the last bit had a ring of truth to it, Malik knew it was a lie, at least coming from him. Because the whole world was basketball. The only opportunities Malik had created for himself were a direct result of basketball. The only thing he wanted to do going forward was play basketball.

"How tall were you when you were my age?" said Michael.

"I don't remember exactly," said Malik. "Tall. But I'm telling you that doesn't matter."

That felt like a lie, too. The fact that Malik was six foot nine and still growing, the fact that he had been pushing six feet when he was a year older than Michael, had a lot to do with his future prospects. Otherwise, what life path might he be looking at after high school? His grades were decent but nowhere near good enough for any kind of academic scholarship. He might get into a state school, OSU or Eastern Oregon, but it wasn't like he had a college fund or any kind of resources set aside. So what would Malik's future have looked like at five foot eleven with an average jump shot? Community college? Selling refrigerators alongside his mom at Consolidated Appliances? The fact was, since Malik was Michael's age, he'd hardly ever envisioned any other life for himself that didn't involve basketball.

Apparently he wasn't fooling Michael either.

"If it doesn't matter about how tall you are, how come I never see seven-foot brothers working at DQ or Safeway? The only seven-foot dudes I ever see are wearing shorts on TV."

Malik would probably miss Michael the most. Funny, vulnerable Michael, almost always the last to leave. Nobody ever came to pick Michael up that Malik could remember. But then, since his own mom had usually been working his whole life, Malik had often walked home from the rec center or caught a bus himself, at least since fourth grade, so maybe things weren't as bad for Michael as Malik sometimes worried they were.

Together they hefted the big net bag into the equipment closet and walked down the corridor to the locker room, where the familiar acrid stench never failed to arouse a certain churchlike reverence in Malik. Same for just about any locker room, but especially this one. The rec center had been a second home to Malik for most of his life. In an unpredictable world, this place had been a model of consistency. Mr. Thorpe and Mr. Green and Mr. Dwyer always had his back. They were always willing to offer guidance when Malik felt outside forces trying to shape him. And these men, they still came around, except for Dwyer, who had died last year in a car accident; they still took an interest in this community, in these kids. Mr. Green sometimes came around on weekends, and Mr. Thorpe was still Malik's supervisor, though he insisted Malik call him Gus now. But Malik couldn't help but call him Mr. Thorpe.

Malik fished his blue hoodie out of the locker and pulled it over his head as Michael hefted his oversized backpack onto his back.

"Yo, Malik. You think you'll ever play for the Blazers?"

"I hope."

"I'd rather play for the Warriors or the Lakers or even the Heat. Anywhere far away from here."

"Why's that?"

"I don't know, I just would."

"Well, make it happen then, little man. You got it. Do the work. Blaze your own trail out of here."

Yet again Malik felt like he was failing Michael, who would probably never grow past six foot one and had done little at this point to distinguish himself on the hardwood or anywhere else that Michael had been. But what could Malik possibly do to prepare Michael for this reality when the kid already saw it coming? And why should he prepare him for it when so much of Michael's life was probably already disappointing? Why not let the little man dream? What bad could it possibly do him?

"Get it, little man," Malik said as Michael walked out beneath the weight of his ragged backpack. "Stay focused."

Malik ducked his head into the office on his way out, where Mr. Thorpe was at his desk, glasses poised halfway down the bridge of his nose as he considered his computer screen.

"Later, Mr. Thorpe."

Thorpe looked up unsmilingly. "Boy," he said, "you bigger than the last time I saw you, and that was yesterday. No wonder your mama works so hard."

Malik suppressed a smile.

"You know, that hurts, Mr. Thorpe, that really hurts," he said. "Do you know how hard it is for a person of my stature to use a bathroom stall, or use an ATM, or eat a taco? Do you have any idea what it's like to have to bend way down to kiss a girl?"

"Seems to me it'd be easier to eat a taco with that big mouth of yours," said Mr. Thorpe. "Besides, what do you know about kissing girls?"

"Touché," said Malik, who turned to leave.

"Malik," said Mr. Thorpe, stopping him.

Malik turned to face him again, half expecting another zinger.

"Be mindful, boy," he said. "Stay out of trouble, stay focused, do the work."

"You got it, Mr. Thorpe."

Consistency was everything. Unwavering

language, unwavering belief. It didn't matter how corny it sounded; it was true.

Once outside in the chill air, Malik pulled his hood over his head and, slouching slightly, strode toward the bus stop. Damn, it was cold; felt like it might snow. Walking the two blocks to the bus stop, Malik started to warm up a bit, though the moment he stood still again, the chill took hold.

One of the disadvantages of being a giant was that you were easy to spot. While Malik was standing at the bus stop about to check his phone, a white Explorer with gold trim, subwoofer banging, shot across the near lane and pulled up abruptly alongside Malik at the curb. The passenger window whirred open to reveal Tavon Clayton, his best friend back in eighth grade, who'd once lived in the same apartment complex as Malik for about four months, though their paths had diverged in high school. Malik had kept his nose to the grindstone, while Tavon had dropped out after sophomore year, drifting ever toward the allure of the streets.

"Yo, baller, hop in, we got you," said Tavon.

"Nah, man, thanks," said Malik. "I'm good."

"Yeah?" said Tavon. "Blue chipper on the shame train? That don't seem right."

"I use the bus to do my reading," said Malik.

"Reading, huh?" Tavon smiled and shook

his head. "Aight then, dog, get after it. Don't stay up too late, now."

No sooner did Tavon begin raising the passenger window than the white Explorer shot off into traffic and down the boulevard.

Even when Tavon was putting Malik down, it seemed like he was propping him up somehow. It was like the whole neighborhood was using him as a vessel for their hopes. This knowledge was at once a blessing and a curse. Yes, he was granted advantages — respect and admiration and even the occasional freebie when he was recognized. He was adored and talked about in gymnasiums and hallways. In a way, he was already a celebrity. His name had appeared in *The Oregonian* many times, and not just in box scores, either. He'd even had a couple of regional TV mentions. Whenever his name was mentioned there always seemed to be big expectations attached to it.

But what if Malik let them all down? What if he tore his ACL, or he flamed out in college and didn't get drafted? What if he came back here and hung around like Mr. Thorpe? Would the respect and admiration and freebies all dry up? Was all of this support conditional? The questions were various and troubling. Yet, when the bus arrived and Malik ducked on board and took a seat near the front, scrunching his legs in close and looking out the window, he was nothing if not grateful to have such problems.

Brianna Flowers

Portland, Oregon, 2019
Brianna was still crying when she drove over the river ten minutes after she'd left Consolidated Appliances. Don LoPriori could go right to hell. Twelve years she'd worked for Don, and aside from the occasional creepy comment on the floor when nobody was around, she'd never had reason to believe he was capable of what had just transpired in his office.

Not giving her an advance was one thing, but propositioning her, well, that was something else. And she'd done the only self-respecting thing she could do about it: She'd walked out, and on a Monday morning, no less. What else could she do about it, report it to HR? Don LoPriori was HR.

The thought gave Brianna shivers. Instantly, she thought about Stacy, or Lacy, the little blonde, from last summer. She'd been relatively bright, and personable (and young), all five foot two of her. She liked working the floor, got along fine with Brianna and Denny and Lawrence. But then she left suddenly on a Friday afternoon. And a few years back there had been Vicky, another youngish blonde, also personable, also simpatico with Denny, Lawrence, and Brianna, who also didn't stick around more than a few months. And back in '07, when Brianna had first joined the Consolidated team, she'd basically ended up replacing Danielle, who, you guessed it, was blond, and on the right side of thirty, and who also left suddenly.

Yep, there was a pattern all right: short, youngish, and blond. Brianna couldn't believe she hadn't seen it before. No wonder it had taken Don twelve years to start hitting on her.

Thank God Malik was still at school, because Brianna was a wreck when she got home. She dropped her purse on the counter, sat down at the kitchen table, and ran her worried hands over her face. What had she just done? How could she walk out like that under any circumstance? Every single decision Brianna had made over the past seventeen and a half years had been geared toward not ending up here, in this exact place: no job, no contingency plan, no safety net, no future, only the awful reckoning.

God, and there she was so close to getting Malik out of the house and on to grander places, unimaginable places, and on the best imaginable terms. With a little luck Malik could write his own ticket. That was, if Brianna could afford a ride on Amtrak and a hotel room in Seattle. How was it possible she couldn't afford that? How could she be thirty-three years old and not have a lousy six hundred bucks? After all she had invested in Malik over the past seventeen years, how could she possibly come up six hundred dollars short?

Every single unnecessary charge Brianna had put on the credit card in the past eight months came flooding back all at once. The takeout from McMenamins one night a week when she was too tired to cook for Malik, the lattes on her lunch hour, the running shoes and the sports bra from Target that she never used. Especially painful were those impulsive purchases she'd allowed herself mostly because she hated her job, though they probably didn't amount to a hundred dollars a month. Whether it was the dark chocolate at the check stand or the Butterfinger Blizzards from the DQ drive-through. It was true Brianna could have dialed back on Christmas, too, for that matter. Malik could have lived without a PS4.

God, but she was tired of having to constantly inventory her purchases and decisions, of having to forever rationalize what felt like her entire existence.

It wasn't until Malik arrived home from

open gym that Brianna realized she'd forgotten to go shopping and didn't have any dinner in the house.

"Why don't we just go out?"

"We can't afford to this week," said Brianna with an edge of impatience.

"Okay, then," said Malik. "What's wrong, Mom?"

"Nothing," she said. "I just had a long day."

"I've got thirteen bucks," said Malik. "Give me the keys and I'll go pick up some Mickey D's. Problem solved."

Brianna could've cried. In an instant, she remembered that it was all worth it: all the sacrifice and penny-pinching and worry. Malik's good-natured smile, his genuine concern for her, his obvious gratitude for the life she provided him, that was the reward. Knowing that Malik's ceiling was so much higher than Brianna's ever had been, or her parents' had been, or her grandparents', or that of any Flowers who ever came before them, knowing that to some degree Malik could set the parameters and define the terms of his own life, was the icing on the cake.

No sooner did Malik snatch the keys from her hand than several things crystallized for Brianna. First, she ought to return to Don LoPriori's first thing in the morning to get her job back, even if it meant enduring another creepy advance. Fifteen more months; that was all Brianna needed to

142

survive. Once Malik spread his wings, God willing, to UW, or Gonzaga, or Michigan State (but hopefully not Kentucky, or North Carolina, or anywhere else in the South), Brianna could start taking care of her own interests again. If she had to endure Don in the meantime, then so be it. He could only get so close. That was the main revelation, and it was an old one: Brianna could and would endure anything for her beautiful boy.

The second thing that crystallized was that Brianna was going to come up with the money for Seattle at any cost. If Don wouldn't give her an advance, she'd go to Moneytree and get a draw against her paycheck. The 20 percent fee would mean that she'd have to suck it up big-time in April. No lattes, no Blizzards, no dark chocolate, no takeout, no problem. Seattle was happening.

By the time Malik returned with their Mickey D's, Brianna was in better spirits and had already abandoned the idea of going back to Don. That bridge was officially burned.

"Tweaked my hammy today at open gym," Malik said over his Big Mac at the kitchen table.

"You ice it?"

"Nah," he said. "It's not bad. Just a little pinch."

"Child, you've gotta stretch," said Brianna. "Before and after. And you got to ice your leg afterward if you feel a pinch. You know that."

Malik smiled.

"Aight, Coach," he said.

They lapsed into silence for a moment, Malik unwrapping his second Big Mac and immediately engulfing a quarter of it in a single bite.

"You wanna split this one?" he said.

"Since when can I eat more than one Big Mac? I can't even finish this one," she said. "You eat it."

"Nah, I'm good with two," he said.

But Brianna pushed it toward him anyway, knowing he could easily eat four, maybe five Big Macs. She felt bad enough, Malik spending his last thirteen bucks, but she couldn't stand the thought of his being hungry. With basketball practice, he could only work but the one day a week after school down at the rec center, where his pay was paltry.

"Mom," he said. "I've been thinking."

"You're too young to think straight," she said.

"Well, you always saying that finishing college is more important than playing in the NBA."

Brianna sighed, shaking her head grimly. "Don't you start getting ahead of yourself again. You ain't finished high school."

"This is just theoretical, Mom."

144

"Dreamin' it don't make it come true," she said.

"I know, I know, it's work and commitment," said Malik. "And having a plan. So, nothing wrong with having more than one plan to fall back on, right? That's the whole reason you say I got to finish college."

Brianna folded her arms.

"See, Ma, your plan has got a hole in it. It ain't —"

"Don't you say *ain't*. Makes you sound uneducated."

"You say *ain't*," he said. "You just said it."

"I ain't going to college," she said.

"Fine," he said. "The point is, the logic of your me-finishing-college plan isn't logical, when you consider that, say I signed on with Kentucky, or Michigan State, or Louisville. And say I play two years and enter the draft."

"Boy, you just stop that —"

"Just hear me out," he said, fashioning a yield symbol with both hands.

Brianna obliged, but only begrudgingly.

"I play two years and enter the draft," he said. "Say I go in the first round. Say that's what the experts project for me, so it's not like I'm just entering the draft blind."

Brianna resisted the urge to interrupt again. She knew she needed to let him have his voice, even if it was teenage-backward.

"Mom, even if I go near the end of the first round, we're talking about ten million dollars over four years. Ten million dollars. You think I can't go finish two years of college any time I want with ten million dollars? I could buy my own college."

Brianna couldn't hold back any longer.

"Malik Flowers, you listen to me," she sputtered. "This ain't about any amount of money. Money ain't the end-all in this world. You made it this far without having any, didn't you?"

"I know money ain't ev— *isn't* everything, Mom. I'm just saying. You the one always worried about me getting injured, so then, why would you want me to risk my health for two extra years, and maybe lose the chance to have everything I ever wanted? It don't make any sense. Heck, I could enter the draft after next year and we'd probably be millionaires."

"This ain't about you the basketball player, Malik Flowers, it's about you the man. Don't matter what you know on a basketball court or what you can do; what matters is what you know in the world. And the more you know, the better — especially if they gonna hand you ten million dollars."

"Fine, you win," said Malik, crumpling the second Big Mac wrapper, leaving Brianna's half-finished burger on the table.

"I gotta study for chem," he said, rising to his feet, ducking low to clear the cheap chandelier.

No sooner did Malik retire to his room than Brianna felt the all-too-familiar pang of a particular guilt: the guilt of stifling her son's imagination. She knew she ought to go easier on him. Why not let him dream? Why not let him make the most of what could very well be the best days of his life? Who knew what would happen after he signed a letter of intent? What if he did go to Kentucky, or Michigan State, and rode the pine for two years? What if he never got drafted? The odds were against it, after all. Thousands of kids played Division I ball, and many of them possessed Malik's size and strength. Yet, each year only sixty of them got drafted. Chances were, nobody would ever hand Malik ten million dollars. But was that any reason not to let him dream? His love of the game was palpable in the twitch of his restless muscles when he watched it, whether from the bench, where he spent very little time, or the couch, which he never sank into so long as there was hoops on the TV. He could hardly bear to watch the game, he wanted to play so badly; he lived to play it. It was both beautiful and problematic, and, in the end, almost tragic to behold — beautiful because it represented an almost divine sense of purpose that few would ever experience, and problematic because it was not eternal. In fact, it could end any day. Even in the best-possible-case scenario, Malik wouldn't be playing the game at an elite level in fifteen years, at which point he'd be Brianna's age. The tragedy was that Malik could not yet see this because all of it was still in front of him, and she ought to let him enjoy that fact a little.

Brianna had half a mind to walk down the hall, poke her head into Malik's room, and apologize. But she didn't want to disrupt his studies.

FINN AND NORA

Chicago, 1851

The director of the Catholic Orphan Asylum was Master Searles, a slight man with narrow shoulders and a remarkably large head, made all the more impressive by a shock of generous side-whiskers that, from the looks of them, had not submitted to any attempt at grooming in the recent past.

When the lady and gentleman from the relief society had picked up Finn and Nora in an alley off of Wabash Avenue that morning, where they'd been sleeping for several weeks in a makeshift shelter among the fruit crates and the vermin, they were immediately consigned to the Catholic Orphan Asylum, located several miles across town. The orphanage was a sprawling and rather ominous-looking brick edifice, three stories tall. There were generous grounds in front, though it resembled nothing so much as a swamp, circumnavigated by a black wrought-iron fence.

Upon their arrival, Finn and Nora had been led by one of the matrons on duty, a Miss Heinlin, to Master Searles's office, which was at once grand and utilitarian in appearance, with its large wooden desk and white walls partially covered in framed portraits of other, more venerable gentlemen in side-whiskers.

"Names?" he said without looking up from his register, in which he was scrawling.

"I'm Nora, he's Finn," said Nora. "Bergen is our family name."

"And what has become of your parents?"

"Our father died of the fever before we ever made the crossing to America, sir. And as for our mother, she also succumbed to the fever, shortly after our arrival in Chicago."

"Mm," said Master Searles. "And you've been living on the streets for how long?"

"Nearly a fortnight, sir."

"And how, may I ask, were you sustaining yourselves during this time?"

"Sir, we were sweeping crosswalks, mostly."

"An honest avocation," he said, still not looking up from the page. "Not like some of these young guttersnipes who would sooner steal a purse from an old woman than sweep a crosswalk."

Finally Master Searles concluded his writing, dotting an "i" with a flourish, and closed the register, at last lifting his big buffalo head to face them.

"Consider yourselves lucky, children," said

Master Searles. "Why, only a few short years ago, you'd have likely been indentured to a family of dubious standing, or committed to the poorhouse — and I daresay you wouldn't want to find yourself there; full of rogues and vagabonds, individuals of questionable moral fiber, to say the least. But lucky for you, those days are mostly gone, thanks to some of our more prominent citizens — Mr. Seymour and Mr. Alton, to name two — who felt it necessary in their hearts to adopt measures for the care and maintenance of destitute children like yourselves."

" 'Twas very kind of them, indeed, sir," said Nora.

"What say you, young man? Finn, is it?"

"Me brother doesn't speak, sir."

"He's an idiot, then?"

"No, sir, he just doesn't speak."

"Well, now, that strikes me as peculiar."

"Ever since the baby died," she said.

"I see," said Master Searles. "And what baby would that be?"

"Our baby sister, Aileen, sir. We lost her shortly before we left Ireland. It was me brother who found her. That's when he stopped talking. The day he found her, I saw with me own eyes a lone magpie on the eave of our home."

"A magpie?"

"Yessir. All by itself."

"And this is significant?"

151

"Yessir. Everyone knows a lone magpie is a bad omen."

"Mm, do they now?" said Master Searles, apparently not pleased with the explanation. "Well, that is an unfortunate state of affairs, but this silence cannot be tolerated for long. To be a productive member of society, a body must communicate. You will need to communicate right here within the confines of the asylum. While I sympathize with this unfortunate turn of events that has struck you dumb, and while it is not my intention to be indelicate, I must ask you to speak, young man. Speak."

Finn looked him in the eye but wouldn't speak.

"Speak, Finn."

Finn only shook his head.

"Boy, I beseech you to speak."

But Finn remained tight-lipped. No amount of entreating or haranguing would succeed in breaking his silence. There was simply nothing to say.

At last, Master Searles relented.

"Very well, Mr. Bergen. You have prevailed for the moment," he said. "However, I will caution you with regard to the near future that this is how it shall be: I shall give you a day or two to warm to this place, to take a hot meal and sleep upon a real bed, impregnable to the perils of street life, safe and secure in our haven. But then, as God as my witness, you will speak what's on your mind, boy. Do you understand?"

Finn cast his eyes down, and a tear escaped him, running down his cheek. Nora clasped his hand in her own and gave it a squeeze.

"Miss Heinlin," said Master Searles, "kindly see to it that these children receive some manner of a cleansing, then assign them to their respective dormitories."

"Yessir, Mr. Searles."

When it was apparent that the twins were to be separated for the purpose of assignment, Nora to the girls' dorm and Finn to the boys', Finn refused to release his grip on Nora's hand until such time that Miss Heinlin forcibly removed it, assigning Finn to the care of second matron, a Miss O'Hara.

Miss O'Hara led Finn down a long, joyless corridor to the head of a wide staircase and down the steps. In the lower corridor, they passed a pale, reedy boy, clutching a mop and bucket, squinting like one who was nearsighted. Within the hour, Miss O'Hara had administered a vigorous scrubbing with a wet rag that left the boy red and chafed. Next, Miss O'Hara brandished a formidable set of shears and began hacking away at his hair inexpertly, though she could do nothing to tame the boy's willful curls. Once Miss O'Hara had achieved a sort of skirted dome around the circumference of Finn's head, she gave up the battle.

Finn was presented with a bundle of clean but ill-fitting clothes, comprising brown, belted trousers of wool; a baggy shirt of cream-colored linen, stained at the lapel and bald at the elbows; and a plain gray neckerchief. For shoes, he was presented a pair of worn half boots with leather side ties.

Finally, late in the afternoon, Finn was assigned to a bed in the boys' dormitory, a long, high-ceilinged chamber with beds numbering twenty along each wall, and a wide aisle running down the center. Finn was flanked by boys on either side, whom Miss O'Hara identified respectively as James, a flat-faced older boy with raised burn scars upon one side of his face, and Sullivan, a diminutive youth with one blackened eye.

"Supper will commence in precisely one hour," said Miss O'Hara. "James will show you the way to the commissary, isn't that right, James?"

"Yes, ma'am," said James.

No sooner did Miss O'Hara take her leave than James attempted to engage Finn.

"I hope you like wood pulp and dog meat," he said.

Finn offered no reply.

"Aw, it ain't so bad as that," James conceded. "I've eaten worse on the streets, believe me."

Finn lay upon his bed and stared straight up at the ceiling.

"Ain't you even gonna ask me about my face?" said James.

But Finn kept his eyes glued to the ceiling, maintaining his silence.

"Not much of talker, are you?" said James.

"You scared or something?" said Sullivan.

"Aw, leave him be. It don't matter how much you talk," said James. "And it's okay to be scared. It'll all be familiar after a while."

Though Finn offered no reaction to these reassurances, he was grateful for this kindness on the part of James. For never had he felt his separation from Nora more acutely than at that moment.

In the girls' lavatory, Miss Heinlin stood to the side while Nora scrubbed herself with a wet cloth and a bar of soap.

"You're not young," said Miss Heinlin. "And you haven't the strong back of a boy, nor the utility. Therefore your placement, if you should ever be so fortunate as to receive one, will depend upon your feminine presentation. You must present yourself in a ladylike manner at all times."

"Ma'am," said Nora, "when will we see the boys?"

"Child, I should say that is a very unladylike question, and a poor start toward feminine presentation."

"It's me brother, ma'am. We're not accustomed to being apart. He needs me to speak for him."

"I daresay that Master Searles has got it right, young lady. It is best that the boy start speaking for himself sooner rather than later. You said he knows how. It is imperative that he exercise this ability, or his placement shall never come to pass. Nobody wants an idiot."

For an institution allegedly conceived under the guise of charity, Nora was finding the Catholic Orphan Asylum to be none too charitable. From Master Searles's unwarranted harassment of poor Finn to Miss Heinlin's gloomy outlook regarding Finn's and Nora's futures, the asylum had shown them little in the way of charity in the few short hours since their consignment.

Nora was presented with a plain cotton dress extending well below the knee, which could not have been more shapeless and less becoming had it been a burlap sack.

"Is this what you meant by *ladylike,* ma'am?" Nora said.

Miss Heinlin turned her nose up and thrust her chin out slightly.

"The dress is modest," she said. "Modest is ladylike. And you must learn to keep such insolence in check, for it is most unladylike. The dress will serve you well. Now come, I'll lead you to the dormitory."

From beneath what old bridge had this dreary Miss Heinlin crawled out, anyway? And how was it she wasn't covered in warts?

After scavenging for weeks on the streets of Chicago, Nora was at least pleased at the thought of sleeping on a proper bed for the first time in months, and eagerly anticipating a hot meal — perhaps a stew of mutton or some cabbage soup. The thought of it cheered Nora somewhat as she walked in single file to the commissary under the direction of Miss Heinlin.

"I do hope it's mutton," said Nora.

"I shouldn't get my hopes up if I were you," said a girl named Penelope.

Indeed, Penelope was right. The Catholic Orphan Asylum proved to be no more a bastion for the culinary arts than it was a bastion of mercy. Supper consisted of a bowl of gray porridge, bearably warm at first but quick to congeal into a mortarlike substance that was quite nearly inedible. Nora was bitterly disappointed. Half a day imprisoned in the Catholic Orphan Asylum and already she yearned to escape.

Though the boys and girls were seated at opposite ends of the cafeteria, it came as no small relief that Nora was able to spot Finn. If it took her a moment to locate him amid the rowdy throng, it was because his beautiful ginger curls had been shorn above the ears, a state of affairs that surely would have brought their mother to tears had she lived to see it.

Nora waved enthusiastically, but Finn,

disconsolate, eyes resting forlornly on the bowl of porridge in front of him, which he was not eating, did not notice her attempts. He wasn't strong enough, thought Nora. He'd already given up. He'd die of heartbreak in here. Nora had to get to him. She stood up and walked past the row of girls, approaching Miss Heinlin, who was stationed stiffly in the aisle, chin up, eyes sweeping the room, ever on the lookout for insubordination.

"Child, why are you out of your seat?"

"Ma'am, I need to talk to me brother."

"I'm afraid visits are not permitted during meals," she said. "Now kindly return to your seat, child."

"I simply must see him," Nora entreated. "He needs me."

Miss Heinlin regarded Nora with the closest thing to sympathy she'd yet to exhibit.

"See here," she said, not unkindly. "Your brother must learn to be self-sufficient. He won't always have you to speak for him or advocate for him. The earlier he learns to depend on himself, the sooner —"

"You can't do this to us," said Nora. "We never asked to be here. You can't keep us apart, you can't!"

Miss Heinlin transformed instantly back to her old, witchy self.

"I must say this impertinence is most unusual, and quite unladylike. You ought to be grateful to be here, young lady. Master Searles would surely be displeased to hear such ingratitude from one of his wards, whom he has snatched straight from the jaws of depravity. And he has been quite clear with regard to the best course of action for your little brother."

"He's not me little brother, ma'am, he's me twin."

"Be that as it may, you shall be permitted to see your brother at the appropriate hour, and according to the established protocol of this institution, but until such time he will have to manage without you."

"When? When is the hour? What is the protocol? When can I see me brother?"

"In due time, according to custom. Now, get back to your seat, child, this instant, or you shall receive a most unpleasant reckoning after which, I daresay, you might find it difficult to sit down."

Nora had little choice but to comply. When she sat again to face her porridge, now a fully formed brick of congealed oats, she had lost her appetite completely.

To be a twin was to never be alone. To be a twin was to have a witness, an advocate, and a buffer to shelter you against the world at large. Prior to their arrival at the Catholic Orphan Asylum, Finn could count on one hand the number of times he'd been separated from Nora for more than half a day. Now such separations were a daily occurrence. For not only did the boys and girls dine and bunk separately, they mostly fraternized independently, but for a brief interval at midday upon the sodden playfield or a stolen moment in the corridor. Finn lived for such moments. And when they presented themselves, he leaned into Nora's assurance like a fire.

"It's not so bad," Nora said as they sat side by side upon the brick stoop, overlooking the playfield.

Finn frowned.

"Oh, you're right," said Nora. "It's dreadful. I'd rather be back in the alleyway, or even back on that cursed boat with Mother."

Nora set a hand on Finn's knee and squeezed it gently.

"We must stay strong in our faith," she told him. "Our fortunes could be worse. At least we have each other."

Indeed, having each other was the single consolation for either of them in a life that had been otherwise unrelenting in its cruelty. To be a twin was to never face the pitiless world alone.

Life in the Catholic Orphan Asylum marched on in uneventful fashion. The children worked, and ate, and slept. Mornings they received instruction, both religious and academic. Afternoons they took their fresh air for a few precious minutes before returning to their assigned tasks. In preparation for their eventual placement, the Catholic Orphan Asylum obliged its denizens to be productive members of society. Thus most of the tasks associated with the upkeep of the institution rested largely on the shoulders of the children.

The only thing that seemed to mark the monotony of institutional life was the occasional and discreet disappearance of a child fortunate enough to be placed. No explanation was ever offered, nor was any hint of said child's fate to be gleaned. They simply disappeared one day, if they were lucky. But as summer progressed, such fortune did not smile on Finn and Nora Bergen.

Master Searles, with whom Finn convened weekly in his office, pursued his zealous campaign to force speech upon the boy. Having exhausted his admonitions and threats somewhere short of physical torture, Master Searles had recently resorted to a number of different tactics, one of which involved jumping out from behind closed doors or behind stairwells in an effort to startle some audible response from the child. Finn never cracked. In fact, his resolve only grew stronger as he grew to suspect that Master Searles now entertained a certain respect for his silence.

"Mr. Bergen," he said from across his giant desk, "it has become increasingly clear to me that in your childlike manner you present a formidable stoicism. As it turns out, I cannot force you to speak. And I have come to understand that to test your mettle is an exercise in futility. For you are made of durable stuff, which in itself is commendable, though let us not confuse silence and virtue."

Here, Master Searles left off to fuss with his great shock of side-whiskers.

"You must understand, boy, that in your silence, whether you mean to or not, you are not only isolating yourself from the rest of the human family, you are complicating in a most detrimental manner what might one day be a better life for yourself. So again, I beseech you to comprehend this: Nobody, that is, nobody wants to adopt an idiot. And if they do, that child's destiny shall almost certainly involve backbreaking labor. Does this not sway you in your misguided conviction, boy?"

Finn shook his head.

"Not in the least?"

Tight-lipped, Finn shook his head once more.

Master Searles continued to occupy himself with his side-whiskers, donning a bemused expression.

"Gracious, child, you are truly unique among men. Find me another man in the great state of Illinois who will stand his ground at any cost, against any foe, counter to any persuasion or reward, at the risk of any amount of suffering, and all not to speak his mind. I'm honestly not sure whether it's courage or cowardice that accounts for your silence, but it is singular, that I must give you."

Meanwhile, at the behest of Miss Heinlin, a most unsentimental mistress, Nora progressed toward feminine presentation and utility: folding laundry, mopping floors daily, dusting, scrubbing, changing diapers, and the one task from which she derived satisfaction, bottle-feeding infants, to whom she cooed and whispered assurances.

Though the day's labor was exhausting, the occupation was welcome, for Nora felt incomplete without Finn at her side. In spite of his needs, disquieting as his willful silence could be, Finn offered Nora a strength and consistency all his own. In the absence of speech, Nora believed Finn capable of feeling things beyond her emotional range, which rendered him pure in Nora's eyes. Though it could frustrate, even infuriate, there was also something reassuring in Finn's silence. He never said the wrong thing, never reaffirmed Nora's fears or burdened her with his own. Moreover, she could confess anything to him without fear of admonishment. And when Nora dared to daydream, Finn did not temper her hopes.

"Oh, Finn," she said upon the brick stoop, accompanied by the cries and laughter of children. "Imagine if we were to be placed with a good family, a well-to-do family who lived in a big house. Wouldn't that be something?"

Finn shrugged.

"Miss Heinlin says that if I make myself useful, and present myself in just the proper manner, there's a much better chance that someone will want me — that is, us."

Finn betrayed nothing in his silence, a condition that Nora took as encouragement.

"Why, imagine eating lamb and potatoes and carrots for supper every night. Imagine a big white house with a white fence. Can't you just see it? I imagine my own room. With a desk, and a mirror, and a chest of drawers, a room where I can collect things that please me, beautiful things, and fragile things. All things that have their own place, things I won't ever have to carry on my back."

Though he never intimated as much, and governed his countenance accordingly, Finn did not share his sister's hope for the future. He doubted whether she believed her daydreams herself. How could she even dare to hope for such things, given her experience? Finn's expectation for the future was consistent with the bleak prospects that Master Searles had already prepared him for: a life of labor and exploitation, motherless, fatherless, and bereft of anyplace to call a home. But even these were prospects Finn could endure as long as he had Nora. His greatest hope was that Nora would one day have her beautiful and fragile things. Thus, it seemed a good omen when one rainy day in early September, Finn, pacing the soggy perimeter of the Catholic Orphan Asylum to no purpose, looked down into a puddle and chanced to discover something flashing blue beneath the surface of the cloudy water. Fishing it out, he stuffed it in his pocket before he dared inspect it. Rounding the corner of the building, certain he was out of sight among the trash barrels, Finn pulled his found prize out and studied it: a heart-shaped locket of blue enamel, a tiny thing, both beautiful and fragile. Inside the locket, upon a gold inlay, was engraved a looping cursive letter L. How such a precious thing wound up in a mud puddle at the orphanage was hard to fathom. Perhaps some wealthy prospective parent had dropped it while touring the grounds? Surely it did not belong to Miss Heinlin, or Miss O'Hara, or any of the matrons thereabouts? The very idea of one of those dour women possessing something so exquisite seemed out of the question. It was as though the locket had been placed there for Finn to find. He was thrilled at the discovery, knowing his sister would treasure such an ornament: the evocative deep blue of the heart, the impossible smoothness of the enamel, the delicacy of the tiny hinges, the brilliance of the gold inlay. Never mind that her name did not begin with the letter L; L was for *love,* and *laughter,* and *light,* all the things his sister provided him. Nora would love the locket. She would cherish it forever. Stuffing the little miracle back into his coat pocket, Finn could not wait to present it to Nora the first chance he got.

Except that he never got the chance.

One rainy morning in early September, as a gusty wind blew off the great, gray lake, Nora's life changed forever.

Miss Heinlin interrupted Nora in her laundry folding and led her without explanation up the stairs to Master Searles's office. Seated behind his desk, Master Searles looked up from his notes to greet Nora with a toothsome smile.

"Sit down, Miss Bergen," he said.

"Have I done something wrong, sir?"

"Quite the contrary, Miss Bergen. Under Miss Heinlin's tutelage, you have rendered yourself quite useful. She has given you high marks for feminine presentation, and your utility has not gone unnoticed."

"T'anks, sir."

"You need not thank me, child, but if you must, please include the 'h.' You should *th*ank instead your good fortune. You see, today is a most auspicious day, Miss Bergen, for your fortunes have changed."

"Sir?"

"You have been placed," Master Searles announced.

Nora's ears began ringing, and her scalp tightened two sizes.

"And, I daresay, very well placed, Miss Bergen," said Master Searles. "For none other than Mr. Seymour, one of our city's finest patrons, has agreed to take you on. As of this afternoon, you are no longer a ward of the Catholic Orphan Asylum. What have you to say about this wonderful news, Miss Bergen?"

"Sir, I . . . well, sir, I . . ."

"Yes, it always comes as quite a shock. But rest assured, Miss Bergen, you have been very well placed. Mr. Seymour will provide you with most excellent amenities and myriad opportunities for betterment. You are indeed the most fortunate of children."

"And me brother?" she said. "Have you told him the good news, sir?"

Master Searles's smile faded.

"Oh, don't misunderstand me, child. It is only you who will be placed. Your brother shall know nothing of this."

"You mean to say, sir, that . . . ?"

"Understand, Mr. Seymour's generosity can only extend so far, child. Your brother shall remain in our care until such time as —"

"No!" Nora exclaimed. "You can't, I won't go, not without me brother."

"I'm afraid that's out of the question, Miss Bergen."

"Allow me to speak with Mr. Seymour," Nora pleaded. "He must take on me brother if he's to have me. Surely, I can change his mind."

"No, child, Mr. Seymour has no interest in your brother."

"Then I won't go," she said. "You can't make me."

"You most assuredly will go, child, and I would caution you to do so graciously. To be placed in the care of Mr. Seymour is a rare opportunity. One could not hope to do better."

"You can't separate me from me brother, you can't!"

"It is done, Miss Bergen, and owing only to the most fortuitous of circumstances. I must say that I'm surprised at your ingratitude. Now make haste and prepare your things."

Nora's devastation was swift and complete, though she did not go without a fight. Such was the fever of her dissent that Master Searles was soon forced to leave his desk and aid Miss Heinlin in restraining the child. When Nora was all out of fight, she surrendered finally to her grief, her body racked with sobbing as Miss Heinlin guided her down the stairs to the girls' dormitory, where she began packing Nora's things as Nora watched on, numb with shock and disbelief.

"Now, pull yourself together, child," said Miss Heinlin. "Mr. Seymour has your carriage waiting."

"I must see me brother first, ma'am," said Nora through the raw ache of her grief.

"You shall not see your brother," she said.

"But I must, ma'am," insisted Nora. "I cannot simply leave him without a word."

"I'm sorry, child. But such an encounter would only complicate matters. It's best that you make a clean break."

"When can I come visit him?" she said.

"You will not visit, child," she said. "It's for the best."

"Will he know where to find me when he gets out?"

"That's up to Master Searles's discretion."

Nora began to sob anew. How could it be deemed good fortune to lose one's only remaining love? How in the name of heaven could anyone account for such a separation? How could God abide such cruelty?

"But why?" she said. "Whyever would you separate us?"

Miss Heinlin looked at her not unkindly and set a hand upon Nora's shoulder.

"So that you might find a home, child," she said.

"Me brother is me home," said Nora miserably.

"There, there," said Miss Heinlin, offering Nora a pat on the shoulder. "Everything is for the best. Today you will begin a new life, a better life. Come now, your carriage awaits you."

Nora would not remember the interminable walk down the corridor, past the curious eyes of a half dozen orphans, all of whom would have given anything to be in her shoes. She would not recall descending the front steps or boarding Mr. Seymour's carriage. Her final recollection of that terrible occasion would be peering out the tiny window of the carriage through the blur of her tears, as the Catholic Orphan Asylum receded and her brother was lost to her without so much as a goodbye, nor even a final glimpse.

WU CHEN

Shasta River, 1851

Wu Chen could not bring himself to feel anything as he squatted over the dead man at the edge of the smoldering fire. Even with the twin streams of blood running out from the pulpy crater in his forehead, the stranger looked surprised as much as anything, his blue eyes frozen wide beneath arched brows and his mouth open slightly. Before yesterday, Wu Chen had had every reason to doubt his willingness, or even his ability, to kill another man. And now, hours later, as the new day began, he had slit three men's necks with an expert proficiency he could not account for and shot another between the eyes, even as the man begged for mercy.

Sorrowful it was to be so far from home, so estranged from himself. And yet, Wu Chen still could summon little in the way of emotion. Perhaps if it were Jimmy Huang staring up at him, instead of the heartless stranger, he might have felt something. Instead Wu

171

Chen was visited only by a queasy physical sensation, which settled heavily into his bones, sapping his strength. It was as though in taking these lives, he had surrendered some life-force of his own. But he knew he must gather his strength and move on immediately. There was nothing to be done about the Huangs, their bodies strewn well downriver by now, probably beginning to bloat. And though it felt somehow improper, he refused to afford a burial for the strangers, leaving their remains to the scavengers.

Shivering as though against the onslaught of a fever, Wu Chen made his way up the bank and back up into the shrubs against the hillside, where he scanned the ground for the abandoned burrow. In the light of day, he could see the wildflowers blooming, red, purple, and orange, but their beauty and promise were lost on Wu Chen. He moved listlessly through their midst, clinging to his lone objective with a dull certainty.

When he located the crescent-shaped cleft against the slope of the hillside, half grown over with river grass, Wu Chen broke a limb free of a nearby spicebush, stripped it of its berries, then lowered himself onto his stomach, poking the limb into the mouth of the warren, wary of snakes and other creatures. Only when he was certain the space was not occupied did he dare plunge his arm elbow-deep into the tunnel and begin dragging out the leather pouches, one at a time.

Accounting for the Huang brothers' three purses, in addition to his own, Wu Chen was soon in possession of seventy-two ounces of gold, only a tiny fraction of what was likely still lying in wait somewhere beneath his feet, running a glimmering vein through the earth. But that ground, once almost sacred as the vessel holding all his hopes, was now worthless to Wu Chen, a scourge that had cost the Huang brothers their lives. He had no more intention of working the claim than he had of staying in this place, strewn with death and already drawing the attention of buzzards. Wu Chen could have never guessed that a place so bountiful, so ripe with the suggestion of its hidden mysteries, a place so bursting with color and so full of promise, could be as dead as the most barren desert.

Dusting off the pouches, he stuffed them in his rucksack. Stepping over one of the slit-necked strangers, whose congealing slough of blood was barely dry in the dirt, Wu Chen left and did not look back. Weighted down with the Huangs' fortune, the sack sat heavier than usual upon his shoulders as he fled down-canyon upon weak legs.

After a half mile, he paused to rinse the dried blood sullying his shirtsleeves. When his efforts failed, he tore the cuffs off altogether and dropped them into the current. Squatting on the bank, he scanned the river for any sign of a Huang brother washed ashore or caught among the snags. Only now did the tears finally arrive, and all at once his chest heaved with grief and bitterness for the Huang brothers, the loyal, hardworking, kind, hopeful Huang brothers, struck down senselessly in the prime of their lives.

This new world was even crueler than the one he'd left behind, and Wu Chen knew that no amount of gold could ever change that. The best he could hope to do was redeem it on behalf of Jimmy Huang and his brothers. But how? With no way to contact the Huangs' family and pass their fortune along to them, how could Wu Chen redeem such a place as this, a place where men killed one another without reservation over shiny rocks pulled from the ground? What good could such a place ever come to?

When his grief finally subsided, Wu Chen resumed his progress down-canyon, winding his way along the river, now and again surveying the banks for the body of a Huang brother. It would have been a comfort to bury someone. Though he was upon the same familiar trail to Shasta City, the question remained: Where to go? Where to run from his past and cast his new fortune? After some reflection, the most reasonable answer seemed to be back where he'd started. And so, a mile before he reached town, he veered left upon the southerly trail as it dipped into the valley, straight toward the formidable white vault of Mount Shasta, wrapped in timber and ancient ash.

Around noon, stiff and hungry, Wu Chen watered by a stream a short distance off the trail. Soon two Indians, a man and a young woman, passed, moving south upon a bow-backed mare. Wary of his fellow travelers lest they somehow guess at his terrible actions on the riverbank, Wu Chen squatted in the reeds until they passed. He lingered there for half an hour, drinking from the stream and organizing his thoughts, before resuming the trail. Three more times along his way south, Wu Chen would encounter the Indian couple. Nearly every night his dreams were tortured, haunted by the Huang brothers, chastising him for his cowardice and greed.

Ten days after he abandoned the claim, Wu Chen arrived in San Francisco with no clear path for his future. He spent his first days back in the city much the way he'd spent the initial week of his arrival not quite a year ago, though much had changed in and around San Francisco in that short time. The city was teeming with activity. Many a burned-out wooden structure was being replaced by brick construction. A number of the central streets were newly graded and planked. Clusters of new houses clung like a rash to the skin of Goat Hill. The harbor swarmed with the masts of countless ships, fixed to quays or anchored in the bay. Parts of the outskirts were utter confusion: a jumble of tents and makeshift houses of wood and corrugated tin, some of them on stilts; streets piled with shattered glass, and broken casks, and discarded clothing.

For days Wu Chen wandered San Francisco aimlessly, through the flats along the bay, past ramshackle saloons and gambling dens, and up the hill through the shanties of Sydney Town. Daily, Wu Chen meandered through the central plaza, past the brass cannons of the customhouse, past the luxury hotels, and grand saloons, and the shops and restaurants, which, in spite of the considerable fortune upon his back, wanted little to do with him. He straggled down Montgomery Street toward the wharf, where the miasma of rotting fish and cabbage assaulted his nostrils. The central wharf, riddled with gaps and holes, extended nearly a half mile into the bay, lined with slop sellers and open-air storefronts, fishmongers, and vegetable stands, and sellers of poultry, live and dead.

He rented an upstairs room in Chinatown, a dank and joyless space a hundred and fifty square feet, with a single window overlooking an alley noisy at all hours with the din of caged fowl. But Wu Chen hardly occupied the space except to sleep, and even then it lacked the charm of his old shack on the river, or even a mat beneath the open sky.

Rarely did Wu Chen linger in any one place that first week. The more he moved about, the more likely he felt it was that the next Jimmy Huang might walk into his life, offering Wu Chen some unforeseen opportunity. Perhaps owing to his lack of imagination, Wu Chen felt he needed somebody who might help him put his fortune to good use. He lacked experience and insight into the ways of this new world. In his young life so far, he had committed himself to only two vocations: farming and mining, both of which were now dead to him. There had to be something more awaiting him in the great city of San Francisco.

After a week of wandering the city without incident or consequence, Wu Chen began to question his own tactic, and was forced to admit that he was only biding time and avoiding any future at all. Thus, he began to view his situation as he imagined his uncle Li Jun might have viewed it.

"Work first, think later," Uncle Li Jun would say. "Do not sit idle, or opportunity will pass you by. Save your money for the future, because you never know what calamity awaits you there. Neither do you know what opportunity might present itself. Do not squander this fortune, Wu Chen. Work. Save. Grow your fortune. Save it for the children you do not have yet."

Wu Chen was grateful for this perceived

guidance. He soon deposited his cumbersome fortune in the San Francisco Savings Bank, an institution that he selected based less upon its name or reputation and more on its sturdy construction: its enormously thick walls, its deep-set windows, and its wrought-iron shutters. For Wu Chen reasoned that in San Francisco, a bank must be fireproof. Five times already the city had all but burned to the ground, including two times just since Wu Chen had arrived the previous year. It was bound to happen again, here, where the very streets were built on piles and the sidewalks upon wooden planks. But the bankers on Montgomery Street were finally getting wise.

Wu Chen felt much the lighter for having the ambivalent fortune off his back, both figuratively and literally. Now he moved about the city with purpose: to find an occupation, to learn a trade, to meet another human soul. While he had managed to unburden himself of nearly five pounds of gold, the loss of the Huang brothers still weighed heavily upon him. Whatever he had lost of himself, the only way he could think to try to get it back was to fill his life with other people. Nights in his rented room had become nearly unendurable. Beyond the loneliness and ugliness of the place, sometimes around his plank bed, he swore he heard the patter of bare feet, and one night he had a vision of the stranger

178

with the hole between his eyes, except there was no blood or pulp, just a clean, empty hole where the ball had entered his skull point-blank. He was naked, the stranger, and ghostly pale.

By the beginning of April, Wu Chen had found employment at a laundry on Clay Street at the edge of Portsmouth Square. The hours were long and the conditions were uncomfortable, between the heat of the stoves and the hand irons and the kettles, and the close quarters. He worked alongside fifteen or twenty other men, some younger and some older, and a few women, in each case younger than himself.

The work was ceaseless, but it got Wu Chen through the days knowing that his fortune was untouched. The repetition kept his thoughts of the Huang brothers and his own gruesome acts mostly at bay, though there were images of prone bodies burned into his consciousness, bloody and defiled by violence, images that he could not unsee. There seemed a part of him that was unrecoverable, or at least unreachable, and this distance was best filled with occupation.

In addition to means, his job at the laundry also provided Wu Chen with the human company he yearned for. Not that he was particularly friendly with anybody, but even the nearness of other bodies working in concert, and the necessity for communication, connected him in some way to the rest of humanity. Eventually, he would find his tribe and become a part of a community, maybe even a family, as in many ways he had become with the Huang brothers.

He soon left his haunted room and found another room on Kearny, this one facing west, a little sunnier, a little less cramped, but the exact same price, a fact that would have pleased his uncle Li Jun, who, in the absence of anyone else to confide in, became Wu Chen's imaginary confidant.

"You will see, Uncle," Wu Chen said, looking out the darkened window. "Things will only get better. I'm learning a trade, like you told me to. And I'm saving my money for the kids I don't have yet."

"Ah, but don't get too full of yourself, Nephew. You have seen more than once the bad fortune that can befall an unsuspecting man."

"I see that now, Uncle. But if I have learned anything in this new place it is that I have to believe in myself. This place demands it of you. So what may sound like foolish pride to your ears, it is only me believing in myself."

"Bah, maybe it's not you I'm worried about, Nephew. I fear you put too much faith in this place. Your friend Jimmy Huang rubbed off on you. He was a kind soul, but also naïve. This optimism, this sureness that the sky is the limit, will be the folly of this place, mark my words."

"What choice do I have but to embrace it?"

"More than you think," said his uncle. "Whatever you do, don't ever forget the ways of your own people. These people, here, Nephew, they do not want to mix with you, they only wish to utilize the Chinese like a service. They wish to have you serve them, and labor for them, but they want you to stay out of sight as much as possible, and stick to your own kind. And you would be wise to do so."

"I will do whatever I must to redeem this place, Uncle, for I am sworn to it."

OTHELLO

Illinois, 1851

For two days after leaving Chicago, Othello berated himself for squandering what might have been his best opportunity to free himself. Now his mental landscape was cluttered with the unwanted furniture of what-ifs, as he resolved not to lose his nerve this time. It was nearly dusk when the carriage pulled into Urbana. Othello, watchful out the little window of the carriage, cataloged streets and alleys, conducting reconnaissance for his ultimate escape route. For tonight was the night. He would not lose his nerve this time.

The Illini Hotel was not so grand as the Tremont House in Chicago; it was a squat wooden edifice all but devoid of decorative flourishes, situated in what amounted to a swamp. Of greater concern to Othello was the stable, set directly opposite the hotel office, which presented an immediate logistical problem. Othello further considered the procedural obstacles upon his first two trips from the carriage to the hotel through ankle-deep mud, portaging Master Worthy's trunks.

Muddy and winded, Othello had further occasion to ponder the difficulties upon a third trip betwixt carriage and hotel, whereupon he was forced to carry Master Worthy through the squelchy morass, much in the manner that a newly wed groom might ferry his bride across the threshold.

"My God, the odor of you," said Master Worthy along the way. "You smell of alfalfa. For heaven's sakes, Othello, haven't I taught you to maintain some basic hygienic standards?"

It took all the will Othello could muster not to drop Worthy Warnock in the morass in that instant. What a joy it would have been to watch him wallow helplessly in the mud. How Othello would have reveled in his master's incredulity and outrage. This thought sustained Othello as far as the front stoop, where he delivered Master Worthy, unsullied.

Upon check-in, Othello learned that he had bigger logistical hurdles to face than the proximity of the stable, when it was revealed that he would be sleeping in the basement, on a pallet among the other servants. There were six other men in all, cloistered in a room the size of a root cellar. Escape would require that he step over four of them in the darkness, and only once he was sure they were all sleeping soundly.

It was a matter of several hours before Othello deliberately eased himself upright on his pallet and drew a slow, deep breath, the pallet issuing a plaintive creak as he rose. Gingerly, he stepped over the sleeping bodies one by one. Reaching the door, he cracked it as discreetly as possible, the hinges squeaking in spite of his efforts. When the door was open enough to slip through, the light from the stairwell slanted into the room, slicing it lengthwise. When he looked back over his shoulder one last time, Othello's heart stopped beating. For the slant of light revealed the nearest man now upright in his cot, staring straight at Othello with an expression Othello was helpless to read.

As he held the man's gaze, his thoughts racing, his eyes beseeching the stranger to take pity upon him, Othello raised an index finger to his lips, denoting silence. The ensuing moment seemed to last a lifetime, during which Othello's eyes sustained their desperate entreaty as the other man's eyes seemed to waver in indecision. In that instant, before his resolve could be reduced to a puddle, Othello slunk through the partially open doorway without further pause, proceeding furtively up the stairs.

The wooden stairwell protested at every step. Arriving at the edge of the darkened lobby, Othello stopped himself at the threshold and surveyed the lobby from his place in the shadow of the stairwell. He found the night clerk asleep facedown on the counter. Heart hammering, Othello took that first tentative step. Instantly the floor creaked beneath him, and the night clerk stirred. Othello stopped dead in his tracks. Suddenly it was obvious he'd made a mistake, perhaps the greatest mistake of his life. As he stood perfectly still on the periphery of the lobby, Othello closed his eyes as though it might make him invisible. When he opened them again he saw that the clerk had settled back into slumber. Proceeding stealthily the five steps across the carpeted lobby to the front door, Othello cupped the cowbell in his hand, pinching the metal tongue between thumb and forefinger, as he eased the front door halfway open without betraying himself. Unhanding the bell gently, he let the tongue slip through his fingers and slithered through the narrow opening and eased the door closed.

Othello stole down the front steps into the chill spring air, crossing the squelchy morass in front of the inn. When he reached the road, he walked briskly toward the nearest alley and through to the next street. Pausing at every juncture to survey the empty streets, Othello darted through the butt end of town in the shadows. Finally, he reached the outer edge of town, which had thinned down to a few clapboard shacks, darkened at this late hour. It was here that Othello began to run for his life. He sprinted until his sides ached and his lungs were fit to burst.

After a mile or so, he arrived at a manageable pace and emptied his mind altogether. He was three miles outside of Urbana before he had the courage to slow his pace. It was at that point he left the main road and followed its general progress from some remove, where he was not likely to cross anybody's path.

After several more miles Othello could go no further. In the dead of night he diverged from the road, across a flat expanse of clump grass, progressing a quarter mile, fighting off a cloud of mosquitoes.

At last Othello stopped in the middle of the pasture and laid his body down in the grass beneath the star-spangled bowl of the moonless night. As his breathing began to slow, a cautious smile spread across his face.

He awoke stiff as iron, shivering in an open field miles from anything, his entire body aching, every muscle knotted like a wet rag, every joint stiff and creaky. Feet blistered and raw, he rose slowly to his knees, where he surveyed the vicinity. All around him the field was awash in a vibrant blanket of yellow, spotted black like a leopard: black-eyed Susans, practically as far as the eye could see, stirring gently in the breeze. How could this spectacle be anything but a harbinger of promise?

Othello allowed himself only a moment to

revel in this possibility before he began moving north through the pasture, through the rippling blanket of yellow flowers, then into the high grass beyond. Only once did Othello pass any sign of life: a small and very distant cabin, its chimney issuing a plume of smoke into the morning air.

Eventually, the pastureland gave way to intermittent woodlands and uneven terrain. Othello encountered few signs of life. Hiking parallel to the road at varying distances, he passed in and out of the scrubby woods, crossing pastures and fording creeks; up and over rolling hills, he marched on. When fresh water presented itself, he drank greedily from it. Food was another matter.

That evening, Othello camped in the woods, huddled in a shallow gulch among the reeds. His sleep was dull and dreamless through the first half of the night, then restless and fitful into morning, a state of affairs Othello attributed to hunger more than nerves. On this occasion, Othello awakened to no magnificent field of flowers, but the persistent thrum of insects swarming about his face. He wasted no time in resuming his journey north.

By late afternoon, carriages were passing regularly on the main road in both directions. The further he hiked, the more his path was cut through with dirt crossroads, and the more houses he passed. Soon it was impossible for Othello to proceed in solitude. The roads, the horses, the people were too many, until finally, like a vision from the future, he saw a great iron steam engine, just as Master Worthy had described it, hissing and churning, and wheezing slowly betwixt the muddy warehouses.

For two hours Othello wandered in the throng of Chicago looking for some marker to lead him to Mr. Seymour's estate. Once he crossed the river and could see the lake sprawling to the north, gray and endless, Othello managed to get his bearings and slogged through the muddy streets toward Seymour's estate.

At last Othello reached the lake and could see the great mansions spread out on the shoreline to the north and the south. And there among the great estates, away from the struggle and noise and industry of the city, lay Mr. Seymour's mansion. And more important, Cora. Poor, unsuspecting Cora, who had not exchanged so much as an actual word with Othello in their few short hours of proximity, Cora, who had no earthly idea or any reason to suspect the force of this total stranger's infatuation, this stranger born into slavery, who amounted to a fugitive, with no legal birthright of his own, in a strange city, in a strange land. This was the rock upon which Othello was currently building his unknowable future: that somehow Cora would save him.

When at last Othello found his way to Mr. Seymour's estate, he recognized it by its wide colonnade of poplars and its long, curved drive, which swung in purposefully to follow the shoreline for effect before arriving at the front of the house. Othello circled round to the service entrance before he ever reached the front of the house.

The sun had already set and dusk was settling in by the time Othello mounted the lone back step and knocked on the service entrance, his welling heart suddenly frozen.

It was a young Black woman who opened the door.

"Who are you?" she said.

"I'm here to see Cora."

"What you want with Cora?" said the woman. "Haven't I seen you before?"

"No," said Othello.

"I could swear I've seen you before."

"Can you get Cora?" said Othello.

"Hold on," she said, pushing the door three-quarters closed before retreating down the corridor.

In a moment, he heard footsteps approaching, and no sooner did his heart swell than a gray-haired man swung the door open to greet him. The man was dark-skinned, and though he was garbed in a grease-spattered white apron, he carried himself with dignity.

"Who are you?" said the old man.

His squinted eyes held the light of suspicion, though his face was not unkind.

"I'm just a friend, passing through," said Othello.

"Friend of who?"

"Friend of Cora."

"Friend from where?"

"How does that matter?"

"I'm her father," said the man.

Othello cast his eyes down.

"What's your name, son?" said the gray-haired man.

"George," said Othello with conviction.

"George, huh?" said the man. "George what?"

"Flowers, sir. George Flowers."

George Flowers, born in a field of black-eyed Susans. No more Othello from Louisville, Kentucky, born into slavery, the son of slaves, the grandson of slaves plucked from the jungles of West Africa like fruit for the white man's taking.

"And what is it you want with my daughter, Mr. Flowers?"

"Actually, I'm looking for work."

"What can you do?"

"Nearly anything, sir."

"You work with animals?"

"Yessir. Horses, hogs, chickens, dogs."

The old man in the greasy apron considered George Flowers at some length.

"I can pay in food and board," he said

finally. "Three meals a day — real meals: meat and vegetables when we can get them. Sundays off. Those are the only terms I'm authorized to offer, son, you understand?"

"Yessir."

"How you feel about sleeping in stables?"

"About what I'm accustomed to," said George.

Indeed, no pay, Sundays off, sleeping in stables: On the surface it sounded an awful lot like the life he had just fled. And yet it felt like so much more. George's heart thrilled at the prospect of sleeping in yet another stable, for this was no ordinary stable. Cora would never be far. Hope, possibility, the unknown, they would all be near at hand.

MALIK FLOWERS

Portland, Oregon, 2019

By his Thursday shootaround at the Y, Malik's hammy felt pretty close to normal. Any remaining tightness all but disappeared with five minutes of stretching, and Malik felt loose when he took to the court and began raining down midrange jumpers.

Thursday shootarounds at the Y had become a custom since the summer after sophomore year, when Haskins, Eddie, and Malik had all started playing varsity together, Haskins and Malik as starters, Eddie a swingman off the bench. A-Jack had started joining them last fall, shortly after his transfer from Southridge, and quickly became one of the Thursday shootaround crew. While these weekly workouts were as much about hanging out as they were about training or preparation, they served an important function in the system, a function Coach M subscribed heavily to: These weekly workouts were an exercise in closeness and chemistry, two big intangibles in Coach M's philosophy. Indeed, the four boys were like brothers at this point, and that familiarity paid dividends on the hardwood even if there was no advanced metric by which to measure it.

"You going to see your girl tonight?" said Haskins, dribbling right to left at the top of the key.

"She's not my girl," said Malik, letting a fifteen-footer fly. "She's my math tutor."

"Uh-huh, sure," Haskins said.

"Nah, Kayla Ramsey way too smart for Malik," said Eddie. "And too good-looking, too."

"Facts," said A-Jack, draining a three from well beyond the arc. "But why she gotta dress like a librarian?"

"C'mon," said Haskins. "Kayla Ramsey ain't all that. Malik's a big man on campus."

"Yeah, dog," said A-Jack. "What do you need with math, anyways, long as you can count in millions?"

Malik relished the chiding and the easy repartee. Normally he would have encouraged more of this banter, but in the absence of his sore hammy something else was troubling him: a slight click in his right knee. Not a hitch, mind you, not a twinge, nothing painful, or anything that inhibited his mobility or the explosiveness of his first step, just an odd little intermittent click, barely perceptible when he bent his knee. Most likely the anomaly was a result of the rapid growth that had caused Malik countless clicks and aching joints since he'd started outgrowing the charts at eight years old. There was nothing unique about the click except that the stakes were now higher than ever before. The giant body whose durability Malik had never questioned, whose agility and dependability he'd come to take for granted through every triple-double, through every turned ankle, and jammed finger, and sprained wrist, was now something more significant: It was the single factor that would decide his future. His high basketball IQ was worthless without his giant frame and athleticism. Malik's prospects were only as good as his knees.

His unspoken reservations were not lost on Haskins, who broached the subject afterward as they dressed in the locker room.

"What's got into you? You were soft today, like you were taking it easy. You in trouble with Kayla Ramsey or something?"

"Nah," said Malik.

"You can tell me if you are, you know that, right?"

"I know," said Malik.

"What is it, then? Is this about Seattle? You worried about those ballers? Because you know, dog, those boys, they only gonna elevate your game," said Haskins. "You're a man among boys, Malik Flowers. Own that shit."

Despite the encouragement of his friends,

and the fact that his knee felt perfectly normal at present, Malik was still a bit uneasy on the walk to the library, where he arrived seven minutes late to meet Kayla Ramsey. She was waiting for him at their usual table near the back, too engaged in her own studies to register his lumbering presence until he was directly above her.

"Sorry I'm late," said Malik.

"It's your money," she said, snapping her textbook closed. "You bring your trig book?"

"Yeah, I got it."

Malik squeezed himself into the chair beside her, his knees pressed to the underside of the table.

"Unit six," she said. "Page forty-two."

Kayla Ramsey was unlike any other high school girl Malik knew. For starters, she didn't surround herself with friends. She was never crowded around a locker or blocking the hallway with a crew of gossiping girls. She seemed unconcerned with being liked or noticed, though she had done plenty to distinguish herself. Malik was more likely to see Kayla talking to a teacher than another student. And while A-Jack claimed Kayla dressed like a librarian, Malik thought she dressed like a woman. He admired her refined if not slightly reserved style: dark skirts with leggings, and sweaters that looked dynamite on her. But more than anything physical, Malik admired Kayla's general bearing, her confidence and composure, and her unflappable demeanor. Kayla exuded the sort of capability that Malik associated with adulthood. She always seemed so quietly self-assured, so prepared, so unintimidated by any given situation, like life was moving slower for Kayla than it was for her peers. Only on the basketball court had Malik ever known such self-assuredness.

"Frankly, I'm surprised they don't just pay somebody to do your schoolwork for you," said Kayla. "I thought student athletes got an academic pass."

"Nah, it's not like that," said Malik. "If I don't make my grades, I can't play. Besides, I don't wanna skate by in life, I want to learn."

"Well," Kayla said, "we'd better get to work on inverse functions, then."

Though she was invariably cogent and always patient in her tutelage, it was often difficult for Malik to stay focused in Kayla's presence, especially when she was so close that he could smell her — not her perfume, or her soap, but her natural smell, earthy and a little savory. Then there was her intelligence, and the perfect straightness of her teeth, the graceful curve of her neck, and the fullness of her lips. Kayla had to know her proximity was causing Malik discomfort, though she never let on.

"Malik, can I ask you a question?" Kayla said at one point.

"Sure," said Malik.

"Don't take this the wrong way. I admire your determination, here. I can see you sincerely want to excel in math, and you're not afraid of the work, but do you really see yourself using trigonometric identities later in life? I mean, isn't the idea that you get a free ride through college and then play professional basketball and make obscene amounts of money?"

"Yeah, sure, that's the idea, but —"

"That must be nice," said Kayla before Malik could finish his thought.

"You must think I'm just a big, entitled jock, is that it?"

"Maybe a little at first," she said.

"Well, I'm not," said Malik, surprising himself. "I mean, supposing all that happens, and I'm drafted, supposing I play for five or ten years in the NBA. Then what, I just dribble off into the sunset? I don't intend on wearing shorts the rest of my life. Who says I won't become an architect or an electrical engineer? And what if I don't get drafted at all? Who says I don't work on a survey crew or become a game developer? All those things use trigonometry, right?"

For the first time ever, Kayla Ramsey seemed somewhat impressed by Malik, arching a brow and looking thoughtfully at him, as though seeing him for the first time.

"Okay, then, let's get back to work," she said.

"It's already six," said Malik.

"That's fine, let's just get through this unit," she said. "Do you have somewhere to be?"

"No," he said. "Let's do it."

And thus they put their heads down again, Malik fighting to focus through the thrill of her nearness, unable to resist an occasional sidelong glance at her lovely profile. Despite his conditioning, Malik was powerless to stop the stirring within him that Kayla inspired. To hear Coach M or his mother tell it, anything or anyone that distracted Malik from his ultimate objective was a potential obstacle. Love would have its day only after his future had aligned itself.

Kayla worked with Malik until they reached the end of the unit around six forty-five, at which point she began gathering her things without ceremony.

"Well done," she said. "I think you've got this. Frankly, I don't think you really need me after today."

"Oh, no, no, I still need you," said Malik with a sudden rush of heat to his face.

"Well, okay, if you say so," Kayla said. "It's your money. Same time next week?"

"Totally," said Malik. "I mean, yeah."

"See you then," she said, turning promptly to leave before Malik could accompany her.

How different would Malik's life look by the time they met again next Thursday? Here he was, less than two days from the invitational in Seattle. The coming weekend might well unlock his future. And yet, one way or another, he knew his feelings for Kayla would abide, whether or not they were reciprocal. Malik was still packing his bag as he watched her stride purposefully down the center aisle, past the reference desk, and out of the front door of the library, following her progress with his eyes as she proceeded halfway down the street to the crosswalk, where she glanced at her phone.

A-Jack was probably right: Kayla Ramsey was too smart and too good-looking for Malik. Kayla Ramsey wasn't impressed by such trivial qualities as athletic prowess, or social standing, or even the allure of a bright future. Still, there was no denying that something significant had transpired between them that evening: If nothing else, Malik had earned Kayla's respect, and that alone was enough to sustain Malik the whole walk home without a single thought of his clicking knee.

Luyu Tully

Shasta City, 1851

For two days Luyu and John Tully rode south on the Siskiyou Trail, until the ubiquitous presence of Mount Shasta was mostly behind them, though its snowcapped dome still peeked at them occasionally as they wended their way through the wooded hills, up and down the little valleys, along the well-trodden path. The days were unseasonably warm, and they paused to rest more than they would have liked. The end of the mountains was only a day or two removed, which would be none too soon for the old bow-backed mare, already in sore need of rest.

And what if the mare should give out on them? It might take them months to get wherever they were going, which was somehow a matter of less import than getting there. Such was Luyu's concern for Sugar that she dismounted and walked up most of the inclines, bearing a good deal of the horse's load up the steeper passages.

Several times along the trail they crossed paths with a Chinese who attempted, unsuccessfully, to hide himself from their view on each occasion, skulking in the reeds or in among the pines. On one occasion they crossed paths with a diminutive Mexican atop a handsome brown-and-white Appaloosa, which was a source of envy to John Tully.

"What do you think of your Sugar now?" said John Tully, nodding toward the mare, once the Mexican was out of earshot.

"I think she has the benefit of experience and the wisdom of a woman," Luyu said, resting her hand gently on the mare's shoulder, as the horse continued to lap water from the shallows.

"And hopefully the endurance, too," Luyu added.

John smiled. "You're a rare one, Wild Dove," he said. "Optimistic, yet practical."

"I can thank the Methodists for the practicality."

"And I suppose the optimism is Miwok?"

"Unlikely," she said.

Now they were both smiling.

"You know," she said, "I've been thinking, and I don't care where we go, John, really, I don't. I just want to go, and we've already done that. So, wherever we end up, I'll be happy."

It was the truth, or at least it felt like the truth. She really didn't care where they landed. And as for stability, she'd tasted her share of it for nearly a decade with the Younts, along with routine, piety, and obedience, just as she had tasted servitude and humiliation at Sutter's Mill. What Luyu longed for now was a freedom she'd only ever heard about, the freedom the whites had stolen from her people. Luyu couldn't say for certain how good things might have been before Sutter and the rest of the whites arrived, but she could say with some confidence — if she were to believe her murdered parents and the rest of her elders — that the Miwok had at least controlled their own destinies before the whites, and for a very long time, at that.

John Tully yearned for much the same freedom, elusive as it was. Most of his life he'd served the white man, on ranches, in trenches, on horseback, and this long before the whites had the numbers to back up their arrogance. In trade, John was of the opinion that his people had been frivolous and short-sighted. In allowing the whites to settle this place, allowing them to live among them, his people had been weak. They should have cast the whites out the moment they arrived, before their insidious presence had polluted their world, which some were now calling a new world.

The world was not new. These mountains, these streams, the flora, the fauna, they were ancient — for John Tully's people, the very measure of ancient. Only the whites were new.

"Will we go to the city?" asked Luyu, once they were back on the trail.

"No," said John Tully. "The city is no place for the likes of you and me. It will only chew us up and spit us out."

The news came as some relief to Luyu. The frenetic activity of the city, at least as she imagined it, with the crowds, the noise, the filth, held no romance for her. Wherever they ended up, Luyu longed for open spaces, for simplicity and quietude.

By the fourth day they could almost see the end of the mountains. Soon the hills would taper into the broad valley, and though it was liable to be hotter, the travel would be less strenuous. In the afternoon as they watered in a meadow beside a small stream, Sugar another day worn down, her spirit and her back another day bowed by the rigors of endless progress, they met with a pair of prospectors on their way north. Presumably weeks on the trail, they did not strike John as a savory pair of individuals, brazen, and unclean, unshaven, sloppy and amateur in their transit, saddles bulging, pots and pans dangling. And drunk well before sundown, which was never a good sign. Even Sugar was uneasy with their presence, as the two travelers settled in needless proximity, sprawling out in the shade. These were not upstanding men, and it didn't take long for John Tully's suspicion to bear fruit.

From his reclining position against the trunk of a pine, the lean, ruddy one would not take his eyes off of Luyu. He whistled his approval as she bent before the stream to fill the bladders, her hair braided back, her lithe figure graceful in the dappled sunlight.

"How much for your squaw, there, digger?"

"She's not for sale," said John without facing the man.

"That right?" said the one with the lazy eye. "I supposed an Indian was always up for tradin'."

"You supposed wrong," said John Tully.

"Well, let's say we're interested in that squaw, anyhow," said the ruddy one. "Let's say it's our intention to have her."

As if on cue, Luyu stationed herself directly at John's side.

"Doesn't change a thing," said John evenly.

"Well," said the ruddy one, "anything can change, if you catch my meaning."

"Not true," said John, maintaining his calm.

"See here," said the ruddy one, rising to his feet. "I'm not at all sure I like your tone, digger, not one bit. Here I was only offering a fair trade, and you get all bent out of shape. As it stands now, I got half a mind to just take what it is I want, trade be damned."

The ruddy one reached out for Luyu's arm

but withdrew it immediately. For before things could play out any further, John drew his pistol so swiftly that Luyu didn't even see it happen.

Impressed by the draw, the ruddy one whistled again.

"Right quick on that draw, digger. Where'd an Indian learn to handle an iron like that?"

"No trading today, gentlemen," John announced. "Now, I'm going to ask you gentlemen once — and only once — to be on your way."

Lazy Eye was incredulous.

"Or what?" he said. "You fixing to shoot us, a pair of white men, and expect to get away with it?"

"If necessary," said John. "But I'm hoping not to."

"Pshaw," said Lazy Eye. "Ain't no Indian no good with no pistol. Drawin' your piece is one thing, aimin' it is another."

"Try me," said John.

Luyu's heart was beating at a gallop.

The ruddy one stiffened and seemed prepared to make a move, until John leveled the iron directly at his chest. He looked John right in the eye but soon backed down.

"C'mon, then, Clinton, let's move on," he said.

"Well hell," said the other. "Ain't you at least gonna let us water some?"

"No," said John Tully.

"You one hard-hearted sonofabitch, you know that?"

"Yes, I do," said John Tully. "Now, on your way."

Grumbling, he joined his companion in standing. They mounted their horses directly and began moving out toward the trail, leaving a fog of whiskey in their wake.

"You best hope we don't cross paths again," said the ruddy one over his shoulder.

"It's you who ought to hope," said John Tully, pistol still trained on his back.

Even after they were out of sight, Luyu's heart continued to race.

"We'd best be on our way, too," said John. "In case the two of them get any bright ideas."

Cinching the bladders to Sugar's saddle, John Tully and Luyu soon led the old mare back to the trail and resumed their progress south.

LAILA TULLY

Red Bluff, California, 2019

Laila's last day at the buffet was a Monday by design. It was the first day of the new pay cycle, and she had no intention of ever seeing another paycheck once she left without giving Dennis notice. While it would probably cost her forty bucks after taxes, and a reference, Laila couldn't afford to let anyone beyond Tam know her intentions. In an ass-backward town the size of this, those intentions were likely to get back to Boaz. Besides, she only intended on staying through lunch, and what she lost in wages, she'd practically make back in food, because she planned on packing four Tupperware containers of buffet fare in her backpack, though she knew from experience it was practically inedible once it cooled down.

Though Laila could hardly contain her nerves from the moment she woke up — indeed, worry had harassed her sleep mercilessly the previous four nights — she tried her hardest not to betray any anxiety or excitement, lest Boaz sniff it out and take her to task for it. Thus, Laila tried to act like her usual self — that was, a doormat, basically.

"I ain't eating Sonic again tonight, so don't even think about it," Boaz said in the kitchen over breakfast, for which he hadn't even bothered to dress. "Cook something decent, would you?" he said. "What about a lasagna?"

"Okay," she said, knowing she'd never have to do the shopping or the prep, knowing that he'd have to put some pants on and fend for himself, knowing he'd have to walk to the Chevron and get his own damn six-pack. That she'd never have to see his stupid skinny, pale legs again, or listen to his drunken snoring, or watch him eat, or feel the brunt of his stupid rage sting her eye or knot her skull, was cause for giddiness. In mere hours she would be free. True, she had no idea what the future held, or whether the truck would even make the journey. Her cousin Genie didn't have a job lined up for her at the lodge in Kalaloch, though Genie assured Laila that summer looked promising.

"What's so funny about lasagna?" said Boaz.

"Nothing," she said.

"Then what are you smiling about?"

"I'm sick of Sonic, too. I thought you liked it," she said.

"Fuck no," he said. "Did I ever say that?"

"Well, you always ate it fast enough," she said, bracing herself for a nasty retort.

"You're mighty satisfied with yourself this morning, aren't you?" he said, slapping her ass suggestively. "Let's say you're a few minutes late to work today."

"Dennis would probably fire me on the spot. You'll just have to wait until I get home," she said.

"Well, then, you best hurry home, girl," he said with a final slap on the ass. " 'Cause I got something waiting for you, right here."

Laila could have barfed. Since the instant she'd finally decided to leave him, the very thought of ever having to touch Boaz again had been repulsive, though she had surrendered to his advances two nights ago, and gritted her teeth through the whole ordeal, even as she talked dirty for him and faked climax, knowing it would end things quicker.

"Well, I gotta go," she said nonchalantly.

"We'll finish this conversation the minute you get home," he said.

God, how on earth had she ever endured him? Even at his best he was a creep. He wasn't even that good-looking, really, aside from his baby-blue eyes. She knew damn well why she stayed with him at this point — fear. But how on earth had her standards ever gotten so low that she'd ended up with him in the first place? The next man she ended up with would be the exact opposite of Boaz, whatever that looked like.

On second thought, maybe she'd be best off winding up with nobody and concentrating on herself for once. Before Boaz it was Dan, and before Dan it was Trent. Dan was okay, stable, nonviolent, pretty passive, really — she probably never should have dumped him — but Trent was basically Boaz Lite. Laila had let all of them absorb her to a large degree, almost like that was her purpose. She always seemed to lose herself in the hopeless task of pleasing, and fulfilling, and serving their endless needs. God, but men were needy. She knew this, and yet she always attached herself to the neediest sort.

As Laila drove to the casino restaurant for the last time, the thought of having a friend and companion in Genie was cause for excitement. Talking to Genie on the phone, Laila could tell she felt the same way. How great it would be to have somebody to talk to and hang out with, somebody besides Boaz to watch TV with, somebody besides Tam to confide in and not fear judgment from. And that wasn't to say there was anything wrong with Tam; on the contrary, Tam was someone to aspire to: Tam called them as she saw them, Tam had the guts to put Dennis or Duane or anybody else in their place, Tam had been nothing less than instrumental — no, central — in helping Laila make the break.

Indeed, it was Tam waiting for Laila by her locker when she got to work Monday. Right away, she thrust a thick envelope on Laila.

Laila had been half expecting such a gesture, but still, the moment caught her by surprise, the sheer kindness of it. What business did thirty-eight-year-old Tam — Tam still working at the casino buffet eleven years on — what business did she have bestowing what little she could scrape together on somebody else, somebody like Laila, somebody young and stupid enough to get involved with Boaz in the first place?

"It's four hundred and thirty-three bucks," said Tam. "You can count it if you want."

Laila wrapped her arms around Tam and immediately began to cry into Tam's fresh apron.

"There, there, girl," she said, absorbing Laila's gratitude. "This ain't the time to get emotional, sweetie. You gotta be strong now more than ever, hon. You ain't nowhere yet."

"But, Tam, I can't take your money," said Laila, knowing that she had to take it.

Her own 308 bucks sure wasn't going to hold out for too long. She couldn't show up to Genie's broke, with no prospects until summer, no matter how much Genie encouraged her to come. And even as Laila was still clinging to Tam, the thought of Tam's kindness, along with Genie's willingness to take her in, caused Laila to weep a little harder.

Who would have guessed that at a time like this, when she was about to flee the failed existence she'd built for herself with the best years of her life, in a broken-down truck, away from an abusive partner and into an unknown future with 741 dollars, she would be overcome by — of all the competing feelings crowding in on Laila — gratitude?

"Honey, you can take it, and you will take it," said Tam. "Heck, I'm countin' on you, girl. You're young, you can do anything you want. I should have left this valley twenty years ago. I should've never even met Duane, though he ain't one-tenth as bad as everyone seems to think, just a little antisocial is all. My point is, honey, you're like a horse I'm bettin' on — though understand I don't expect any money out of it. This money here is a gift, Laila. I don't want to be paid back, and I mean that. I just wanna invest in you, that's all. It's kinda my way of investing in what I might have been. Provided you send me a postcard now and then, it'll be worth it. And if you're too busy, that's okay, too. You just be sure and let me know if anything is wrong, that's all."

Just when Laila thought she couldn't cry any harder, there she was crying harder into the bleachy bouquet of Tam's apron. It was true; sometimes you didn't know what you had until it was time to leave it behind.

"Aw, hell, Tam," said Laila through her

sobs. "That's the nicest damn thing anybody ever —"

It was amazing how quickly Laila was able to turn off the waterworks the instant Dennis entered the room, clipboard in hand, wide-eyed and gnashing his teeth. If nothing else, being with Boaz had taught Laila how to manipulate her emotions at a moment's notice as a matter of survival, though in this case what was she really risking that wasn't going to be in the rearview mirror in a few minutes anyway?

"Uh, ladies," said Dennis, "it's Monday, and that means Swedish meatballs, and that means thawing."

She ought to throw a frozen meatball at Dennis, the tooth-gnashing sonofabitch.

Tam rolled her eyes. "Way ahead of you, Dennis," she said. "Why don't you go to the bathroom? Oh, and by the way, can I get you a tissue? Maybe some Visine?"

Laila shot her a look.

Dennis stormed off.

Tam winked at her.

"You're like my lucky charm, girl. I'll get you paid for today," she whispered. "Just send me an address. If Dennis doesn't like it, I'll go to HR and tell them he's a tweaker. Then where will he be?"

Laila tied her apron off and donned her white hat. She felt like a different person as she thawed the meatballs and the sausages and heated the gravy, while Tam scrambled bottled eggs on the grill. She hardly paid Dennis any mind as he came and went with his clipboard and his newest tic, a frequent twitching of the neck, as if a mosquito were biting him but he couldn't be bothered to slap at it with a hand.

After the breakfast rush, as Laila was prepping the penne and the fettuccine, while Tam shuttled the salads and the sides out to the buffet, Laila found opportunities to secretly fill her Tupperware containers with pasta and sauce and meatballs and sausages, and stow them all in her backpack in the locker room when Dennis wasn't looking.

After the lunch rush, as they filled their own plates in the kitchen, Tam said:

"Grab your bag and your coat from the locker."

"You think?"

Tam nodded.

Laila stopped at her locker and hefted her overstuffed backpack.

Tam carried both their lunch plates as they retired to the "patio" together, a rectangular slab of concrete out back, overlooking the employee parking lot, adorned with a lone plastic table with a broken umbrella, where Tam immediately pushed her plate aside and fired up a cigarette.

"Why come back after lunch?" she said. "Dennis will be so gacked he might not even notice. You might make the border by dinnertime. Get through the mountains while it's light. Enjoy the views. And don't you worry, hon. You're doing exactly what you're supposed to be doing."

For about the third time in her life, Laila wanted a cigarette.

"Oh, God, I dunno, Tam. The truck, the heat, what if — ?"

"What if you stay?" Tam interjected. "That's the question you ought to be asking yourself."

Gently, so she could smoke the rest of it later, Tam stubbed out her cigarette on the concrete, kicked away the ashes, then set the butt beside her plate and began stabbing at her steamed vegetables.

"It's like yanking a tooth," said Tam, pulling back her lip to expose an empty spot where a bicuspid ought to have been.

"You yust yotta yew it," she said, still contorting her mouth.

Tam was right. You yust yad ya yew it.

"You're the best," said Laila.

"Thanks, doll," said Tam.

Laila never came back from lunch. After she ate half of her Swedish meatballs and most of her coleslaw, she watched Tam smoke the rest of her cigarette. When Tam snuffed it out once and for all, Laila shed her apron and her hat and, leaning across the table, planted a kiss on Tam's forehead, at which point, for the first time, Tam let her emotions show.

"Get out of here," she said, wiping her eyes.

Leaving her apron and hat on the chair, Laila strode across the lot toward the truck.

"Don't you dare look back," said Tam.

And by God, Laila vowed not to, not ever.

After she swung out of the lot in Boaz's dented truck and picked up the interstate, Laila shot north through the scorched brown valley at sixty-five miles per hour, which was all the truck could handle. Within an hour, she was winding her way up into the foothills, sputtering up the inclines, being passed frequently by impatient drivers in newer cars. Yet every time she crested a hill, Laila felt more alive than she could remember.

"Fuck you, Boaz!" she yelled, turning up the radio.

Soon the great white dome of Mount Shasta was visible to the north, and Laila felt the full power of possibility coursing through her. Grandma Malilah would've been proud.

With seven hundred bucks and two dozen meatballs on her person, Laila was feeling relatively comfortable and prepared when she got the first text from Boaz, around 5:20.

Wear u at?

Laila almost threw her phone out the window then and there but resisted the urge, knowing she'd need her phone going forward. And it certainly helped that the window wouldn't open.

Around Yreka, Laila got the second text.

WTF? Did you break down or something?

It was pure joy to imagine Boaz in a state of discomfort, any state of discomfort, and thus Laila relished her phone silence, resisting the urge to reply.

She couldn't resist, however, the thought of making Boaz squirm as long and as uncomfortably as possible. Once she was settled in Washington, she could change her Verizon account, and by extension Boaz's, and Boaz would never have access to her again. He didn't know Genie's last name. He didn't know Queets from Australia. Even if Boaz could track her down, he was too lazy and didn't have the resources to actually pursue her. Who knew how long it might take him to even get cell service again once she cut the cord with Verizon?

Laila took Tam's advice and enjoyed the views through Yreka and Weed, pushing the past and future aside as best she could and soaking up the present: the pink glow of sunset on Mount Shasta, the wide green valleys cradling it like a tea saucer, the furrowed green ranges to the north, still to be crossed. With the radio muted, Laila allowed herself to live in the moment for the first time in weeks.

By the time she hit the heart of the Siskiyous at dusk, she felt like she could drive all night, or as far as the little truck would take her. Maybe she could make it all the way to Eugene before she'd need a motel. The difference between her new life and her old life was that Laila didn't know what to expect.

When Tam got home from work with two bags of groceries, Duane was on the roof of the trailer with a can of Coors, a paintbrush, and a bucket of rubber roof coating. Though it had only rained twice all spring, when it had rained it had come down hard, first inundating, then breaching the old sunbaked roof, where the pantry and the kitchen received the brunt of the water damage. Tam had been after Duane for weeks about the roof and the curling linoleum in the kitchen, so it came as no small relief to finally find him up there, albeit just in time for the dry season.

"If I break my neck it's your fault," he said without so much as a hello.

"I should be so lucky," she muttered on her way through the screen door.

Inside, the TV was on and the ashtray was still smoldering, so Duane couldn't have been up there more than two minutes. Tam set the groceries on the counter and immediately put the hamburger, the milk, and the Coors in the fridge, leaving the rest of the groceries in the bags. She lit a cigarette and sat down in the splotchy yellow recliner in front of the TV.

AMC was playing an old western with Joel McCrea. Duane had quite the romance with old westerns. He liked to think of himself as a modern-day cowboy even though he couldn't ride a horse, or wrestle a steer, or shoot from the hip, or do anything else a damn cowboy could do. Apparently just watching TV and drinking Coors was enough.

Tam guessed that Laila must've been somewhere in the Siskiyous by then. Good for her. Sure, the 433 bucks stung, but God knew it certainly wouldn't have gone toward anything worthy in Tam's life anyway. The whole hope was to help save Laila from Tam's life, because that was where Laila had been headed. Another few years with that loser Boaz and Laila would never have gotten out the rut. Tam ought to know.

As if on cue, Duane pounded on the ceiling.

"Hey, bring me a beer up here," he shouted.

"Hold your horses," she shouted back. "I'm unpacking the groceries!"

Tam exhaled a plume of blue smoke. From where she was sitting now it was hard to believe that she'd ever had aspirations. Twenty years ago she'd wanted to go to beauty school and open her own salon. Granted, nobody had taken that opportunity away from her but herself. She might have found a way to make it happen. But it wasn't like the outside world had been there to offer a helping hand. More often than not it seemed to be giving her a big middle finger.

Ever since she was six or seven years old, Tam had had a way with hair and makeup. Not like Laila, who couldn't even hide a black eye. Tam had been quite the beauty back in the day, but she'd let her looks go along with the rest of her ambitions. Not everybody could live the American dream. Somebody had to pay the passage for the lucky ones.

A long time ago Tam had started sacrificing her personal development to the hopeless endeavor of being an instrument in the service of other people's causes. It wasn't the sacrifice that was the problem, it was the causes: mostly, Duane, and you could see how well that had worked out. In a way, Tam's giving Laila her savings amounted to the same thing, but this time it seemed like a worthy cause, and that little bit of redemption made it worth every penny of 433 bucks. The fact was, Tam didn't know Laila all that well, and she'd never gotten the sense that Laila particularly liked her. What mattered was that somebody somewhere had a chance, and that Tam had incrementally increased their odds about the only way she could.

Duane pounded on the ceiling again and a few particles of foam rained down onto the kitchen linoleum. From her place in the recliner, Tam could hear his empty aluminum can hit the porch and bounce off onto the dead grass.

"What's the holdup down there?" he shouted.

Stubbing out her cigarette, Tam stood up with a sigh and walked to the refrigerator.

WALTER BERGEN

Oregon, 2019

The Coast Starlight was just north of Eugene when the snow began to fall in earnest. A thin white sheet soon blanketed the valley floor and began accumulating upon the trees, and roofs, and fence posts. Walter supposed he was a little more sentimental than usual, this being his final run, but the snow all around was as beautiful as it was unseasonal: the way it accentuated the lay of the valley, the way it buffered the abruptness of the hills, and the way it seemed to still all activity, but for the rhythmic churning of the Coast Starlight over the rails, locomoting north through the white wonderland.

Walter sped up the wipers and stared out the window of the engine into the oncoming snow, which played tricks on his eyes. The tracks before him were still clear, as far as he could see. Though he had a schedule to keep, Walter was in no hurry for his day to end. The last thing he wanted to do at the moment was step into the future.

Everything was changing so fast, it was hard to keep up at sixty-three: technology, culture, climate, the country, the world, all of them accelerating toward new and previously unimaginable places, speeding like runaway trains into the unknown. That was how it felt, anyway. Identity politics, political correctness, same-sex marriage. It might have been easy to turn his back on all of it, but for Wendy. His daughter's gayness, as a practice, no longer shamed him, though he still cringed every time she announced herself as "queer," which seemed such a vulgar label for something Walter had come to understand as perfectly natural.

He accepted it, but he still couldn't understand it, and it had nothing to do with not liking Kit, though it was true he found her difficult to like at times, sharp and pointy as her personality could be. The crux of it was that no matter how much Wendy insisted she had been born that way, Walter couldn't help but feel he'd had a hand in making her gay. He knew it didn't matter. He knew it was perfectly acceptable in the twenty-first century. Yet the very idea of it still made him uncomfortable. Perhaps it was the readiness with which such things were now accepted. Walter couldn't get his brain around the idea of "nonbinary" or "transgender," any more than he could get his brain around Wendy's vocation (nonpaying) as a Socialist Alliance activist, which seemed to comprise a lot of browbeating around dinner tables, and hostile picketing in front of government buildings and financial institutions.

Walter could not help but admire Wendy's conviction, and her passion for what she deemed justice. He did not doubt his daughter's good intentions, nor question her earnestness. But it would've been disingenuous to pretend that Wendy's brand of progress wasn't more than a little unsettling to Walter. It seemed sudden and rash, and often lacking in foresight. Perhaps it was old-fashioned to believe that there were fundamental differences between men and women, perhaps it was old-fashioned to believe that society served the majority even if it was flawed on some level. Maybe it was old-fashioned to cling to the past. And that was what unsettled Walter the most, the idea that he was old-fashioned, that the world was passing him by. As the Coast Starlight forged on through the snow, Walter felt sure that he was destined to go the way of the steam engine.

Walter sounded one long blast on the horn as they pulled into Albany right on schedule, despite the snow.

Macy poked his head into the cab just before deboarding.

"What do you think?" he said.

"So far, so good," said Walter. "Nothing

from dispatch."

The Starlight pulled out of Albany, Walter sounding the horn, picking up speed through the back end of town, past the business park, and the subdivisions, and the wrecking yard, before hurtling into the broad valley, shrouded in white. Walter sounded the horn again at the crossing. The wind started picking up and the snow began to swirl and eddy.

Once the snow had drifted to about four inches along the edge of the track, Walter picked up the handset and radioed ahead for a status report. No sooner did he get word from dispatch than Macy poked his head into the cab again.

"Anything?"

"Yeah, your pants are too tight," said Walter.

"You wish," said Macy.

"Put the cheeseburger down, Macy."

"Ha! You should talk," said Macy. "Really, though, it's getting nasty out there, Wally."

"Plow's are ready. Probably nobody to staff them, but what do I know?"

Generally speaking, Walter dreaded operating an engine in foul weather. Though he was prepared, at least in theory, sometimes the conditions arrived without warning to shatter Walter's routine, whether it was flooding along the slough, or wind ripping through the valley, downing limbs, whole trees even, or rails mired in snow. The current conditions, the sudden combination of wind and snow, did make Walter a bit anxious. And apparently, Macy, too.

"I don't like the looks of it," said Macy.

Neither did Walter. But whatever lay ahead, it wasn't likely to test him, or inconvenience him beyond a few minutes, so, why not go out with something memorable? Stressful as it could be, there was a certain glory to plowing through a blizzard, as long as the tracks weren't frozen, and as long as there wasn't more than a foot of snow.

By the time the Starlight was nine miles out of Albany, the snow and wind out of the west had begun to abate somewhat.

"False alarm, I guess," said Macy, ducking his head into the cab for the tenth time.

"I wouldn't be so sure," said Walter, peering out the window of the cab.

"I hope you're wrong," said Macy. "Maddie's got a concert tonight at the school, and I promised Tanya I'd take them all out to Mountain Mike's."

"Are you gonna change your pants?" said Walter. "Because I'm telling you, they're too tight."

"I'm serious, here," said Macy. "Are we gonna get screwed?"

"Fingers crossed," said Walter.

Any kind of delay would actually be welcome, a pardon, if only temporary, from his future — a future without purpose, without significance beyond the act of giving away his only child, paying his massive debts, clearing out the garage at Annie's behest, all the while getting bullied into yoga and plant-based diets. Walter was still not ready to confront a future without the brassy blare of the horn sounding through crossings or the curt one-two of passing a station. It was hard to imagine a future without the bone-rattling power of a diesel engine, or the great steel wheels hugging the rails as the train sped ever onward toward somewhere of consequence, somewhere people needed to be.

Just as Walter expected, the snow soon started up again, about two minutes after Macy left the cab. It began falling slantwise, faster and more determined than before. They were fifteen miles outside of Salem when the onslaught began, and soon the snow was drifting to a half foot along the edges of the tracks. There was no sign of its letting up any time soon. In spite of protocol, Walter ran the lights on high, his uneasiness nosing toward anxiety as the Coast Starlight barreled north.

NORA BERGEN

Chicago, 1851

"You gonna like it just fine at Mr. Seymour's," said Henry, the carriage driver, a Negro as black as any Nora had ever seen. "Mr. Seymour's house is a whole lot nicer than any old orphan home," he observed, ushering Nora down the front steps of the Catholic Orphan Asylum toward the waiting carriage.

"Food's a whole lot better, too, I figure," Henry observed. "Yes, ma'am, you gonna be real glad Mr. Seymour 'dopted you, young lady. Mr. Seymour, he's a great man, a very important man. Why, he personally knows President Millard Fillmore himself. What do you think of that? Mr. Seymour, he gonna build an iron horse, bigger and faster than any other, and one day he gonna steam it clear across the great frontier. He gonna make the whole world smaller, so that one day a body can get from wherever he at to wherever he want to go in just days instead of weeks or months. Yes, ma'am, Mr. Seymour got big plans. First, he gonna build a rail all the way to New York City. Watch your step there," he said, helping Nora into the carriage.

Then Henry mounted the carriage, took his place on the little perch, clutched the reins, and off they rode, clackety-clack, into the unknown future.

From her seat in the coach, Nora could hear Henry talking to nobody in particular.

"Yessir, every day this city getting bigger and bigger. Getting to where a body can't even recognize the place. Used to be I could see from one end to the other end of Chicago. Used to be I could understand what-all everybody was saying. But not anymore. Folks speaking in tongues I ain't even heard before. They coming from all over the world on account of America supposedly being the greatest nation that ever was. Sure be nice if a body could understand just what they was all yammering about."

It did not take long for Nora to figure out her standing as a ward of the illustrious patron Mr. Seymour, for upon arriving at the great estate on the lake, Henry delivered her to the service entrance at the back of the manor, where she was greeted on the step by another old Negro man, this one in a spattered white apron.

"Who she?" he demanded.

"She the new help," said Henry. "Mr. Seymour 'dopted her from the orphan home."

The old man in the apron shook his head woefully, as if this information were disappointing.

"Man got no shame," he muttered beneath his breath. "What's your name, sweetheart?"

"Nora, sir."

"Well, Nora, welcome. My name is Clifton, and I'm gonna see to it that you're treated right around here. You come on in, now, and we'll make you at home."

Clifton did not really look old beyond his white hair. There was hardly a wrinkle upon his face, and he possessed the sturdy figure of a younger man, though he walked with a slight limp as he led Nora down a long, dim corridor, past a half dozen bedrooms on either side, doors ajar, each small and unadorned. At the end of the corridor, they pushed through a swinging double door, which opened up into a large, noisy kitchen, bustling with Negro help. Pots were boiling and bodies were hurrying about. The air was thick with steam and redolent with the smell of cooking.

Clifton led Nora by the elbow like a dance partner between bodies and around butcher blocks to a young Negro woman of considerable and effortless beauty who was peeling potatoes expertly over a large metal basin.

"This here is my daughter, Cora," said

Clifton. "Rhymes with Nora, how about that? She gonna show you to your room and teach you how things work around here."

Cora set her knife aside and wiped her hands on her apron before taking both of Nora's hands in her own and looking kindly into her face.

"Now, don't you have pretty eyes," she said.

"T'anks, ma'am, they're me father's eyes."

"And what a musical voice," said Cora.

Cora was a revelation. Such was her kindness and soothing manner that for a few short hours Nora stopped thinking about poor, doomed Finn, destined to languish the rest of his days at the Catholic Orphan Asylum, never so much as knowing the fate of his twin sister.

"It's the sunniest room in morning time," Cora announced, showing Nora her quarters.

Sunny though it may have been in the morning, in the afternoon the little room, ten by ten feet square, was as dark and uplifting as a tomb. The room was scarcely furnished: a bed, a nightstand, a candle, and a chamber pot. The lone shaft of sunlight penetrating the darkness was swimming with dust. It was not the room Nora had dared to imagine upon learning that wealthy Mr. Seymour was to be her custodian. But at least it was private, and that was something. After months at the asylum, Nora longed mostly for one thing: to be beside her brother, every minute of every day, no matter how silently, so long as she could feel the warmth of his nearness, the comfort of his presence. Short of that, Nora only wished to be alone, where she could take refuge in her thoughts.

Perhaps sensing her loneliness, Cora was around frequently those first days to buoy Nora's spirits.

"On Sunday, you can come to church with Daddy and me on the South Side. We can go to the beach after service, and have a picnic and swim."

"Can I see me brother?" asked Nora.

"That's not so likely."

"But why?" Nora said, the tears welling up in her eyes.

Cora wrapped Nora in an embrace and held her close as Nora sobbed into her apron.

"Honey, sometimes there's no real why in this world," Cora said. "There just ain't one, not one that makes any sense, and not one that's any comfort to a soul. Most of the time in this world it's just a bad case of the way things are. You gotta just absorb the world as best you can and look for the bright spots."

The bright spots in Nora's life were few in the absence of Finn. Her daily existence at Mr. Seymour's was hardly different from her life at the asylum, except there was no hope of ever seeing her brother, if only to pass him in the hallway and steal a moment, or to sit shoulder-to-shoulder with him for a few minutes each day on the stoop overlooking the playfield.

Just as at the orphanage, Nora's life consisted mostly of labor. More than any task, Nora was assigned to laundry, where she found herself for hours on end among the great boilers in the stultifying confines of the cellar, alongside a handful of colored women, dunking and wringing, dunking and wringing, until her hands were wrinkled and her skin bleached ghostly white. Sometimes, on sunny days, in the rear courtyard, stringing linens on lines, Nora turned her face to the sun and closed her eyes, and tried to leave herself behind.

But it never worked. Nora's life might have been bearable if not for the absence of Finn, or the persistent memory of her mother as Nora had seen her last: dull-eyed and listless, skin like parchment, her ravaged figure racked with coughing as she spat blood by the mouthful into the muddy streets. Worse than anything they'd left behind in Cork were those first days in Chicago, homeless, totally bereft of means, without anyone to call a friend.

And to think that the Bergens had once dared to believe that America would be their savior, that behind the Golden Door lay the promise of a better life. America had only finished the job that Ireland had already begun.

Nora had now been a fortnight at the Seymour estate and still had yet to encounter the elusive Mr. Seymour himself, who had apparently been away on business since shortly after Nora's arrival. Though conspicuously childless, the Seymours always kept a full house. For even in her husband's absence, Mrs. Seymour entertained constantly: Whether it was tea, or supper, or the meeting of one charitable society or another, there was always something that required the staff's attention.

Mrs. Seymour rarely deigned to issue her instructions to the staff personally; that was a matter left to the butler, Edmund, a Negro so fair-skinned he was nearly white. It was only Edmund's tightly knit hair that betrayed him. Upon but one occasion had Nora seen Mrs. Seymour enter the service area, and not once, not even upon the hour of Nora's arrival, did Mrs. Seymour ever inquire about Nora or her well-being. She seemed unaware of Nora's very existence until one afternoon when Mrs. Seymour, dressed for town and clutching a parasol, wandered into the service yard, hiking her skirts above the mud, seemingly lost in her unfamiliar surroundings.

"Oh, Henry, where have you gotten off to, now?" she muttered. "You're like a child. And who are you?" Mrs. Seymour demanded as she came upon Nora stringing linens.

"Nora's me name, ma'am."

"And to whom do you belong?" Mrs. Seymour demanded.

"To the staff, ma'am."

"Hmph," said Mrs. Seymour. "I'm looking for my driver."

"Mr. Henry, ma'am?"

"Yes."

"I believe he'd be in the stable, ma'am."

"Well, go on, fetch him, then," said Mrs. Seymour. "What did you say your name was?"

"Nora, ma'am. Nora Bergen."

"Bergen," said Mrs. Seymour, as though the name were an unpleasant taste.

As summer approached, Cora seemed to intuit Nora's yearning for open spaces and fresh air, and saw to it that Nora was assigned two days a week to the stable, where she shoveled dung, and laid down fresh straw, and sometimes stroked the horses' snouts affectionately, or scratched softly behind their ears, or ran her hand gently down their withers, speaking to them like she'd once spoken to Finn, without reservation or fear of judgment. And like Finn, the horses never spoke back. Yet she was certain she could feel the force of their understanding, and it was a comfort.

The stable man was a Negro named George Flowers, who also talked to horses, though unlike Nora, whose interactions were one-sided, the horses actually talked back to

George, or at least in George's head they seemed to. For one afternoon in July, Nora heard George Flowers in the adjacent stall, shoveling the floor.

"That's right, Governor, it won't be long now," he said to the gray stallion.

"Come Sunday, George is going to sit down with Miss Cora and have a little talk. If not this Sunday, well then, the next one or the one after that. But it's going to happen, Governor, you can bet on it."

There followed a brief silence, while George continued to shovel straw and dung into the wheelbarrow.

"What's that, Governor?" said George. "Is that what you think? Well, not so fast. It may seem like a lack of conviction to you, but that's just not the case, Governor. It's a matter of proper timing. You can't just rush into something like this. People, they're not like horses, and I mean no disrespect by that, Governor. It's just that horses seem to get on easier than people do. Horses got a more easygoing nature. Folks, they need a proper warming up. They've got to develop a little familiarity among one another before they up and run off together for parts unknown."

Nora grew to adore George for his optimism, which was hard to account for. The man slept in a stable and talked to horses all day, and yet somehow he managed to keep his chin and his spirits up, most of the time.

One afternoon while Nora was enjoying a visit with George in the stable, two rough-looking men showed up, and no sooner had they stepped into the stable yard than George stopped talking in midsentence and darted off into the depths of the stable without explanation. Nora left the stable and took cover behind the big willow in the side yard, watching as the two men, both heavily bearded and brandishing holstered pistols at the waist, approached the service entrance and knocked on the door, where Clifton soon greeted them.

Though she could hear their voices, Nora was unable to make out the words as the three men conferred on the back steps, the two white men exchanging doubtful glances each time Clifton addressed them. The men lingered for a few minutes before they finally turned and began walking down the long drive. Not until they reached the main road did George reemerge from the depths of the stable, straw clinging to his shirt and hair.

"Who are they?" said Nora.

"Slave catchers, I reckon," said George uneasily.

"Mr. Seymour hasn't any slaves," she said.

"No, he don't," said George. "Not that he know of."

And suddenly Nora understood the gravity of George's dilemma. Poor George, forever a refugee in the world, worse off than an orphan. That George had chosen to divulge his secret to Nora was not a gesture that she received lightly. Her fondness for George hardened instantly into a fierce love, and she clutched him tightly about the waist and wouldn't let go.

"You can't let them find you, George, you just can't."

"Don't you worry, they're not gonna catch me, I'm too smart, and too slippery besides."

More and more as the months wore on, Nora began to think of the staff as something akin to a family, and not just George, but Mr. Clifton, and Cora, and Henry, and Tilly, everyone save for Edmund, who was caught between worlds. Mostly, the staff stuck together, they identified with one another, they suffered, and toiled, and commiserated with one another, just as the Bergens once had before the ravages of starvation and disease and flight had torn their family tree out by the roots, scattering them from County Cork to Chicago.

What need of iron horses? It was already a small world when it came to suffering. Nora was grateful to be fed and housed, beholden to Mr. Seymour for taking her on, and to the staff for their kindness and acceptance. If nothing else, life at Mr. Seymour's was the most stable life she'd ever known. And yet Nora could never feel complete, not for a moment, for without Finn, she was the very definition of incomplete.

Nora became increasingly irritable as the summer wore on. The crippling anguish of separation that had marked her early days at the Seymours' soon gave way to a simmering resentment, which, stoked by the heat and humidity of the unventilated service quarters, blossomed into outrage.

Nobody had any right to separate her from Finn, not Abraham Seymour, nor the Catholic Orphan Asylum, nor anybody else. And so, one sweltering Sunday in August, Nora skipped church, despite the entreaties of Cora and Clifton, and instead walked the three miles from Seymour's manor to the Catholic Orphan Asylum, where she passed through the wrought-iron gate, crossed the soggy field, walked up the brick steps and through the front door, and proceeded directly for the boys' dormitory. She was halfway down the corridor before she met Master Searles himself, with his gigantic head and his shock of side-whiskers, as he descended the stairs.

"I came to see me brother," said Nora. "And you can't stop me. Not you or anyone else."

But Master Searles blocked her way and took hold of her wrists before Nora could pass.

"You can't," said Master Searles.

"I will," said Nora.

"It's not possible," he said.

"I don't care about the rules," she said.

Mr. Searles loosened his grip slightly and looked down into her face meaningfully.

"Child, he's gone, your brother is gone. He was placed with a German couple not long after you left the asylum."

"Where?" she demanded. "Gone where?"

"West," said Master Searles.

"Where west?"

"That I cannot say," said Master Searles.

"But you can, you must."

"Not with any certainty," he said. "They went west to settle, child. They left by wagon train months ago. God only knows where they might be by now, or where they'll end up."

In that instant, it was as though a flame in Nora's chest had been snuffed out forever, and only then was her despair complete, for she knew that whatever lay ahead of her, whatever the Seymours, or God, or the world at large had planned for her, she would never be whole again without Finn.

ABRAHAM SEYMOUR

Chicago, 1852

"Abe, in all our years, I've never complained," said his wife, Marilyn, from the divan. "But certainly it is not imperative that you leave the county every time you have a bit of business to conduct? Why, there is the postal service, and the telegraph office. I'm beginning to think you're trying to get away from me."

"Nothing of the sort, my dearest," Abe said from his place by the window, watching two of his fox terriers frolic in the side yard. "You must understand: Business is, and always has been, about forging relationships. And these relationships, they cannot be established by telegraph, my pet. Men of business must look one another in the eye."

"If I may be candid," said Marilyn, "I am not at all fond of this young Warnock fellow. I find him to be an insufferable bore, and most un*worthy* of your partnership. Why you

241

would want a relationship with him is beyond me."

"And the answer is business," said Abe.

"Of course," said Marilyn with an edge of bitterness. "It's always business."

"Would you prefer we discuss the other matter?" said Abe. "The matter of the g—"

"There's nothing to discuss. If such a thing were ever to have been, Providence would have allowed for it," she said. "By all means, go back to your business."

Marylin was not wrong in her criticism, and Abe knew it. While amassing and consolidating wealth was perhaps not the noblest of all causes, Abe had learned to be good at it, and business had been without a doubt the primary focus of his adult life. The Seymour name was synonymous with financial success in the state of Illinois, and yet, the name itself was a lie. Though Seymour was a noble surname predating the Norman invasion, it was an assumed name, for Abe's parents, Aleksander and Devorah Silberstein, had fled Poland after the Second Partition, on the heels of the failed uprising. Their safe passage to England was in large part owing to their considerable wealth, which allowed them to broker a pass out of Warsaw. Upon their liberation, the Silbersteins had settled in Gloucester, assuming the names Alex and Deborah Seymour, and ceased practicing their faith, at least publicly, lest they be cast out again.

Young Abe was sent to board in Bristol, where he was to receive his primary education in grammar and literature. Looking back at the Bristol School, Abe was haunted by loneliness. Not a sociable animal by nature, Abe had never been quick to attract companionship, and Bristol proved to be no exception. Abe barely survived the isolation of his first year. He missed his parents, and especially his brother, Silas, and their afternoon romps through the pasture with Dash, Abe's wire-haired fox terrier. Some nights in the dormitory Abe hid his face in his pillow, muffling his sobs, praying that someone, anyone, would save him from the place.

Then one morning in March of Abe's thirteenth year, Headmaster Hollingsworth, a bloodless and prematurely aging man with but a few fine wisps of hair still left upon his crown, summoned Abe to his office.

"Young Mr. Seymour, it is with a heavy heart that I must inform you of the death of your brother."

Out the window Abe watched the rising tide of the Avon in the distance as the news of his brother's terrible fate washed over him. In Abe Seymour's recollection it was during this very instant that part of him died and another part of him was born. Perhaps it was the instantaneous passing from childhood to adulthood, but Abe was never the same after his brother's death.

Though he was reeling emotionally, his studies did not suffer in the coming year, or the following year, as he gutted out fourth form. However, near the end of the year, Abe was once again summoned to the headmaster's office. On this occasion Headmaster Hollingsworth, hollow of eye and sallow of cheek, looked even worse for wear than usual. In fact Abe's first thought was that Headmaster Hollingsworth himself was dying. But the reality was much worse.

"Mr. Seymour, there's no easy way to tell you what I must tell you, so I'm not going to sugarcoat it. There's been a house fire back home in Gloucester. Your parents, I'm sorry to say, did not survive the unfortunate event."

Abe could not believe his ears. It was too much to process. He had a thousand questions.

"Again, I am terribly sorry for this misfortune, Mr. Seymour," said the headmaster. "I am informed that your inheritance has been placed in trust, where it is to remain until you are of sufficient age."

It soon became apparent that this was the only comfort Hollingsworth had to offer Abe.

"I'm afraid, Mr. Seymour, that another issue has come to light as the result of this misfortune."

"Sir?"

"It has come to the attention of administrators here at Bristol that your parents — and by extension you — are of a, shall we say, non-Anglican persuasion."

"Sir?"

"You are Jews. From Poland, Mr. Silberstein."

"Yes, sir?"

"As I am quite sure you are aware, Bristol School is a Christian academy. We, or shall I say they, unfortunately do not enroll Jews, Mr. Sey—er, Silberstein."

As the weak sun peeked out from between the clouds and angled in through the window of the headmaster's office, Abraham Seymour resolved forevermore to be self-sufficient. He knew in that moment that he must construct himself into someone infallible and impenetrable, someone who could control his own destiny, lest destiny control him, lest he be thrown out wherever he went for the unforgivable offense of being born a Jew.

"Suffice it to say, young man," resumed Hollingsworth, "that I do not intend to see you tossed out into the street. As it happens, Mr. Silberstein, I've managed to secure you an apprenticeship in —"

"No," said Abe.

"Pardon me?"

"I don't want your help."

Hollingsworth was aghast. "Well, I must say, I —"

"There's nothing you must say. It would be

best if you said nothing more. I've heard quite enough for one day. I shall leave this office and pack my bags straightaway, and be gone from this place. To where, I do not know, but it shall not be on the recommendation of you or anyone else."

And with that, Abe marched out of the headmaster's office. He was two steps outside the door before the tears began to stream down his face, and even then he managed to fight them back. That was the day Abe Seymour galvanized the sense of self-sufficiency that would mark the rest of his life. Self-sufficiency became his creed, in life and in business.

"Dearest," Abe said to Marilyn. "Please understand that my intention was never to —"

But when Abe turned toward the divan to apologize to his wife, he found that she had already left the room.

FINN BERGEN

Chicago, 1851

Forty-seven days had passed since Nora's sudden departure from the Catholic Orphan Asylum, and every night as he lay awake in bed in the boys' dormitory, Finn clutched the little blue locket that was meant for Nora as he listened to the trains moving in and out of the yard downtown. Impossible as they were to ignore, even at such a distance, the trains had never warranted Finn's attention particularly, let alone captured his imagination. Not until the night he knew Nora was gone forever did it begin to feel like she might be on any one of those trains. The plaintive moan of their whistles receding in the darkness served as a nightly reminder that Nora could be bound for anywhere, and that he would surely follow if ever given the chance.

For forty-seven nights Finn's sleep was haunted by trains.

On the forty-eighth day, Master Searles summoned Finn to his office, which smelled as always faintly of tobacco and moldering paper. The sun slanting through the window illuminated the crowded desktop, where a large register lay open, surrounded by bric-a-brac.

"Do be seated, Mr. Bergen," said Master Searles.

Finn took a seat in the straight-backed chair directly across the desk from the director, who was presently thumbing through the register.

"Well, now," he said brightly, looking up for the first time. "How are we today, young Mr. Bergen?"

Finn offered no reply, prompting Searles to sigh.

"Still not utilizing our faculties of speech, are we, Mr. Bergen? Tsk tsk. I should think that the Vogels would be most pleased to hear you speak. It would be a shame to disappoint them."

Finn's expression was a study in blankness, though his heart began to beat faster.

"Gracious, child," said Master Searles. "Have you no blood in your veins? Aren't you curious as to who the Vogels are? I should think you ought to be. For the Vogels have adopted you."

Though Finn betrayed nothing upon hearing this news, the last pale flicker of hope died inside of him. His removal from the asylum under any circumstance would essentially complete his separation from Nora, rendering their estrangement permanent and unresolvable. Nora could always find Finn so long as he was a ward of the Catholic Orphan Asylum.

"That's it?" said Searles. "Not so much as a smile or a nod or a bat of an eyelid? Perhaps you do not fully comprehend the magnitude of this development, young Mr. Bergen. You have a family, a family who wants you in spite of your — *ahem* — considerable shortcomings. If ever there was a time to break this confounding silence of yours, this is it, child! You have a family! What have you to say about that?"

Finn had exactly nothing to say about that. If anything the news made him want to crawl deeper inside himself, where he might avoid the dreadful realization that his sister would be forever lost to him.

Searles shook his shaggy head in disenchantment.

"Once again, Mr. Bergen, you astound me with your resolve. I should think that with such adherence to your misguided cause you might withstand a considerable deal of torture. Let us hope that never comes to pass. Now, shall we meet your new family?"

Searles stood up, circled the desk, and poked his giant head out the office door.

"Miss Heinlin, would you kindly send in the Vogels?" said Master Searles, who then resumed his seat.

Like the countless intrepid souls who'd ventured to America before them, the Vogels longed for freedom: freedom to worship, freedom to own, and the precious freedom of isolation, away from the intervention of the civilized world. The endless prairie, buffered from the outside world by an ocean of grass, was a veritable Garden of Eden. In Iowa, the Vogels planned to make a life for themselves independent from the machinations of the larger world. They could live and worship as they pleased. Hans and Katrin also yearned for a child, which Katrin was unable to provide, a cruel state of affairs since Katrin ached for nothing more; girl or boy, it didn't matter, so long as she could nurture it and provide for it, and be the beneficiary of its unconditional devotion. Only once they numbered three could the Vogels call themselves a family. It was that very wish for a family that had delivered the Vogels to the Catholic Orphan Asylum, prior to their departure for Iowa. Though Katrin had had her heart set on an infant, Hans had insisted that the child be of sufficient age and hearty enough to make the journey west to help establish the farm.

A moment later the Vogels made their entrance, a youthful and handsome couple, blue eyed and blond, their faces both beaming with satisfaction as they looked down upon Finn.

"What is your name, boy?" said Hans Vogel.

Finn did not answer.

"Why he cannot speak?" said Hans.

"Oh, no, Mr. Vogel, that is not the case at all," Mr. Searles assured him. "It's not that the child cannot speak. It's that the child — owing to traumas I've never been given to fully understand — chooses not to speak."

"Hans, we can heal the boy," insisted Katrin.

Hans could not belie his skepticism.

"You say he work good, the boy? Strong?"

"I can vouch for the young man's work ethic without reservation, Mr. Vogel. In the arena of labor it must be observed that silence can be advantageous, which is to say that the boy keeps his head down. He's not easily distracted. Moreover, he is quite obedient. Though he ventures not to speak, he has no reservations about submitting to guidance."

"Mm," said Hans, mildly impressed.

"We heal this little boy, Hans," said Katrin. "He will be our boy now. He will speak again."

Seeing the enthusiasm in his wife's eyes, Hans had no choice but to grant his consent.

Katrin kneeled down beside Finn and, with tears pouring from her eyes, wrapped the boy fiercely in her arms, while the husband stood behind her, smiling stupidly.

Caught by surprise, Finn felt a welling of gratitude in his throat. How long since anybody had held him close? How long since he had enjoyed any physical contact at all?

The woman finally relinquished her hold on Finn long enough to hold him at arm's length and admire his blue eyes and his fair, freckled complexion and his generous head of red hair before she clutched him to her chest again, her teary eyes brimming anew.

"Beautiful boy," she said into the nape of his neck.

And that was when Finn could no longer contain his own tears.

Thirteen days later, the Vogels and their new son left Chicago in a wagon train bound for Iowa, a journey that saw Katrin, and to a lesser degree Hans, tirelessly endeavor to coax Finn out of his shell. Though they enjoyed little success, they refused to abandon their efforts, questioning the boy frequently, soliciting responses as though they might trick him into answering reflexively.

"What do you think will be your favorite thing about Iowa?" Katrin would say.

And when Finn wouldn't answer, Katrin would speculate on his behalf.

"I think you will like most the wide-open space. A boy, he need wide-open space to run."

252

Hans's attempts tended toward the more direct.

"Well, what is it on your mind? I'm your father now, you can talk to me."

Yet as much as Finn had grown to admire Hans for his strength and his patience and his generosity, he did not once offer him the benefit of a reply. Finn could not begrudge the couple for their efforts any more than he could begrudge them their native enthusiasm or unsolicited kindness. Still, he offered them little in the way of encouragement beyond a nod or the occasional hint of a smile.

Nora remained ever in Finn's thoughts. Her voice was burned into his memory. If he closed his eyes he could visualize her animated face. There were points along the trail through western Illinois when Finn, clutching the little blue locket in his fist, convinced himself that Nora might still hear his thoughts. If only he could concentrate his focus to the necessary degree, they might reach her directly. It seemed possible that he could send his thoughts out like a beacon and that Nora might follow them across the sprawling prairie.

Despite his silence, the Vogels' devotion to Finn was not unrequited. Finn made himself useful at every opportunity along the trail, whether it was leading the cows, or scavenging firewood from beneath the oaks, or fetching water from the river. By the fire at night, after they circled the wagons, Finn scooted so close to Katrin that their shoulders would graze. And when she set her hand upon his knee, or planted a kiss upon his cheek, he no longer flinched but welcomed it.

Traveling with the Vogels began to feel almost natural. There was a rhythm and purpose to Finn's new life, which he preferred to the cloistered routine of the asylum. He enjoyed the wide-open spaces, the flat, expansive landscape that rendered everything small in its midst. He enjoyed the smell, almost like bread, of the endless grain having baked in the summer heat. He appreciated the constant occupation and the sense of accomplishment that came with putting miles behind them. He marveled at the ever-changing sky and gave thanks to the soft breeze out of the north as it cooled the sweat upon his face. And in the evening he was comforted by the chorus of crickets.

What Finn appreciated most of all was the progress. After months in captivity, he yearned for movement. If given the choice he would have preferred to keep right on moving through Iowa and beyond, as far as the trail would take them, if only to keep from standing still. For, when he was not occupied, as was the case at night, on his back in the middle of the prairie, gazing up at the unfathomable starlit firmament, the absence of his other half overwhelmed him. The prairie, and even the night sky, seemed puny next to his longing for his sister.

After seventeen days of travel, upon arriving at a seemingly arbitrary point in an endlessly repeating landscape, Hans decided that the Vogels were home. To say that there was nothing distinctive about the location would be an understatement. Indeed, the flat, grassy topography and the absence of shade were indiscernible from anywhere else as far as the eye could see.

But to Hans, the place was singular, not because it looked different, rather because it felt different. Hans claimed to feel the land vibrating up from beneath the surface of the earth. He claimed that when he put his ear to the ground he could hear the heartbeat of the world. Thus, he wasted little time in securing rights to the land from the patent office to the tune of a dollar and a quarter an acre.

It was much too late in the season to plant crops, so the Vogels set to work clearing the scant timber they could find for their cabin. The footprint would be twelve feet by twenty. The structure would have a steep-pitched roof to shed snow. Finn would have his own room for the first time in his life. There would be a hearth of river rock to keep them warm through the winter. But not that first winter. The cabin was only half built when the snow and blistering cold arrived to thwart their efforts. And there began the nights of sleeping under the wagon, huddled beneath their mounded furs as the arctic winds howled south over the prairie, hissing eerily through the grass and battering anything in their path, which wasn't much. By the time the Vogels, and twenty thousand other settlers, had streamed across the river valleys in wagon trains, ferrying across the Mississippi at Dubuque or Prairie du Chien or Burlington, the timber had thinned out and given way to the boundless high grass prairie.

In retrospect the Vogels might have been wise to settle the ridgelands, covered with white oaks and dense undergrowth. As it stood, there was barely enough timber on their hundred and forty acres to construct a shelter, let alone enough for split-rail fences. Instead they marked their claim with walls of stone and mounded dirt. Timber being such a precious commodity, they burned hay and corn and cattle droppings to warm themselves through the interminable winter. Yet even the rigors of a prairie winter could not temper Hans Vogel's optimism. What was a little sleet and ice, what was four feet of snow or an arctic blast so frigid it could freeze livestock, next to freedom?

"Without winter there is no spring," Hans said on at least a dozen occasions that first winter. "Everything has its season."

For months on end, Katrin and Finn leaned

into Hans's optimism like a campfire until finally winter relinquished its grip on the prairie. After the thaw they began plowing the tough prairie sod, cultivating corn and wheat and potatoes. They yielded barely enough for sustenance and used much of the corn to feed the pigs, which they sold for a profit in Davenport. The Vogels relied heavily on poultry and eggs, and were diligent in protecting the chickens from predation, allowing them to roost, much to Katrin's chagrin, in a makeshift pen in the corner of the cabin at night until such time as they amassed ample timber to build a barn, or a proper chicken pen. The few pigs they didn't sell they butchered and hung to dry in the little smokehouse behind the cabin.

At last the Vogels had a working farm. While it may not have been profitable, it was at least sustainable. And that was enough for Hans and Katrin Vogel. But not for Finn. It was not the backbreaking work he objected to, nor the meager rewards. It was the lack of movement, and the lack of possibility, that he found stultifying. As much as he'd grown to care for the Vogels, he yearned to move. Specifically, he yearned to find his sister, no matter the improbability. No matter that Nora could have been anywhere under the sun, never mind that he wouldn't know where to begin such a search. What else was there but to find her? What future but to look for her?

Were it not for his debt to the Vogels, Finn might have embarked on this journey. Instead, he rewarded the Vogels' loyalty and worked harder, the sun beating down on his face and shoulders and neck, searing his pale Irish flesh to a feverish pink. He labored until he was nothing but lean muscle and sinew; he toiled until he was so exhausted that he could hardly read himself to sleep at night. And in this manner he suppressed the impulse to stray. Most nights he was too exhausted to dream and slept like the overworked earth beneath him. But one night, a few weeks before harvest, he had a troubling vision.

He dreamed of Nora standing in a wide field of marshy stubble, her back turned to him, her arms folded defiantly. It was raining in the dream, and Finn was angry with Nora for reasons he could not comprehend, though there was no mistaking the rage that coursed through him. Face streaked with mud, feet sinking into the blighted muck, he kept yelling her name, commanding her attention, but Nora refused to turn. Furious, Finn grabbed her by the shoulders and swung her around to face him, totally unprepared for the visage that confronted him. For Nora was not Nora but a wraith, arms crossed over her chest, blood completely drained from her lifeless face, only the whites of her eyes showing.

Gasping, Finn let go of her shoulders and awakened with a shudder. He bolted upright in the darkness, mopping the sweat from his forehead. When he looked out the window toward the east, dawn was still but a faint ribbon of gray on the horizon. He slipped out of bed, and pulled on his trousers, and slid into his boots, stealing quietly out of the cabin. Shaken to the core by the horrific vision of Nora, the empty silence of the prairie was little comfort to Finn as he crossed the clearing toward the barn squatting in the darkness. It was only a dream, he told himself half-heartedly, Nora could not be dead. Even God, ruthless despot that he was, could not be cruel enough to snuff out Finn's last dim hope of connection.

But as Finn tended the animals in the dark quarters of the barn, minding the water and turning the hay, collecting the eggs and scattering the feed, a relentless doubt pervaded his consciousness. Even as the farm came to life all around him and the sun made its appearance, pinkening the eastern horizon with the promise of a new day, Finn felt a cold certainty settle into his bones. Shortly after dawn, as Finn was walking the fence line, his grim confirmation arrived in the form of a lone black-beaked magpie perched upon the mounded rocks, regarding Finn with its impenetrable black eyes. Just as on the morning he'd discovered his infant sister lifeless in her crib, here again was the mateless magpie to portend the unthinkable.

And that was when Finn knew that his sister was irrevocably lost to him, and that he, like the magpie that had gone beyond its range, was alone in the world.

WU CHEN

San Francisco, 1852

For a year Wu Chen had continued to work at the laundry on Clay Street, returning each evening to his rented room on Kearny, where he taught himself to read English by candle-light. Heeding the advice of his uncle Li Jun, Wu Chen lived frugally and saved the bulk of his modest pay for the children he did not have yet, amending his fortune weekly at the San Francisco Savings Bank, which had survived yet another fire since his initial deposit the prior spring.

Over a year removed, the bloody fiasco at the Huangs' claim was still fresh in his mind. His sleep was tortured by images of the murdered Huangs: Johnny with his pants around his ankles, caught by surprise. Tommy, tears streaming down his face, begging for his life. Jimmy, hunched forward, face in the dirt, the back of his head blown to pulp. Wu Chen was haunted, too, by his own barbarous acts, the four men he'd murdered

261

with the same hands that now scoured and folded other people's laundry.

To think that because of these horrors he was now a wealthy man was almost inconceivable. Thus, he did not feel like a wealthy man, any more than he lived like one. Wu Chen was not one to smarten up on Sundays and stroll the plaza, nor did he splurge on fancy meals, or even the better lodgings he might easily have afforded himself. He lived instead a small, quiet life well below his means, filled largely with educating himself in the ways of America.

One of the few things Wu Chen allowed himself in the way of leisure was long walks. In summer, when the days were long, Wu Chen spent his late afternoons and evenings exploring the ever-expanding city. So perpetual was the change that in a matter of weeks, whole new neighborhoods popped up, and dozens of new businesses appeared: banks, grocery stores, restaurants, laundries, and, of course, saloons by the handful, which Wu Chen never patronized.

On sunny evenings he enjoyed the many vistas the hills had to offer, or the wharf and surrounding harbor, swarming like an anthill. To the east, the great blue bay, bordered on the western shore by the burgeoning port, bristled with masts.

From Nob Hill, Wu Chen could see northwest, beyond the Golden Gate, clear to the frothing ocean that had brought him there.

Even on days when the city was enveloped in impenetrable fog, Wu Chen wandered the streets, on occasion getting lost. There was something magical about the way the fog quieted the restless city, the way it shrouded its beauty in mystery, as though protecting it from those who seemed to arrive on its shores hourly.

Each day on his way home from the laundry, Wu Chen passed countless storefronts and stalls, including a little open-air Chinese grocery just off Portsmouth Square on Clay, which Wu Chen never noticed in the blur of commercial enterprise, until one particular day. It was a Monday, cloudy, and unseasonably cool. The laundry had been uncharacteristically slow, and Wu Chen was released from his duties early. He left the laundry and crossed the square as usual en route to his room.

What caught Wu Chen's attention that particular day in July was not the little grocery itself, with its bruised fruit and caged chickens, but more specifically, who was attending the stalls: a young, beautiful Chinese girl of eighteen or twenty, with the fairest skin, and fullest lips, and kindest eyes he'd ever gazed upon. Wu Chen nearly tripped over a mongrel dog in passing, then falteringly, as though against his own will, turned back and soon found himself scouring the stalls of the little grocery for nothing in particular.

"May I help you?" said the young woman.

Her voice was like soft music. Breathless, Wu Chen could scarcely find his tongue at first.

"Uh, um, just looking for uh, yes, yes, one of these," he said, plucking a sad lemon off the pile. "Oh, and yes, one of these, too," he added, palming a small cabbage, already beginning to wilt.

"This one is better," she said, handing Wu Chen a fresh head, just as a little frowning man appeared behind her, arms folded, presumably displeased at the girl for not unloading the wilting inventory in favor of the fresh.

"How much?" said Wu Chen, blushing.

"Half dime," replied the frowning man, even as he cast a disgusted glance sidelong at the girl.

"Father, you are incorrigible. Here, take this one, too," said the girl, defiantly foisting the wilted cabbage upon Wu Chen.

The little man glowered at her, then waved her away.

Upon departing with his sad lemon and two cabbages, Wu Chen could not help but look back over his shoulder for a last glimpse of the girl, who bestowed a smile upon him, despite the fact that her father was scolding her.

The rest of the walk home was a blur. He retreated to his little room, where he lay on his mattress and stared at the ceiling, trying to conjure the girl's face out of the dusty air.

As if he could hear his nephew thinking, imaginary Uncle Li Jun took Wu Chen to task.

"Don't be foolish with your daydreams," said his uncle. "Be practical. You don't even know this girl."

"But, Uncle, did you not see her eyes, how kind and understanding they were? Did you not see her conscientious nature on full display when she insisted on giving me the better cabbage?"

"Bah," said Uncle Li Jun. "Did you see her father? She's a disappointment."

"Impossible," said Wu Chen dreamily.

"Don't be stupid," said his uncle. "At least learn something about her and her situation before you go acting the fool. For all you know, she is already spoken for."

"No," said Wu Chen, more as a protest against the very idea than a denial.

"If you haven't noticed, the men far outnumber the women in your new promised land. What does she want with a laundry boy when she might have a real professional, a business owner, or a restaurateur?"

"Please do not take offense, Uncle Li Jun, you have been like a father to me. I trust your guidance always. But must you always be so gloomy?"

"I am not gloomy, Nephew. I am realistic. I'm practical. I am forward thinking."

"But you said yourself I must one day find a wife."

"I said one day, not *in one day,* Nephew. You can ill afford to be reckless in these matters."

"Oh, very well, then, Uncle. I will investigate."

And Wu Chen was more than happy to investigate. In the coming days he bought many heads of cabbage that went uneaten. He bought beets, and carrots, and unripe oranges that more closely resembled lemons. His exchanges with the girl were not expansive and were invariably interrupted by the scowling father. Though the information he gathered during these investigations was scant, he was able to divine her name, if only by way of her father's grumblings.

Ai Lu. Ai, like mugwort, which hardly did the girl's beauty justice.

Each day his affection grew stronger. He could barely endure a day without her melodic voice, her hypnotic eyes, or the slight brush of their hands as they exchanged money, usually beneath the watchful gaze of her father, who appeared willing, though not thrilled, to accept it.

On those precious few occasions when Wu Chen and Ai Lu were left to themselves, Wu

Chen, though terrified of her beauty and kindness, pushed himself to develop intimacy with Ai Lu.

"I have an uncle from Guangdong. And many cousins," he offered.

"There are many people here from Guangdong."

"I miss them," said Wu Chen.

"I have two sisters," said Ai Lu. "This is perhaps the primary reason, but not the only reason, for my father's unhappiness."

"But you are so beautiful and kind," said Wu Chen, blushing to the roots of his hair.

"It is you who is kind," she said. "What need has anybody for so much cabbage?"

"I'm afraid you've found me out," confessed Wu Chen. "I only come to see you."

Indeed, on those days when Ai Lu was nowhere to be seen, Wu Chen walked right past the little grocery on his way home. This pattern was not lost on Ai Lu's father, under whose scrutiny Wu Chen fell with each passing. Until one day, Ai Lu's father stopped him before he could pass.

"You," he said. "How come you only come when my daughter is working?"

"Do I?" said Wu Chen, feigning innocence.

"She's the oldest daughter," he said. "Maybe not the smartest, but beautiful."

Wu Chen was nearly taken aback by such unsentimental candor.

"With all due respect, sir," said Wu Chen,

"Ai Lu strikes me as very intelligent. And not only that, she is kind, and curious."

The slightest hint of a smile played at the corners of her father's lips.

"Okay, you've passed the first test," he said. "Now, you buy something."

Wu Chen left several minutes later, his arms heaping with cabbage.

Lying upon his mattress, staring up at the ceiling, he reported to Uncle Li Jun.

"You see, Uncle. I am making progress. I have earned her father's first blessing."

"You were fleeced of your money. You have a year's worth of cabbage, and frankly, this room is beginning to stink of it."

"Ah, but what are a few coins next to love, Uncle?"

Wu Chen could envision his uncle shaking his head in disappointment.

"I suppose you'd do better to ask for her hand now than to spend your fortune on wilted cabbage."

Midway through fall, Wu Chen resolved to ask Ai Lu's father for her hand.

On an afternoon when Ai Lu was not present at the stand, Wu Chen stopped to buy some carrots and turnips he had no use for. After pretending to select these items with a discerning eye, and presenting Ai Lu's father with the money, Wu Chen finally summoned the courage.

"Sir, I would like to ask for your daughter's

hand in marriage."

Her father didn't bat an eye.

"Ha! Why should she want to marry you?" he said.

"I believe she likes me, sir. I believe we are a good match."

"What prospects have you that I should want to give her to you?"

"I would not own her, sir. You would be giving me nothing. And together, perhaps, we could give you some grandsons."

"Hmph," said her father. "Anybody could say as much. It does not take anyone extraordinary to produce offspring. What have you to offer my daughter beyond the burden of bearing children?"

"Everything, sir. My devotion and undying loyalty. My every resource."

"What resources? Do you own the laundry in which you toil?"

"No, sir, but I have plans."

"This place is full of plans," he said. "They are more plentiful than fish. What is so special about your plans?"

"I am a wealthy man."

Ai Lu's father looked at him doubtfully.

"Oh?" he said. "I would not have guessed you a wealthy man."

"That is because I am wise with my money. Just as my uncle Li Jun in Guangdong taught me."

"Mm. And what evidence of this wealth

269

have you to offer, beyond the fact you spend freely on vegetables?"

"I could show you a savings note, sir, from the San Francisco Savings Bank."

"And how did you come by this wealth, young man? Surely, you did not bring it here from Guangdong."

"Gold, sir."

"And how was this gold gotten?"

"By the sweat of my brow, and the strength of my back, and by my shrewd ability to locate the stuff, sir, where many before me had failed. For every shrewd miner like me there are a thousand who fail."

"So, luck?" said her father.

"Yes, to some degree that is also true."

"And what are your big plans for this fortune?"

"Why, sir, for starters, to invest in this very grocery," said Wu Chen.

The truth was that Wu Chen had given little thought to how he might invest his fortune. He only knew that he was saving it for the children he did not have yet, and that he wanted more than anything in the world to spend his life with Ai Lu, to wake up beside her, to stroll through the city with her, hand in hand, and one day, to have a family with her.

"Tell me more," said her father.

Wu Chen flew by the seat of his pants through what began to feel more and more like a negotiation. He shared with Ai Lu's father all the wisdom and foresight he had gleaned from his uncle Li Jun pertaining to matters of commerce, foresight, prudence, and general pragmatism, but also love.

"Sir," he said, "even with your blessing, I am only interested in Ai Lu's hand if she wants me. I should never horse-trade for somebody so kind and decent, so smart and beautiful, as Ai Lu. If she does not want me, I shall disappear from your lives."

"No more customer?"

"Well, I suppose I could still be a customer."

"It's not good to lose a customer."

"It's settled then, sir," said Wu Chen. "One way or another I will continue to be a customer."

For the very first time, Ai Lu's father donned his smile in its fullness, which might have been fuller. But still, Wu Chen found it far preferable to his customary scowl.

"You let me think about it," said her father.

JENNY CHEN

San Francisco, 2017

When Jenny emerged from the bedroom, ten-year-old Winston was there to greet her in the hallway, his face buried in his tablet, his thick, dark hair in sleepy disarray.

"Aw, do we have to go?" he said without looking up from his screen.

"Yes," said Jenny.

"Why?"

"Ask your father," she said.

"But it was your idea," he said, looking up. "Dad doesn't care. He'd rather watch basketball."

"Just get dressed," said Jenny. "We're going to spend some time together as a family."

"But we can do that here."

"We're going to see your grandparents, Winston. Doesn't that mean anything to you?"

"We just saw them on my birthday, remember? They gave me a check for nine bucks."

"Do you realize how ungrateful that

sounds?"

"Well, c'mon, Mom, nine bucks?"

Did her children really have no understanding of how fortunate they were? Could they truly not see the extent to which their parents, and grandparents, and even their ancestors had their best interests at heart? Had Jenny failed to instill this sense of continuity in them? Had she failed to instill gratitude in them?

It wasn't too late to save them.

"Turn the tablet off and get ready," she said.

"Fine," he conceded, though he didn't turn the tablet off — not that Jenny had expected him to do so on the first go; she knew better by now.

"Off," she said.

It was like he couldn't even hear her voice.

"Off!"

Still, Winston didn't budge, his focus trained exclusively on the screen. It was a wonder he remembered to breathe.

"OFF!" she shouted.

"Geez, Mom, don't have a cow," he said, finally powering down the tablet as he turned and strode down the hallway. When he was halfway to his bedroom she called out to him and he turned to face her.

"What?" he said.

"Let me ask you something," said Jenny. "And I want you to really think about it."

"What?"

"Do you like your life?"

"What kind of question is that?"

"Just answer it."

"Sure," he said. "It's fine."

"Just fine?"

"Yeah, it's fine, it's great. What do you want me to say, Mom? Can I get dressed now?"

Jenny almost pushed him further, almost took Winston to task for his shortsightedness, but decided to err on the side of finesse. Today's outing would provide a good opportunity to impress a few things on her boys; no need to rush anything.

It was noon by the time she went downstairs, where Todd was fully dressed and watching a basketball game.

"Oregon," he said.

"Again with Oregon? Seriously?" she said.

"No, the game, Oregon-Cal."

Jenny almost let Todd off the hook right then and there. Everybody would be happier. Todd could watch his basketball game, Jenny could go back to bed, and the kids could play on their devices. But Jenny was determined to see this outing through. They needed this time together. Still, in spite of herself, she couldn't resist testing Todd.

"Do you not want to do this?" she said.

"Of course I want to do this."

"I understand if you don't want to."

"I want to," he said, turning off his beloved Ducks game as though to prove his point.

Obviously, he was lying, but she loved him for it. He'd always been such a good sport about her parents. And despite their somewhat disinterested manner, they really liked Todd more than they let on.

"You know my parents don't actually hate you, right?" she explained for the hundredth time in eleven years.

"Yeah, I know that. Of course I know that," he said. "I'm fine with your parents. Round up the boys and let's get moving."

Why was Jenny making them all do this against their wills? Because it mattered. History mattered. It was time for her children to acknowledge once and for all that nobody in the Chen-Murphy household had gotten where they were without help. Virtually every opportunity that had ever been available to the Chens was owing directly or indirectly to the struggles of their forebearers. For all their good fortune, they were beholden to their ancestors. And Jenny was determined that her children honor them, willingly or not.

They escaped the city without traffic. It took less than fifteen minutes to get to the cemetery, and yet not one time in the past eight years had Jenny made the effort or even had the thought to visit the graves of her ancestors, despite the frequent hectoring of her mother. When the city had outlawed new burials at the end of the nineteenth century, the cemeteries had been moved south. Nearly a hundred and fifty thousand bodies had been exhumed and relocated, eliminating the health hazard, but more important, freeing up prime real estate.

Thus Colma became the home of seventeen graveyards parceled out along various racial and denominational lines, but the Chinese cemetery was not among them. Instead the Chinese cemetery had taken shape just outside Colma on a dry hill all by itself, situated above what was now the Serramonte neighborhood. The numberless graves lay beyond a simple wrought-iron gate marked "Chinese." To be Chinese in America was to be separate, to be displaced.

"They all look the same," said Winston.

"You're not looking close enough," Jenny said, annoyed at the laziness of the observation. For though they were small markers all, and mostly unadorned, every grave site was different. They spread out for acres in every direction, yet hardly two stones reposed at the same angle. Size was about the only thing uniform among them.

"He's not wrong, you know," said Todd. "How are we going to find them? Do you remember where they are?"

"Pretty much," Jenny lied, though she vaguely remembered the Chens somewhere near the northwestern corner.

As it turned out, Jenny wasn't far off. It took only ten minutes of exploration to find the markers, which were situated near the western edge of the cemetery, adjacent to a potter's field of unmarked graves.

It wasn't until they were all standing above the gravestones that it occurred to Jenny that she had not brought so much as a bouquet of flowers or a stick of incense to honor the deceased.

"Who were they?" said Winston.

"Those two there are your great-great-great-great-grandparents," said Jenny. "And those are your great-great-great-great-great-grandparents, who came from Guangdong."

"What did they do?" he said.

"They were shop owners."

"All of them?"

"Yes," she said. "Even when your grandfather was a boy, his parents owned stores all over the city."

"But you always said they were broke when they came to America."

"They were."

"So how did they own a bunch of stores?"

"They worked their tails off. Your great-great-great-great-grandpa Chen was a forty-niner."

"He played football?"

"No, he was a gold miner who had a bit of luck in the hills. He came to the city, where he met your great-great-great-great-grandmother Ai Lu, and they began opening stores. Then they had children, and they opened more stores."

"So, what happened to all the stores?" said Winston.

"Grandma and Grandpa sold them."

"All of them?"

"Yes."

"Did they make a lot?"

"Yes."

"Were they rich?" said Tyler.

"I suppose," said Jenny. "At least by some measures. But they didn't live like it. They lived frugally."

"So, what did they do with the money?"

"They bought some real estate in China-town, and the rest they saved."

"For what?"

"For you."

"Sweet," said Winston. "When do I get it?"

"What about me?" said Tyler.

Todd cleared his throat.

"Not like that," said Jenny. "They saved so that we would have a future here."

"So we don't get any money?"

"No."

"Bummer," said Tyler.

Jenny sighed, knowing she was no better than her kids. Her ancestors had had the foresight to save their whole lives on behalf of the unborn, and Jenny hadn't had the foresight to bring some flowers to their graves.

"So like, Great-Great-Grandpa was a miner?" said Winston.

"Great-Great-Great-Great-Grandpa," said Jenny.

"That's epic," said Winston. "And he found a bunch of gold?"

"Yes."

"You never told us that before."

"I didn't think you'd be interested."

"Duh, Mom, gold mining? That's epic."

After the cemetery, they drove the three miles across town to Jenny's parents' house.

"Are you sure they're home?" said Todd. "Maybe we should have called first."

"Where else would they be?"

But Todd was right. Her parents' car wasn't in the driveway when they arrived. Only Kevin's scooter. Of course, Kevin's scooter. Talk about somebody who didn't have anything better to do. He still rode a scooter. No job, no real plans, and no prospects.

Jenny, Todd, and the boys all piled out of the car. Kevin met them at the door before they could even knock. To his credit — and Jenny's surprise — he was fully dressed.

"What are you guys doing here?" he said.

"We just dropped by to see Mom and Dad."

"You should have called first," he said. "They're not home. Hey, Todd, hey, guys, come in."

"Where are they?" said Jenny.

"Shopping."

They walked through the foyer and took a left into the sprawling but faceless living room full of new furniture. Jenny would always miss the old cramped Victorian on Clay Street she'd grown up in.

"Can we go in the den?" said Winston, before anyone sat down.

"Fine," said Jenny, knowing that they'd only turn on the television.

"So, what's new?" said Kevin, seating himself in his father's chair.

"What's new for you?" Jenny said.

"Not much," he said.

Big surprise, thought Jenny.

"I'm learning Mandarin," said Kevin.

"Mom told me."

"And I've been taking culinary classes."

"She told me that, too."

"What about you?" said Kevin.

"Well, I just got a bunch of people in Oregon laid off at Amtrak, so I've got that going for me."

"Ouch," he said. "I mean, congratulations, I guess."

"Pays the bills," she said.

"I'm gonna check on the boys," said Todd, before he ever sat down.

As much as Jenny loved her little brother, she had a hard time respecting him. Kevin had made none of the sacrifices Jenny had made upon entering the adult world. He'd dropped out of college, never gotten a real job, never applied himself to anything remotely profitable. She resented the fact that

Kevin had managed to circumnavigate duty and achievement; she resented that he'd managed to eschew ambition and expectation when these qualities comprised nothing less than a Chen family imperative. Meanwhile Jenny had picked up all that Chen slack and nobody ever seemed to notice. Kevin could buy a new pair of slippers and it didn't escape his mother's notice.

Sometimes Jenny wanted to strangle him.

"I miss you," he said. "You never come around."

You never go away, she almost said.

"So, really," said Kevin. "I mean, what's new? We haven't talked in forever."

His curiosity, which seemed genuine, disarmed Jenny immediately in spite of her misgivings.

"Todd wants to move to Oregon," she said.

"Wow. Do you?"

"Not really. Kind of."

"What's holding you back?"

"I mean, I think it would be great for the kids and Todd, but I'd have to quit my job."

"Do you like your job?"

"No, but it pays well."

"Couldn't you find a job in Oregon?"

"Probably."

"Then maybe you should do it," said Kevin. "I'd totally do it."

"Why?" said Jenny.

"I don't know, why not? Oregon. It sounds

exciting. Isn't Todd's family there? Besides, this place is deadsville."

"So why do you keep hanging around, then?" Jenny said, regretting it immediately.

As if on cue, her parents pushed through the front door, arms loaded with groceries.

"Why didn't you call?" said Jenny's mom.

"We were just in the neighborhood," Jenny said.

Todd promptly emerged from down the hallway to unburden Jenny's mom of her grocery bags in the foyer, knowing that this consideration would likely be unappreciated.

"Where's the boys?" said her mom.

After three or four prompts the boys finally peeled themselves from the television screen to grace the family in the kitchen, where small talk ensued. Within five minutes, however, Jenny managed to establish that they wouldn't be hanging around long.

"You're not staying for dinner?" said her mom. "Kevin's such a good cook."

"I promised the kids we'd go to Chinatown," said Jenny.

"No, you didn't," said Winston.

"Yes, we talked about it this morning," said Todd, coming to Jenny's rescue.

"Sorry, Mom, but I promised them Good Mong Kok," said Jenny.

"Mm," said her mother.

What was Jenny trying to escape? Wasn't this day supposed to be about teaching the boys about family and a sense of legacy? Wasn't spending time with their grandparents and their uncle Kevin the perfect opportunity to instill these values in them? So, why was she so restless, why did she yearn to run from her family? Was it because she felt underappreciated?

After the groceries were put away, they all moved to the outsized living room, where they sat awkwardly, knowing it was to be a short visit.

"Do you ever miss the old house?" said Jenny.

"No," said her father from his chair.

"Sometimes," said her mother.

"I do," said Kevin.

"I don't remember it," said Winston.

"Me either," said Tyler.

"It was small," said Jenny's father. "And expensive."

"It was paid for," said her mom.

"Not the taxes," said her father. "Outrageous."

"You sure you won't stay for dinner?" said her mom, appealing to Todd.

Jenny flashed Todd a look, but he was way ahead of her.

"We promised the boys humbows," he said.

"Besides, Mom, I've got to fly to DC Monday," Jenny said. "It's been a grind, lately. I've hardly been home."

Her mom could not belie a sullen disappointment.

"Always so busy," she said.

"Well, you taught me to be a hard worker."

"Hmph," she said.

From there on out the conversation was mostly stilted. When it came time for good-byes twenty minutes later, they all walked out to the driveway. Hanging back, Kevin pulled Jenny aside.

"Look," he said. "I know you think I'm a loser, and my opinion probably doesn't count for much."

"I don't think you're a loser," Jenny lied.

"But maybe you should go for it," said Kevin.

"For what?"

"For Oregon," said Kevin. "Do it. I'll hold down the fort here."

"We'll see," she said, hugging him for the first time in recent memory.

LAILA TULLY

Highway 101 North, 2019

Laila's gutless pickup was sluggish through the Siskiyous, barely managing thirty miles per hour up the steeper grades. She made the pass at dusk. Darkness gathered as the twin spears of her headlights lit her way down the back side of the range into Oregon. Laila couldn't help but smile inwardly when she crossed the border. It was really happening. There was no turning back now.

No doubt, Boaz had texted a dozen times by then, but Laila had turned off her phone just north of Weed. Rather than speculating about the current state of Boaz, Laila did her best to keep her thoughts focused on the future, and the state of Washington, where cousin Genie eagerly awaited her arrival. But even these speculations were colored by anxiety. What if Genie's plan of getting her a job at the lodge didn't work out? Shouldn't she have some kind of plan for herself, one that didn't depend on Genie? It was hard to figure when she had no idea what her options might look like in Queets, Washington. The place was hardly a thriving metropolis. When Laila had googled Queets, she'd learned that it wasn't even a town, but an unincorporated area with a population of . . . wait for it . . . 174. One restaurant, one gas station, one store. The image search, however, gave Laila much reason to hope. For Queets, at least the larger setting, was beautiful, with its lush green terrain and its proximity to the mountains, both of which would be a welcome departure from the flat, scorched valley she'd left behind.

After the dark passage through the Siskiyous, it was a relief to see the lights of Ashland, nestled in the wedge of the basin. Inconceivably this was the furthest north Laila had ever traveled. Except for a car trip to Carlsbad with her parents when she was eight years old, two dozen visits to Sacramento, and four or five trips to the city, Laila hadn't been much of anywhere in her life. How was it even possible that she'd never left the state of California before today? To hear Grandma Malilah tell it, in all the generations she could count, for all their wandering, and displacement, and relocation, whether forced or chosen, no Tully had ever left California. The closest anyone had come was Eureka. But here was Laila, officially in Oregon.

Twenty-eight years and what did she have to show for her life? Most of a high school education, no career track, and a handful of romantic involvements ranging from the vaguely unfulfilling to the unmistakably abusive. Laila didn't even have any kids. All she could call her own was what she was wearing and what was stuffed into a single, sausage-shaped canvas duffel she'd found working housekeeping at the Ramada hotel five years ago: her crappy Dell laptop, a couple pairs of jeans, an extra pair of black work pants, an extra white work shirt, four or five blouses, socks, underwear, makeup, and an envelope full of cash comprising every penny she had to her name. Not a single dress. Even this crappy pickup wasn't registered in her name. Her only meaningful keepsake was the tiny blue heart-shaped locket Grandma Malilah had given Laila for her thirteenth birthday, the significance of which Laila could not even remember, beyond the fact that it had once belonged to her great-great-great-great-grandmother Luyu. How Luyu had come by it Grandma Malilah could not say, but likely it came from her husband, John Tully. Laila had treasured the blue locket because it was old, and because she loved the smoothness of the enamel, and the delicacy of the tiny hinges, which she rarely opened, knowing well what was on the inside. Engraved in gold within its tiny chamber was a cursive letter L.

And that was it: a laptop, some laundry, and an old locket. This far into her life's journey, that was all the baggage Laila could claim.

In spite of this grim accounting, Laila felt with every mile as though she was shedding the trappings of her old self. In Queets she would develop new habits. She would set goals, though from here she could only guess at what those goals might look like. She'd start eating better, start getting more exercise, start reading more books and watching less Netflix and Hulu. She would take her job — whatever it might be — more seriously, so that she could possibly work her way up the ladder, whatever that looked like. All of it would add up to more dignity and more self-respect. She would hold herself to a higher standard. And under absolutely no circumstance would she leave the measuring and defining of herself up to somebody else, especially not a man.

The interstate was mostly deserted through Rogue Valley on a Monday night. Laila gassed up at the Circle K in Talent to the tune of thirty-eight bucks, not to mention the two-dollar coffee, feeling every penny of it as she merged back onto the interstate sipping the lukewarm sludge north through Phoenix and Medford.

By the time Laila reached Central Point,

her eyelids began to grow heavy in spite of the coffee. Restless as she was to outrun her old life in one long sprint, she decided to play it safe and pulled off at the rest area at Gold Hill, where she locked both doors and lay sideways on the bench seat. Using her sausage bag as a pillow and her fleece sweatshirt as a blanket, Laila fell asleep almost immediately in spite of her worries.

She awoke shivering against the chill and immediately cleared the fogged-up windshield to peer out. The eastern horizon was just beginning to pale. In spite of the early hour an elderly couple in matching green caps and green parkas braved the morning cold, manning the free coffee station. Dropping thirty-three cents into the plastic donation jar, Laila gratefully procured a Styrofoam cup of weak coffee and loaded it with Sweet'N Low and nondairy creamer. Following some brief pleasantries with the old couple, Laila retired to the truck, where she washed down a pair of free chocolate chip cookies, stale but sweet, and called it breakfast. Sweeping the crumbs from her lap, she started the truck on the second try and wasted no further time in resuming her journey north.

By Rogue River the snow had begun to fall. Laila gripped the wheel tighter, praying it wouldn't stick, as she left the broad valley and began winding her way into the hills. By

Grants Pass the snow was sticking on the shoulders. Gripping the wheel still tighter, Laila practically had to remind herself to breathe. To make matters worse, the little truck continued to struggle up the inclines as motorists, even semis, passed her on the left.

Maybe she ought to turn back, or pull over and wait out the flurry. But what if it only got worse? What if she got stuck in Grants Pass and had to pay for a motel? What if it lasted more than a day? Think of the precious time and money she would lose not putting miles between herself and her old life, specifically Boaz.

Laila decided it was best to forge ahead and keep praying. Though the snow continued throughout her steady ascent out of Grants Pass and on through Canyonville, the accumulation kept mostly to the shoulders except for a dirty swathe of slush running down the middle of the interstate until Myrtle Creek, where the snow began to find a thin purchase on the roadway. The truck, with its balding tires and no weight in back, began to get squirrelly, further increasing Laila's dread and anxiety as she forged north. If she could only make it through the mountains to the lower elevations, the road conditions were bound to improve. But the mountains turned from green to white in a matter of minutes. Meanwhile the truck was having a tougher and tougher time ascending the inclines. There were hills so long and steeply graded on the approach to Roseburg that the truck could barely manage, and Laila thought for certain she would lose her momentum entirely.

When the mountains finally relented fifty miles later, and Laila descended at last into the Willamette Valley, she let out the breath she'd been holding in for an hour. But her relief was short-lived, as the snow continued falling. The wind had picked up considerably. Laila could feel it blowing in from the south-west, forcing the truck toward the snowy shoulder. On one such occasion the truck began to fishtail at forty miles per hour, but Laila was able to correct it. The damage to her nerves, however, may have been permanent. Proceeding more cautiously than ever, she leaned forward in the driver's seat, stomach in knots, both hands clenching the wheel fiercely. Though she needed to pee desperately, she held it all the way until Cottage Grove, at which point her bladder nearly burst.

The exit ramp was blanketed in several inches of snow. As Laila depressed the brakes ever so softly, the truck began to fishtail again, and nearly slid into the ditch before Laila corrected it. When she finally came to a stop in front of the bathrooms, she had to pry her fingers off the steering wheel.

The rest stop was all but deserted, but for a

few idling rigs in the truck lot.

Laila scampered over the snowy walkway, relieved to find the women's bathroom un-locked. As she squatted, hovering inches above the toilet seat, she considered once again whether she might be better off waiting out the snow. But the fact that she'd made it through the mountains alive was enough encouragement to press onward.

Back in the truck, Laila paused only long enough to dig a small Tupperware container of cold Swedish meatballs out of her bag. She forced a few down, cold and congealed as they were, before replacing the container in her duffel. She started the truck on the third try and pulled out of the rest area at a crawl, stomach still growling, nerves fried.

Eight miles south of Salem the truck began to slow down inexplicably until she was go-ing twenty miles per hour, at which point it began to lurch. Though still running at a weak idle, it refused to accelerate. Finally, after a quarter mile or so, cars racing past her in the left lane, the truck lost power al-together, and the engine went silent. Laila barely had enough momentum to coast to the shoulder, where the truck was soon mired in the snow.

Though she'd already envisioned this very scenario in advance, the development was no less devastating. She should have listened to Tam and signed up for AAA. But the hundred and twenty bucks felt cost prohibitive. Surely she couldn't afford to have the truck towed, let alone afford to repair it, so what now? How would she get to Queets? She was still over two hundred miles away. And what would she do without transportation, provided she ever got there? Was she supposed to depend on Genie to shuttle her around?

Laila had to act quickly, for it would only be a matter of time before the highway patrol spotted her on the shoulder. Being that the truck was registered in Boaz's name, and without proof of insurance, Laila didn't want to answer any questions about the truck. If Boaz had figured out what had happened, Laila wouldn't put it past him to report it as stolen. As it was, Boaz was likely to be contacted eventually once she abandoned the truck, at which point he'd know that Laila had fled north.

As close as Laila was to breaking down completely in that moment, she resolved to stay focused and do like Tam had once told her: "Eat the elephant one bite at a time."

Hefting her oversized duffel off the seat, Laila jumped out of the cab. Breath fogging in the cold air, she began clomping through the snow at a hurried pace down the shoulder of the interstate, trying to put as much distance between herself and the truck as possible, never looking back. In a strange way it was almost a relief, walking away from the truck, as it was one less connection to Boaz, one less responsibility, one less piece of baggage weighing her down. Her biggest regret was the half tank of gas still left in the truck, amounting to about twenty bucks.

After almost a mile, Laila finally looked back and saw that the truck was out of sight, whereupon she hoisted her duffel over her shoulder, turned to face the oncoming traffic, and stuck out her thumb.

It only took a matter of minutes before an old blue Subaru wagon with California plates, and an Obama/Biden sticker on the back window, pulled to the shoulder twenty yards in front of her. Before she reached the car, Laila could hear the heartbeat of reggae music. She swung the passenger door open and ducked into the car to discover a smiling young white woman with dreadlocks.

"Hey," she said, turning down the stereo. "Oh my God, you must be freezing."

"Sweating, actually," said Laila.

"Was that your truck back there?"

"No," said Laila, stuffing her duffel down by her feet in the wheel well.

"You can shove that in back," said the girl.

"It's okay," said Laila.

The girl fixed her blue eyes on the rearview mirror, waiting for the opportunity to merge, then pulled back into the right lane a little too abruptly and practically floored it as an eighteen-wheeler bore down on the Subaru.

"Don't worry," she said.

"I'm not worried," said Laila.

"Maggie may be old, but she's got lots of spunk left in her," said the girl, patting the dashboard. "And she's good in the snow, too. Good tires and all-wheel drive. I'm Becka, by the way."

"Hi," said Laila without offering her own name.

"I can only take you as far as Salem," said Becka. "I hope that helps."

"It does," said Laila. "Thanks."

In Becka, Laila had lucked into her first ally along her new life's path, somebody she might have connected with or opened up to, somebody who had already proven herself to be helpful and concerned. And yet, in the fifteen minutes it took to get to Salem, Laila offered Becka virtually nothing in the way of conversation beyond the fact that she was headed for Seattle from somewhere in California for reasons she was unwilling to divulge.

Becka tried to elicit conversation on a half dozen occasions, only to be met with curt responses from Laila. Though Laila knew it had to be uncomfortable for the girl, she maintained her silence. Why? Was it fear of exposing herself? Was it because she was ashamed of her dilemma? Or was it because she resented this smooth-faced white girl on her way back to college, the one with the reliable car and the good tires, and the dread-locks, and the Bob Marley, and probably a boyfriend who wasn't abusive, and a set of parents who gave a shit, and probably gave her money, and paid for her college, along with an already established idea or expectation of what her future looked like, though she must have been at least five or six years younger than Laila?

The fact of the matter was that however little Laila offered Becka in the way of companionship, or even courtesy, no matter how she deflected her friendly inquiries, if not for Becka, Laila might never have arrived at her next course of action.

"Oh, God, not Greyhound, don't do it," Becka said. "I took it once, and a lady flushed a dirty diaper down the toilet five miles out of town, and for six hours they didn't do anything about it. It smelled like rotten eggs the whole time. And the baby never stopped crying. I felt sorry for it. I'd get the Amtrak if I were you. It's not too far from campus. It's basically the same price as Greyhound but faster and way nicer, I swear. It's really pretty, they call it the Coast Starlight."

"Okay," said Laila. "That'll work, I guess. So like, how much is it?"

"I dunno," she said. "Like fifty dollars, maybe. Do you have enough? Because I could—"

"Thanks," said Laila. "I have enough."

Five minutes later Becka dropped Laila at the curb in front of a squat old building of yellow brick.

"Good luck," said Becka as Laila wrestled her giant duffel out of the wheel well. "It was nice meeting you."

"You too," said Laila.

"Are you sure you don't ne—"

But Laila shut the door behind her before Becka could finish the sentence, proceeding straight to the front entrance. Laila could feel Becka waving at her across the passenger seat.

Before she pushed her way through the heavy old door of the station, Laila watched the blue Subaru pull away from the curb, and for some reason — Laila couldn't even say why — a deep sadness washed over her and she began to cry.

LUYU AND JOHN

Northern California, 1851

Upon the sixth afternoon of their journey, Luyu and John emerged from the thick of the mountains and began at last descending into the wide golden valley below, where the shade of the pinewood gave way to the scorching heat of the basin, and the sky opened up, cloudless and cornflower blue, rolling on forever to the south.

In the heat of midafternoon they took shade beneath the canopy of a lonely clutch of live oak, where Sugar watered from a tiny slough, hardly a foot across and no deeper than a few inches. Exhausted from the heat, they leaned against the trunk of a gnarled oak in silence, the only sound the trickle of the little stream.

Now where? That was the question upon which Luyu's mind was sluggishly at work as she mopped the sweat from her brow. What opportunities might this long, broad valley have to offer the likes of two Indians, homeless and adrift?

"I'm open to ideas," said John Tully at last, as though he could read Luyu's mind.

"All of our lives we've been displaced," said Luyu.

"But now is different," observed John Tully. "Now we are displaced on our own terms."

They spread out their blankets and slept beside the little stream that night, its ceaseless burble weaving its way through Luyu's dreams. They awoke in the cool of dawn and wasted little time before hitting the trail. Barely had the disc of the sun cleared the eastern horizon before the heat of the day settled into the valley. The new day offered Luyu renewed hope. The world seemed a great, wide-open place full of possibilities. Even if they never stopped, would that be so bad, to live as nomads in the California wilderness? They had each other, and that alone was enough to sustain them.

It seemed impossible that they had known each other only a week, when already they could share the comfort of silence and guess at one another's thoughts. Luyu could hardly imagine life before or after John Tully, and judging from the way she caught him looking at her when he thought her unaware, this burgeoning affection seemed mutual.

As they proceeded southeast toward the Sacramento River, the terrain in the hollows alongside the trail became progressively marshier with runoff, and the temperatures began to cool slightly, as a gentle wind off the river, still miles off, blew in from the east. Twenty or thirty miles beyond the river, the foothills swelled on the horizon, like muscles rising out of the basin, the saw-toothed ridges of the High Sierras behind them. Only one day removed from the Siskiyous, and already the mountains were calling to John Tully again. In a world where his kind was mostly unwanted, something about the shelter of the high country appealed to him. To live, hidden amid such a vast wilderness, away from the scourge of the white man's insatiable greed and the Mexican's misplaced propriety, free to carve out a life according to his own desires, like his people had for eons before the Mexicans came north, and the whites came west, and the whole world sought to eradicate them.

"What would you think of building a cabin in the mountains?" he said as they led Sugar on foot across the delta.

"I was thinking how I was already missing the mountains," she said.

"Then we're agreed," said John Tully. "We will continue east, and into the hills. At the first settlement we encounter, we shall come by hatchets and saws. We will stake out a little parcel of land, in the forest, near a stream, and we will build our home."

"More, tell me more," said Luyu.

"It will be a cabin of pinewood, straight and true," he said. "And a chimney of river rock and mud. It shall have a wooden floor, and shuttered windows, and a hearth to cook upon. And there we shall spend the rest of our days."

"Will we have a family?" she asked, her face blushing.

John Tully stopped his progress, turning to take her about the waist and pull her close, so that her face was pressed against his beating heart.

"Anything you wish," he said.

And with these wonderful revelations, the miles seemed to pass effortlessly through the remainder of the morning, until late in the afternoon, when they reached the west bank of the Sacramento, where it ran flat and wide through the valley.

Here John Tully and Luyu kneeled side by side upon the silty bank and drank greedily from its chill waters. Sugar, too, drank her fill, as Luyu refilled the bladders and John mused upon their newly discovered destiny. A fine, honest life it would be, taking what they needed, and nothing more, from the land, as their people had since the beginning of time, with no obligation to anyone but each other.

Chest-deep in the current, they forded the river with some difficulty regarding the old mare, who halted her progress frequently, resisting the crossing on several occasions. They emerged twenty minutes later, drenched to the bone and gasping for breath. After a short rest, during which John re-cinched the saddle and the gear, they resumed their progress east across the delta. Within a half hour, their sodden clothing had dried completely in the afternoon heat. The foothills, though drawing nearer with every mile, were still but a smudge on the eastern horizon, maybe two days' travel.

They stopped near sunset and made camp in the low brush bordering an irrigation slough, where the slow-running water was murky but digestible. Exhausted, they did not start a fire, but ate their oats cold and dry, then spread their hides and blankets in the clearing and lay on their backs as the pink light of sunset began to fade.

Soon, the darkness gathered, and the stars were splashed across the sky. As John lay shoulder-to-shoulder with Luyu, their hands intertwined, his eyelids grew heavy.

"Sweet dreams," he heard her say, just before he succumbed to sleep.

Sweet dreams, indeed.

John Tully awoke in the darkness with a violent start. Gasping for air, his flailing limbs soon attached themselves to the boot presently pinning his neck to the ground.

"Well, now, what have we got here?" said a voice in the darkness.

Startled from her sleep, Luyu bolted upright, recoiling at the sight of the stranger, who eased his foot off of John's windpipe.

"This here is Colonel Whitworth's land," said the man.

He was carrying a rifle in one hand and a darkened lantern in the other.

"Colonel of what?" said John Tully defiantly.

"First United States Dragoon Regiment," said the stranger. "Kicked us some Mexican ass, we did. Anyway, you ought to know that the colonel don't take kindly to folks squatting on his land."

"We're only passing through," said John.

"Oh, you're passin', all right, tres-passin'. And like I say, the colonel, he don't much care for trespassers, especially not no pair of flea-bitten prairie niggers like yourselves."

"How were we to know this land belonged to anyone?" said John. "I see no fences."

"Who you suppose dug that irrigation ditch?" said the stranger.

"I didn't think of it," said John Tully.

"Well, now you be wishing you had. 'Cause don't nobody pass through Colonel Whitworth's land without paying a price. And just looking at you pair of sad-sack mongrels, I get the distinct feeling you ain't got much to give. So, I'm giving you to the count of five to get on your way. Go on."

Dawn was still an hour off as Luyu and John mounted the old mare and headed in a straight line toward the foothills. Sitting behind John in the saddle, as the sun began to peek over the High Sierras and a foot of mist clung to the valley floor, Luyu wondered why trouble always had to follow her. Was it her own destiny, or the destiny of the Miwok, to be forever harassed, forever chased off the land that had once been their home?

When the sun cleared the eastern horizon, Luyu fell asleep in the saddle, clutching John Tully tightly about the waist.

GEORGE FLOWERS

Chicago, 1852

The storm came howling off the lake late in the afternoon, a wicked spring squall that gained full force shortly before dusk and sustained its power through the night, ravaging everything in its path, rattling windows and shearing a pair of shutters clean off of Mr. Seymour's manor. Swells ten and twelve feet high assaulted the shoreline, exploding against the bulkhead. The sky was a living thing, a roiling purple-gray mass hurrying south on gale-force winds.

All through the night George did his best to settle the anxious horses in the stable, stroking their snouts and backsides, talking to them in his calmest, most comforting voice.

"Now, now, Colonel, just you relax. This here ain't nothing but a little wind and rain. You're safe and sound right here. George ain't gonna let nothing happen to you, boy."

Despite his assurances the horses nickered

and reared up at each thunderclap. Torrential rain swept the stable in sheets, finding its way through the smallest gaps and flooding the north bank of stalls. George never once lay down upon his straw mattress, but ministered to the nerve-worn animals through the night.

Finally, near dawn the wind and rain relented, and in the wake of the storm, the whole world seemed quieter than ever before as George set about restoring order to the ravaged stable, re-securing gates, tying down loose canvases, gathering up windfall and debris, all the while reassuring the horses with a kind word or a pat on the haunches.

After several hours working in the yard, George felt eyes upon him and turned to face a gentleman in a tall top hat and overcoat who seemed to observe George's labor with keen interest.

"You have a way with the animals," he observed.

"I reckon that's true," said George. " 'Specially horses. Been around horses my whole life."

"And you care for all these horses?"

"Yessir."

"And the carriages, who maintains those?"

"That'd be me, too, sir," said George. "I clean them, service them, right the wheels — I do everything but build them, sir."

The gentleman looked impressed.

"A wheelwright is indispensable," he said.

"Yes, sir, that's true."

"The name is Best," said the gentleman. "May I ask what Seymour is paying you?" said Mr. Best.

"Why, just food and board, sir," George said.

"Board where? Here, in the stable?"

"Yessir."

Mr. Best frowned as though the answer were most unsatisfactory.

"And you're a freeman?"

"Yessir," George lied.

"How would you feel about earning five dollars a week? Plus food, of course, and a real room."

"Well, sir," said George, "I reckon I'd feel just about how you might imagine, which is to say mighty good."

"Ever been to Springfield?"

"No, sir, never have been."

"It's quite beautiful downstate. How would you like to make such a trip?" said Mr. Best.

"I reckon I'd like that," said George.

"Very well," said the gentleman. "Then how would you like to come to Springfield and manage my stable?"

"Well, sir, as much as I like the sound of that, I have a wife to think about. Or, that is, I will soon. And I can't rightly say how she'd feel about me up and leaving for downstate."

"Then you must bring her along, of course," said Mr. Best. "I can always use an extra domestic hand, and I shall compensate both of you, and provide you with quarters sufficient for a family, if indeed you plan on starting one."

"Well, sir, I . . . see, I just don't know about that. I reckon I'd have to ask Miss Cora what she thought of Springfield. And also, I'm none too sure Mr. Seymour would be pleased to let me go."

"Leave Seymour to me," he said. "I'm certain I can sway him. Abe and I have considerable history. Surely something can be arranged. What is your name, boy?"

"George Flowers, sir."

"Well, George Flowers. My stay in Chicago is to last one more week, whereupon I shall return to Springfield. And it is my hope that you, and your woman, will accompany me."

"Well, now, sir, to be honest, I'm not rightly sure whether Miss Cora or her father know about my intentions specifically at the moment."

"That gives you seven days to make them known," said Mr. Best.

Though he hadn't gotten a wink of sleep the previous night, George was wide awake through the day as he busied himself in the stable, sweeping out the flooded stalls and undoing the damage of the storm. Mr. Best's proposition had pushed George's timeline forward by weeks, even months, regarding his intentions with Cora. He had no money to buy a ring. He had nothing to offer Cora as a symbol of his undying affection beyond his heart and his word. George Flowers was but a fugitive slave pretending to be free, with not a change of trousers to his name. Even his name, George Flowers, hardly belonged to him — for George Flowers had not even existed a year ago.

So what about George Flowers could possibly inspire Cora's confidence? Surely not the smell of sweat, dung, and alfalfa that perpetually clung to his person. He was currently employed at no material gain with no tangible prospects but the vague promise of an unknown life hundreds of miles away. With so little to offer, how could he possibly expect to win Cora's hand and inspire her to relocate with him on hardly a week's notice?

George did not propose to Cora that first day, nor on the second, or even the third. By the fourth afternoon he had almost managed to talk himself out of proposing to Cora at all. But every time George so much as caught a glimpse of Cora, whether he was admiring the intelligence that shone in her eyes, or her rangy, athletic figure as she hung the linens to dry, or the grace of her stride as she fetched water from the well, George was certain all over again that he did not wish to endure any future that did not include Cora.

And so upon the morning of the fifth day, just two days removed from their would-be departure, George Flowers cleaned himself up as much as possible, wringing his shirt clean in the horse trough, shaving his face with a dull razor, patting his nappy hair into submission, washing his teeth, dousing himself with a concoction of muddled lilac and dried lavender procured from inside his makeshift mattress.

He thought about bringing Cora more poached flowers, but instead he brought her the tiny figurine in her likeness he'd whittled from wood in the evenings before the light faded. He stuffed the keepsake deep in his pocket, thinking he would offer it in lieu of a ring.

Shortly before lunch George tracked down Cora in the basement, hunched over a steaming cauldron of linens, her breathing a bit labored, her forehead slick with sweat.

"Hello, George," she said. "What can I do for you?"

"Seems I have a question for you," said George. "And it's kind of a big one. So, I was wondering if maybe we couldn't have the conversation out in the yard under the sun instead of down here in the dark."

"I suppose I could duck out for a moment," she said, mopping her forehead with the sleeve of her blouse.

George followed her up the stairs and down the corridor to the back door, where they stepped out into the glare of afternoon.

When he passed by closely, she put her nose to the air and sniffed.

"What's that smell?"

"Must be something on the breeze," said George, blushing.

"It smells like lilacs," she said.

"Hmph," said George. "Lilacs, huh?"

"And lavender," she said. "Really strong like lavender. It's lovely. And what a beautiful day out. You wouldn't know it down in the dungeon."

"No, ma'am, I suppose you wouldn't," said George.

"What is it you wanted to speak with me about, George?"

"Well now, maybe you want to sit down for this," he said.

He led her by the wrist to a nearby bench flanked by flowerpots, where he invited her to sit, though he remained standing himself.

"Now, I realize I ought to go to your father first about this, but then I figured, well, if you weren't interested in my proposition, what was the use of going to anybody else first? And if you like the idea then I'll take my chances with your father."

"Proposition?" she said.

"That's right, Miss Cora," he said. "A proposition."

And at this juncture George got down on one knee, but forgot about the little figurine in his pocket.

"Miss Cora," he said, "it is my hope to marry you and take you to Springfield and make a life with you there."

Cora's face was a prairie of blankness.

"Springfield?" she said. "George, what are you talking about? Why, that's downstate."

"I ain't never gonna feel free here," he said. "Long as I'm here I'll just be skulking and hiding, anyway. Slave catchers been nosing around here since the week I got here, and they'll be back, you can count on that. How long before they figure out George Flowers ain't the freeman he pretend to be? How long before Mr. Seymour figures out as much? Master Worthy, he sure to be looking for me. Best chance I got is to get as far away as possible. And Mr. Best, he's offered me an opportunity I'd be a fool to decline."

"Oh, George," she said.

"Now, I realize I might have caught you a little off guard with this," said George. "I had another plan that was slower to unfold than this one, but unforeseen circumstances demand that I must have an answer within two days if we are to realize a future in Springfield, which I can assure you is a better opportunity for both of us, and for the future prospect of having a family."

Cora's mouth was agape, though there was not a word on her lips. The reaction was not what George had hoped for. She was clearly at a loss, as though she'd never once guessed at George's intentions. Had he not made his affection perfectly clear in a thousand little ways? Could she not feel his longing every minute of every day? Could she not feel the force of it every time he hurried to open the back door for her or unburden her of a bucket of water? Had he not on three different occasions gifted her flowers, filched on the sly from the back garden, blue hyacinths and daffodils and, yes, lilacs? And on each occasion had she not made the identical comment, "So, that's why they call you George Flowers, eh?" And hadn't on each occasion Cora's pleasure been palpable? Had she not reciprocated his gift with an easy smile or gentle caress of his wrist?

But now she was not smiling. Not even close.

"George, I . . . this is my home," she said. "My father is here, my job is here, my church, and my friends, and everyone and everything I've ever known is here. I could never leave Chicago."

"Well then, it's settled," said George. "Never mind Springfield. We'll make our lives in Chicago, if you'll have me. I will find myself another good opportunity, one that pays more than food and board, one that allows us to live in our own home, right here close to everybody and everything."

"But, George, I couldn't. I'm not ready for that."

"So it's me, then?"

"No, it's not. It's . . . George, you should go to Springfield. I beseech you to go. Don't let me hold you back. Seize your opportunity, George Flowers. Make a life for yourself downstate. Surely you'll find someone more worthy than me to start your family with. My roots are bound here. But not you. The world is a much bigger place for you."

"I don't want to live in a world without you," George said. "Don't matter what size it is."

"I can't marry you, George, I'm sorry."

"But why?" said George.

"It's all very complicated."

"Why not? At least you owe me that," he said.

"Because I have my father to think about, George. He needs me. I'm all he's got left. My home is here at Mr. Seymour's. The staff, they're like my family. Nora, she is like a little sister. I can't leave them."

George cast his eyes down into her lap. Though crestfallen, he was not ready to give up.

"You don't have to make up your mind now," he said. "You've got two days. Think about it. Me and you, we could be good together. We could stay right here at Master Seymour's," he said. "I don't need it to be a new life, it could just be our old life, but together."

Cora looked him in the eyes and George thought he saw a lot of things there: pity, and affection, but also something more, a certain sadness that looked like genuine regret.

"Go, George, do it for me," she said. "Go to Springfield and make good for yourself."

"Come with me, Cora."

Cora set a hand upon his shoulder and looked kindly down into his face.

"You are a good man, George. A woman would do well to accept your hand. But I can't," she said.

Only then did George reach into his pocket for the figurine. Looking down to sneak a peek at his handiwork, it seemed now, in the full light of day, such a paltry and homely offering that he quickly stuffed it back in his pocket as he rose to his feet.

"I do wish you'd reconsider," he said.

"I'm sorry, George."

George turned, and slowly made his way back toward the stable.

Leaving Cora was the second-most difficult decision George had ever made, the first being his frantic dash to freedom in the thick of the Illinois night, a decision that had ultimately led him straight back to Cora. And just as George had left part of himself behind when he'd fled into the Urbana night, so, too, he was certain that in leaving Cora he would be forsaking another part of himself.

Presently George was all packed up and

waiting outside the stable for Mr. Best's carriage. The previous night, he had walked to the house and knocked on the back door. Nora had let him in, and no sooner had George crossed the threshold than she clutched him about the midsection as though her life depended on it.

"Now, now," said George.

But the girl would not stop crying, nor would she stop clutching George for dear life.

"Everything going to be just fine, Miss Nora. You going to be just fine."

"But you're me best friend, George," she said. "You make me laugh. You teach me things about horses and life. Who will I play checkers with? Who will bring me apples to feed to the horses? Who will tell me stories about me brother, Finn? Oh, George."

Nora redoubled her grip on him and began sobbing into his shirt collar all over again. And once more, George was overcome by doubt. Why should he leave love behind for the promise of a living wage and the freedom to define the terms of his own life? Which was greater, love or freedom?

Cora emerged from her room clearing her throat. Only then did Nora relinquish her grip on George. Still in tears, the girl took one last look at George's face before running off to her quarters. Watching her go, George's own eyes began to burn.

"God bless you, child," he said beneath his breath.

Moments later, on the back step, as the moon was rising on the eastern horizon, George beseeched Cora one last time to change her mind.

"Think of it," said George. "Think of what we might have."

"I'm sorry," she said. "But my place is here."

George slept fitfully that night in the stable, his heart torn between Cora and the promise of the future. By the light of dawn, he packed the last of his things and squatted in the dusty yard in the shadow of the stable beside his meager belongings, waiting for his new life to begin, still overwhelmed by doubt. Leaving this place was foolish.

Gazing off down the tree-lined lane, he listened for the telltale clop of horse hooves and the squeaking protest of the wagon over the uneven ground. He tried for the hundredth time in two weeks to imagine Springfield.

"I can't hold this all day," said a familiar voice, startling him.

George turned to see Cora burdened by a small trunk.

Jumping to his feet, he relieved her of the trunk and set it by his own effects, then wrapped her in his arms, even as she stiffened slightly in his embrace.

"What's this?" he said.

"Guess I just couldn't stand the thought of you cooking and cleaning for yourself," she said.

George almost died of happiness then and there.

"You won't regret this," he said. "Mr. Best, he going to treat us right," said George. "He's going to pay us a living wage, and put us up in a real house, and ain't nobody going to be our master, just our employer, like here at Mr. Seymour's, but better. And we'll have a baby and —"

"Don't get ahead of yourself," said Cora. "Nothing in this life is ever what it promises to be, especially not for the likes of you and me. Could be that we're fools to leave this place."

Looking back at the house, George saw Cora's father standing at the downstairs window.

"What say we walk up the road and meet the carriage?" he said.

Slinging his two bags over his shoulder, George hefted Cora's trunk and they proceeded down the lane on foot, away from their old lives. George looked back only once, and there was Cora's father, still standing at the downstairs window like a ghost.

Since the world was still a big place in the spring of 1852, since the iron horse had yet to fully deliver the heartland and points west from the rigors of overland travel, the journey from Chicago to Springfield proved a slow one.

Two weeks from the day they'd started up the shady lane from Mr. Seymour's estate, weary from travel but hopeful for their future, George and Cora got their first glimpse of Springfield, the capital city of Illinois, laid out in a broad plain not far from the Sangamon River. The city was tiny compared to the metropolis of Chicago, comprising only a small assemblage of structures hugging the courthouse square, with the tower of the old statehouse rising above it all.

"Looks a mighty nice place to me," George said.

"Yes it does," said Cora, clasping his hand.

And here, at last, George Flowers, once a slave and now a fugitive, would make his home with his beloved Cora, or so he dared to hope.

BRIANNA FLOWERS

Portland, Oregon, 2019
Determined to secure some manner of employment before she got on that train for Seattle, Brianna wasted little time on her job search. By midday Wednesday she'd already delivered a handful of résumés and lined up three interviews for the following day. As it happened, the interviews were scheduled chronologically according to Brianna's employment hopes, in descending order from upward, to lateral, to desperate.

Brianna was a little nervous for the first interview, which was downtown at Roche Bobois, an upscale furniture retailer presently hiring a sales manager. The package was considerably better than anything Don had ever offered her at Consolidated: base salary plus commissions, good benefits, even a 401(k). Brianna dressed the part in a crisp navy business skirt and a flattering blouse, knowing that if she ever made it to her third interview, at Taco Bell that afternoon, she would be overdressed.

Brianna felt immediately out of place in the showroom, where she was left to wait for nearly fifteen minutes amid the exorbitantly priced "contemporary furnishings from international designers." Seven thousand dollars for a sofa? Sales by appointment? This was not Consolidated Appliances.

Though out of her comfort zone, Brianna was up to the challenge of acting the part and feeling quite positive about her prospects until the manager whisked into the showroom looking like she'd walked off the pages of a J. Peterman catalog. A white woman in her midforties, she had no business looking so natural in a baby-blue boatneck dress, cinched at her twenty-five-inch waist. Her hair was a lush helmet of auburn with dark highlights, not a hair out of place. Her body looked like you could crack walnuts on it. All the confidence drained from Brianna in an instant. She felt frumpy next to this woman, who introduced herself as Melanie, even her voice possessing an elegant sheen of sophistication, an affectation, but a persuasive one. Melanie sounded perfectly natural pronouncing *Roche Bobois*. Brianna supposed Melanie lived in a thirty-five-hundred-square-foot home in Lake Oswego and drove a Lexus. Her husband was probably a banker or an anesthesiologist. Melanie probably didn't have to work. For Melanie, being a professional was likely a choice.

Brianna scolded herself for making these assumptions, but she never quite recovered from those first impressions.

"My apologies for keeping you waiting," she said. "Please, join me in the office."

Brianna followed her to the rear of the showroom to an office that looked nothing like Don LoPriori's cluttered office. Though small, the space was airy and tasteful, as though it were on display itself.

"So, I see you have retail experience of a sort," said Melanie. "Do you have any background in home décor?"

"Not per se," said Brianna. "Although, appliances are part of that."

"So, décor is more of a hobby?"

"You could say that," said Brianna.

"Do you have a particular style?"

"I guess you'd say I'm eclectic."

"Ah," said Melanie. "So, for example . . . ?"

"If I like it, I like it," Brianna said. "As long as it works together."

The interview proceeded awkwardly from there, Melanie trying to draw out Brianna's inner interior decorator. When the interview mercifully ended, Brianna couldn't get out of Roche Bobois fast enough.

Walking back to the Camry, she found the meter expired and a forty-four-dollar ticket pinned beneath her wiper. She might have cried from frustration and hopelessness. But she didn't. Instead, on the drive back to the east side, Brianna managed to pull herself together for the next interview, at Cascade Auto.

The office at the rear of the showroom smelled like carpet cleaner. Kyle, the floor manager, who introduced himself twice, was younger than Brianna. Clean-cut and freshly shaven, Kyle wore a starchy white shirt and a red tie that somehow managed to be conservative with its dull pattern of tiny black polka dots. His features were sharp and ferretlike, his eyes quick but not curious, peering out from behind his fake wood desk.

"So, then, no experience selling cars?" he said to break the ice.

"No," said Brianna. "But a lot of sales experience. I think that's the main thing, knowing how to follow through, knowing how to inform the client and hold their hand. I'm sure there's a lot of parallels between selling walk-in coolers and selling cars."

"Mm," said Kyle. "So, what kind of car do you drive?"

"Camry," said Brianna.

"What year?"

"Old," she said.

"How old?"

Brianna wanted to say: "About as old as you," but she didn't.

"To be honest, I don't remember the year,"

she said, glad that she'd parked a half block away.

"Mm. What do you like about your car?" said Kyle, almost as though he were getting ready to sell Brianna a car.

"It's reliable," she said.

"What else? I mean, if you were looking to step up from your old Camry, if you had a little extra money to spend, and you're looking for an update, what qualities would you be looking for?"

"You mean like extras?"

"I mean, like what would be your dream car?"

"Something safe and reliable," she said.

"That's good," said Kyle. "Safe is good, safe is a good place to start. But say you're going a little over budget, what's really going to sell you on the car?"

"A good heater?"

"Okay," said Kyle. "Heat is good. I guess I'm looking for something a little more aspirational, here, you know? Like, how is your dream car going to make you feel?"

Brianna wanted to say: "Safe and warm," but didn't.

"Look," she said. "I find that selling is less about persuading people and more about listening to them."

When she said it, Brianna felt like she'd nailed the interview, but looking at twenty-five-year-old Kyle's expression, somewhere between doubtful and a mild gastric disturbance, it was apparent that he was not hearing what he needed to hear from Brianna. The remaining three minutes of the interview were little more than a technicality. When it was over, Brianna was almost relieved to be walking back to her '99 Camry with the broken heater.

Her last interview of the day was at the Taco Bell on MLK, where she and Malik had used the drive-through on more than a few occasions after practices and games. Grim as the prospect was, it was only nights, and Brianna figured it might hold her over while she spent her days looking for something better. The manager was an acne-scarred guy named Rueben, who, like Kyle, was younger than Brianna.

Rueben conducted the interview in the dining area, at a two-top in the corner, four feet from a woman and her two toddlers gorging themselves on chalupas.

"So, it looks like you have a lot of floor management experience. What did that look like at Consolidated Appliances?"

Brianna briskly ran through her litany of responsibilities as a floor manager under Don, though they were clearly bulleted on the résumé, a list that included supervision of new employees, administration of policy, supervision of the sales team, stock and inventory, resolution of point-of-sale discrepancies, and on and on.

"So, a little bit of everything," she concluded.

The manager scratched his neck, gazing down at the résumé as though he'd been reading along.

"To be honest," he said, "you seem a little overqualified."

"Look," said Brianna, in the spirit of honesty. "It's nights. If something better comes up, I promise I'll give you plenty of warning. I need this job."

Brianna's spirits were flagging when she left Taco Bell with no guarantee, though Rueben assured her he'd let her know by early next week.

On the drive home, skirting the gentrified blocks that seemed to crowd in on Albina every year, every month, practically every week, Brianna wondered if she shouldn't get her real estate license. She was already a pro at sales, and she wasn't afraid of paperwork, and she cleaned up well. But how would she support herself in the meantime? How was she going to pay down the credit cards? Eventually, she'd need to replace the Camry, which had become a money pit the past nine months — first the timing belt, then the alternator, then the brakes. She couldn't file for unemployment since she'd technically quit Consolidated, and if she filed any kind of grievance about Don's misconduct, who knew how long something like that might take to sort itself out?

When she got home, Brianna flopped her purse on the kitchen counter and kicked her shoes off. Malik was probably just leaving the library after his math tutor, a meeting that represented his last paid session. He might have to take next week off unless the Ramsey girl was willing to work on credit.

It was nearly seven thirty by the time Malik finally got home.

"What took you so long?" she said. "I was starting to worry."

"Starting? You always worrying," said Malik. "I was just late with my tutor is all."

"How's the trigonometry?"

"Great," he said.

"What are you smiling about?" she said.

"Am I smiling?" he said. "I dunno, I guess I'm just excited for this weekend."

"I saved you some dinner. It's in the oven. Careful, that plate is liable to be hot."

"Thanks, Ma. You're the best."

Opening the refrigerator to grab the orange juice for Malik, Brianna allowed herself to be hopeful. Tomorrow she'd have Malik all to herself as they set out together on an adventure, just the two of them, as it should be, for that was how it had been for the last fourteen years, since Darnell left. The thought of having Malik's undivided attention, the idea of a four-hour train ride, of staying in a hotel room, maybe even a room with a view, the knowledge that Saturday Malik would take to the court in Seattle and, God willing, would save them both, all of it seemed like a welcome diversion to Brianna as she stood in the light of the refrigerator.

ABRAHAM SEYMOUR

Downstate Illinois, 1853

Frilly had never been the Seymour way. Thus
the carriage presently transiting Abe Seymour
and his young business partner Worthy Warnock from Chicago to Springfield was of
sturdy construction and excellent maintenance, and was not short on comfort, though
neither was it long on frills. What need was
there of decorative flourishes and needless
amenities, when an object's function was
simply to convey people from one place to
another? Better to have sturdy wheels and a
sturdy axle than lace curtains and gilded
hardware.

Though his worth was substantial, Abe Seymour was a pragmatist who preferred to keep
his wealth out of sight as much as possible,
which accounted for the unmarked drives
leading to both his modest summer home on
Lake Winnebago and his considerable though
comparatively unpretentious estate on the
shores of Lake Michigan. This furtive ap-

proach to wealth was not due entirely to modesty, but was also in the service of preserving said wealth from those who might covet it. To perpetuate wealth at all costs was the primary function of Abe Seymour's existence. As he was childless, with no heir to his fortune beyond his wife, one might be tempted to wonder, for whom was Abe Seymour preserving this fortune? But that was a question Abe went to considerable lengths to avoid, occupying himself instead with business in the form of whatever vocation or opportunity meant amassing more wealth while incurring the least amount of risk.

In the four decades that had followed Abe's expulsion from the Bristol School for the offense of being Jewish, he had managed almost without exception to avoid partnerships, particularly in the arena of business. Yet such was the scope and ambition of this railroad venture, and so formidable and well capitalized the field of competitors, that partnerships had become a necessary evil. Already Abe had cultivated a handful of partners, with young Mr. Warnock being his least favorite by a considerable margin. But it was Warnock who had brought Seymour the New York-Chicago line, the construction of which was already in the works, to be completed within the year, a connection destined to change the face of industry in America, as promised by the young Southerner. Thus, in spite of his misgivings with Warnock, which were primarily superficial, Seymour persisted in the partnership, guessing he was bound to turn a tidy profit for many decades to come.

Sure enough, barely a year after their first venture, Warnock came to him with the proposition of connecting Chicago to St. Louis. Here again, according to Worthy Warnock, was another opportunity to revolutionize not just passenger travel but freight and distribution, so long dependent on the Mississippi. But St. Louis was roughly where Seymour's interest waned, or perhaps as far as western Missouri, but not into the territories, that was for certain. If there were profits to be made west of the Mississippi, let other, more intrepid and less risk-averse investors than himself carve the passage to those probabilities. Only a fool or a gambler would rush into something so uncertain.

If Abe was being honest with himself, even the possibility of a railroad line from Chicago southwest to St. Louis seemed like a stretch. Bureaucratically and logistically, it was an enterprise destined to travel uphill. As far as commerce was concerned, the river was an awfully big rival to contest. While the land acquisitions between Chicago and St. Louis were likely executable, and the market might be there, the cost overruns and the inevitable schedule hurdles, along with moving the necessary labor, would possibly spell financial risk to Abe's way of thinking. But not ruin, and that was key. It was a calculated risk, and one he was willing to take, particularly as it had the confidence of his old acquaintance Montgomery Best, whom he and Warnock were to convene with at his Springfield manor.

The possibility of a railroad as far as Missouri seemed like a well-reasoned gamble. While the riverboat forever depended upon the Mississippi and its various moods, seasons, and currents, travel by rail was not beholden to these factors. While the maritime vessel was ever accountable to the winds and the rains, railroad ties, on the other hand, were unyielding, predetermined paths, not unlike Seymour's own path, firmly grounded and plotted every inch of the way. And as for the mighty conveyors themselves, what were these steam-driven "horses" if not mobile furnaces, which Abe knew plenty about? That these engines were powered by steam, the very same property that had revolutionized the river and would soon conquer the seas, was only further reason to be optimistic.

To hear some men talk, the coasts would be linked by rail within the decade, though Abe Seymour was dubious with regard to this timeline. To begin with, many of the charters had a ten-year shelf life. Abe had observed that it was often the case with business ventures that people overestimated their capacity to execute or deliver upon their promises. This seemed particularly true in the case of the transcontinental railroad. For while the hills and valleys of the east and mid-Atlantic, and the prairies of the Middle West, were navigable terrains, the passage through the great Rocky Mountains, and beyond them the Sierras, presented obstacles of an altogether different magnitude.

This was not the case for Abe's carriage companion, young Worthy Warnock, whose zeal for the venture, along with his confidence in its ultimate success, seemed to know no bounds. It was true that Abe had entertained doubts about young Warnock from the very first night he arrived in Chicago from Louisville, upon which occasion he'd proceeded to permeate the Seymour estate like an unpleasant odor. It was not so much Warnock's southerly affectation that Abe objected to, rather Mr. Warnock's general conceit, which seemed, if not unearned, at the very least out of proportion, a roosterlike bravado that Seymour found particularly hard to endure in the close quarters of a carriage. For young Warnock talked incessantly. He gassed, he gabbed, he lectured, and he exhorted. He illuminated, he elucidated, and he waxed without ever waning. This in itself was an affront to Abe Seymour's modest sensibilities.

But the deeper problem abided in the fact that for all his disquisition, young Warnock was limited in scope almost entirely to his own concerns. Rarely did he ask questions of Seymour, or elicit his opinions or insights. Had Worthy Warnock been a shrewder man, he would have talked less and listened more. No doubt Abe could have imparted much to the younger man in the ways of business and general worldly wisdom. But that possibility seemed increasingly unlikely with each mile the carriage rode roughshod over the countryside.

"Indeed, Seymour," Warnock was saying, "were it not for the likes of you and me, that is to say, the forward thinkers, the captains of industry, this young country would no doubt have been stunted in its infancy. For who would account for its nurture and growth?"

"Mm," said Seymour, who had been feigning sleep for half an hour, a fact that was apparently lost on Worthy Warnock.

"Let us consider the common man," Warnock resumed. "Particularly that variety newly arrived from Europe and elsewhere. This immigrant, he comes for opportunity — but make no mistake, he is no opportunist. For that would require a brand of speculation beyond his capacity. This commoner, he is hardly more imaginative than the slave or the savage with regard to the possibilities which abide beyond his daily purview, let alone those that might require enterprise. Thus he cannot conceive of real progress, because he's too busy feeding and pleasuring himself, always a slave to his appetites. And the baser the appetite, the more ravenous his hunger seems to be. The immigrant has no gumption, and no foresight."

"And no capital," muttered Seymour dryly.

"Perhaps not, but that too is his own fault, because he makes foolish decisions with his money at every turn. He cannot visualize a future for himself, but envisions only more of the same. He is forever beholden to the past. And thus he only brings his old slovenly ways to a new land and stubbornly clings to them, expecting good fortune to provide for him as if it were his God-given right. But you and I, we know different, don't we, Seymour?"

"Er, yes, yes," mumbled Seymour, pulling his hat further over his eyes. "Whatever you say."

At this juncture, as he often did, Warnock proceeded to remove both his shoes and socks, releasing the fetor of his imprisoned feet as he presently began to wiggle his misshapen toes.

"Seymour, I would wish these bunions on no man," said Warnock. "Not my most bitter rival."

"Mmph," said Seymour.

"Anyway, as I was saying," said Worthy, kneading the big toe of his right foot. "Who, pray tell, provides the only good fortune these commoners shall ever know, Seymour? Who provides the jobs, and the opportunities, and the industry to grow this young nation, the one they've come to from all corners of the world — bringing their disease, and poverty, and hedonism — to insinuate themselves upon?"

"Mm, yes, okay, point taken," mumbled Seymour, eyes clasped shut.

"We," resumed Worthy Warnock. "You and me, Seymour, *we* are the providers. Not God, not country, but us, the stewards of industry. The future comes to pass by our design. We give the laborers purpose, and sustenance, and mobility. We improve the quality of their lives, Seymour. Without us, they are aimless. This entire nation is aimless without us."

For all of that, Worthy Warnock was apparently just warming up. Mercifully, after he'd feigned sleep for three-quarters of an hour, real sleep finally came to rescue Abe Seymour. He dreamed of a gentleman's farm in Gloucester, of a sunny room with a partially open window, the breeze gently stirring the white shade. In his dream Abe walked down an airy corridor to the kitchen, past the housekeeper in her crisp white apron, and out the back door to the pasture, where in a field of waist-high grass, his gap-toothed brother, Silas, awaited him.

As the nameless carriage rattled south toward Springfield and the estate of Montgomery Best, Abe Seymour dreamed of Dash, his wire-haired terrier, sprinting to meet them in the pasture, cleaving the golden grain in his wake. And all the while, running like a current beneath Abe Seymour's dreams, came the steady drone of Worthy Warnock's voice.

Nora Bergen

Chicago, 1854

August 27, 1854

Dearest Finn,

   I know in my heart that you are alive and in tolerable health, and I hope that you are able to intimate the same about me. I write you this letter on the eve of our fourteenth birthday, knowing that as with a half dozen letters I've written you before, you will never receive it, as I have no address, not so much as a state, or even a territory, to which to send these correspondences. Four times I have been to the asylum to demand information from that deviant Master Searles, who saw fit to separate us against our will. All four times I have been turned away with no information beyond the fact you are somewhere "out west."

   But that is a start. Someday I will find you if it is the last thing I do. I pray that you know that. One day I will somehow achieve the means to track you down, my brother. It is your responsibility to care for yourself in the interim, to keep yourself healthy, and right in the eyes of God. There is only so much I can control, but what I can control in this world going forward, what I know I must control, is to find my way to you.

I write this late in the evening as my long workday has finally come to an end. I sit in my little room by candlelight at the little desk George fashioned for me years ago out of stable scraps, though I fear my candle is burning low and I shall have to ask Edmund for another. I have never taken much of a liking to Edmund, who comes and goes between the staff quarters and the house at all hours. I find the man difficult to trust, though he has never explicitly done anything to earn this mistrust in my years at the Seymours', where he has been since long before my arrival. Let us say that Edmund is of an inquisitive nature, though I suspect *nature* is a misnomer, for his curiosity does not seem native so much as required. He always seems to be spying on the rest of us, as though he were reporting back to the Seymours on the goings-on down below, which consist almost exclusively of work.

Mrs. Seymour has been in poor health of late, and Mr. Seymour is mostly absent on business. The various social gatherings have ceased in recent months, yet still there is never any shortage of work to be done here. You would think that the linens were sullying themselves. The Seymours did not replace Cora. Clifton, despite his age, and the fact that he was no lover of animals, took over George's duties in the stable, an undertaking that ran him straight into the ground. Last month he dropped dead one afternoon in the corral. Clifton was replaced almost immediately by a man named Willem, recently arrived from Germany. In the house, meanwhile, the extra work and responsibility have fallen largely on me. I am now working harder than ever before.

It angers me beyond reasonable measure to think that when they took me from that dreadful orphanage, separating me from the only flesh and blood I could call my own, I actually dared to believe for a few short hours that I was being delivered to a family who wanted me. Forced to leave you behind, I had to believe that, brother. Perhaps I would wind up in the care of a kind mother who could not conceive a daughter of her own, or maybe a family who had lost a child, or perhaps even a family with many children already that was willing to absorb another.

But as it turned out, I was not adopted to be anybody's daughter. I was adopted to be a housemaid. And here I am nearly three years later, an orphan all over again, or so it feels, for everybody that I grew to love here at the Seymours' is gone. I suppose I ought not to complain, as my life still contains small pleasures. Like writing you these letters and reading whatever I can get my hands on. For two years I was reading so prodigiously by candlelight that my eyes could hardly stand the strain of it. But since Clifton passed it has been nearly impossible to get my hands on the printed word. It's enough to ask Edmund for a new candle or a new broom. Somehow I cannot bring myself to ask him for books. But if I don't do something soon, I fear I will go mad.

To add to my isolation, with Cora's departure, and the passing of Clifton, I have not been to the city once, not even for church, though I still have my Bible, which has come apart at the spine. You must forgive me for saying so, but the Bible is not my favorite reading material. While I sometimes fancy the stories, I find the writing tepid and disjointed and, like my life, altogether lacking in romance. Novels are the seat of my new faith. For novels offer me an escape from this place and a respite from my own restless thoughts, and a vessel for my hopes. Novels are grand entertainments, full of adventure and intrigue and romance. Often they are funny, and I usually find myself in need of laughter, for my life has become suffocating. Novels are whole worlds of their own. Lost inside a novel, I am myself invisible, which is how I long to be much of my waking life. For Edmund is not the only one who makes me feel spied upon.

When he is not at large on business, I sometimes catch Mr. Seymour standing at the window as though he were watching me as I hang the linens to dry, or haul the water, or pick up the dog waste strewn upon the grounds on the west side of the house. The little fox terriers, of which there are no less than five, all of them male, are called Sprite, and Teague, and Jip, and Rags, and Dash. Apparently the little curs like to do their business while they watch the sun descend on the western horizon, for it is always the side yard where I find their droppings, regarding which I will spare you further details beyond the fact that they are numerous, and one must tread carefully through the side yard. I, for one, if given the choice, might look at the lake while doing my business, for Lake Michigan is quite beautiful, and moody. Like an ocean, it has no discernible end. And oh, how I love the crying of the seagulls, which never fails to conjure a sense of great remove. No matter their numbers they always sound lonely, and I suppose I find that easy to relate to. The proximity of the lake is one more thing to be grateful for because the water makes me think of home, though the wind that comes ripping off the surface can be a holy terror, the likes of which I cannot recall back in Cork.

So much of what I once remembered of Ireland has either dimmed or faded in my memory, as much the bad as the good, which I suppose is a blessing. The other day I couldn't remember whether baby Aileen had light or dark hair, or whether our mother was left or right handed, because in my memories both of her hands were usually occupied. But your face, brother, your face I remember as clear as if I had seen you this morning. At night in bed I can hear your breathing next to me. My fingers still know the warm clasp of your hand. I can still see your smiling eyes. I can still hear your silence and guess at your thoughts. I have only to feel my heartbeat to know that yours is beating the same rhythm. For we were born together and will abide together, no matter what the world puts between us. And one day we will sit side by side looking out over the world together like we did before. No matter how vividly you live in my body and my imagination, I shall always feel incomplete until that day.

Who knows where you are, brother, or how often you think of me? I can't help but feel that you must because in me it is like a compulsion. I try to imagine what you must look like three years older. I wonder whether you have resumed talking or whether you still live inside yourself. I pray that your tongue has been freed and that you are using your voice, and that it is connecting you in some meaningful way to others. Because you and I, of all people, were not intended to be alone.

Well, my dear brother, the hour is getting late, or perhaps *early* is a more accurate description, and duty shall call me at dawn, which is only a few hours distant. And so I will blow out this nub of a candle and end my correspondence here, though your likeness may stalk me in my dreams. Do take care of yourself, brother, wherever you may be, and I beseech you, I beg you, think of me, so that I may continue to exist outside of myself.

Yours always,
Nora

II
FORTUNES

FINN BERGEN

Iowa, 1855

Now a grown man of fifteen years, Finn set his childish hopes aside and no longer dared to think of himself as anything but an orphan, bereaved, and dispossessed. As portended by the mateless magpie, the grim certainty of Nora's fate abided, even in the face of Finn's most hopeful defenses. All that was left of Nora, all that he could touch, was the tiny, heart-shaped locket engraved with the letter L. L was for luck, of which he had none; L was for the loss, and longing, and loneliness that filled his life. And now it was clear he would never give it to her. His isolation was complete. Tethered to the prairie by his devotion to the Vogels and their hopeless cause, Finn worked like a machine, joylessly and efficiently, through the seasons.

Three years cultivating the hard prairie ground had yielded little more than bare sustenance for the Vogels in Iowa. Rains had destroyed most of the first wheat crop, and a fungus had claimed most of the potatoes, a tale all too familiar to Finn. Then, late that third summer, mere weeks before harvest, ranchers from the south had run four hundred head of cattle over the wheat. Thank God for the chickens and the hogs, or the Vogels may not have survived. By the fall of 1855 they were practically fighting the chickens for grubs.

Yet, no amount of privation seemed to temper Hans Vogel's belief in the land he had chosen to call his own.

"We will coax plenty from this land," he said, his face scorched red from the prairie sun, his hands worked so thick with calluses that the shank of a nail could not penetrate them.

"You shall see it, boy. Time, it will take time, but we shall succeed. We must only work harder each day."

As much as Finn had grown to trust his adoptive father, and to respect his resourcefulness, to revere his ingenuity and dogged determination, the young man assessed Hans Vogel's unyielding faith in the land, to which he attributed capacities bordering on the supernatural, as wholly unfounded, if not altogether foolhardy. For three years they'd worked themselves half-blind in the Iowa heat, turned the soil until their bodies ached and their muscles seized up from dehydration. And how little they had to show for it.

Two months they'd spent working their lone ox to the edge of death dragging timber for miles across the prairie to build a barn they could not fill, either with wheat or with stock. And already, having endured but two winters, the sagging structure was showing signs of collapse.

It pained Finn to see the Vogels fail in their mission. They yearned for nothing more than a simple life of farming and a place to call their own. They did not wish for the development of the region, or for the coming of the railroad. It was the isolation of this place that had drawn them halfway across the continent, and it was this same wish for solitude and an honest livelihood that kept them here, feeding their relentless aspirations, if not their bellies.

As much as the Vogels asked of Finn and as little as they managed to provide for him in the way of nourishment, they unquestionably cared for him and wanted the best for him. Finn knew that his silence vexed them, and that they wanted so badly to be privy to his thoughts instead of forever guessing at what was on his mind. Often Finn could feel Katrin's loving gaze upon him as he ate or studied at the kitchen table. Finn was certain that Katrin could guess at his gratitude and affection, and yet he still withheld the words for reasons he himself did not understand.

Likewise, Finn shared intimate moments

with Hans. Occasionally when they were working side by side, Hans would pause in his labors long enough to set a heavy hand on Finn's shoulder and let it linger there as he stared silently off toward the horizon.

"You are a good boy," he would say, giving Finn's shoulder a pat.

And each time Finn felt his face color with pride.

All summer long Finn and the Vogels prepared to harvest what wheat the cattle had not trampled or gorged themselves upon. Beyond the monotony of their labors, their lives were uneventful. Until one fall evening, shortly before harvest, a pair of men both dressed unseasonably in black vests and coats arrived at the farm. Stepping off the carriage, they regarded the Vogels' farm with keen disinterest and proceeded to the front steps of the cabin.

The two gentlemen promptly introduced themselves as Mr. Baxter and Mr. Anderson. Mr. Baxter was a short, heavy man of labored breaths and a phlegmy voice, which he would soon employ at great length. Conversely Mr. Anderson was a morbidly thin personage with the sober disposition of an undertaker, who was in no way disposed to his companion's appetite for loquacity. In fact Mr. Anderson was nearly as silent as Finn throughout their visit, which began when Katrin, her dusty apron slung about her neck and tied at the waist, showed the two gentlemen to the Vogels' humble sitting room, none other than the kitchen table, where she served them a weak tea made of chamomile and pineapple weed.

After some brief pleasantries and light conversation, during which Mr. Baxter was moved to comment upon the dust, the heat, and the humidity of the farm, he proceeded directly to the business that brought him to the Vogels' little Garden of Eden.

"Now then," proclaimed Mr. Baxter, proceeding to work tongue and palate together vigorously, as though trying to elicit some elusive flavor from his tea. "I have come to you today with an offer, Mr. Vogel, and a very prosperous offer, as it were. I presume you have heard of the IMIRC?"

"No," said Hans Vogel.

"Ah, well, then," said Mr. Baxter, as though it pleased him to elucidate on the matter. "The Illinois and Missouri and Iowa Railroad Corporation is a public entity in part federally granted, which shall be responsible in the coming months and years for the laying of rail in this region in loose association and indirect collaboration with the transcontinental railroad as this miracle of modern locomotion forges its way west."

"What has this to do with me and my family?" said Hans. "Why have you come here in the middle of my work, when harvest is coming?"

Mr. Baxter smiled. "I like your way of doing business, Mr. Vogel. Yes, yes, right to the point," said Mr. Baxter, eliciting a slow roll of the eyes from Mr. Anderson.

"I have come today, sir," continued Mr. Baxter, "bearing both an olive branch and a grand, dare I say singular opportunity for the Vogels. You see, on behalf of Messrs. Best and Warnock and Seymour, along with the shareholders of the IMIRC, we are prepared to offer you fifteen dollars per acre for your farm. Er, such as it is," he added limply.

"But this is my land, it's not for sale!" said Hans. "I have deed."

"Yes, sir, that is precisely the matter that brings us here," said Mr. Baxter, a slight rattle in his throat. "And that is precisely why Messrs. Best and Warnock and Seymour, by virtue of the IMIRC charter drafted upon their merger with the then recently formed DQI and M in October of last year, have granted me permission to buy out your interest at a hugely inflated sum."

"What is the meaning of *buy out*? This land belongs to me, I have deed to prove so. I will not sell ever."

Mr. Anderson, in a rare display of expression, hoisted a single eyebrow at this observation, which was met by a knowing nod on the part of Mr. Baxter, who cleared his throat before resuming.

"Mr. Vogel," said Mr. Baxter reasonably, "I have come this afternoon prepared to offer you a great deal more than you currently have invested in said land, which, while admittedly quite unremarkable, happens to dwell within the bounds of our easement as stated in the terms of our federal grant."

"I will not sell my land," insisted Hans.

"You can't stop progress," said Mr. Anderson matter-of-factly in what would prove to be his lone contribution to the dialogue.

"What my associate means to say," Mr. Baxter hastened to add, "is that progress has beckoned you into its service. Progress begs you to light the way as neighboring farms have seen fit to do. You have come to America to prosper, to assimilate, to become part of the great American experiment. And I, Mr. Vogel, have come to offer you your destiny on behalf of your newly adopted country. For the railroad is America's destiny!"

Mr. Baxter left a moment of pause so that this rousing observation might be fully appreciated, but Hans just sat there at the table, hands folded in front of him, his face a total blank.

"Well then," said Mr. Baxter with a strained joviality. "What say you, Mr. Vogel? Are you prepared to answer destiny's call?"

"I do not understand this talk," said Hans, shaking his head. "I want only my farm, and nothing else. I have deed, which I will not surrender at any price."

Mr. Anderson shook his head grimly, then fished out his pocket watch. Reading its face perfunctorily, he then eased it back in his trouser pocket.

Undaunted, Mr. Baxter manufactured a pleasant, if strained, smile while appearing to suppress a belch with a series of short, gavel-like reports to his sternum.

"Now, understand, Mr. Vogel," said Mr. Baxter. "Our wish is not to drive you off — oh, quite to the contrary. We want you to settle in these parts. We want you to reap the benefits of this development. There are many parcels of land still available along the perimeter of our federal easement, which can be yours at a fraction of the price I am presently offering you. Were you to take our generous offer, you might secure yourself five times the land — and better land, too, from what I understand, nearer the watershed."

"I will not sell."

Here Mr. Anderson drew a deep breath through his nose, clasping his eyes shut for an instant as though quelling some tempest deep within him. However, once again it was Mr. Baxter's patience that prevailed in spite of the increasingly gassy condition that seemed to threaten his good spirits.

"Perhaps, Mr. Vogel, you are not understanding the significance of the coming railroad," said Mr. Baxter, appealing to Finn on this occasion more than Hans. "Why, neighboring communities are scrambling to finance such an endeavor. They are literally throwing their money at it. They are actively wooing the railroad interests to develop this country. You mustn't fail to consider the vast benefits the IMIRC will bring to the region, particularly to farming communities. The movement of goods and the shipping of crops will mean the end of sustenance farming and the beginning of commercial farming in the state of Iowa! No more scratching out a meager existence in the prairie heat with these miserable chickens. What a profitable enterprise it shall be, Mr. Vogel, to be the breadbasket for the whole of a nation! Just think of the possibilities! Think of the towns that shall sprout up along this route! The towns you could feed with your crops!"

"My crops are for feeding my family," proclaimed Hans. "Not for feeding your railroad."

In the end, much to the chagrin of Mr. Baxter, and particularly Mr. Anderson, whose inner tempest had begun to show in the furrowed lines of his forehead and the downward crook of his mouth, the railroad was forced on this occasion to concede.

"While your decision is most unusual, Mr. Vogel," said Mr. Baxter upon the front landing of the cabin, "I shall at least for the time being honor it. Though I assure you that you've not seen the last of us, or the IMIRC. And should you fail to change your mind, I daresay you will live to rue the day that you refused to accept the IMIRC's generous offer."

After Mr. Baxter and Mr. Anderson left, Finn and Hans and Katrin lingered in the kitchen for a few silent moments, unsure what to make of the situation. In spite of Hans's stubborn insistence that the farm was not for sale, there hovered in the thick, humid air of the cabin a palpable sense that a final decision had yet to be reached. It was at this juncture that Finn nearly broke his silence.

After a brief period, without so much as a verbal prompt from Hans, they all resumed their work on the farm. Working beside Hans, Finn could feel the decision weighing on him. Hans was a dichotomy — an idealist, but also a pragmatist. The advantage of all that extra capital could not possibly be lost on Hans, who could still have his dream if only he were willing to defer it. Though it could be argued that in selling the farm their labors might be lost in the end, the capital would offer them a degree of security presently well beyond their reach. And though Finn could intimate clearly that the sound decision was to sell, he was no less sympathetic to Hans Vogel's dream of a self-sufficiency born and beholden to nothing more than soil and toil, and indefatigable will.

They paused for dinner as the sun began to sink below the western horizon, so close it seemed that they could reach out and touch it. They ate their modest dinner in silence, the weight of the decision still heavy in the air. Afterward, at dusk Finn accompanied Hans to the barn, where they penned the two remaining hogs and the ox, and shepherded the stray hens to their roost.

It was fully dark on the prairie by the time they secured the barn. Halfway to the cabin, they paused upon the hard, dusty clearing beneath the prairie sky and gazed up at the vast firmament. Here, they lingered in silence amid the trilling of crickets.

Standing there under the stars, Finn recollected how Hans had decided on this location, how he'd stuck his ear to the ground right there in the very spot they presently occupied, where Hans had claimed to hear a promise from the center of the earth. Now it occurred to Finn that what Hans had heard was neither his salvation nor any promise from the earth, but the coming of the railroad.

In that instant the imperative to express himself verbally after so long welled up inside of Finn to such an extent he could no longer ignore it. Here at last was a way out for Hans and Katrin, and a way out for Finn, too. If he could not be moved to speak now, when their collective fates hung in the balance, when the promise of the New World was finally offering them a foothold, when then could he be counted on? For all the Vogels had done on his behalf, from adopting him to feeding him to calling him their own, Finn was obligated to say something.

When he finally ventured to speak he did not recognize his own voice, though the words, practiced in silence, came out clearly.

"Take what they offer you, Papa," he said. "The railroad will not go away."

Jenny Chen

San Francisco, 2018

The boys were finally asleep by the time Jenny lay down in bed beside Todd and began flipping through the channels on the muted television, unable to soothe a restlessness that had been festering beneath her skin all day, all week, all month. CNN sure wasn't going to scratch that itch, nor was HGTV, or Animal Planet, or HBO, or anything else on what her father swore would be the end of civilization, cable television.

She turned off the TV and thought about having a glass of wine but knew that would only be a Band-Aid, the kind she'd been using more and more of late, even on work nights. What ailed Jenny wine could not cure. She was miserable in a way that wasn't likely to change. And given the advantages she'd had, given the resources bequeathed to her, there was really no accounting for how she'd arrived at this place. And there was really no excuse for dragging Todd and the boys along.

It was Jenny who'd led them to this dead end.

What was she making of their lives? Though this was a question she aimed at herself fleetingly from day to day, tonight she aimed it like a laser, determined not to flinch, or evade, or rationalize. Yes, okay, they were raising kids, two somewhat entitled, device-addicted, bordering-on-obese boys who would rather lie on their beds all day in a Cheeto-induced stupor playing Splatoon 2 than go out and make a few bucks mowing a lawn. Not that there was a lawn within two miles of Hayes Valley. Sure, Tyler and Winston performed at a high enough level academically to skate by. Sure, they looked good on paper, and they were not petty or unkind, nor were they exceptionally spoiled in comparison to their peers. They were ostensibly happy and healthy, and they'd probably go to good colleges one day, but what could they actually do?

If Jenny and Todd were to disappear tomorrow, if the boys were to become orphans overnight, what skills had Jenny and Todd imparted to Tyler and Winston that might serve them in this life? If anything, Jenny and Todd had infantilized them. If the Wi-Fi was down, the boys were lost. They were given zero responsibility. They could barely make a sandwich. They didn't spend nearly enough time outdoors. They had been camping exactly twice, both times in Oregon with

Todd and his dad.

Todd was right. They'd be better off hunting and hiking and running free in Oregon. The city was over. At least it was for the Chen-Murphys. It was too much work. They had to step over junkies to get to the Yerba Buena Center for the Arts. The Haight, the Mission, Castro, North Beach — they were all just shells of their former selves. They didn't know their neighbors, they hardly ever saw their friends, and they didn't feel a sense of community in any way, really, besides the larger bubble of California in which they were living.

"Screw it," said Jenny. "Let's do it."

"What are you talking about?" said Todd.

"Let's move to Oregon," she said.

"Very funny," he said. "It's not such a crazy plan, you know. If we cashed out we could —"

"I'm serious, Todd," she said. "You're right, there's nothing here for us. We hardly spend time together as a family, we never hang out with anybody or do anything particularly memorable."

Todd lowered his book, still skeptical.

"What happened?" he said. "Why are you saying this stuff now?"

Jenny sat further up in bed. "Because I'm really not happy, and I think I could be," she said. "I realize I'm so fortunate to be in my position financially, but I think I could do

361

better for my whole self, you know?"

"Yes," he said, a grin spreading across his face.

"Ugh, but it sounds like one of those movies on Lifetime about the career woman who moves to the country and becomes a housewife."

"Nobody's asking you to be a housewife," he said. "You can be whatever you want to be."

"I don't even know what that is, Todd."

"You can figure it out."

"Maybe you're right," she said. "I haven't decompressed in so long I don't even know what that feels like anymore. I don't have time to think about what really matters to me, I'm too busy trying to maintain our outsized life. It's like I'm on a hamster wheel most of the time. Screw it. When I was a little girl it's not like I dreamed of being a corporate consultant when I grew up, someone who lays people off. Am I being rash?"

"Yes, totally," he said. "You're totally being rash. And I love it."

"You hate staying home, don't you?" said Jenny. "You want to work."

"I don't hate it at all," he said. "I just think our lives could be more if we were away from the city.

"I don't care what I do at this point," said Todd. "I really don't. I just want to be near trees and open spaces — and I don't mean parks. I want to recognize people when I walk down the street, you know?"

"I'm getting it," she said. "And even if I hate it, what am I really leaving behind? Some history that doesn't even mean anything anymore. I wish it did with all my heart, but it just doesn't. San Francisco is no longer the future."

Todd laid his book aside. "Babe, I can't even believe we're having this conversation, this is great! Should we wake the boys?"

"No," she said.

"Yeah, you're right," said Todd. "Do you think they'll be, you know, resistant to the idea?"

"Yeah, probably," she said. "God knows I was. But it's not like we'd be moving them to Arkansas or something."

"Ugh," said Todd. "Now you've got me second-guessing the idea. What if they hate the schools? What if they don't fit in and make friends? What if we can't find decent jobs? What if the rain drives us crazy?"

"Stop," said Jenny, clasping his wrist and looking him in the face.

It was the closest she'd felt to Todd in years, probably since Tyler was a baby. And she was sure Todd must be feeling the same thing. Here they were, finally on the same page again, wanting the same things. Maybe it was like one of those movies on Lifetime, but what was so bad about that?

Jenny leaned in and gave him a peck on the lips.

"I'm excited," she said.

"Me too," he said. "But honestly, Jen, I still don't quite believe you. I feel like you're just in a rut, and work is going to call you in the morning, and you'll get sucked right back in, and we'll keep talking about moving to Oregon for a while, but something else will come up, then something else, then we'll be back to square one again."

"No," said Jenny. "I promise. This is for real."

"Aren't you even a little bit scared?" he said.

"Yes, I am, really scared," she said. "And I like it."

Jenny and Todd discussed the move to Salem nightly in bed for a week. Jenny hadn't given her notice at work, and they had yet to list the house. They wanted to be sure they were making the right decision before they turned their back on the life they'd built in the city. A chief point of their nightly discussions was the matter of when and how they should inform the boys.

"Maybe we should wait until school is out," said Jenny.

"Then they won't be able to say goodbye to their friends," Todd said.

"Good point. Are we being unfair?" she said.

"No, I don't think so," said Todd. "We're

trying to give them a better life, Jen. Somewhere less crowded, somewhere where they won't have to step over homeless people to walk down the street. Somewhere they can actually afford to live someday."

"You're right," she said. "I guess I'm just nervous. I mean, I hate my job, our mortgage is ridiculous, the city is awful at this point, I hardly recognize the place, so, what are we risking?"

"We can buy three houses in McMinnville for what we'll get for this place," said Todd. "We can have an actual rec room and an office and a freaking yard, for once. I can have a shop. We'll have more time together as a family."

Tyler and Winston were dubious when it was announced at the dinner table that they'd be having a family meeting afterward.

"What the heck's a family meeting anyway?" said Winston. "Since when do we have family meetings?"

That the boys were not allowed to bring their devices to the meeting was further cause for discontent. The boys sprawled impatiently on the sofa while Jenny and Todd sat opposite on the identical green wing-back chairs that had cost them an arm and a leg at the 9th Street Designer Clearance.

"Are we in trouble?" Tyler asked right out of the gate.

"No, honey," said Jenny.

"Did someone die?" said Winston.

"Nobody died," said Todd.

"Then what are we doing here?" said Tyler.

"We've got some exciting news," said Jenny.

"Are we going to Hawaii or something?"

"Not Hawaii," said Jenny. "Oregon."

"Cool," said Tyler. "Do we get to see Uncle Ted?"

"Yeah," said Todd. "We'll be seeing a lot of Uncle Ted. And Grandpa Paul, too."

"When are we going?" said Winston.

"As soon as school gets out," said Jenny.

"That's cool. But we do it like every summer. Since when do we have a meeting about it?" said Winston.

"Buddy, the thing is, we're staying this time. We're actually moving to McMinnville," said Todd.

"Wait, what?" said Winston.

"Isn't that great?" said Todd.

"You mean like permanently?"

"Yeah."

Both boys were dumbstruck. Winston looked like he might cry.

"Why?" demanded Tyler, bolting upright on the sofa. "I don't want to move. I like it here."

At which point Winston did in fact begin to cry. Jenny left her seat to offer him comfort on the sofa.

"It's okay, honey," she said.

"Why are we even moving?" said Winston.

"I won't go, I don't want to go. All of my friends are here. My school is here, our house is here. Why didn't you tell us? What's the use of a family meeting if we don't even get any say in anything?"

"We're your parents," Todd snapped. "You do whatever we think is right for you until you turn eighteen."

Winston folded his arms across his chest.

"Honey," said Jenny. "McMinnville will be a better situation for you. For all of us."

"Says you," said Winston.

"That's right," said Todd. "Says us. We're the adults here."

"We thought you'd be excited," said Jenny. "You love Oregon."

"Not to live," said Tyler. "There's nothing to do there."

"Sure there is," said Todd.

"Like what?"

"Like hunting," said Todd.

This one got both boys' full attention.

"You mean like with guns?" said Winston.

"Maybe," said Todd.

"Hunting what?"

"Well, Uncle Ted goes deer hunting, and I think even elk," said Todd. "And fishing, too."

"Fishing is boring," said Winston, wiping his eyes. "He took us last summer. I didn't catch anything. But hunting is awesome."

Jenny had to admit, as much as she disapproved of hunting, it was a pretty brilliant enticement on Todd's part. Once access to guns was on the table, it was all downhill.

"Well, that went okay," she said in bed that night.

"Could've been worse," he said.

"Are you nervous?" said Jenny.

"Not at all," he said. "I can't wait. I feel like it's our destiny to move."

"Destiny? I wish I felt so certain."

Within the week, Jenny gave her notice at work and managed to wiggle out of the trip to DC for the last of the Amtrak purge. Todd called Dave Mitchell, his old frat brother from Davis, who was a big agent at Keller Williams. They listed the Hayes Valley apartment at one point three million, which was four hundred and fifty thousand more than they'd paid ten years ago.

Meanwhile Todd and Jenny browsed real estate listings on their laptops in bed at night. They found dozens of houses in McMinnville that were well under their budget, including a four-bedroom outside of town on — get this — two point five wooded acres with river views, a swimming pool, and a detached shop for . . . wait for it, wait for it . . . four fifty! Good heavens, they could practically retire at that price.

"Why did we wait so long to do this?" said Jenny.

"I know, right?" said Todd.

"God," she said. "If we played our portfolio

right, we wouldn't have to work at all. I mean, we will, but I'm just saying, we wouldn't necessarily have to."

It was true. With or without Jenny's job, the Chen-Murphys were sitting pretty. In McMinnville, they could live like gentry on nothing but the wealth they'd accumulated in the past ten years, that and what was left of Todd's trust.

It had taken six generations of Chens and five generations of Murphys to get here. They had crossed the seas as refugees and had not been greeted kindly upon their arrival, except by their own kind. They'd started with nothing. They'd scratched and saved and dreamed against all probability of the golden fortune this place had promised them. And though it may have come at a heavy toll, they had been delivered stupendous good fortune along the way. They were the lucky ones.

WALTER BERGEN

Oregon, 2019

The snow continued to fall, funneling down in big, wet flakes like ash against the windshield. The wipers made quick and blurry work of them as the Coast Starlight hurtled north. Despite the snow, Walter still operated at max speed, and thus far it hadn't been a problem. The plows had been active, and all things considered, travel remained relatively smooth through the Albany-Salem corridor. No trees down, no ice on the lines, no clogs at the points nor impacted snow, and the drifts along the edge of the tracks were still well under a foot. Moreover the wind had once again abated somewhat in the past twenty minutes.

"Looks like I'm gonna make Maddie's concert after all," said Macy, ducking his head into the cab.

"We'll see," said Walter. "Nothing from dispatch to make me think otherwise."

"Still on schedule," Macy said.

"Always," said Walter.

No sooner had Macy retreated, resuming his duties, than Walter was visited once more by a bittersweet nostalgia.

Always. As if there were such a thing as always. Nothing was always that Walter could see, not a damn thing in the whole world, and that included the polar ice caps and the night sky. You grew up, you got married, you had kids, you gave your life to them, then they grew up and left you, at which point you couldn't even remember life without them. And all of it happened quicker than you could see it coming. My God, and you hardly had time to look back, and when you did it all blurred together like some long-forgotten weekend. And when it was over, your head was still spinning.

Wendy's first ride-along had been in a snowstorm, though really it hadn't been much more than a November flurry. She must have been a five-year-old. Walter was still pretty green at that point, but he'd already developed a good reputation as an engineer. For at least one snowy afternoon in her life, Wendy had been interested in trains. Walter could still see Wendy's eager, round little five-year-old face blossom with expectation, glowing with some irrepressible energy that only children could seem to harvest.

God, where did the time go? Nearly twenty-five years had passed since that afternoon.

Walter still had a chain saw and a pair of shorts that old, so how could everything else have gotten away so fast? It was hard to fathom that retirement was already upon him. He didn't feel sixty-three. Not on the inside, anyway. It seemed like only last week he'd married Annie, and they'd bought the house on the edge of town, not too far off campus, the little rambler with the blue shutters and the shady yard, and the attached two-car garage with one broken door, the same house in which they were still living. Walter still hadn't fixed the garage door; wasn't that proof enough that whole decades could not possibly have passed?

It seemed like last summer that they'd brought Wendy back from Sacred Heart and tried unsuccessfully to get her settled into the crib in the nursery, only to spend the next two and a half years co-sleeping, Walter forever exiled to the very outer edge of the king mattress, lying so frequently and exclusively on his left shoulder that he eventually developed bursitis, while the baby awoke every two hours to nurse on poor Annie, and nobody got any sleep.

And yet from this remove, those two and a half years seemed like the bat of an eye. It seemed like last summer that the three of them had taken their trip to the south of Ireland, thirteen-year-old Wendy complaining constantly about the food, the accommodations, the activities or lack thereof, underwhelmed by the rocky coves and windswept headlands of West Cork, uninspired by the verdant hills, and gently rolling valleys, and the miles upon miles of sprawling pastures and furrowed fields, laid out like carpets over uneven terrain, dotted with structures so old they almost seemed part of the landscape itself, a disarming landscape cut through with ancient stone barriers and gravel roads. The only thing Wendy cared a whit about was the ice cream.

The Bergens stayed at charming little inns, with fireplaces in the lobbies and tiny pubs attached, where they ate lamb kabobs, and meat pies, and bangers and mash, and Walter drank stouts and malty ales at room temperature. Walter fell in love with County Cork. There were points during their ten-day stay when he daydreamed of pulling up his life in Eugene and moving his family to Cork without so much as a thought for what future the place might hold for them. After a week, like the old sod structures squatting in the fields, he felt himself a part of the landscape.

But even Blarney Castle, despite eight hundred years of history, could not arouse Wendy's thirteen-year-old imagination.

"It's kinda cool, I guess. But it's boring. Everybody is like two hundred years old."

The stone, of course, was lost on her. Wendy refused to lie on her back.

"Okay, it's a rock, wow," she said. "I'm supposed to kiss a rock? No thanks."

The wishing steps were the closest she came to any kind of concession.

"Fine, I'll make a wish," she said. "I wish the next six days will go really fast."

The main objective of the trip, for Walter, anyway, was a two-day visit to Magh Eala, the Crossroads of Munster, on the river Blackwater. Magh Eala, now called Mallow, was the very village that Walter's great-great-grandfather Finnegan and his twin sister, Nora, had left behind in the mid-nineteenth century to begin their American odyssey. Magh Eala offered green hills, a castle, a racetrack, and a donkey sanctuary — to be sure, nothing much to excite Wendy, or even Annie. But to Walter the place had felt sacred somehow, whether owing to its antiquity, a wistful yearning toward history, or some pastoral aspiration that abided in the green hills themselves. But to Walter, Magh Eala felt like a return.

"Ugh, this is the most boring place yet," Wendy had said.

Looking back, if there was ever a time that seemed to move slower than the rest of Walter's life, both then and now, it was Wendy's early teenage years, when neither Walter nor Annie, nor anybody else, could seem to impress a thing upon Wendy, who was the very definition of defiance, yet another quality her mother attributed to the Irish.

"Baby, this is where our ancestors came from," Walter said, standing astride a marker in the garden, the great stone fortification of the castle rising up behind them.

"Well, they left, didn't they? And besides, Dad, that was like forever ago. We are so not from Ireland. Sian O'Connell from Algebra Two is from Ireland — she was born here. You can hardly understand what she's saying half the time. The boys think she's exotic or something. Please. Ireland is not exotic. It's about as exotic as Germany. Thailand is exotic. Brazil is exotic. But no, we had to come to rainy old Ireland for spring break, because our ancient freaking ancestors almost starved to death here."

Now, in the autumn of his years, given the choice, Walter would gladly live his life all over again, though he'd skip Wendy's early teenage years. It was true, the two of them had butted heads a lot on various subjects, especially Wendy's freshman and sophomore years, subjects ranging from — but not limited to — wardrobe, diet, academic achievement, adult responsibility, respect for elders, punctuality, reliability, accountability, music, cinema, politics, hygiene, history, technology, and NPR.

It was also true that Annie had often found herself in the middle of the fray, and largely because of her diplomacy, father and daughter's relationship had remained intact.

"You both have the damn Irish temper," said Annie, a Lutheran from Wisconsin, a patient soul, a good listener, and a driver who invariably acquiesced at four-way stops.

"And your Irish stubbornness," she hastened to add. "And your Irish logic, and your Irish flair for the dramatic, and your general Irish hardheadedness."

Thank God for Annie, or Walter and Wendy might have done permanent damage to their relationship.

Things got better once Wendy self-actualized. That was, once she started dating other girls, though these arrangements were not formally acknowledged as dates or dating, but "hanging out." It started when Wendy went out for softball junior year, and it continued through fall, when she went out for volleyball, both of which she was good if not great at. That didn't matter. Walter watched on with relief as Wendy grew into herself, becoming a more positive voice, a more engaged and constructive personality. And yeah, Walter did a little growing, too. He cut his drinking in half, for starters. He went to the pub but one night a week, making himself more present. Finally he stopped taking Wendy so personally, as Annie had told him to do all along.

By the time Wendy went off to Southern

Oregon University in Ashland after senior year, Walter and Wendy were simpatico again. The night of Wendy's graduation, near the end of the family reception at the Paddock, Walter and Wendy hugged in the corridor by the bathrooms when they thought nobody could see them, crying big Irish tears together.

The first time Wendy came home for winter break, she'd put on fifteen pounds and pierced her lip, and cut her hair short except for one big swoop of bangs on her forehead, which she'd dyed red — not red like her grandmother's hair, not Irish red, but red like a fire engine, or a stop sign. Walter had no problem with that. After all, what was a little misguided fashion next to the fact that Wendy was engaged in her studies and excited about learning and life, and that she wasn't doing drugs, as far as Walter could tell? And that she no longer begrudged him merely for being her father.

In the years since Wendy graduated, remaining in Ashland long after graduation, where she worked first as a bartender, then a personal trainer, and finally, a physical therapist, Walter and Wendy had become friends. From Walter's perspective, at least then, this turn in their relationship had happened once Wendy earned Walter's respect as an adult, once she started demonstrating the responsibility to match her independence.

That was when Walter began to listen to his daughter in a different way, to really hear her, to consider her beliefs and conclusions about the world, and understand her evolving values, so many of which she had learned and adopted outside of Walter's sphere of influence, and so many of which were nothing like the values or conclusions or opinions Walter had grown up on and come of age with. And a funny thing happened: Some of Wendy's crazy progressive ideals began to not seem so crazy anymore. In fact, some of them made a lot of damn sense, given the state of the modern world.

And really, at the end of the day these new "millennial values" of Wendy's were not so much departures from the traditional Irish Catholic values he'd grown up with: community, family, service, loyalty. No, these new values were just more nuanced and evolved expressions of the old values — more versatile, more inclusive, less competitive, less punitive, and more aspirational, less ambitious in the ways of consumerism. Walter appreciated all of this. He believed in social justice, and equality, and freedom of expression, and opportunity, and feelings, but . . . it was also true, objectively speaking, that you could not have a bathroom for every damn individual according to how that individual identified outside the parameters socially agreed upon probably sometime back in the

Pleistocene epoch, or the whole of public life would consist of bathrooms. There would be no room for theaters or restaurants or hospitals. Better that everybody just share the same bathroom.

So while Walter and Wendy still couldn't always quite get on the same page with regard to identity politics, they fundamentally agreed more than they disagreed, and they exchanged ideas openly. Even as Walter made himself available to his daughter's ultra-progressive worldview, even as he tried to recontextualize the modern world from her millennial perspective, Wendy betrayed more and more the traces of her father's influence. For instance, after college she'd grown to like pubs — real pubs with darts and music, pubs without TVs. She shared Walter's derision for reality shows, and social networking, and the majority of modern music. She'd even grown to appreciate some of the music of Walter's own burgeoning adulthood: Dylan, Floyd, CCR, and even Tom Waits.

But more important, Wendy had begun to demonstrate in adulthood some of the qualities — loyalty, punctuality, accountability — that Walter had tried to instill in her from the beginning. It was satisfying to see that some of it had stuck, that in spite of those rough patches, beyond the years of willful defiance, his efforts had not been wasted. Perhaps Walter's greatest triumph in this regard was that all these years after she'd lamented the endless scenery and refused to kiss the Blarney stone, Wendy and Kit were going to the south of Ireland for their honeymoon. If that was not consolation enough, there was the fact that in marriage Kit would be assuming the Bergen name.

Walter sounded the horn twice in quick succession as the Coast Starlight slowed into the station. The tracks were clear and the platform was dry, though snow was beginning to accumulate on the metal roof of the covered landing and pile on the eaves of the station.

Wu Chen

San Francisco, 1852

The afternoon that Ai Lu not only refused to change Wu Chen's half dime for a head of cabbage but would not speak to him, and abstained from so much as looking at him, was the same afternoon Wu Chen was forced to accept that Ai Lu had no intention of ever marrying him.

"She change her mind, you see," said her father. "I make her change it. You give me one week."

But Wu Chen's heart had already decided. In spite of custom, he did not want Ai Lu, or anyone else, under such conditions, nor could he bear the thought of making Ai Lu his unwilling partner in life. And while he did not formally withdraw his proposition, Wu Chen left the store, his heart sitting like a rock in his stomach, with every intention of never coming back. He was stunned as he walked down Clay and wove through a crowded Portsmouth Square, past the cannons and the customhouse.

His body guided him straight to the laundry by force of habit, but when he got there, he stood dazedly upon the boardwalk for an instant, before he turned around and walked away.

He did not return to the laundry that day, nor did he exhaust a single thought contemplating the consequences of his absence. Caring about anything seemed suddenly beyond his reach. His whole life at that moment seemed totally meaningless, a waste of a life, really. That a genuinely good soul like Jimmy Huang should die senselessly so that an ineffectual coward like Wu Chen could live, and could make nothing of his fortune, who could not so much as attract a poor immigrant girl from a grocery stand with his fortune, seemed patently unjust. It should have been Jimmy Huang who lived. Jimmy Huang would have gotten the girl.

Wu Chen zigzagged his way back through the crowded square like a man struck by lightning. The world was a blur. His own heartbeat was but a distant drumming as he careened down Columbus Street to Kearny. When he finally reached his apartment, he immediately retired to his stuffy room up the stairs and pulled the horse blanket over the window, blocking out all offending light, and lay down upon his loveless mattress in the dark, overwhelmed by a sense of his own impotence.

For two days he did not leave his room but to empty the chamber pot in the privy out back. For two days he ate nothing but wilting cabbage, which was in no short supply in his apartment, as he'd purchased eighteen heads in the past three weeks. Nobody from the laundry sent for Wu Chen, for his labor was easily replaced. That he technically did not need the income was a bigger relief than he was ready to admit.

In his heart of hearts, he understood that this was no tragedy, for ultimately he deemed himself unworthy of Ai Lu and considered himself a fool for ever proposing to her father. But that didn't make his heartache any less agonizing. For he could see her round, alabaster face, like a moon in his mind's eye, and smell her earthy goodness, and feel the touch of her fingers as they exchanged coins, and even, in his imagination, taste her lips, though he'd never really had occasion to taste them, and he imagined the warmth of her mouth upon his, and the smallness of her hand nestled inside his own.

In Wu Chen's imagination he had already possessed Ai Lu, he had already witnessed their future together. He had even managed to anticipate their prospective children, a girl and a boy. In his imagination Wu Chen had already pursued the growth of the store, and the purchase of a home, and the architecture for their children's futures. Wu Chen had already daydreamed practically every minute of their future together. To lose her after all that was unbearable.

Along with Wu Chen's lovelorn despair came another troubling development: The visions returned. The bloodletting at the claim once more pervaded his thoughts without warning or control. When they arrived he could not force these recollections from his consciousness. It was not just the terrible undoing of the Huangs, shot at point-blank range as they begged for their lives, but the chilling revelation that was Wu Chen's own capacity for violence. The muscles of his hands remembered; they knew what it was to slit a man's neck open like the belly of a carp with no thought or emotion. He could still feel the warm blood running over his fingers. His arms and legs knew the sudden dead weight of his slumping victims as one by one he eased their lifeless bodies to the ground under cover of night. Most troubling of all was that ultimately he could not deny the overwhelming sensation of invincibility that had accompanied looking into the eyes of a begging man, a man on his knees, and mechanically planting a bullet between his eyes.

These terrible visitations were invariably accompanied by a familiar guilt and anguish and heartsickness, reminders all of the barbarism and effortless violence of which he was capable. Maybe he couldn't hide it. Maybe Ai Lu had glimpsed this terrible potential, maybe she could see it in his eyes, and maybe that was why she'd refused his bloodstained hand.

To make matters worse, Wu Chen had nobody to confide in, not another living presence, save for his uncle Li Jun, as he imagined him.

"Quit pouting," his uncle said. "I told you before, there are other fish in the sea."

"No," said Wu Chen. "Not others like her."

"You hardly knew this girl, Nephew, how can you even say that? And look at the father, the hairless pig. You dodged a bullet there."

"He's a good man."

"I doubt whether he would say the same of you," said his uncle.

"He wished for me to marry his daughter, did he not?" said Wu Chen.

"He was after your fortune," his uncle said.

"What do you want, anyway?" said Wu Chen. "Leave me to myself."

"It was you who summoned me, Nephew."

"Well, I didn't mean to, so go away."

"Very well," said Uncle Li Jun.

"No, no, stay," said Wu Chen.

"As you wish, Nephew."

"Oh, but, Uncle, what do I do? I've made nothing of my opportunities here. I have nothing to show for my fortune — a fortune I didn't even earn myself."

"You earned twenty-five percent of it."

"But it should have been me, Uncle. It shouldn't have been Jimmy Huang or his brothers. I was the impatient one. I was the one who wanted to cash in my share. I was the one who met the white man on the trail. I should have stopped it somehow. I should have known, I should have warned them. I should have drawn my iron and shot the man before he ever went to the claim. It was clear he was no good. How much blood-shed might have been avoided had I done that? I could have saved them, Uncle."

"At least you avenged them."

"But I could have saved them. I was there, squatting in the brush. I could have done something. I could've snuck up from behind. I could've created a diversion, at least. Anything would have helped."

"Almost certainly you would have died, Nephew."

"Maybe that would have been better. To die trying to save them instead of cowering in the bushes. I had the thought, Uncle, even as it was happening: I knew where their shares were stashed in the rabbit den. I don't know why I had it, but that I should have that particular thought must say something about my character. How could I not risk my life for the Huangs, the very people who for no good reason at all took me into their confidence and offered me a life in this strange country where I had no prospects?"

"You did what you had to do," said Uncle Li Jun.

"I did what my cowardly instincts told me to do," said Wu Chen. "And it was my cowardly instincts that told me to show Ai Lu's father the bank note, too. Because, Uncle, it is just as you say: He had no respect for me previously. He could see me for exactly who I was: a fraud. That was my mistake, trying to impress her father. To hell with custom, Uncle, I should have asked Ai Lu directly."

Shortly after that conversation, though his fortune was secure behind the formidable walls of the San Francisco Savings Bank, though he was in no danger of starving for the foreseeable future and beyond, Wu Chen managed to lose himself for weeks in a morass of self-pity and regret.

AI LU

San Francisco, 1853

There was much to admire about Wu Chen:
He was kind and considerate and a little shy,
qualities Ai Lu appreciated in a man. In her
limited experience, vulnerability was in short
supply when it came to men, especially the
ones who washed up half-starving on the
shores of Alta California. Wu Chen was also
thoughtful and not so quick to make up his
mind like most men she knew. Why, it took
him at least three minutes to pick a cabbage
he would probably never eat.

In the right light, Wu Chen was handsome,
though not traditionally so — a bit short,
perhaps, a little pigeon-toed, soft-spoken,
slightly nearsighted, a little hunched (presumably from his weeks and months huddled over
other people's laundry, or dredging the river),
but handsome, still. His face was kind and
symmetrical, and he was not afraid to show
his teeth. Moreover, his eyes were engaging,
and here more than anywhere you could see

his vulnerability.

Not only was Wu Chen kind and handsome and willing, but if you were to believe the bank note from an institution that had burned to the ground on no fewer than three occasions since Ai Lu's arrival in San Francisco, Wu Chen was allegedly a wealthy man.

And therein lay the problem, at least as far as Ai Lu was concerned.

It was obvious from the start that Wu Chen's frequent and prolonged patronage of her father's store had everything to do with her presence there, and nothing to do with their inventory. Nobody needed that many heads of cabbage, nobody consumed lemons in that quantity. It was only recently, however, that Ai Lu had become aware of Wu Chen's intentions, which were not in themselves disagreeable to her. Anything that might expand the parameters of her experience in America, anything that might offer her some degree of influence or freedom — entitlements all but absent from her life — would be an improvement over her current state of servitude.

Coming to this new land had not provided much in the way of opportunity for Ai Lu. The benefits were virtually none. But she'd had no choice but to leave Guangdong with her father. Ai Lu had enjoyed more freedom in China than she enjoyed here in America. In the absence of her mother, dead a year before they ever left the mountains of Guangdong, and her two younger sisters, left behind with their aunt and uncle, her father's needs were left exclusively to Ai Lu. At least in Guangdong, she could come and go in her village as she pleased. In Guangdong, she was permitted to frustrate the monotony of her labors by prolonging her errands or visiting friends. But here in America she was at her father's side from the moment she awoke to the moment they retired to their rented room on Grant Avenue at night. Indeed, they slept in the same room. And her father was a needy and very particular man, and one who snored like a wild boar.

Ai Lu had begun to resent her father's demanding and inflexible ways, though up until now, she had never defied his will. But his intention to marry her off for his own benefit offered Ai Lu a perfect opportunity to exercise her defiance. Thus she refused to let her father marry her off simply so he might profit by the arrangement. Her father had not even cared much for Wu Chen, whom he considered to be a rube and a poor judge of cabbage. That was, until the day Wu Chen had produced the bank note. And for this reason, and no other, Ai Lu was resistant to the arrangement that her father wanted so badly to force upon her.

"He will come back, and when he does, you will do the right thing," her father said as they closed the shop, crating plums and melons, and stacking the crates upon splintered pallets in the rear of the store, where they would eventually be locked.

"You marry this man," he said, "and he will invest in our store, he will invest in us, you understand, in us. All together we make our store bigger, and more profitable. We make our way in this place. We make a better future here."

Ai Lu cast her eyes down but issued no reply.

"Oh, you will learn to love this man," said her father, not unkindly, believing no doubt that he must have been anticipating her thoughts. "But sometimes you must think beyond yourself, Ai Lu. You must learn to think of your children."

"I have no children."

"Not yet," he said. "But you will, my daughter. Our family will grow with our store."

"Why is everything about the future?" she said. "Why can't we enjoy our lives now?"

"And what is to enjoy when it can all disappear overnight?" he said.

Ai Lu looked him in the eye.

"Being alive," she said. "Moment to moment, meal to meal."

"Bah," he said, waving her off. "Life does not happen in a moment. That's foolishness."

"There is more to the world than tomorrow, Father," she said, packing the overripe melons into a crate, as though to prove her point. "Maybe tomorrow isn't always better."

For weeks, her father hectored Ai Lu for resisting his will. But she was determined to take her father out of the equation. Ai Lu wanted once and for all for her life to be predicated on her own decisions, whether or not they aligned with the preferences or the will of her father, Wu Chen, or anybody else. If Ai Lu was going to surrender her will, she was going to do it on her own terms.

And so, much to her father's frustration, Ai Lu firmly maintained her resistance to the arrangement in the coming weeks. The more her father pushed, the more Ai Lu refused to comply, and the more defiant she became.

"We will find this man, and you will marry him," he said more than once.

"I will marry the man I choose," she said each time. "And that is if I marry at all."

"I am your father, and I say you will marry this man."

"You can say whatever you want, but I will act as I choose."

One afternoon after such an exchange, Ai Lu whipped her apron off, lobbed it atop the cabbage bin, and walked straight out of the store and down the street without explanation.

Ai Lu stopped after a half dozen steps and turned back toward her father, who was standing in front of the store, clutching her apron in a state of discomfiture somewhere between agitation and confusion.

"You do not own me," said Ai Lu, shaking her fist. "You do not decide for me."

She stomped down Clay Street, past the old herbalist's clapboard shop, fuming. It was not a woman's destiny to be kept, nor to be traded according to a man's will. Where would men even be without women to forever serve their needs? Yet they apparently had no conception of their dependence upon the women they treated as their property. Without women, the world would fall to pieces in two days. For men were like children.

After a block or so, calmer moods prevailed, and Ai Lu allowed herself to forgive her father once more. He was only obeying tradition. She could not begrudge him this, for she knew that leaving China meant that he had to cling to his old ways more firmly than ever. Still, she would not return to the store directly. Instead, she would let him sweat it out for a few minutes.

And so, she walked about Portsmouth Square, twice passing the laundry where Wu Chen worked, hoping to sneak a glance at him. If only Wu Chen could know that he was not the problem. If only she could have chosen him herself.

A week passed, and Wu Chen did not make a single appearance at the store. Every afternoon since the day she had taken leave of her own volition, her father permitted her a short break for her lunch, which she had formerly taken hunched in the rear of the store. But now daily she strolled past the laundry at the edge of the square, ever on the lookout for Wu Chen. But she did not see him. And as the days passed she began to curse herself for resisting her father's wishes, for indeed, they were her wishes, too.

ABRAHAM SEYMOUR

Spring field, Illinois, 1853

They were less than half a day outside of Springfield, and much to Abe Seymour's exasperation young Worthy Warnock was still holding forth unchecked on a variety of subjects, including, but by no means limited to, immigration, industrialization, big-boned women, labor, commodities, interstate commerce, slavery, peaches, and of course his favorite subject of all, the transcontinental railroad.

"Yes, Seymour, once we have succeeded in bridging Rock Island to Davenport, the prairie shall lie open before us, nothing but high grass and flat passage until the Rockies. Just imagine."

But Abe did not imagine. In fact, on this occasion he neither feigned sleep nor pretended to listen, but rather stared out the tiny window and let Warnock's relentless blather wash over him. Mercifully, when they reached Springfield, Abe would be rid of the insufferable Worthy Warnock, or at any rate, no longer confined to close quarters with the man. Unless, heaven forbid, Best should see fit to seat Abe next to Warnock at dinner.

Gazing out the window at nothing in particular as the carriage bumped and squeaked over the Illinois terrain, Abe ran his fingers absently over the ancient scars still barely perceptible upon his inner wrist, and instantly his thoughts turned to those painful days of adolescence following the death of his parents, those gruesome years of self-exile in London he rarely dared to revisit, though they had molded him into the man he was today.

After his expulsion from the Bristol School, and his subsequent refusal to accept any assistance from Hollingsworth, fourteen-year-old Abe had found his way to London. He could not explain his stubborn refusal to accept help. He only knew that the necessity for self-sufficiency sat hard in the very middle of him like a walnut that could not be cracked. Nor would the world ever crack him, no matter how hard it tried.

The filth and depravity that greeted young Abe in the East End of London were unlike anything he'd encountered in Gloucester or Bristol. He had seen poverty, beheld dirty children, overworked and underfed, their faces streaked with coal from the mines. He had witnessed the sallow, drawn faces of their parents. But nothing had prepared him for the unwholesome streets and alleyways of the East End. Nothing had prepared him for the parade of urchins, hollow eyed and joyless, orphans like himself, but unlike Abe without a fortune awaiting them, the lot of them forced to grovel and steal for their livelihood in an urban wasteland, amid the great stink of London, its gutters and hovels and stultifying air running rampant with typhoid and diphtheria, cholera and measles, starvation, brutality, and exploitation. Streets flowing freely with sewage, paths littered with manure and animal carcasses, swarming with flies. If ever a place had been hellish, it was London's East End. And yet, nothing could compel Abe to return to Gloucester, where the lives of the Silbersteins had been reduced to ash.

After three days and two perilous nights wandering the streets, afraid for his life, Abe finally consigned himself to the mercy of the Whitechapel Working Home, a squat brick edifice in a notable state of disrepair. As Abe soon learned, the Whitechapel Working Home was an institution short on mercy and long on profiteering. Within the week Abe, to no benefit of his own, was placed in a blacksmith apprenticeship in an alley off of High Street with a childless and unmarried man named Spragg, who was to provide him two meals a day in exchange for his labor.

Suffice it to say that Thom Spragg was a

drinker and a rough man, whose rotten teeth, a veritable Stonehenge in miniature, were attended by a sickly-sweet odor that even alcohol could not mask. His forearms were marked with dozens of nearly identical burn scars, each running horizontally up his wrist toward his elbow, roughly an inch long, pink, and slightly raised, blemishes presumably owing to the great brick forge within whose depths he cast his arms countless times each day. Spragg's heavy apron, smeared with soot and charcoal, was marked by a constellation of little holes, the results of errant sparks leaping from the molten mouth of the forge.

"And what have we here?" he said, clutching Abe's arm upon their first meeting. "You 'aven't got an ounce of muscle on you, 'ave you? It's a wonder you can climb out of bed with those arms. I've seen more meat on a neck bone."

Spragg presented a craggy smile, wholly devoid of mirth, a smile that might have wilted cabbage.

"What's your name?" he said.

"Abe, sir."

"And you're the best they've bloody got?"

"That I cannot say, sir."

"Well, go on then," said Spragg. "Put on an apron."

Thom Spragg soon proved himself to be a cruel and stern taskmaster given to mood swings and frightful bouts of drunkenness, during which he would sometimes sing in a warbling tenor, his brogue so thick and his tongue so heavy with drink that Abe could not begin to understand the words, as Spragg listed this way and that, spinning wildly from forge to anvil, searing-hot iron at the end of his tongs. That he could practice his trade without burning to death or mashing his hands to jelly was a small wonder.

Abe was forced to labor six days a week, twelve hours a day, and Spragg was not much of a cook. Meals generally consisted of drippings and bread or potatoes with the occasional sheep trotter. And of course for Spragg, said meal was invariably accompanied by gin. At night Abe returned to the workhouse, his hands blistered, his wrists burned like Spragg's, his eyelashes curled, and his face singed red from the blast of the forge. At Whitechapel Working Home he was afforded a cot barely wide enough to accommodate his teenage body in a cloistered hall he shared with two dozen other boys ranging in age from eight to seventeen.

The boys at Whitechapel Working Home received no formal instruction, nor were they afforded any form of worship or leisure, lest they take the time out of their sleep. Sundays were reserved for licking their wounds and scaring up a meal. Their feeding during the week was left to their guardians, for whom they all toiled daily for no gain. The smallest among the younger boys were forced to work in the textile factories, scrambling perilously under the machines to sweep beneath them or catch rats. Others were forced to work as chimney sweeps, lowered by rope down impossibly tight spaces to scrape soot for hours on end, gasping for fresh air, their knuckles scabbed and their faces blackened. Like the children from the mines, they wheezed and rasped as a result. Next to these unfortunate souls, Abe felt lucky to apprentice for Spragg. In his endless toil and crusade for self-sufficiency, he had all but forgotten the fortune that awaited him in Bristol, for that future was simply too far off to imagine.

Throughout the months and years of Abe's apprenticeship, Spragg showed Abe little patience or kindness and was frequently abusive, mostly verbally, but occasionally dispensing a slap to the head or a kick to the backside. Though Abe was generally a quick learner, he did not take to blacksmithing with any particular zeal or aplomb, though with time he became just proficient enough to avoid further abuse at the hands of Spragg.

While Abe had no appetite for the trade, the big brick forge did not fail to make an impression on him. It was not the power or grandeur of the hearth, but the clumsiness and inefficiency of the thing. Surely, a more worthy forge could be manufactured.

At this juncture, an unpleasant odor startled Abe from his ruminations, the source of which he soon discovered to be none other than Worthy Warnock's tortured feet, now exposed to the open air of the carriage, toes wiggling. Disgusted on any number of levels, Abe turned his face back to the tiny window, resuming his reflections.

At sixteen, Abe left Whitechapel and his apprenticeship with Spragg, securing himself a position with a rival, and notably more successful, blacksmith named Snell, who paid Abe a modest wage and provided him a room. Like Spragg, Snell was a bachelor and not much of a cook, though thankfully not a drinker. Snell could not be characterized as a mentor, but Abe learned enough from the man that in addition to hammering iron he was soon handling the books.

Sundays were reserved for dreaming, if you could call it that. Abe would often walk to the river and watch the filth and the rubbish wash steadily past, and formulate his plans for his future in America, where he would put his considerable means to work for him if he managed to live that long. Capital was everything. Without capital, possibility hardly existed; there was only sweat and toil and the flimsy stuff of dreams.

At eighteen Abe finally returned to Bristol to claim his family fortune, if indeed such fortune still existed. The solicitor assigned to the administration of his parents' estate was a Mr. Hickinbotham, a ghoulish persona whose sunken eyes and bloodless lips seemed to portend bad news.

"Gads, young man, we were beginning to think you'd met your end. Whyever did you not return sooner?"

"There was nothing here for me, sir."

"There most certainly was a quarterly allotment available to you, which in your absence you deferred. Needless to say, those funds are still intact. Where have you been?"

"London, sir."

"Doing what?"

"Building character, sir."

Hickinbotham eyed Abe's dirty fingernails with apparent distrust.

"Have you a plan, Mr. Seymour?"

"Yes, sir, it is my intention to go to America."

"I see," he said doubtfully. "And what awaits you in America?"

"Nothing in particular, sir. We shall see when we get there. But in America I intend to expand my fortune."

"Why not here?"

"America wants me," he said.

"I see," said Hickinbotham, more doubtfully than ever. "Well then, let us proceed with the necessary legalities."

Abe left England within six weeks and made the harrowing trip across the Atlantic to America, losing nearly twenty pounds during the twelve-week crossing. He arrived at the Port of New York with every intention of making the great city his home. But after three weeks' stay in New York, Abe found that the place did not appeal to him any more than London. All the activity and possibility of the young city could not disguise the filth and depravity and suffering it harbored — the same graft and corruption, the same dirty-faced children of the East End.

Abe hired passage to the newly claimed Illinois Territory, where he purchased forty acres from the Illinois-Wabash Company along the shore of Lake Michigan and contracted the modest home that would one day be supplanted by his sprawling manor. He purchased an additional forty acres on the shoreline, which he sold back to the Illinois-Wabash Company four years later at a tidy profit. While Illinois-Wabash would subsequently lose their holdings in a merger, a shrewd Abe Seymour negotiated a land patent to preserve his holdings on the lakefront.

Soon after, he negotiated another patent on the west side of the river, where he would eventually double, then triple his fortune in the manufacture of iron forges and furnaces, still a cottage industry in America, but a very profitable one. All of this he would achieve before the age of twenty-five. That Abraham Seymour was born into sufficient means to allow for these business opportunities in the New World was beyond debate. But that didn't make him a natural at amassing wealth. He quickly learned some hard lessons in business, and made more than a few mistakes. But he always managed to recover, and along the way honed his skills until he was shrewd in both his investments and his business interests. Along with the sufficient means to thrive, Abe Seymour possessed an undeniable knack for identifying opportunities and anticipating the needs of the people, collectively speaking.

What Abe did not possess then or now was a knack or desire for partnerships, whether in business or personal life. He had not allowed himself the intimacy of a friend since the deaths of his brother and his parents. He confided only in himself, trusted only himself, and once free of Snell answered only to himself. He had become an island. That he should meet Marilyn in his twenty-fifth year was almost a fluke.

The daughter of a printer, Marilyn Minor grew up with ink-stained hands. Raised under modest conditions, she was unaccustomed to leisurely pursuits or frivolity in any guise. Between working for her father and looking after her five younger siblings, she had no time for frivolous things. She was hardworking, straightforward, and forthcoming. In short, Marilyn Minor was a partner Abe could trust: tireless, pragmatic, and virtually guileless. Abe met her by chance at an auction where Marilyn was liquidating her recently deceased father's printing machine. So taken by Marilyn was Abe that he overpaid for the apparatus, which he had no use for.

"I'm on to you, Abraham Seymour," she said. "Don't think for one minute I'm not."

In the coming months Abe courted Marilyn dutifully, finally proposing to her one blustery afternoon along the lakefront.

"Will you have me?" he said, the wind rocketing past his ears.

"Speak up," she said.

"Will you have me?" he shouted.

"For what?" she said.

"For your husband?"

"I could do worse," she said.

Theirs was a civil union without fanfare at the Chicago courthouse. They deferred their honeymoon to a later juncture but in the end never took it. Marilyn quickly proved herself a worthy partner. Though it took her nearly six months to get used to living in the relatively luxurious and expansive environs of Abe's lakeside estate, Marilyn was up to the task. Within a year she had managed by the sheer force of her loyalty and dependability to succeed in getting closer to Abe than anybody else in his adult life, anybody since his vow of self-sufficiency in Headmaster Hollingsworth's office upon the day of his expulsion. He would have been crazy not to wed Marilyn.

And for the next thirty-three years Marilyn stood beside him. Eventually, she grew into leisure somewhat, but never frivolity. She remained for three decades a steady force in a life otherwise dominated by the vagaries and imperatives of business. Her tireless hosting of charitable events, her civic involvement, and her adept navigation of all social strata kept the Seymour name in good standing even as Abe, like a machine, kept his eyes almost exclusively on expanding his wealth and influence, knowing all the while that the pursuit was destined for emptiness, that he could never fill the hole left by a lifetime of abandonment and loss, or a history of persecution.

For decades Abe and Marilyn had practically lived separate lives, Abe forever tending to his business concerns near and far, and Marilyn back at home holding down the fort. All those years Abe had taken Marilyn for granted. It was almost like he was avoiding her. That they could not conceive a child was the great tragedy of their lives.

And now she was dying. Abe knew it in his bones. Helplessly, he'd watched her grow progressively weaker over the months, watched the light of her eyes dimming, felt her receding from him. There seemed to be nothing a procession of doctors could do. No two of them could even agree on the nature of her illness. That nobody could save her was not for lack of effort on Abe's part. But the question remained: Where was he in his wife's hour of need? Off making deals, that was where. Escaping. That Abe had left her in such a condition while he embarked on this ill-conceived business trip to Springfield shamed him. Suddenly he wished to be back in Chicago at her side.

As the carriage neared Springfield, Abe drew a deep breath and swallowed the hot lump in his throat, and vowed to be better if only given the chance.

"Our path is manifest," said Warnock, disrupting Abe's meditations. "It is destiny. And that is precisely why we cannot fail. Am I right, Seymour?"

"Er, yes, yes," said Abe.

GEORGE FLOWERS

Springfield, Illinois, 1853

Mr. Best's estate was spread out along the Sangamon River north of Springfield, a colonial in the Georgian style, four rooms over four with flanking wings on either side of two rooms over two. There were twin white pillars in front, a sprawling gambrel roof, corniced windows, and a chimney on each end. While Springfield may not have been grander than the great city of Chicago, Mr. Best's estate was certainly grander than Mr. Seymour's.

Mr. Best made good on his promise to pay George five dollars a week to run his stable, while Cora was paid an additional two and a half dollars a week to work in the house. They boarded on the property in a one-bedroom cottage out back of the stable. Though their workdays were no shorter than they had been at Mr. Seymour's estate, the lives that George and Cora led were fuller and more eventful, if only because of the newness of their surroundings.

At the end of each day, when George laid his head down beside Cora's, an act in itself that seemed miraculous given where his journey had begun, George set his right hand upon her swollen belly and felt the life burgeoning inside of her. That he was going to be a father any week now was yet another miracle.

Some Sundays Mr. Best permitted George the use of a carriage so that he and Cora could attend services at the Baptist church. One Sunday after church George and Cora drove the carriage along the river with George at the reins. That evening, they ate outdoors on a blanket beside their cottage, looking out across the Sangamon. Never in his life had George imagined that such an existence was possible. In the eyes of the law he was still a fugitive, but there he was, living and loving freely on Mr. Best's estate. It was almost too good to be true.

In September 1853, Mr. Best was scheduled to host a group of his business partners associated with his newest railroad venture. Mr. Best's business meeting was to be preceded by a grand feast and followed by a number of entertainments, the sum of which kept the entire staff busy for weeks in advance. Cora, in spite of her condition, prepared rooms and polished silver and china endlessly, while George received deliveries almost hourly in the stable, some of them perishables from as far away as New York and Philadelphia.

A week before the event, the butler, Malcolm, began gathering the staff daily for briefings to ensure that every logistical consideration would be smoothly executed. George would greet each arriving carriage at the entrance so that no guest should have to suffer the unpleasant smell or even the sight of the stable. George would proceed to open the carriage door, then stand aside. Ezra would then greet the guests at the base of the landing and lead them up the front steps. From there, Esme and Charlotte would show the guests to their rooms, as assigned by Mr. Best, briefing them on the schedule for the evening and inquiring after any present needs they might have. Franklin and Braddock would proceed to carry the luggage up the stairs. George would lead each carriage to the stable and show the drivers to their accommodations in the bunkhouse. Conspicuously pregnant Cora was to stick to the kitchen with the rest of the staff, away from the public eye.

When the day of the big event finally arrived, the staff, who had prepared meticulously, leaving not a napkin nor a spoon out of place, performed exquisitely. George greeted the first two carriages with the requisite mix of dignity and invisibility, and without so much as a hiccup, Ezra, Esme,

Charlotte, Franklin, and Braddock all proceeded to execute their charges. The elegant choreography of it all almost made serving pleasurable.

When the third carriage came rattling down the long gravel drive, nothing about the conveyance distinguished itself from the others immediately. Thus George poised himself, hands clasped behind his back, as the driver brought the team to a halt before the entrance. George swung the door open and held it thus as the first partner disembarked, a lean, gray-haired gentleman whom George recognized immediately as none other than Mr. Seymour, who walked right past without recognizing George. Ezra then greeted Mr. Seymour with a slight bow, a gesture that the latter, who appeared to be in a state approaching exhaustion, neither acknowledged nor seemed to notice. Then the second man stepped down out of the carriage with a winning smile, and George nearly fainted at the sight of him. Though the man had recently cultivated some facial hair, even as his hairline had receded slightly, there was no mistaking the Kentucky gentleman as he drew a deep breath of the humid Springfield air upon disembarking.

Had Worthy Warnock simply proceeded up the steps like Mr. Seymour, he would've probably never taken notice of George standing in the shadows, partially obscured by the carriage door. But it was Warnock's signature flair for the dramatic, his genius for pomposity, that caused him to turn back toward the river with a sweeping gesture and proclaim:

"It is the smell of promise."

When Master Worthy's eyes fell upon George for an instant, George was grateful for the ten extra pounds he was carrying, and the relatively recent salt and pepper that colored his hair. Still, a curious look, which may or may not have been recognition, crossed Master Worthy's face before he turned back toward the house and began mounting the steps in Ezra's wake. It was only upon reaching the landing at the top of the steps, when Master Worthy looked back over his shoulder toward the carriage, that George was certain Master Worthy had recognized him in spite of the weight he'd put on and the flecks of white that had in the last year appeared at his temples.

Though George managed to maintain his calm outwardly, his heart was beating at a gallop as he directed the carriage to the stable. He needed to get to Cora in the kitchen immediately. As soon as the next carriage arrived, George's absence would be felt, and that could be at any minute. George began to sweat profusely. Five minutes ago his life had been better than he ever could have reasonably expected it to be, and now, with the arrival of Worthy Warnock, every prospect looked grim. Such was his desperation and dread that George had to fight back tears in order to keep his wits about him. That in all the great wide-open expanse of America, a land so vast that steam and rail had yet to conquer it, Worthy Warnock should find his way back to Othello seemed as though it must have been by some malevolent design. What a cruel place the world was to be so small.

Once George had directed the driver to the carriage house, he hurried back to the main house in the fading light of dusk, slipping in through the servants' entrance. He made his way quickly up the stairs to the rear kitchen entrance and ducked in, surveying the chaos in search of Cora. He found her peeling potatoes, her swollen belly pressed fast against the basin. He took hold of her elbow so that she might understand the urgency of his request.

"Meet me around the side," he said.

"George, in case you can't see, I'm —"

"Now," he said. "Cora Lee, it's gotta be right now or you may never see me again."

He released his grip on her arm and hastily retreated from the kitchen, down the stairs, and out through the servants' entrance, where he hurried across the side yard. He waited for her beneath the cover of the old willow, peering out now and again from behind its massive trunk. From this vantage

413

George could see the front of the house, where Ezra waited attentively, likely already wondering what had become of George. To George's relief additional guests had yet to arrive, though that was bound to change any minute, for two more carriages were due.

A moment later, Cora emerged from the servants' entrance and looked around for George in the gathering darkness.

"Pssst," he said from behind the willow.

She strode purposefully across the yard, both hands on her belly for support.

"George Flowers, what on earth is going on here?"

"I'm in trouble, Cora Lee," he said.

"What did you do?"

"I didn't do anything," he said. "Master Worthy is here — he's seen me, and he recognized me. Oh, Cora Lee, this is bad." George could barely hold back his grief and anxiety. "I thought I made it," he said. "I really thought I made it."

"Shush now," said Cora. "Calm yourself. You heard what Mr. Best said right from the beginning when he brought you here. He said you belong to no man, George Flowers. He said you're your own man."

"Tell that to Master Worthy," he said.

Just then George heard the distant crunching of wheels over gravel as the next carriage approached from the top of the drive, its cab glowing orange in the last light of dusk.

"See here," said Cora. "Mr. Best, he paid Mr. Seymour to bring you here, isn't that right?"

"I never belonged to Mr. Seymour," said George. "I was not his to bargain with. I only came back to Mr. Seymour's because I had to see you. Master Worthy owns me."

"Maybe you can pay him yourself," said Cora.

"I can't buy my freedom. Even if I did have that kind of money, Master Worthy would never have it."

"Maybe Mr. Best will help us," she said. "We can work it off."

"I'm a fugitive, Cora Lee," he said. "Ain't nothing for a fugitive to do but run. We've got to flee this place and find somewhere else."

"But, George, look at me," she said. "I can barely walk. This child wants out of me. I can't run from nobody."

"If they catch me they'll just as like kill me as anything," he said.

And even as he said it George watched as Master Warnock emerged on the front landing, conferring with none other than Mr. Best himself, the former motioning toward the stable.

George swallowed what felt like a lump of coal.

"You stay," said George. "I'll come back for you."

"No," she said. "I'll pack my things."

"We ain't got no time to pack things," he said.

"I need my papers," she said. "And we gotta have our money."

"Hurry up, then, woman."

George huddled behind the shelter of the big willow, watching Worthy Warnock and Mr. Best as they descended the landing. They were already crossing the side yard toward the stable when George and Cora took flight into the Illinois night, Cora waddling as best she could at eight months pregnant, clutching to her chest only those meager possessions she could gather at a moment's notice, among them her papers and what little money they'd managed to save since their arrival in Springfield.

Harried by the possibility of George's capture, they crossed the wide field to the south in the moonlight, Cora laboring under her burden. They reached the road and crossed it into the trees, where they navigated by the moonlight penetrating the cover of the forest.

"We crazy to run off like this," Cora said, gasping for breath.

"We got no choice," said George. "We got to get as far away from here as we can."

"And how we going to do that, George Flowers, when we ain't got but thirteen dollars and I'm so big with child I can't hardly walk?"

"We'll find a way," said George.

"A way to where?"

"North," said George. "Or maybe west."

"And what are we gonna do there?"

"We going to make a life for our little girl," said George.

"What makes you so sure it's a girl?"

"Intuition," said George.

"Same intuition that makes you think we going to make some kind of life up north out of nothing?"

"Maybe so," said George. "You got any better ideas?"

"Maybe a better idea is I ought to have stayed back in Chicago in the first place, or leastwise at Mr. Best's."

"You're probably right about that," he said. "Maybe you ought to turn back."

"No," she said. "This baby wants a father."

They hurried on in silence, emerging from the woods and crossing into the next field. To their relief, they heard no dogs. Behind them, Mr. Best's estate was well out of sight. Before them in the distance they could just barely make out the string of glowing lamplight that comprised the city of Springfield.

"Where are we going, George? Curfew can't be far off. We can't just walk around the city all night to no purpose. We've got to get us indoors."

"We're going to Cobb's," he said.

"Why Cobb's?"

"Because the Cobbs is good Christians, and I know they'll take us in tonight."

"And then what?"

"Will Cobb, I hear he knows a man who can help folks that's on the run and looking for freedom."

"On thirteen dollars?"

"There's more than money to make a thing happen," said George.

They skirted the center of town. Will Cobb was a free Black who owned a barber emporium downtown, where some of the city's wealthiest white men went for their grooming and their gossip. As a result there wasn't much Will Cobb didn't know about the comings and goings of the city of Springfield, not to mention its inner workings. Though he wasn't part of the so-called colored aristocracy, there wasn't a man who attended the Baptist church who knew more about the events of the nation and the larger world than Will Cobb.

Will lived with his wife and six children in a ground-floor apartment on the far edge of town. The moon had already sunk back down below the horizon when George tapped on the Cobbs' front door. After a moment, Will himself appeared on the stoop in his nightshirt, holding a candle aloft.

"George Flowers, that you?" he said softly

in the quavering light.

"Sure enough," whispered George.

"What you doing out at this hour, son? You supposed to be indoors by now."

"We're in trouble, Will. Can you take us in for the night?"

"Of course," said Will. "Hurry on in here. Mind, the children are sleeping."

They tiptoed into the apartment in a puddle of candlelight and stopped in the living room, where a number of sleeping bodies were scattered in the darkness.

"As you can see, we ain't got much to offer you in the way of room," said Will. "But we can make a place for you right here on the floor, and I'll fetch what I can in the way of blankets. Can't promise you a pillow, though."

"God bless you," said Cora.

Will Cobb lowered the candle a little bit to get a look at her distended belly.

"You're not fixing to have that baby tonight, are you?"

"No, sir," she said. "I'm still a few weeks out."

"Anything I should know right off about this trouble of yours, George?"

"I'm a fugitive. They after me."

As if on cue, one of the children stirred on the floor, but in the ensuing silence settled back to sleep.

"Fugitive?" said Will. "Why, you ain't even

a slave."

"Not anymore," said George. "I'm a free man to my way of thinking, but not in the eyes of the law. I ran off in Urbana and never looked back. Never had any trouble until tonight."

Even in the dim light George could see the gravity written plainly on Will's face.

"We got a lot to talk about," Will Cobb said softly. "But I suppose it'd be wise if we wait until morning. You two hungry?"

"No, sir," said George.

"You?" said Will to Cora.

"I'm fine, thank you, sir."

Will left for one of the back rooms and returned shortly with a pair of well-worn blankets, piled one atop the other. He then retreated to the kitchen and came back with a half loaf of bread and a drinking tin.

"Sorry I can't offer you more at this hour," said Will, presenting Cora with the bread. "Whether or not you're hungry, you ought to eat in your condition, and drink some water."

"We can never repay you for your kindness," said Cora.

"I knew we could count on you," said George.

"We got a lot of figuring to do in the morning," said Will. "But the two of you best rest up for now."

As soon as Will took his leave for the back of the apartment, George and Cora laid themselves out side by side on the floor. Almost immediately Cora fell asleep. George, however, was not so fortunate. In spite of his exhaustion and the late hour, his heart and mind were racing. He lay awake most of the night on his back, his thoughts speeding out in front of him like a runaway locomotive.

Having dodged slave catchers in Chicago on no fewer than three occasions, George must have been cursed for Master Worthy to stumble upon him some hundred miles and two years since he ran off. Surely it was his destiny to be caught and thrown back into slavery, no matter his talents, or aspirations, or goodness of heart. He was just a thing, a commodity, a living, breathing resource to be exploited.

Lying in the darkness of Will Cobb's crowded living room, his expectant wife sleeping beside him, George vowed never to be objectified again so long as he still had breath in him. He would not get caught. He would find his way to freedom once and for all, if it meant Canada or the western frontier. If America would not grant him his freedom, he would steal it, so that future generations of Flowerses might know the condition of freedom as he had never known it — as something they were born into.

In the morning George and Cora consulted with Will Cobb in the confines of the tiny kitchen. George told him about his encounter with Master Worthy at Mr. Best's estate, and how they'd run off.

"He's bound to be looking for me," said George.

"What if you could buy your freedom?"

"I'd be a long ways from affording such a thing," said George. "And knowing Master Worthy, I doubt he would allow for it. Master Worthy fancies himself to be a sympathizer of the Negro, but he's far from it. He's deep down mean-spirited on account he never had to do anything on his own, which don't even make sense. You'd figure that would make a body agreeable. But Master Worthy, he relished owning me. He liked nothing more than to have me tend his rotting feet. If he ever manages to get his hands on me, I'll be lucky to come out of it half the man I am now. No, there's no other way that I can see. We've got to get us north, or maybe west."

"Maybe you should wait for the arrival of the child," said Will. "Lay low right here among us."

"It's a generous offer," said George. "But to my mind we'd best move as soon as possible."

"You'll be lucky to make it upstate before that baby comes," said Will. "The trail is no place to have a baby."

"So long as it's the trail to freedom, it's as good a place as any," said George.

"And what about you, Cora?" said Will.

"What do you think about all this? You're a free woman. Maybe it's best you stay right here until George finds himself settled."

"I won't let him leave without me," she said. "When I made the decision to put in with George, I made it the whole way."

Will ran two weary hands over his face. "Well, then, I guess it's settled."

"Then, you can help us?" said Cora.

"I believe I can try," said Will Cobb, the lines of his face furrowed with worry.

MALIK FLOWERS

Portland, Oregon, 2019

Sleep was having nothing to do with Malik on Thursday night. The promise of his future was so palpable, his impatience to live it so urgent, that it seemed to course through his every muscle and hum in his every nerve ending. His harried thoughts were not unwelcome. On the contrary, they were irresistible, arriving feverishly one on top of the other quicker than he could catalog them, until the velocity and pitch of his jubilation threatened to overwhelm him.

As he shifted from side to side on the mattress, endlessly flipping his pillow, the compulsion to unburden his imagination of this budding promise began to ache within him. If he could acknowledge his good fortune aloud, perhaps it would relieve the pressure. He considered waking up his mom, but that seemed unfair — cruel, even — knowing she'd never get back to sleep. He thought about calling Haskins, or A-Jack, or Eddie, but the thought of unloading all his excitement on one of them seemed rather heartless. They were all invariably supportive and unyielding in their belief in Malik, yet whenever he discussed his future with the guys he felt like he was rubbing it in somehow, for every one of them had harbored the same dream most of their lives, and only Malik would ever enjoy the opportunity to realize it. Haskins and A-Jack might have the skills but not the size or the grades to play past junior college, and Eddie would be lucky to crack the starting five next year.

If Malik could have called Kayla Ramsey, he would have. The thought of calling Kayla quickened his pulse still further. Kayla, always so poised and in control. Surely the sound of her voice, or better yet, the graze of her elbow or the flash of her smile, would've had a soothing effect on him. Kayla would know how to untangle all the excitement coursing through him; she would master it like a trigonometric equation. But calling Kayla Ramsey, who in all likelihood had no inkling of his burgeoning affection, was not an option, especially not in the middle of the night.

Finally, Malik rolled over and plucked his phone off the nightstand and stole out to the tiny balcony in his T-shirt and underwear. All but shivering against the chill air, he dialed before he lost his nerve.

"Malik, is that you?" said Coach M groggily. "What is it, boy, is something wrong?"

"No, Coach, nothing to worry about," he said. "I know it's late, I'm sorry I woke you."

"What's on your mind, son? You in some kind of jam?"

"Nah, Coach, nothing like that."

"Girl troubles?"

"You know me, Coach, I pretty much steer clear of the ladies."

"You got a case of the nerves?"

"Not exactly, sir," said Malik. "I guess I just wanted to say thank you. You know, for everything you've done for me."

"Well, I must say you chose a strange hour to thank me, Malik, but I'll take it. I'm damn proud of you, son. You're more than just a baller, you're a fine young man. You sure you're okay?"

"Yeah, Coach, more than okay. I don't even know how to describe it. It's like a shot of adrenaline that won't stop. It's like that high after winning a big game, except I'm not coming down, and the game hasn't happened yet. I thought maybe if I just talked to somebody I might be able to settle down and get some sleep. I gotta be rested for tomorrow. I don't know, maybe I should run around the block or something."

"Don't do that," said Coach M. "For God's sakes, not at one in the morning."

"Coach, something big is gonna happen, I

just know it, I can feel it."

"I don't doubt that, son, not for one second," Coach M said. "But don't forget to keep your feet on the ground. You didn't get here overnight, and you're not likely to be delivered anywhere overnight. Everything is a process, everything has an order. Right now, it probably feels like everything is happening all at once."

"Yeah, exactly," Malik said.

"Well, it's not," said Coach M. "It's a process like anything else. You know this. There's a protocol, a sequence of preparedness. Your job, the key to your success, is to trust the process, son, to engage it one step at a time, and don't get ahead of yourself. And right now you need to rest your body and your mind, so that you're better prepared for the next step."

The familiarity of Coach M's voice, the unflagging consistency of his messaging, eased the nervous tension a bit.

"You always know what to say, Coach."

"Ha, tell that to my wife," he said.

Just then, a light snapped on in the apartment, puddling on the little balcony, and Malik knew he'd awoken his mother.

"Well, Coach, I'll let you go," Malik said. "I just wanted to thank you. And now I guess I owe you another thank-you."

"I'm glad you called," said Coach M. "You get some rest, Malik. Trust the process."

"Aight, Coach."

Malik found his mom standing in the kitchen wrapped in her puffy white bathrobe, looking drained in the light of the refrigerator.

"Boy, ain't you got no sense? What are you standing outside in your underwear for? You wanna catch your death?"

"Sorry I woke you, Ma."

"You think I was sleeping? Pfff. Child, you don't know me very well. Who were you talking to at this hour?"

"Just Coach M."

"Last-minute advice?"

"Something like that, yeah."

"So, you can't sleep either, huh?" she said.

"No, ma'am," he said. "I just can't seem to turn my thoughts off."

"Well, you best figure out how pretty quick. We got a train to catch tomorrow."

"I know it," he said.

"You nervous, is that it?"

"No, excited more like. Ma, you ever feel like everything is happening all at once?"

"Yessir, every time I pay the bills."

"No, really. Like back when you were young did you ever f—"

"Malik Flowers, I'm thirty-three years old and you make me out to be an old woman — stop that."

"I didn't mean it like that. I just meant was there ever a moment when your whole life

428

felt like it was gonna change overnight?"

"How about the day I got pregnant with you? You want to talk about a game changer. I was six months younger than you, barely a junior in high school. Think about that for a minute."

"Were you scared?"

"Of course I was scared."

"You were happy, though, right? That you were pregnant with me."

"I was feeling a lot of things, believe me."

"But happiness was one of them, right?"

"Child, it's nearly one thirty in the morning. We've got no business talking about ancient history at this hour, not tonight of all nights."

"You weren't happy at all?"

"Of course I was happy. And I was even happier when I saw you for the first time. Now, get yourself to bed," she said. "We've got the rest of our lives to have this conversation."

THE CHEN-MURPHYS

Northern California, 2018

With the Prius packed so tight there was hardly room to move, the Chen-Murphys left San Francisco for McMinnville, Oregon, on a Wednesday morning in mid-August just as the fog was burning off south of Market. Jenny drank in the city around her as though it were the last time she'd ever see it, the skyscrapers huddled in the bowl of the Financial District, as though they were colluding; the hills rearing up beyond, Nob and Russian, and the most distinguished of all, Telegraph, with its shaggy green hillside, Coit Tower adorning its top like an ancient birthday candle. And to the south Bernal Heights, a towering presence above Castro and the Mission, the red prongs of the TV tower reaching skyward in triplicate out of the bald saddle of Mount Sutro.

Fortunately, Jenny had plenty of time to drink it all in, for, as always, traffic was bottlenecking at the junction of 280 and 101 as they inched their way through the industrial flats. It took nearly forty-five minutes to reach 80, and twenty more to make the bridge.

"This sucks," said Winston, wedged in the backseat. "Why didn't we just fly?"

"Somebody's got to bring the car to McMinnville," said Todd. "Besides, it's all about the journey."

"Well this journey sucks," said Winston.

"Yeah?" said Todd. "You think this is bad? My ancestors had to cross the Atlantic in coffin ships."

"What about my ancestors?" said Jenny. "They had to cross the Pacific. That's twice as far."

"Yeah, but we crossed the entire continent to get west," Todd said. "You guys landed three miles from here."

"So?"

"So, our journey was actually harder."

"Ha!" said Jenny. "But they practically rolled out the red carpet for you when you got here. My people were treated like animals."

"What are you talking about? Your people practically owned the city."

"Oh?" said Jenny. "O'Farrell, O'Shaughnessy, Geary, McAllister — where are the streets called Wang?"

"Um, Chinatown?"

"Okay," said Winston. "You guys win. This is stupid. Can you guys not argue?"

"You're right," said Jenny. "It is stupid."

"How much further?" said Tyler.

"Only about ten hours," said Todd.

"You mean, about ten days the way we're going," said Winston.

The truth was, part of Jenny was grateful for the traffic. Her face to the side window, she cataloged every detail of the city for future consumption.

Todd, though, was itching to leave the city in the rearview mirror.

"List of things I won't miss about California, number four thousand three hundred and thirty-eight," he said. "The traffic."

Indeed, the gridlock persisted through Oakland and Berkeley. They were halfway to Walnut Creek before they were driving the speed limit.

In spite of Todd's frequent assurances, in spite of the irrefutable financial advantages and the vastly affordable housing market, in spite of the fact that Jenny had already lost eight pounds not eating in airports and felt infinitely more energetic since leaving her job in July, she remained uneasy about the relocation. She wasn't quite ready to stop shaving her legs and start eating at unironic diners. She was still a city girl, and in spite of Todd's insistence McMinnville was not a city — it was a town half the size of Stockton, a mere fraction of the size of Sacramento. And it wasn't even in California. It was in the cultural backwater that was Oregon, a bastion of bad Chinese food, a state with only seven electoral votes and three professional sports franchises, one of them being soccer, which barely counted. Compared to California, Oregon was still a territory, an outpost, a stopover on the way to somewhere else.

"List of things I won't miss about California, number four thousand three hundred and thirty-nine," said Todd, as though in direct response to Jenny's thoughts. "Walnut Creek."

They stopped in Vallejo for lunch at an Olive Garden, in a sprawling mall off the interstate.

"Are we still in California?" said Tyler as they crossed the parking lot on foot in the furnacelike heat.

"Yes," said Todd.

"No duh," said Winston.

"How much further?" said Tyler.

"About nine hours," Todd said.

"How many miles is that?"

"A lot."

"Do we have a house yet?" said Tyler as they stepped into the immediate relief of the air-conditioned foyer.

"Not yet, honey," said Jenny.

"So, we're homeless?"

"Not exactly," Jenny said.

After lunch, loaded with carbs and Alfredo sauce, the boys fell asleep in the backseat as

Jenny and Todd traveled mostly in silence through Williams and Maxwell and Willows, Orland and Corning and Red Bluff. With each flat, miserable, sun-scorched little town they passed on their way north up the long valley, Jenny had the same thought: They could do a lot worse than McMinnville.

"Are we still in California?" said Tyler upon awakening just south of Redding.

"Yes, honey."

"That sucks," said Tyler. "I want to be in Oregon."

"Me too," said Jenny, half lying.

Late in the afternoon they started climbing the north end of the basin, and the great white dome of Mount Shasta took center stage out the front windshield. They wound their way into the foothills, Shasta's dome like a beacon in front of them, Winston and Tyler reading the signs through Lakehead, and Castella, and Dunsmuir, and finally Weed.

"Weed?" said Winston. "Really? Are you sure we're not in Oregon yet?"

They stopped for dinner in Medford at the Cobbler, which they later all agreed had been a big mistake. It was dusk by the time they hit Central Point, and everybody was gassy. They stopped briefly to fuel up in Gold Hill and were on their way again, the boys farting every twenty seconds from Grants Pass to Roseburg. They drove nearly a hundred miles with the wind whistling in through the cracked windows. Above them, away from the lights, the stars were showing like they never showed in the city, the Milky Way a wide brushstroke of pale luminescence spread across the sky.

"This doesn't suck," said Todd.

"Are we in Oregon yet?"

"Yes, we are," said Todd, sounding about as satisfied as Jenny could remember him sounding in years.

Looking out the window at the dumbfounding spectacle of the night sky, Jenny could not ignore a distinct sense of possibility written there, a thousand possibilities. All her anxiety regarding her unknown future dissipated in an instant. Cracking her window halfway, Jenny set her face to the night air and took a big breath of the possibility.

"Things I like about Oregon, number one," she said. "The stars."

Jenny reached across the seat for Todd. He took his right hand off the wheel and clutched Jenny's hand in his own and gave it a firm squeeze.

"Almost home," he said.

WALTER BERGEN

Oregon, 2019

The Coast Starlight began picking up momentum as soon as the train cleared the station, the engine reaching maximum speed about two miles outside of town. The bureau called shortly thereafter for a report, at which point Walter estimated the drift to be somewhere around nine inches. None of the platforms were shoveled. So far, no bucking from the brakes, the wipers were fully functional, and Walter wasn't experiencing any slip-slide. Now and again a side wind caused the train to shudder.

About ten minutes outside Salem, Macy ducked his head into the cab again.

"Mr. Punctuality," he said.

"That's me," said Walter.

"Jesus, I'd kill for a cigarette right now," Macy said.

"Might be able to sneak one in at Portland if they go over the brakes."

"What I need to do is quit," he said.

"You said it, not me," said Walter.

"Yeah, I know," said Macy. "It ain't easy, though. Believe me, I've tried."

Despite all the years he'd worked with Macy, Walter didn't really know much about the man besides the fact that Macy had been talking about quitting the coffin nails for over a decade. And yet, his fingertips continued to yellow, his voice grew raspier by the year, and his uniform continued to stink of stale tobacco, though nobody had ever complained, at least not formally.

But what did Walter really know about Macy at the end of the day? What was Macy's biggest fear? What was the worst thing that ever happened to him? Was he a Protestant, a Catholic, an agnostic? How did he feel about Walter's lesbian daughter?

Though Walter could answer not one of these questions, he felt nonetheless bound by familiarity to Macy, just as he did to these diesel trains and the lovely old stations up and down the West Coast from San Luis Obispo to Bellingham. It was hard for Walter to imagine a life without these reliable benchmarks. The closer his day came to ending, the more he resented the reality of retirement, which he'd begun to view as the end of his usefulness.

He was certain he still had something to offer the world. But according to his own daughter, Walter had already had his day. According to Wendy it was time for Walter and the rest of the old white guys to step aside and get out of the way. Walter was part of what Wendy called the patriarchy, another concept Walter was certain she had adopted from Kit, the Californian, a woman who deferred to no one, who sharpened her teeth on anyone who didn't agree with her. Ideologically speaking, Walter managed to sympathize with Kit for the most part. Women had a tougher go of it in virtually every way. Hard to argue with that. They got paid less. They rarely got the credit they deserved. That their reproductive rights were even an issue in the twenty-first century made Walter ashamed to be an old white guy. But it wasn't actually Walter legislating women's bodies, it wasn't Walter paying them less or belittling their accomplishments. Kit had to see that. If Kit truly loved Wendy she'd have to recognize that Walter had done his part to shape the person that was Wendy, wouldn't she? Kit would have to acknowledge that Walter had helped account for Wendy's self-confidence, that he'd empowered Wendy every day of her life, that he'd never judged her or tried to change the person Wendy wanted to be, even if Wendy's ideals were confusing to Walter. So why did Kit always make Walter feel like the bad guy? What had Walter ever done to oppress anybody?

It would have been a lot easier to give

Wendy away to somebody he actually liked. And Walter tried to like Kit, he really did, which was more than Walter could say for Kit, who never seemed to give Walter much of a chance. Apparently it wasn't enough being a decent husband, friend, and father. Never mind that Walter gave blood at every drive. Never mind that he pledged money to PBS annually and shopped locally, and even recognized meatless Monday, if only to appease his vegan daughter. Never mind that Walter had voted for Obama twice. Somehow Walter had become the villain.

The snow started coming down harder around McMinnville. Walter switched the lights to high at the crossing and sounded the horn, its prolonged bleat muffled by snowpack. About three miles south of McMinnville the snow started coming in sideways. For the first time the train began to experience a little slippage as the wheels tried to find steady purchase. The side wind was accounting for a little wobble. In spite of Walter's efforts to look through it, the snow began to play tricks on his eyes.

Walter took a deep breath and redoubled his focus. But hard as he tried to concentrate, his misgivings about Kit continued to harass him. The problem with Kit was that everything was political and she refused to engage in civil discourse. Political action, the way Walter conceived of it, was supposed to be grounded in debate and diplomacy and compromise, and yet Kit would not so much as listen to dissenting opinions, no matter how well reasoned the arguments. It was as though she was constitutionally incapable of compromise or even civil discussion, whether the subject was social justice or caterers. Walter might have forgiven Kit all of this had he not felt that Kit was actively turning his daughter against him.

Thankfully the bureau called again for an update, chasing off Walter's misgivings like pigeons. Increased wind. Increased snowfall. A little slip-slide. Drift approaching a foot. But no windfall on the tracks and no ice. Walter was still running at max, and on schedule to the minute.

Oh, the holy schedule, that stern master, the standard by which every train and every engineer was doomed to be measured. All other considerations defaulted to the schedule in the end. Even safety. For time was money. If only Walter's life could adhere to such an uncompromising imperative as the ever-pressing schedule. Think of what Walter might have achieved in his lifetime had he shed every other concern but the singular consideration requiring timely passage from point A to point B without a moment's diversion. Maybe that was what it took to be great: an inexhaustible subservience to the almighty schedule. If one could avoid all diversions,

440

there was no limit to what one might accomplish. What if he had buckled down and applied himself harder? What might he have been? Where might he be right now besides on the eve of a retirement that was all but forced?

For the fifth time that day Macy came to Walter's rescue, ducking into the cab.

"Wally, you're an animal," he said. "You better slow down or we'll hit Portland ahead of schedule."

"That's the idea," said Walter. "So you can choke down that cancer stick."

"Nah, I'm quitting," said Macy.

"Good for you."

"Maybe not today," said Macy, gnawing at a cuticle.

"Screw it," said Walter. "You can smoke right here as far as I'm concerned. It's my last day, what are they going to do, fire me? Just blow it out the back."

"Ha, wouldn't that be nice?" said Macy, ducking out of the cab. "I'm the one they'd fire."

No sooner had Macy left again than Walter wished he could've enticed him to stay, so that Macy might have actually smoked a cigarette in the cab. Hell, Walter might have even taken a drag for the hell of it, and he and Macy could have shared a moment. Who knew, it might have made for an amusing little anecdote by the coffee machine. Anything to assure that the name Walter Bergen might be summoned after he was gone.

At 2:23, soon after the train hurtled north-ward across the county line, downtown Portland revealed itself in a blurry panorama, the hills of Southwest all covered in white, cradling the skyline in their open palm. With the low sky pressing down upon them, the towers of steel and glass seemed to huddle together for warmth, while at their feet the slate-gray Willamette cleaved the city in two. As Walter skirted the river at a crawl, only the slow rhythm of the rails and the hypnotic thrum of the wipers marked the silence. The snow fluttered down like confetti as Walter sounded the horn. Macy's scratchy voice came over the intercom, announcing their impending arrival. Moments later, the engine sighed as the Coast Starlight pulled into Union Station right on schedule.

NORA BERGEN

Chicago, 1857

Nora Bergen's seventeenth birthday passed without fanfare. That she remembered the date herself was no small miracle, as her birth seemed an occasion of so little significance. She paused only once in her otherwise routine workday to contemplate the milestone. Mopping the downstairs corridor, the dreary light of late afternoon funneling through the lone window at the end of the hallway, Nora wondered whether somewhere in the great unknown West, in Iowa or Nebraska or even California, her twin brother's adoptive family was recognizing this day, perhaps with a small cake, or a gift of new trousers, or a hat to keep the sun off his face. Nora hoped desperately so, and tried to imagine such a scene. Were there other children in her brother's adoptive family? Master Searles would divulge nothing, but Nora liked to think so. That Finn, already having lived, and perhaps still living, in the isolation of his silence, should ever know the loneliness that Nora had known in the years since their separation was almost too painful to contemplate. In that moment, in the murky light of the corridor, gripping her mop firmly, Nora held Finn as close as she could in her heart, willing the invisible force of her devotion down the hallway and out the window and west across the plains, over endless fields of wheat, straight into the heart of her brother.

Nora thought of Cora and George Flowers nearly every day, trying to imagine their lives together in Springfield. Did they have children? She liked to imagine them living their lives just as George had promised: in a little house of their own, going to church every Sunday. She liked to imagine them on a riverboat, Cora wearing a white dress and a white hat, clutching a parasol like a proper lady in a novel, and George wearing a fine gray suit of clothes. Oh, if only they would send her a letter. That they did not write could only mean that Nora was forgotten to them, a thought so disheartening that she was forced to chase it from her mind. It seemed that to be alone was Nora's destiny. Whatever companionship she managed to foster would only take leave of her in the end.

Meanwhile big changes were afoot at the Seymour estate. A week before Christmas, Mrs. Seymour died suddenly. Edmund descended the stairs late one afternoon to inform the staff. Preparations were to be made for guests soon arriving to pay their condolences. Despite the somber occasion, the kitchen and the laundry were buzzing with activity the rest of the afternoon and through the following day, when the guests began to arrive in considerable numbers, carriage after carriage pulling into the stable.

Nora was among those serving the mourners. Even the grieving must take nourishment, and so there came from the kitchen an unending flow of stuffed eggs and jellies, olives and nuts and radishes. Mr. Seymour touched none of it. In fact he seemed to be absent through the majority of the proceedings. From his quarters in the rear, he drifted into the great room every few hours and shook hands dazedly before retreating back to his isolation. Each time he seemed as though he were floating somewhere above himself, a stricken look Nora recognized all too well from her grieving mother. Seeing Mr. Seymour this way offered Nora the unlikely occasion to feel sorry for the man who had stripped her of her brother, who had exiled her to the downstairs and made a servant of her. But to see Mr. Seymour like that, present but unreachable, alive but numb to every possibility, was heartbreaking. Never had it been clearer to Nora that wealth could not solve everything, that all the coddling and convenience and comfort of abundance, all the dividends and profits in the world, could not solve the problems of loneliness and loss.

Though Christmas graced them with just enough snow to be festive, the holiday was a somber affair around the Seymour estate. No more carriages came or went from the stable, no caroling was to be heard from above, no gifts came down the stairwell, nor loads of freshly soiled linens. And for the first time since Nora's arrival, there was no grand party to christen the New Year.

In the coming months Mr. Seymour postponed all of his business travels and confined himself mostly to the rear quarters upstairs, where sometimes late at night Nora could hear his footsteps above her room. Were it not for the staff, the estate surely would have gone to seed. That Mr. Seymour managed to keep himself relatively shaven and somewhat in order was astonishing given the apparent state of his mind, which seemed to roam of its own agency anywhere and everywhere but the present. The one thing that seemed to reach him at all was his beloved fox terriers, whom he watched from the window, his arms crossed behind his back, occasionally venturing out of doors to stand in their midst and talk to them, though never to frolic. Nora was given to wonder what it was he said to the dogs, but she never drew near enough to eavesdrop.

Mr. Seymour's behavior extended into

spring, whereupon he began taking to the outdoors more frequently as the weather improved. If ever there was a man in need of fresh air, it seemed to be Mr. Seymour. He wandered about the estate in a fog, paying no particular attention to anything, often with a dog or three in tow. After weeks on end of this conduct, he finally seemed to take a turn for the better. You could see it in his step, the slightest of bounces. You could see it in his carriage, shoulders upright, and in his eyes, once more engaging the world. Sometimes he would pause at the stable long enough to share a brief exchange with Willem the stableman, who was good with the horses but in no way George's equal as a companion.

One fine day when the lake was flat and calm, reflecting a cloudless sky back up at itself, Mr. Seymour, whom she knew to watch her from the window upon occasion, surprised Nora in the yard, where she was hanging linens to dry.

"Hello, sir," she said. "You gave me quite a fright."

"I apologize for that," he said. "The day is magnificent, isn't it?"

"Yes, sir. You can't help but notice."

"No, you can't," he said, gazing out over the lake. "A long, cruel winter we had."

"Yes, sir, and, well, I'm sorry for your loss, sir, if I may say so. I hardly knew Mrs. Seymour, but it is clear that you loved her very much."

"She was a complex woman," he said. "But yes, I did, and thank you."

"I'm Nora, sir."

"Indeed, I know who you are, young lady."

"You do?"

"It was I who brought you here against my wife's wishes. I've been following your progress since the day you arrived here."

"You have?"

"Indeed, I have."

Nora had no clue how to respond to this news, and retreated into silence just as a stiff gust of wind off the lake set the linens to flapping crazily.

Mr. Seymour closed his eyes, and seemed to enjoy the wind and the silence.

Why? Why had he brought her here against her own will and the will of his wife? Who benefited from this arrangement?

"If I may be so bold, why did you adopt me, sir?" she said, surprising herself. "If it was not a daughter you wanted, why did you not simply hire another housemaid?

"But I did want a daughter," he said. "And so did Marilyn. But she wanted her own, and I could not give her that."

"And she didn't want me," said Nora.

"Though it shames me to say it, there is some truth to it," said Mr. Seymour, leveling his eyes sympathetically upon Nora. "I made arrangements to bring you here because I believed it would please my wife. An orphan myself, I suppose I thought you might save us all. It just seemed right."

"But . . . ?"

"I was wrong. My mistake was arranging for your adoption before I ever told Marilyn. When I broached the possibility of adoption upon the eve of your arrival, she was resistant to the idea. In fact, she refused to so much as entertain the possibility. She said that if God had intended her to have a child, he would have granted her one. I tried to persuade her further, appealing to her sympathies, citing the possibility of an unfortunate child, say, a young immigrant girl for whom we might provide a better life. But Marilyn wouldn't have it."

"And so you abandoned me to a life of toil as one of your servants? And never once did your wife wonder at my presence here? You never dared to tell her of the little girl whom you snatched from the only family she had?"

"And for that I am ashamed."

"How could you do it? And why did you not take any interest in me yourself if you were the one responsible for bringing me here?"

"I cannot answer that except to say that I have judged myself harshly for not doing more for you. God knows, it's a cruel enough world for the dispossessed. I deeply regret

449

any further misery I have caused you by bringing you here."

Nora wanted to berate him for separating her from her brother. What gave him the right? But she held her tongue and stewed in a silent rage as Mr. Seymour looked back over the lake.

"I was an orphan myself from the age of fourteen," he said. "Did you know that?"

"No," she said, leaving off the requisite *sir.*

"Of course not, how would you?" he said. "My parents were killed in a house fire. If I am to believe certain people in Gloucester, my mother may have killed my father in the fire, but I shall never know for certain. It seems she blamed him for the loss of my brother, Silas, who was the light of her life."

Nora almost softened at the horror of this confession, but she could not forgive Seymour for bringing her there under false pretenses.

"Of course, it wasn't my father's fault," observed Mr. Seymour. "How could it possibly be? Silas had weak blood from the start, but a strong heart, mind you. He may have been an angel. But none of that mattered in Gloucester, any more than it mattered in Poland. They wouldn't let my mother bury Silas in the Gloucester cemetery."

"Why?"

"Because he was a Jew. No matter that he didn't practice, no matter that he was just a boy. I believe it might have pushed my mother over the edge."

"That's terrible," said Nora, letting her guard down.

"When Silas died I abandoned part of myself. And when my parents died it was as if my life had been erased. Those more than anything else are the events that made me the man I am today."

"And who is that?" said Nora.

"A fair question," he said. "What do you think I am?"

"I think you're a very wealthy man."

"That I am, by the measure of most people, but not in spirit, child. No, my spirit was dashed out like a flame before I ever came to this country."

"Why did you come?"

"For the same reason I imagine your people came," he said. "There was nothing left for me there, not on the whole continent it seemed. A Jew in Europe was unwanted. I was told that America welcomed the Jews, and what choice did I have but to believe it? I was a young man, a few years older than you. But unlike you I was a young man of means. Here I could make something different of myself. I could distinguish myself as someone different. I could rewrite my history."

"Is such a thing possible?" said Nora.

"Perhaps not."

"Sir, I can't help but wonder, why are you telling me all of this now?" said Nora.

"That, too, is a fair question," he said. "It is true I have been unfair to you all along."

"Why did you take me away from me brother?" Nora blurted. "You must have known I had a twin, they must have told you! Banish me from your home for saying it, but who would do such a cruel thing?"

Mr. Seymour looked somberly at his feet as a ringing silence gathered around him. After a moment, to Nora's shock and surprise, he began to weep.

"I did so against my own better judgment," he said. "It was that clod Searles who convinced me. He said you were an exceptional child and that the boy, your brother, would come to no good, that he would only drag you down in this life. He convinced me I'd be doing you a favor."

"That's not true!" she said.

"I can see that now," he said miserably. "God knows, I should have seen it then. Or maybe I did and I was only being dishonest with myself. Oh, child, I don't know why I do the things I do. Only in business do I seem able to reason. Only in the matter of dollars and cents, risks and rewards, do I seem to make sound decisions. You are right to despise me, for I am despicable. There is nothing I could ever do to repay you for what I have done to you. Perhaps you would have been better off in that dreary asylum."

"It is hardly less dreary here, sir, not since Cora and George have left. Not since Clifton died."

"The Negroes were the closest thing you had to a family," observed Mr. Seymour.

"I do not think of them as Negroes, not anymore. I think of them as the people who cared for me. But even they have forsaken me."

Nora broke down in sobs until Mr. Seymour, wiping the tears from his own eyes, took her about the shoulders and pulled her close, a little awkwardly.

"I am sorry, child," he said. "God as my witness, I am sorry."

Though Nora allowed his embrace, even welcomed it if only for the warmth of another body, she despised Seymour at that moment. She despised him for depriving her of Finn, and she despised him for the presumption that he had the power to improve her life, then or ever. Above all, she resented that he had used her, first as his servant, and now as his confessor.

"Help me find me brother," she said.

"Yes," he said. "Yes, that's it. Searles, the lout, I will press him for information. I will do everything within my means."

It seemed to Nora that Mr. Seymour looked suddenly lighter and more alive at the thought, as though he had found a way to deliver himself.

FINN BERGEN

Iowa, 1856

A dark cloud hung over the Vogel farm as September passed into October. Even Hans's optimism was no match for the failure of his crops. All his hard work and determination and faith in the land had yielded nothing but exhaustion and heartache. What little was left of their already meager savings would surely not be enough to sustain them through the long winter ahead. And still there was the thankless work of prepping the fields for next spring, once a hopeful task, now a grim drudgery that felt as if they were merely going through the motions.

That Finn had rediscovered his voice was one of the few bright spots in the Vogels' lives as the days grew shorter and the prairie winds grew colder.

"Next year will be better, Papa," he assured Hans, hurling a clump of stubble aside.

"If we live that long," said Hans. "You are right, Finn. We'd be better off to sell the land.

I'm no farmer; I was once a bookkeeper, and an innkeeper, but I am no farmer."

"Papa," said Finn, straightening up, "I know that you want to do things your own way, and that you don't want to depend on other people. But what if they depend on you, like I depend on you?"

"That's the problem!" said Hans. "What good has depending on Hans Vogel done for you, what has it done for my dear Katrin? We are all half-starving from doing things my way. That people depend on me only makes my failures worse."

"It doesn't have to be this way, Papa," said Finn. "You can still do things your way. You don't have to work for anybody. You could do what you already know in a place that needs you."

"What is this you are talking about?"

"Davenport, Papa."

"What about it?" said Hans.

"You could open an inn in Davenport. It's a busy place. Many people are coming to Iowa, and many more are passing through. Papa, if you were to sell this land at the right price you could buy an inn and make your fortune, and maybe someday you could be a farmer again."

"Never again," said Hans.

"Papa, everybody is coming across the river just like we did. If ever a place needed an innkeeper, it is Davenport."

Hans smiled for the first time in what seemed like weeks and set a hand upon Finn's shoulder.

"You are a smart boy," he said.

"I am no longer a boy, Papa."

"You are right," said Hans. "Overnight you have become a man — and a very smart one."

"I have learned much from you," said Finn.

"Perhaps. But you are smart in a way that I did not teach you. You are smart because you listen. Everybody else, they talk, talk, talk. But not you. All these years of you watching, and listening, and observing. All the time you reserve your opinions. While other men talk, you reason. When they called you an idiot, I always knew they were wrong."

Finn felt the blood rush to his face at the compliment. He had yearned for Hans's approval from the first time he met the Vogels in Searles's office, but more so Finn blushed because he knew it to be true, he was smart, and to hear it acknowledged for the first time filled him with pride.

"I knew because I could see it in your eyes," said Hans. "I could see you watching and learning, always. I even saw you moving your lips when you thought I was not looking. I could see it in the way you . . . what is the word? In German is *vorhersehen.* The way you see what needs to be done before. The way I never have to tell you something after one time."

"I don't know the word, Papa," said Finn. "But I do know that the railroad men will come back, and when they come you should have a plan."

"What plan? There is only sell, or not sell."

"Yes, Papa. But there is the matter of price."

"You think I should ask for more?"

"Yes, Papa, I do. They need this farm, Mr. Baxter said so himself."

"But what if they don't come?"

"They'll come, Papa, they have to."

"And what do we tell them?" said Hans.

"You tell them what you always tell them, that you won't sell," said Finn. "And I will help you with the rest."

"How?"

"I have given it much thought, Papa."

Indeed it was only ten days later when, upon a morning thick with October frost, Mr. Anderson and Mr. Baxter arrived once more by carriage. Had either Mr. Baxter or Mr. Anderson any understanding of farming, they would have noted as they stepped down from the coach that the wheat field was tilled and stubble free, and that the potato mounds were freshly turned. Instead Mr. Anderson surveyed his general surroundings with his customary skepticism, with particular interest to the drooping front landing of the house and the roof of the barn, already beginning to sag near the center. Mr. Baxter hoisted his trouser legs several inches as he walked across the rutty hardpan as though he were avoiding manure, though there was none to avoid.

As on their prior visit, the men convened at the dining room table, although on this occasion Finn was seated beside Hans. Once seated, Mr. Baxter removed his hat and set it upon the table in front of him, while Mr. Anderson left his perched upon his head.

"As I'm sure you've surmised, Mr. Vogel," began Mr. Baxter, "we have come again on behalf of the IMIRC, and are here to extend to you another offer for your farm. You should be relieved to know that despite the wishes of my associate, Mr. Anderson, I am prepared to make the same offer and not a lesser offer, as is our custom. Isn't that right, Mr. Anderson?"

Anderson grunted.

"That is to say," proceeded Mr. Baxter, "we are authorized to offer you — and the offer is final — ten dollars per acre."

"Last time you say fifteen," observed Hans.

"Oh, right, yes, yes, pardon me, fifteen per acre," said Baxter.

"It does not matter," said Hans. "Five dollars does not change anything. My farm is not for sale."

Mr. Anderson shook his head grimly.

"Mr. Vogel," said Mr. Baxter, "it behooves us to warn you and your family that should you refuse our offer, the federal government is more than likely to side with us in any subsequent land dispute. There exists many a precedent for such a decision, particularly where the public interest is at stake. And if that's the case, you may not be compensated at all. Do you see my point?"

"But I pay for this land! I have deed!"

"Yes, yes, the deed, we've been over that," said Mr. Baxter. "The other families also had deeds, Mr. Vogel. But in light of the easement, these reasonable people saw the advantages — and they are advantages, make no mistake — of accepting our offer. It was for the betterment of themselves and the nation that they accepted this offer."

"Five times, I say: I will not sell. But still you come. Why?"

Here again, Mr. Anderson could not belie his agitation, clearing his throat several times as though something substantial were lodged in it.

"Yes, yes," said Baxter in response to this cue. "Perhaps, Mr. Vogel, you fail to fully comprehend our sphere of influence. The federal government has every reason to want this rail to go through. Gracious, the people of Iowa have every reason to want to see this rail go through. At present, Mr. Vogel, you are the only thing standing in the way. I've told you what this rail means to the state of Iowa and to the nation at large, and yet you still resist reason. Now, that almost seems unpatriotic."

"Mr. Baxter," said Finn, surprising nobody more than his silent counterpart, Mr. Anderson. "If I may speak?"

Mr. Baxter glanced sidelong at Mr. Anderson.

"Of course," said Mr. Baxter. "I didn't know you could."

"My parents have worked this land for years," said Finn. "They started with nothing and have managed to sustain themselves on the strength of their hard work and commitment. Understandably, my father is very attached to this farm. That said, we are not unreasonable people. We see the great advantage to Iowa and the nation that this rail represents. We understand the prosperity that will follow in its tracks. After further consideration, we see the value in selling our farm. Isn't that right, Papa?"

Hans nodded his assent.

Mr. Baxter smiled. "Now we're getting somewhere."

Even Anderson looked cautiously optimistic at this concession, hoisting a curious brow.

"Now, I ask you to view all this from my father's perspective," said Finn. "Being that the advantages to this rail are so substantial, and let us not forget profitable, particularly for your company, the fact that this farm is the last parcel necessary for the completion of the line makes it of particular value, does it not?"

Anderson nearly keeled over in his chair.

"Gentlemen," said Finn, "considering all that, we would be foolish to accept anything less than forty dollars per acre for this farm."

Here Anderson's eyes bulged out of his head as he forced a breath out of his nostrils like an agitated horse.

"Well, sir," said Mr. Baxter, more than a little taken aback himself, "I do believe I liked you better when you were an idiot. I'm afraid that is out of the question. We are authorized to offer twenty dollars per acre, and not one penny more."

"I'm sorry, Mr. Baxter," said Finn. "Our price of forty dollars per acre is not negotiable."

"Absurd," blurted Anderson, finally unable to resist speech. "That's what it is. It's my opinion we should take the matter to the federal government and have this land by decree."

Finn shook his head. "Very well, then, if that's how you wish to proceed, so be it. I am bound to honor the wishes of my father so far as I can," he said. "Though I should think that any dispute over this land would only serve to slow the progress of construction down, and at a comparatively small savings. More likely, the result would be a loss when you consider the delay. And being that this farm is located closer to the eastern border than the west, it would seem in the best interest of the Illinois and Missouri and Iowa Railroad Corporation to acquire it as soon as possible, am I right?"

"You are not wrong, young man," conceded Baxter. "But while it may seem incumbent upon the IMIRC to proceed with haste, I can assure you they will not take kindly to your counteroffer; in fact I can almost assure you that they shall rebuke such an offer."

"Still, we will stand on principle, Mr. Baxter, and take our chances then," said Finn.

Baxter looked to Hans. "Is this your wish, Mr. Vogel?" he said.

Hans nodded in the affirmative.

"You are going to let this boy speak for you?"

"He is not a boy."

"And you realize what is at risk here? Knowing that the IMIRC is more than likely to have this easement one way or another, you are willing to risk everything you've worked so hard for over the matter of a few dollars?"

"Maybe your company should ask itself such a question," said Hans. "I did not come to this country to be bought."

WU CHEN

San Francisco, 1852

For nearly two weeks after he had given up on the prospect of a life with Ai Lu, Wu Chen confined himself to his darkened room, leaving only to visit the privy out back in the alley. During that time he barely ate or washed, and he abandoned his studies in English altogether. It wasn't that Wu Chen was feeling sorry for himself, he simply found himself powerless to stop the spiral of despair that had gripped him. In the absence of hope, the unwanted visitor in his troubled past came calling.

The terrible events at the claim harassed him. The irresolvable knowledge of his own savagery and his hidden potential for cruelty stuck to him like a shadow. That he should escape these unforgivable acts of violence not only with his life but with a small fortune only increased his crippling sense of unworthiness. If sitting on this tainted fortune were not debilitating enough, Wu Chen was daily shamed by the knowledge that he was engaged in the unthinkable and unforgivable practice of frittering it away, while not generating a penny of income. This was a state of affairs that his uncle Li Jun deemed most unsatisfactory.

"Look at you," he said. "Wasting your life, squandering your savings. Have you no sense of pride?"

"I am unworthy of my fortune, Uncle. I am unworthy of a life."

"Bah," said his uncle. "You're going soft in the head. You need to get out of your own way and stop taking the world personally. You must cease with all this introspection, and work, and save, and secure a future."

"But, Uncle," objected Wu Chen, "I have no vitality, no will to move, no appetite for this world."

"You have a responsibility," said his uncle.

"To whom?" said Wu Chen.

"To future generations."

"Better that I spare the world my rotten legacy."

"Now you sound like a poet, which you are not," said his uncle. "See here, boy. You must put all this behind you. You only did what you had to do. You saved yourself, and when that wasn't enough, you avenged the Huang brothers. You proved yourself courageous and loyal in an unfortunate situation."

"Blood stains my hands, Uncle. My violence solved nothing. The Huangs are no better for my vengeance."

"Enough!" said his uncle. "Pull yourself together. Wake up and look around you at this filth. This apartment, it reeks of rotten cabbage. You've got an infestation of flies. It's a wonder the other boarders have not complained."

"Please, Uncle, do not berate me."

"Your father would be ashamed," said Li Jun.

"Yes, he would," said Wu Chen.

"Then do something about it."

Despite his uncle's encouragement Wu Chen only resumed his backslide into impotence and apathy; horse blanket pulled over the window, cabbage festering in the corner, flies proliferating until their buzzing was so constant he could no longer hear it, Wu Chen huddled atop his dirty mattress. Most days he encountered no one. Once the landlady rapped on his door to make inquiries regarding his health and he sent her away with half-hearted assurances. Even Uncle Li Jun had forsaken him following their last spat. Wu Chen stopped eating altogether and began the curious habit of scratching himself compulsively as though he were host to an army of nits, though he could find no evidence of them. It seemed to Wu Chen that his mental and emotional deterioration was nearly complete.

Then one morning there came a knock on the door. Wu Chen did not register the knock until it picked up an urgency he could no longer ignore.

"Wu Chen, Wu Chen, open up!" came a voice.

But Wu Chen remained inert upon his mattress until he was no longer able to dismiss the insistence of the interruption. Finally, he rose to his feet and moved mechanically to the door, unlocked it, and swung it open. Standing in the hallway was none other than Ai Lu, a small steamer trunk at her heels.

"I have quit the store and left my father," she announced, stooping to drag the cumbersome trunk past a dumbstruck Wu Chen and into the fetid environs of his room.

"What is that smell?" she said. "Open a window."

Wu Chen stood there bewildered as his heart began beating a confused rhythm.

"What happened to you?" she said. "Are you ill?"

Unable to find his tongue, Wu Chen only shook his head.

Ai Lu looked him steadily in the eyes and her countenance softened from alarm to genuine concern.

Slowly his numbness began to wear off, and a riot of conflicting emotions seized him: relief, shame, gratitude, and exhilaration, all at once.

Ai Lu marched across the room through the miasma of decomposing vegetables and threw back the horse blanket, stirring the fruit flies. Wu Chen shaded his eyes as the light flooded the room. Covering her nose, Ai Lu promptly pried the window open.

"Ech!" she said. "The smell. How can you stand it?"

Wu Chen cast his eyes down and felt himself blushing. But beneath his embarrassment he felt a welling of hope in his chest that had been absent for weeks.

"Wait here," she said.

And Wu Chen waited.

She returned ten minutes later with a broom, a mop, a bucket, several burlap sacks, and a heap of rags. Immediately, she began filling sacks as Wu Chen stood by dumbfounded.

"Don't just stand there," she said, foisting the broom on him.

For twenty minutes, as Wu Chen dutifully swept every corner of the room, Ai Lu tore through the apartment like a tornado, disposing of virtually everything in her path, which comprised mostly rotting fruits and vegetables, but also a few rags of soiled clothing and several bowls of moldy rice. By afternoon the apartment was transformed, though the stench of moldering cabbage still lingered.

Wu Chen wanted so badly to ask what any of these developments meant to their future:

her coming, leaving her father, bringing the trunk. But he was afraid to ask.

"Now, off with those rags," she said when there was nothing left to clean.

Obediently Wu Chen began removing his clothes, blushing once more when Ai Lu did not avert her eyes from the spectacle of his half-naked body. Only once he was down to his skivvies did she turn her attention toward the window.

When his filthy clothing was heaped on the floor, Ai Lu stuffed it in a burlap sack with the last of the spoiled produce and set it in the hallway. Proceeding to the far corner of the room, she began rooting through the pile of clothing, smelling each item until she arrived at the most passable ensemble.

"Put these on," she said.

Wu Chen complied without protest, just as he complied when she forced him outdoors, where the sun had finally managed to burn through the gloom of fog, just as he complied when she led him on an aimless stroll north out of Chinatown and up the hill and past the cemetery. Eventually, Wu Chen recovered his nerve.

"Why have you left your father?"

"He thinks only of himself and his own interests," she said.

"I believe that he means well," said Wu Chen.

"Ha!" she said. "To him, I am something to barter."

"I'm sorry," said Wu Chen. "I should never have gone to him. I should have professed my love to you first."

"Yes, you should have," she said.

"In doing so I, too, acted as if you were his property."

"Yes, you did."

"I only meant to honor tradition," he said.

"I know that," she said. "And that is why I'm here."

"Does this mean you will have me?"

"This only means I forgive you."

Only now did Wu Chen see that he must earn her affection. Tentatively, he reached for her hand, and to his profound relief she took it. If Ai Lu could forgive him, he must now find a way to forgive himself.

"Thank you," said Wu Chen, just as they crested the hill.

She replied with a squeeze of his hand.

With the glare of the sun in their eyes, they continued at a leisurely pace down the back side of the hill toward the wharf. Even at a distance they could hear the frenzied activity and smell the rot of fish upon the breeze.

When they reached the chaos of the wharf, they did not linger, but proceeded west along the edge of the bay, then up the incline and halfway across the wooded plateau. When the forest gave way to the wide open, they passed the sprawl of the abandoned fort and continued west, the wind kicking up as they neared the ocean.

Upon the bluff they paused at a scenic overlook, where Wu Chen breathed deeply of the salty air, his long hair blown back, shirtsleeves flapping in the breeze. Only hours ago he'd been huddled on his mattress in the dark, breathing the rot of cabbage and the stink of regret. And now he was standing at the edge of the world in awe, looking out at the great gray-blue distance. Still, he could not shake the sadness.

"So far from home," he said.

It took nearly a week with both windows open to rid Wu Chen's apartment of the stink of cabbage. No sooner had Ai Lu accomplished the objective than she insisted they look for a different apartment. It was only a matter of weeks before Ai Lu took hold of the financial reins. Within the month, Ai Lu had found them an even smaller room just off the square at a considerable savings.

The second-story room did not receive the good western light in the evenings, as Wu Chen's old quarters did, nor did the apartment confer any desirable vista beyond the narrow alley directly facing the rear of another building.

"It's so dark," said Wu Chen upon entering the empty room. "And so small."

"It's closer," she said.

"Closer to what?" he said.

"You'll see," she said.

Wu Chen was thrilled to surrender control of his fate. So far he had managed to accomplish nothing on his own, thus it was no small relief to step aside and let Ai Lu manage the planning of their lives. It was more than sufficient to be a tool in her hands.

One cool foggy morning, Ai Lu led Wu Chen down the street from their little hovel toward the square, right past her father's fruit stand, where her father paused in his labors to fold his arms and leer at them as they passed. Ai Lu was undaunted by this display, marching right past her father without so much as a glance, towing a befuddled Wu Chen in her wake.

"Where are you taking me?" he said.

"You'll see," she said.

They crossed the street to an empty storefront, a large but poorly organized space, half covered and half exposed to the open air.

"This is it," announced Ai Lu.

"This is what?" said Wu Chen.

"Our future."

"It is?"

"Yes. Here, we will open our own grocery."

"We will?"

"Yes," she said. "I've already started making the arrangements."

"But it's right across the street from your father's."

"Exactly," she said.

"He's not going to like this," observed Wu Chen.

Indeed, even as he said it Wu Chen could see the old man scowling at them from across the street.

"Of course he won't like it," she said. "It's a bigger space. It's on the better side of the street. It's closer to the square."

Wu Chen could not deny any of this, but he was still uneasy with the idea.

"You will make an enemy of your father," said Wu Chen. "Are you sure you want to do this?"

"Yes," she said. "In the end, it will be better for everybody, including my father."

"How is that?"

"We will break him," she said. "We will run him out of business so that he will have no choice but to join us. You must understand that my father, he knows the farmers, he knows the business, he can attain the goods cheaper than us. What he lacks in grace he makes up for in hard work. He is a good resource, just not a good leader. My father will be an asset to us."

Ai Lu was an unstoppable force of nature. No obstacle seemed to discourage her will. Within a week, they were readying the storefront for business, ever under the incredulous gaze of her father from across the way.

Ai Lu and Wu Chen handled all of the

preparations themselves. They mended shelves and stalls, painting the stalls red and yellow and green to symbolize luck, power, and prosperity.

Not since his days on the Huangs' claim had Wu Chen known such purpose. Never had his life felt so full as it did when he was working side by side with Ai Lu, whom he came to view in a different light than before, no longer as the innocent girl, the shy daughter of a grocer, but as his fierce and capable better — brighter, more resourceful, and more decisive than himself. Yet somehow she maintained a softness around the edges, something she certainly did not inherit from her father, whose grocery stall was now his second order of business, the first being to stand in the middle of the boardwalk with folded arms, glowering across the street at the new grocery that was busier than his own.

Ai Lu relished this pastime, often smiling and waving across the way at him.

"Oh, the poor thing," she said. "Just look at him. He's miserable."

"Perhaps it is time we invite him to join —"

"No. No," she insisted. "Let him swallow his pride and come on his own."

But for weeks her father did not come, only watched their bustling grocery from afar as his own business fell off precipitously. Over those weeks he made sad attempts to doll up his store, painting the stall a dreary gray and rearranging the footprint and displays. He stayed longer hours. He even attempted to engage passersby like a wharf monger. But nothing seemed to help. His little grocery seemed doomed.

Gradually Wu Chen could see the fight dying in the old man. He abandoned his folded arms and glower. Instead he swept the boardwalk in front of his stall endlessly and forlornly, only occasionally stealing a glance at the brisk proceedings across the way.

"It won't be long now," said Ai Lu.

When their long workdays ended they sometimes strolled through the plaza arm in arm past the cannons and past the laundry where Wu Chen had formerly been employed. With twelve men to every woman in this town, Wu Chen was the envy of every bachelor they passed. He could hardly contain his pride. Ai Lu filled him up like a pitcher, imbuing him with an optimism, a belief, a hopefulness that had formerly died a violent death along with the Huangs.

Through the lens of Ai Lu the whole city of San Francisco was transformed from a filthy, lawless hub of vice and depravity to a golden city of opportunity. With Ai Lu at his side it seemed there was nothing Wu Chen could not achieve.

Late one night, when Ai Lu was soundly sleeping and Wu Chen could not contain his enthusiasm for this new life, he summoned his uncle Li Jun with a whisper in the darkness.

"You see," he said softly. "I told you she was the one."

"You have done well for yourself, Nephew," said Li Jun. "She is a formidable woman. She makes you better."

"And is she not beautiful?"

"There is that, too," he said.

"Oh, Uncle, if only the rest of the family could see me."

"The time has come to start a new family," he said.

"We shall make a big family, you will see," said Wu Chen. "We will name a boy after you, Uncle, and one after my father. We shall provide for them and teach them the ways of this new world, build for them a better future just as you always instructed me, Uncle."

"But don't neglect the old ways," said Li Jun. "Those, you must preserve. The ways of this new world are not always the best."

"Of course, Uncle," said Wu Chen. "I shall never forget who or where I came from, nor shall my children or their children ever forget. The Chens will make their mark on this city, Uncle. We will dig ourselves in here and never leave this place."

Ai Lu stirred just then, rolling over onto her back.

"Who are you talking to?" she said.

"Nobody," he said, grazing her shoulder in the darkness.

Throughout the spring and into summer, as the little storefront she and Wu Chen had opened at the edge of the square thrived, Ai Lu could not fully embrace her good fortune. Not until all the pieces were in place would she allow herself this pleasure in fullness. Thus even as she thrilled at the brisk pace of business, even as she mentally tracked the day's receipts with a cautious optimism, even as she felt the graze of Wu Chen's shoulder, or the brush of his hand as they crossed paths in close quarters throughout the day, Ai Lu felt the heat of her father's gaze from across the street as he swept the boardwalk in front of his failing grocery looking bitter and crestfallen.

Ai Lu knew he was judging her, and she couldn't blame him. In leaving her father she had broken the ranks of family and the calling of tradition; in refusing his attempt to arrange her marriage she knew she had been disloyal, disobedient, and willful. Still, she couldn't help but feel that she'd been right in standing her ground, and not just for her own sake, either, but for everybody involved. She truly believed that they would be stronger as a whole with her making the decisions. Had she not already proven as much with the success of the store? Sooner or later her father would acknowledge it.

Wu Chen was gradually becoming the man she'd always known he could be, the man he was meant to be. While he was neither the shrewdest nor the most confident man, he was more than capable when set to a task. He had a strong back and a good heart and a fierce sense of loyalty. And beyond all these qualities, it was also true that Wu Chen was winsome in a way that spoke directly to his experience in life and his outlook, his face marked at once by ruggedness and somehow, still, innocence. To see him smile in spite of himself, to feel his fingers running through her hair, to see him looking gratefully into her eyes as though he might get lost there, was to want to complete the circle and make a father out of him. But only in due time.

Wu Chen continued to give her father the benefit of the doubt.

"Was he so wrong to try to marry you to me?" he said. "You did it, after all. Maybe he saw something in me beyond my money."

Wu Chen need not have lobbied for her father, because Ai Lu, too, yearned for her father to rejoin the fold, but on her own terms. And she knew the day would come eventually, for the more her business grew, the more his little stall struggled to compete, and once it failed completely where else could he turn? Together with her steward-ship, and Wu Chen's strong back, and her father's experience and contacts, their store would prove even more prosperous. To execute her designs in such a way seemed cruel in a certain light, but it was necessary if they were to thrive in America.

Sure enough, they drove her father out of business by midsummer, and it was a painful thing for Ai Lu to watch; less and less traffic, emptier and emptier stall, more and more nervous sweeping along the boardwalk. As predicted, her father appeared one foggy morning late in July before the store was open for business as Ai Lu was stocking the stalls with turnips and potatoes.

Her father did not come with his tail between his legs as Ai Lu had expected. He came instead with a straight face and a somber bearing, hands behind his back as he took silent inventory of the storefront without touching anything.

"Your store is doing well," he said. "You have put your resources to good work."

"I learned from you," she said.

"Hmph," he said. "Only what you wanted to learn. The stone fruit should be out front. Nobody wants to look at sweet potatoes."

"Father," she said. "I want you to understa—"

"Most of this citrus is overripe," he said, moving down the aisle. "Where's all the cabbage? Did your husband buy it all?"

As if on cue, Wu Chen poked his head out from the back room, but immediately withdrew it again, leaving father and daughter to themselves.

"Father, I feel I must explain myself," she said.

"Your actions have explained themselves well enough," he said. "Save your words."

"Join us, Father," she said. "Help us run this store. Together the three of us will —"

"No," he said. "I am done with America. You are out of my hands, and that's what I came to achieve. May your future be bright, Ai Lu."

"But, Father, you can't leave me."

"Like you left me?"

"But I didn't," she said. "Only temporarily."

"You made your choice," he said. "And so far as I can tell it was a wise one. You chose a young man over an old man."

"It was not just for myself," she said. "What I did, I did for us both. It was just as you had planned it."

"No," he said. "It was better than I planned it. What need have you and your wealthy husband for a stubborn old man?"

"Father, you know how to run a store better than either of us."

"If that were true it is you who would be out of business, not I," he said. "Do not try to talk me out of it. My mind is made up and cannot be changed. Where do you suppose you got your stubbornness from?"

"Stay," she said. "I beg you."

"There is nothing here for me," he said.

"And what is left for you in Guangdong?"

"Your mother is buried there," he said.

Despite continued attempts to induce him, Ai Lu's father could not be persuaded to stay in America. And so, within the month he was set to leave on the steamer *Hong Kong*. Ai Lu was filled with doubt as his departure approached. What if she hadn't made the right decision after all? What if the success of their store was only short-lived? What if somebody else took a page out of their book and opened a bigger and better store right down the block? What if Wu Chen surrendered once more to those dark spirits that haunted him, those moods she knew nothing about? What if something else happened to him, some horrible accident befell him? What if she were forced to make her own way in America? With each successive doubt, Ai Lu tried harder to persuade her father to stay.

On a cool morning near the end of summer, Wu Chen and Ai Lu somberly walked her father up over the hill and down again to the bustling docks, where a half mile offshore an impenetrable wall of fog slowly closed in on the city. Ai Lu had packed her father a large parcel of food to help him get through the journey: sourdough and rice and potatoes, smoked fish and carrots and turnips, and precious little fruit, some of it not yet ripe.

The three of them stood in the shadow of the hull of the great steamship, the dock all around them swarming with life as the crew busied themselves readying the vessel. If there was one thing to be grateful for, it was that thanks to the miracle of the steam engine her father's journey back to China would not be nearly so arduous, the conditions not nearly so brutal and the voyage only half as long as the journey that had brought them to America six years prior.

"It's not too late to change your mind, you know," said Ai Lu.

"You know me better than that," he said.

"Oh, Father, why must you be so stubborn?"

"Why must the ox be so stubborn?" he said.

Oh, but she would miss her father, especially his faults. She'd miss his scowl, and his angry sweeping, and the way he answered a question with another question. She would even miss his pouting. It was with a heavy heart that Ai Lu watched her father board the steamship *Hong Kong.* Up the plank he proceeded with slow, measured steps, dragging his tiny trunk and his parcel of food, and never looking back. Not even once.

THE CHEN-MURPHYS

McMinnville, Oregon, 2018

The first weeks in McMinnville did not unfold according to anyone's plan, least of all Jenny's. For weeks the Chen-Murphys squatted at the Comfort Inn waiting to close on the house. Despite the promise of its name, the Comfort Inn conferred little in the way of actual comfort. Not only was the tan and yellow décor nauseating, and the room impossibly cramped, but the walls were paper-thin, the mattresses hard as travertine, and the pillows shapeless and utterly exhausted. Moreover, there was no bar at the Comfort Inn, and the complimentary breakfast buffet consisted of muffins and cereal.

The saving grace was the indoor pool, which occupied the boys for hours. Afternoons and weekends they explored McMinnville and the surrounding area in search of cultural enrichment, outings that included a sculpture garden best described as wildly eclectic; a small aviation museum, home to the illustrious "Spruce Goose"; and the Yam-hill Valley Heritage Center, a hulking yellow edifice amounting to a converted barn, housing antique farm equipment in endless rows. Alas, each excursion proved less thrilling than the last. Evenings were spent in the hotel room, eating takeout and flipping endlessly through cable channels, arguing over what to watch.

The holidays offered a brief respite from the Comfort Inn. The Chen-Murphys spent Christmas Eve and Christmas Day with Todd's parents in nearby St. Joseph, engaged in various fetishistically wholesome activities, including Christmas Charades *and* Christmas Carol Pictionary, not to mention the making of salt dough ornaments (Tyler's snowman looking like a deformed penis) and mason jar snow globes. When that wasn't enough Yuletide merriment, they all drank spiced apple cider and watched *Miracle on 34th Street.*

"So, are Papa and Nana like the whitest people ever?" Winston asked Jenny confidentially.

Three days into the New Year, still marooned at the Comfort Inn awaiting escrow to close, winter break ended and the kids resumed school, Tyler at Newby Elementary and Winston at Duniway Middle School. They both hated school.

"Everybody's weird," Tyler opined.

"I've made like zero friends," Winston complained.

Mercifully, at the end of January, the Chen-Murphys moved at last into their new home. The house itself was wonderful: a drafty four-bedroom, two-and-a-half-bathroom craftsman near the center of town. The closets were gigantic. The front porch was sprawling. The neighbors seemed nice enough. But if Jenny was being honest, it wasn't quite the situation she'd dared to imagine.

Never mind the ubiquitous wineries and brewpubs, quaint little McMinnville wasn't nearly enough town for Jenny. Her hopes for nearby Salem were dashed in a single afternoon of exploring. Tree-lined avenues, shuttered storefronts, and empty sidewalks. It could have been a town in Ohio or Missouri. A middling college town simply wasn't enough to scratch Jenny's urban itch after life in San Francisco. And while a Saturday trip to Portland initially offered more enticing prospects, Portland lacked the sophistication, diversity, and cosmopolitan veneer that Jenny was accustomed to. Portland was quirky, for sure. Dynamic, yes. But it failed to possess anything approaching the outsized metropolitan flavor, the canyons of steel and glass, or the deafening urban pulse of San Francisco. Though unfamiliar and ripe for discovery, Portland didn't have the grit, or the density, or the ceaseless thrum of activity to excite

Jenny in the way San Francisco did.

Was she wrong to expect so much of her new home? She knew her disappointment was yet another iteration of her entitlement, but she couldn't resist it. She had gotten used to a certain lifestyle. She knew she should feel blessed to be the owner of a four-bedroom house on three acres in a mostly liberal community practically free of crime. She realized she was ridiculously lucky to have money in the bank, and the luxury of taking her sweet time in deciding on a new career, or even entertaining the possibility of retirement. How many people anymore had that kind of safety net or those kinds of options? How many families in America could embark on frivolous weekenders, could afford hotels for months on end, own a four-bedroom house on acreage outright, and contemplate private schools for their children? Yes, Jenny knew she was wrong to expect so much, and yet she could not seem to help herself.

Todd, meanwhile, was apparently satisfied with their new living situation, and that didn't help. With little financial pressure to hurry him, he seemed to relish his half-hearted job search.

"Maybe I should go back to school," he ventured at one point.

They were moving backward. In Todd's case, willfully.

In the evening and on weekends Todd tended to projects, puttering around in the yard or the garage like his father. Jenny thought it was cute at first, but after six weeks of fruitless job hunting, Todd purchased a thirty-five-hundred-dollar Tuff Shed at Lowe's and began accumulating various power tools, mowers, and gardening implements.

Finally, Jenny confronted him in the hallowed confines of his "shop," the aforementioned eight-by-twelve windowless shed where two days prior while looking for a screwdriver she'd happened upon a bright yellow, twelve-inch rubber bong stashed behind a pair of paint cans.

"Don't you think this is all a little much, Todd? Neither one of us is working, we have no prospects, and here you are spending a small fortune on . . . on what exactly?"

"Relax, babe. We're sitting on a pile of cash," he said.

That much was true. They'd nearly doubled their money on the Hayes Valley house.

"And don't forget equity," he said.

It was also true they'd paid cash for the McMinnville house.

"Besides, this isn't an apartment, Jen, we've got acreage here. At least some of it has to be kept up. We're just getting started around here. Don't you see? This is the dream, babe, to have our own homestead in Oregon."

"Homestead? We're not pioneers, Todd."

"In a way we kind of are, though, right?"

"When did you buy a bong?" she said.

"I dunno, a month ago, maybe."

"You haven't smoked weed since college."

"When in Rome," he said. "The stuff is everywhere here. The retail stores are ridiculous. That thing is made of silicone, isn't that rad? You can drop it, the guy at the store says you can even put it in the dishwasher."

"Todd, I'm concerned."

"Concerned?"

"You just said *rad.* You're spending countless hours in a dark shed, smoking weed and . . . doing what exactly?"

"I'm gonna wire up some lights. I'm working on that."

"How long until you're out here listening to Dave Matthews?"

"I hate Dave Matthews."

"Todd, what's happening to you?"

"What do you mean?"

"I mean, who are you?" she said. "Who is this pot-smoking, new-pioneer overnight handyman? Where did he come from? Because I don't know this guy."

"You married this guy," he said.

He was right. It hadn't occurred to Jenny that in addition to returning to where he came from, part of Todd's dream may have been to return to who he once was, the same guy from Oregon she'd met at Davis eons ago, the one wearing cargo shorts and a backward baseball cap. All these years Jenny had assumed that Todd had outgrown his old self, when really he had lost his old self by default. The job at Chase. The cloistered urban environment. The countless responsibilities of parenting, particularly in tandem with a largely absentee partner. The nearly complete lack of self-care, or even self-interest; the impossibility of a yard, or even a shed, in the city.

Todd donned a big, affable grin. "What's wrong, babe? Relaxed doesn't look good on me?"

Jenny knew at once that she couldn't begrudge Todd's wanting to be himself, as long as he got a job eventually, and didn't start listening to Dave Matthews. She had to hand it to him; his tireless optimism was impressive. His capacity to adapt, his easygoing but methodical approach to his goals, his blind trust in his own vision, they were all so . . . so what? So Irish? No, that wasn't it. So Catholic? That wasn't it, either. So American? Yes, that was it. No wonder he thought of himself as a new pioneer.

Suddenly Jenny wished she could see their new life in Oregon through the same rose-colored glasses as Todd. Maybe then the charm of McMinnville would grow on her. Maybe she'd start wearing sweatpants to the grocery store. Maybe she'd learn to love gardening. Maybe she'd buy a greenhouse and linger in it the way Todd lingered in his shed. Would that be so bad? Maybe they really could open up some kind of shop. If all those wineries could survive in McMinnville, why not a shop? Or maybe Jenny would find a job that paid somewhat less than her old job but didn't demand as much of her, didn't dominate her every waking moment with its meaningless urgency. Maybe it would awaken some new appetite for adventure in her. Maybe Jenny too could see herself as a new pioneer. But as much as Jenny wanted to embrace Todd's vision, to lean into his optimism, she couldn't. Somehow it all smacked of a lowering of expectations.

To Todd's credit, he could sense Jenny's restlessness and disenchantment.

"Hey, let's take the train up to Seattle this weekend," Todd said, striding through the back door and into the kitchen, sawdust clinging to his baggy overalls and collecting on the tile at his feet, still more sawdust marking his progress up the back steps and across the room from the back door.

"You said Portland was too small," he said. "Well, Seattle is way bigger. I mean, it's pretty much the city ten years ago. We can stay somewhere nice downtown. Maybe we could leave the boys with my folks."

Though the idea of being childless for a weekend in a big city sounded marvelous,

Jenny knew she had a responsibility to the boys, who were almost as restless as she was in McMinnville.

"No," she said. "They'll want to come. We'll pull them out of school after lunch so we can get an early start."

By evening Todd and Jenny had booked a room at the Sorrento (a Condé Nast favorite) and made reservations on Amtrak to board the Coast Starlight in Salem early Friday afternoon. The very idea of mobility was a comfort to Jenny, allowing her for the first time in weeks to take a more deliberate view of her current situation. Thus, she envisioned McMinnville less as somewhere that she was stuck, and more as a starting point, a base of operations, an outpost on the edge of further discovery. This weekend Seattle, next weekend, why not Vancouver, BC? Todd was right. They had the means. Provided they found any kind of employment, they were sitting on enough money, and, more important, enough time, to support such whimsy, a lifestyle that their former lives, while lucrative, could never support, mostly because of Jenny's relentless job obligations. Somehow the idea of returning to quaint little McMinnville over and over was more appealing than being stuck there.

Four days later, the Chen-Murphys stood on the snowy platform at the aptly (if unimaginatively) named Salem Railroad Station, Tyler clutching Jenny's hand while Winston projected his usual slump-shouldered, aloof manner, still pouting about having to leave his iPad behind for all of forty-eight hours. Beside him Todd seemed invigorated, possibly stoned (no, probably stoned), looking every bit the new pioneer beneath his nappy, three-week-old beard, already starting to show a little salt and pepper at the chin.

"This is gonna be epic," Jenny heard him say to Winston as they filed across the platform and onto the train.

Laila Tully

Oregon, 2019

After Becka dropped her off at the station in Salem, Laila finally caught a couple of breaks. Her ticket to Seattle was less than the fifty bucks Becka had prepared her for, and she even managed to secure a window seat on the west side of the train. The wait was only thirty-five minutes before boarding. Laila changed into dry socks and began the task of reorganizing her oversized duffel, a job that included rinsing out her now-empty Tupperware containers in the bathroom sink before brushing her teeth and refreshing her makeup, all the while resisting the temptation to check her phone.

Upon boarding, Laila took her seat by the window and began biting her already bitten nails. There was truly no going back now, a knowledge that was at once terrifying and exhilarating. Alone and far between way stations, Laila couldn't help but wonder how she had wound up so alone with no safety net but a cousin she'd met no more than five times. While she and Genie may have held each other close, they really were not all that familiar. It had been over five years since Laila had last seen Genie in person, though they kept up on Facebook and Instagram.

It wasn't until about ten minutes out of Salem that Laila realized she'd left her charger in the truck. She knew she ought to save her battery for emergencies, but she powered the phone up in spite of herself to find no less than eight texts from Boaz, three from Tam, and one from Genie. She almost didn't read them, but she couldn't resist the urge. She always liked the good news first, so she started with Genie:

Thursday, 1:35 pm

Where u at? Excited to see you! Will you be here in time for dinner tonight?

Laila texted back:

Long story, but I'm like a day behind schedule. Halfway there! Can't wait!

Next she read the three texts from Tam:

Thursday, 2:39 pm

Girl, just you keep moving and don't let nobody talk you out of nothing

Thursday, 2:56 pm

LOL, you should see Dennis! He's off the rails! I hope he has a heart attack

Thursday, 3:34 pm

Don't forget to send me an address.

Laila texted Tam back:

So far so good! Halfway through Oregon! I will send you a postcard when I get to Queets!

Laila was heartened by these messages. See, she wasn't alone. There was cousin Genie, who'd encouraged her to come north, cousin Genie, who'd opened her home to Laila with nothing to gain. And there was Tam, who'd given her what probably amounted to most of her savings so that Laila could make this break and start a new life. So, no, she was not without allies in this world. She left off biting her cuticles and allowed herself a brief moment of hopefulness before turning her attention to Boaz's messages, even though she knew they'd only piss her off.

Thursday, 5:40 pm

Where the fuck are you, what the fuck, I'm hungry?????

Thursday, 6:05 pm

WTH, did the truck not start? Make sure the battery cable isn't crusted.

Thursday, 6:23 pm

You better not be pulling any shit

Thursday, 7:54 pm

Where's my fucking truck???????

Thursday, 8:05 pm

Answer your fucking phone!!!!

Thursday, 8:38 pm

Ok I'm starting to worry . . .

Thursday, 9:24 pm

WTF, your work said you walked out!!! WTH is going on?

Thursday, 9:49 pm

I want my fucking truck!!!

Before Laila could power down her phone to conserve the battery, another string of texts buzzed in, every last one of them from Boaz:

Thursday, 10:34 pm

We need to talk . . . Please answer your phone!!!!

Thursday, 11:39 pm

WTH is this about the other night? I said I was sorry!!!

Friday, 1:07 am

Whatever I did, I'm sorry. Let's talk this out.

Friday, 1:53 am

I'm worried about u

Friday, 2:11 am

You're probably fucking someone right now. If it's fucking Dennis I'll kill him.

Friday, 9:11 am

I said I was sorry. We can work this out. I've just been stressed out

Friday, 9:38 am

Fucking answer me!

Friday, 10:27 am

Why aren't u at work? WTF? Did u quit for good?

Friday, 11:17 am

Fine. But don't bother crawling back this time, whore. I want my truck!!!!

Friday, 1:12 pm

At least tell me where my truck is!!!

Laila powered her phone down before a new string of texts could arrive, gazing angrily out the window at the snow. God, how she loathed him. The way he lied, then flat-out denied that he'd ever said the shit he said. The way he tried to turn their friends against her. The way he tried to convince her that he was the only one who ever told her the truth about herself, that her friends were just humoring her, that he was the only person she could trust to tell her what she really was. Worried about her? Ha! Boaz only cared about himself, every second of every day. Laila was just another tool in his belt, something to be manipulated and used for his own utility and convenience. She hated the way he projected his own shortcomings onto her. She hated every single thing about him: the way he ate like an animal, the way he slept, the way he breathed through his mouth, the way he always left his jeans in the middle of the floor, the way he walked around in his dirty, moth-eaten underwear, the filthy, demeaning shit he said when he was fucking her, like it was supposed to be some kind of turn-on.

Laila did her best to push all thoughts of Boaz out of her head and turned her attention to the only thing that really mattered now: the future. Yet the closer she got to Queets, the less she had to work with. No truck, no phone charger, no confidence that she could make anything happen with what few resources she now possessed, and no faith that anything would work out for the better.

Bad enough she was showing up on Genie's doorstep practically destitute. Now she'd be dependent on Genie for transportation. Who knew how long it might be before she could afford to buy another car? At the moment her whole plan seemed like a mistake. Maybe in Seattle, she should hock the old locket Grandma Malilah had given her; maybe it was worth a couple hundred bucks to somebody named Lucy or Laverne.

But looking out the window at the snowy landscape soothed her anxiety almost immediately: the wide white valley spreading out to the west, the snow-covered hills beyond buffering the coast. How small her problems seemed compared to the huge frozen world outside the train. At least she was warm. At least she had money in her pocket. At least she was still moving in the right direction, away from Boaz and her unfulfilling nowhere life.

LUYU AND JOHN

Northern California, 1851

Throughout the morning, squinting against the glare of the sun, John Tully and Luyu rode the old mare east across the delta, away from Colonel Whitworth's ranch, bound for the sanctuary of the hills. As she clutched John Tully about the waist, Luyu's teeth chattered in the dawn. One moment they had been sleeping soundly, wrapped snug in the coverlet of their dreams, and the very next moment they had been sent packing.

Shortly before midday, the flats east of the river began their grassy climb into the sprawling foothills, golden in the sunlight and dotted with live oaks. Eventually the oaks and the high grass gave way to thick pinewoods as they gained elevation. The air, cooler beneath the canopy, came as a relief as the trail switchbacked every hundred feet up the side of the mountain. The old mare seemed to slow with each switchback until Luyu dismounted voluntarily to lighten the load, walking beside the old mare, encouraging her now and again with a stroke of her snout.

Occasionally the sound of a stream infiltrated the silence. In the afternoon they watered at such a stream, swollen in spring as it hurried westward beneath the wooded canopy. Luyu and John hunkered against a hillside in the shade of a giant granite outcropping, nerves worn, stomachs protesting.

"Where are we going now?" said Luyu.

"If I remember there's supposed to be a town up ahead."

"You've been here before?"

"No, I've only heard. Not a big town to hear it told, but big enough to stock up before we move on. Last stop before Reno."

"Move on to where?"

John Tully scratched at his neck and sighed.

"I don't know," he said with an edge of irritability.

It was the first time he'd ever spoken to Luyu in such a tone, and somehow it made her ashamed of herself.

"All that I know is that I'm done letting the whites take from us. From now on, we will live according to our own desires."

"What is it that we desire?" she said.

"You tell me. What do you want from this life?"

It was not an easy question, nor one she was prepared to answer. Just shy of sixteen years old, Luyu was unaccustomed to naming her desires or even quantifying them. Her yearnings were so many as to be overwhelming at times, and yet they were so undefined. Her yearning was like a force within her, like the opposite of gravity. How could she say what she wanted specifically when she had seen and knew so little of the world? While she could cut her life into even halves, both were under lock and key one way or another, neither founded on her desires in any way. At Sutter's Mill the prison had been real, while at the Younts' the trappings had been ideological.

Now her life had splintered once more, assuming a third manifestation, one in which her own agency was being called to duty for the first time.

"To be in one place," Luyu said at last. "But also to move around freely. To come and go as I please."

Once Luyu began naming her desires it was like a dam had given way to the swelling current. Suddenly they all had names.

"And believe what I want to believe," she rejoined. "And worship how I want to worship, and work when I want to work, not when I'm told to work. Free, I want to be free."

"Now you are free," he said.

"No," she said. "Now we are homeless."

Grimly he concurred with a nod of his head.

"Maybe so," he said. "For a while, anyway.

But at least this time it is our own choice. That is progress. We go where we want to now, not where they tell us."

After their brief respite by the stream, Luyu and John readied themselves to resume their journey, mounting the old mare. Over the next hour they gained an additional seven hundred feet of elevation, pausing in their progress long enough to take in the vista below: the abrupt green hills tapering and turning to brown before opening up into the broad, flat basin with the river flashing silver in the distance, marking the valley lengthwise like a scar.

By late afternoon they began passing the occasional traveler in the opposite direction until they came to a junction, where they confronted a not-so-sturdy signpost pointing straight ahead to Mariposa Springs. *Mariposa Springs* had a nice ring to it. Maybe it would be different from other California towns — cleaner, quieter, less rowdy. Surely, it would have more to offer them than Shasta City. Within the hour they reached the western edge of the outpost, a ragtag assemblage of commercial enterprises ranging from hardware to whoring, nestled in the green foothills of the Sierras. It was undeniably a beautiful setting for a town, though what comprised the town itself was ugly like any other town.

"Well, at least it's someplace, I guess," said John, surveying the collection of structures huddled together like gamblers.

"It doesn't look so bad," Luyu said.

"Maybe there will be a hotel."

They rode through the center of town atop the bow-backed mare, either drawing suspicious looks or invisible to people altogether. On the surface Mariposa Springs was a town much like the one they'd left behind, but quieter, less urgent in its activity. They passed a livery and a wheelwright, a single saloon, a barber, and a mercantile before they arrived at the only hotel in town, the Mariposa Inn. Dismounting the mare, John hitched her to the post, and side by side he and Luyu ascended the wide wooden steps.

Never in her life had Luyu stayed in a hotel, or even set foot in one. Only once, upon her last day in town, the very day she'd chanced to meet John Tully, had she so much as put her face to the front window and peered into the Cypress Hotel. To hear the Younts tell it, not only was a hotel needless luxury and expense — in itself just the kind of gratuitous indulgence that God frowned upon — but it was most often something even worse: a den of iniquity and sin, and no place for a Christian.

But after days on the road, grit piled upon grit, her muscles aching, her feet swollen, her nerves ragged, the mere possibility of a wash pan and a bed seemed nothing less than a small miracle. The thought was almost enough to buoy her flagging spirits. Mariposa Springs was a savior.

The white man behind the desk, a gray-haired personage with ruddy cheeks and one blue eye that was clouded over as if by milk, could not hide his distaste as he looked Luyu and John over, then back down at his ledger.

"Haven't got any work for you here," he said, scribbling a notation.

"We're not here to work," said John.

"Oh?" said the clerk.

"How much for a night?"

"Dollar and a half," he said without looking up.

Luyu could see the muscles in John's jaw tighten.

"The sign says a dollar," he said.

"High season," said the clerk, looking up to face them with his milky blue eye.

John set his jaw and narrowed his eyes in anger. Begrudgingly he reached for his purse, but Luyu stopped him.

"No," she said.

"But —"

"No."

She took him by the hand and practically had to lead him as they turned around and walked out of the lobby.

WORTHY WARNOCK

Springfield, Illinois, 1853

Following a four-hour pursuit of Othello and his pregnant wife through the fields, thickets, and woods of Central Illinois, an exhausted Worthy Warnock checked into the Belle Riv-ière, the finest hotel in Springfield, just before midnight, having once again been bested by his former servant. Two and a half years he'd been hunting the ungrateful devil, and when Worthy had finally caught up to him, purely by chance, the rogue had managed to elude him yet again.

Worthy had to hand it to Othello; he was resourceful, just one of his many attributes, which made losing him all the more difficult. Worthy had come to depend on Othello for a thousand little things. His absence had been keenly felt these past two and a half years. But Worthy was livid at having suffered the embarrassment of losing him again, an indignity his business partners had all witnessed. Certainly, none of it cast Worthy in a capable light. Thus he resolved to spare no expense in bringing the scoundrel to justice this time.

In the morning, Worthy met with a most unsavory character by the name of Knox with the aim of bringing Othello (or George, as he now had the audacity to call himself) to justice and returning him safely.

"We ought to castrate the runaways like we used to," Knox told him. "Those South Carolinians had it right. There ought to be militias and citizen patrols. It ought to be a requirement for the American citizen, a mandate to police the runaway slave. But society is growing weak. People are bending too much in their beliefs."

"The immigrants are watering us down," Worthy noted. "These Germans and Irish and Eyetalians, these mongrels from Eastern Europe and beyond, they have no vested interest in America. They don't understand the American ideal."

Knox nodded in agreement.

"And the Negroes, well, they're just plain ungrateful," said Knox.

"Exactly," said Worthy. "Like children. We provide for them, we house them, and the next thing you know, they run off."

"Well, this one calling himself George, he won't get far," said Knox. "I'll see to that."

Having contracted Knox that morning, along with three additional bounty hunters, Worthy Warnock spent the remainder of the day resting his sore muscles and bruised ego at the Belle Rivière. As evening fell upon Central Illinois and the sun cast its dying light upon his western-facing quarters, Worthy Warnock, his supper resting heavily upon his delicate constitution, was still livid, his pride still smarting. After such an embarrassment it would surely be a long trip back to Louisville. But he consoled himself with the certainty that in the end, justice would be served.

GEORGE FLOWERS

Springfield, Illinois, 1853

For eight days George and Cora took refuge in Will Cobb's crowded apartment on the edge of Springfield, and for eight days Will and George tried endlessly to persuade Cora that her best course of action would be to stay behind in Springfield, at least for now.

"There's no sense in a free woman skulking around like a fugitive," Will insisted.

"Listen to the man, Cora," said George.

"Once you leave these parts, you're as good as a fugitive yourself," Will cautioned. "That's a fact. They catch up with you, you're no better off than George."

But Cora could not be reasoned with. She was determined to make the journey with George, regardless of the risks.

"We go together," she said.

"But your condition."

"Our condition. I didn't get this far alone, and I don't intend to go any further without the father of this baby. It belongs to both of us."

George understood that he had done little to earn this loyalty.

As if luring her into sacred union weren't enough, George had promptly separated Cora from her father, along with the only home she'd ever known, all so he could bring her south to Springfield, where their fortunes had taken this awful turn, and all because of him.

And this was Cora's thank-you, to steal north like a fugitive.

On the ninth day at Cobb's, a free Black man named Rankin arrived at the apartment. Though he was still in the prime of his life, Rankin's cropped hair was showing some salt and pepper, and his thirty-or-so years had already worn deep crow's feet about his eyes. That — and a whole lot more — was the cost of being Black in America.

Shortly after his arrival, Rankin briefed George and Cora in the kitchen, step-by-step running over the arrangements and preparing them for the journey ahead.

"We don't want no surprises," he explained. "Every little detail got to go off without a hitch, or you'll soon find yourself in a mess of trouble."

It was Rankin himself who was tasked with delivering them through the first leg of their escape, an exploit he voluntarily undertook without compensation, and at great risk to his own freedom. If Rankin ever got caught, they'd lock him up and throw away the key.

Rankin readied himself to take leave of the apartment shortly after dinner.

"You best get some rest while you can," he cautioned them. "You gonna be traveling awful hard."

"I don't even begin to know how to thank you, sir," said George.

"You can thank me by getting yourself free."

Shortly before dawn the next morning, Rankin returned to the apartment and proceeded to smuggle George and Cora out of the neighborhood and clear across town in a heaping rag cart. That he managed to push all that weight and never betray his burden seemed miraculous.

For George and Cora, covered from head to toe in filthy rags, the heat was stultifying. The stench was nearly unbearable. That pregnant Cora was forced to endure such conditions through no doing of her own was a shame George would surely bear the rest of his days.

An hour into the ordeal, beneath the growing pile of fetid cloth, George groped for Cora's hand and found her clutching the little figurine he'd carved for her in lieu of a ring. That was his promise to her. Not a band of precious metal symbolic of the endless circle of devotion, but a crude wooden carving, the work of a rank amateur. George clutched Cora's hand in his own and did not let go the remainder of the morning, through the heat, and the cramping, and the ceaseless discomfort.

In a barn north of the city, still uncomfortably close to Mr. Best's estate, George and Cora were transferred to the suffocating confines of a pair of wooden caskets placed unceremoniously in the back of a covered wagon. The driver sat tall upon the box seat, all dressed in black, humming a spiritual as though the whole world were watching him pass, though as far as George could tell from the sweltering interior of the casket, they encountered no one along their way, for not once did they stop their progress, and not once did the driver talk to anyone but himself.

For hours the caskets tossed and heaved as the wagon wheels churned over the rutty road. As the miles wore on it seemed to George that if they didn't get out of those coffins soon they were surely going to abide in them for eternity.

Eventually, the wagon pulled to a stop, and George and Cora were finally liberated from the suffocating confines of their caskets. Breathing deeply of the fresh air, they found themselves on a primitive road at the edge of a deciduous forest.

"What now?" said George.

His question was answered a moment later

when they were greeted by a young boy, barefoot and dressed in rags, who beseeched George and Cora to follow him as he led them a quarter mile through the trees, then up a narrow path and through a thicket to a dingy white house at the edge of a sprawling field of high grass.

The boy promptly led them to the barn and guided them up a ladder to the hayloft, where he left them in the darkness. A few minutes later he returned with a loaf of bread and a bucket half-full of water.

"They's a privy out back of the house, but my daddy say be careful coming down that ladder in the dark."

With that, the boy, whose name they would never learn, left them alone in the darkness, where they settled down upon their backs in silence, still too frightened to breathe a word. Once again George clutched Cora's hand, itself still gripping the little wooden figure tight, and felt her pulse beating in unison with his own.

"Everything gonna work out, you'll see," he whispered at last.

But George's assurances fell upon deaf ears, for Cora was already fast asleep.

Morning arrived in an instant, the sunlight slanting in through the slats of the roof, dicing the musty loft into narrow sections. The boy appeared again shortly after sunup with two biscuits and a tin of bacon grease, of which George and Cora partook greedily.

"They gonna put you in that hay wagon yonder," he said. "Gonna be a mite itchy, my daddy says."

Indeed, following their brief repast, George and Cora were whisked onto the cart and soon covered in hay. The driver, who would also remain nameless, was an elderly man with a pronounced hump in his back, half-toothless, with two missing fingers on his left hand. Upon his head perched a beat-up straw hat.

"Anybody stops us, you just stay real still back there, understand? And don't you draw so much as a breath until we moving again, right?" he said as he took the reins.

It was apparent within thirty feet that the hay wagon itself was in a state of sorry disrepair comparable to its humpbacked driver. The front wheels exhibited a pronounced wobble upon the axle, and the undercarriage creaked ceaselessly as they trundled up the narrow road fronting a small river. After a few miles they diverged from the river's path and continued heading north across the marshy flats, Cora still clutching the little figure.

The old man would take them halfway to Galesburg, where once again George and Cora relied on the kindness of strangers to see them through to the next depot, and the next. Like human freight they made their way north, sleeping in gullies, weathering rain and cold, holding their water until their bladders were fit to burst, crowding in crawl spaces, hunkering beneath hay and lumber and rubbish, subsisting on whatever scraps were provided for them, and all the while Cora's belly growing bigger by the day.

NORA BERGEN

Chicago, 1858

May 21, 1858

Dearest Finn,

It is late and I write this by lantern light, the lantern recently left in my quarters by an anonymous donor, whom I fully suspect to be Edmund, presumably because he's grown tired of slipping me candles and feels sorry for me. Whatever the case, I am grateful for its light, which is brighter and much easier to read and write by. I've decided to spare you my customary preamble about the unique futility of writing undelivered letters and proceed straight to recent developments, some of which are hopeful, while others are not.

On the hopeful front Mr. Seymour continues to help me locate you, and I should think his vast resources and influence might make all the difference in finding you.

Unfortunately, Mr. Seymour, like Mrs. Seymour before him, has recently taken ill, which has become a source of great anxiety for me of late, as I have not the foggiest idea what would become of me in the event of Mr. Seymour's passing. I suppose I would be free to go where I pleased. But my chances of ever finding you would no doubt be greatly diminished by such a circumstance. Why must every blessing be a mixed one? Still I remain hopeful that Mr. Seymour's health and vitality will return so that we might soon resume our search for you.

The weather is turning cold and the leaves are just beginning to change colors here. The sight of their orange and yellow plumage is at once lovely and melancholy. As ever, I am lonely. But somehow autumn always seems the loneliest season, and this autumn is no exception. While the staff remains familiar and certain intimacies are shared, it does not feel like the family it once did with Clifton gone to heaven, and Cora and George to Springfield. Mostly those novels and manuscripts that I manage to get my hands on see me through.

I will trust that you are well, as I cannot bear to contemplate you in any other condition. I trust that you have found your voice and that you are a formidable and useful young man, and no doubt handsome like our father. When I close my eyes I can see that you still have your beautiful red locks, and your sly smile, and your sympathetic eyes.

In a reasonable world the ruinous effects of time and distance should render your absence increasingly less painful to endure. Yet, I only seem to feel your absence more as the years separate us. The further you stray from me, the further I stray from myself, and so, lest I disappear completely, I cling harder to your memory and to the knowledge that I will one day find you.

Please know, wherever you are, that I love you dearly and unconditionally, and that I will find you, I will, I will, I will.

Forever your loving twin,
Nora

Three days before Thanksgiving upon a crisp early morning fresh with a light dusting of snow, Nora was mopping the long corridor in the servants' quarters when Edmund appeared at the bottom of the stairwell.

"Your presence is required upstairs," he explained.

Nora propped the mop in its bucket and wiped the sweat from her brow, refastening the bun of her hair as she followed Edmund up the stairs. To her surprise Edmund proceeded past the upstairs kitchen and the pantry directly to the library, where an unfamiliar gentleman in a frock coat and necktie sat in a leather armchair with his hands in his lap, awaiting Nora.

"Miss Bergen, Mr. Trompette," said Edmund, bowing before vacating the room.

"Please sit down," said Mr. Trompette.

For the first time in all her years at Mr. Seymour's, Nora took a seat in the library, surveying her surroundings. The room was replete with burnished wood and fine furnishings, but in the style of Mr. Seymour, neither extravagant nor conspicuous in its décor. What immediately captured Nora's imagination were the books lining the walls, hundreds of leather-bound editions of varying sizes and shapes. Nora was seized with the impulse to stand up and inspect each one of them, to circle the perimeter of the room and read their leather spines as she ran her fingers across them. What a fortune and blessing it would be to possess so many books, to live and love and prosper inside of them, each one a small world in itself.

"Good morning, Miss Bergen," said Mr. Trompette, disrupting her meditations.

"Top of the morning to you, sir," said Nora, her hungry eyes still seeking out the wall of books behind him.

"Miss Bergen, it is with a heavy heart that I have summoned you here today," he said. "A very heavy heart, indeed."

"Sir?"

"I am afraid that last night our dear Mr. Seymour passed from this vale of tears," he said. "If it is any consolation this passing was painless and likely happened in his sleep, for that is where Edmund discovered him, tucked in bed, the lamp snuffed out, and a novel still open at his bedside."

Surprising herself, tears began to fill Nora's eyes immediately. While she'd resented Seymour until the bitter end for separating her from Finn, she had, in recent months, particularly since the death of Mrs. Seymour, grown cautiously fond of him. That the man had died reading a novel only further endeared him to her.

"First," said Mr. Trompette, "know that all arrangements regarding Mr. Seymour's memorial service are presently being tended to by my office expressly in compliance with Mr. Seymour's instructions. So you have nothing with which to concern yourself there. Edmund shall fill you in on the details once the arrangements have been set. Every detail shall be seen to, I assure you."

Why was he telling her any of this? Nora's thoughts began to scurry in every direction. But before her thoughts could pursue any path in particular, Mr. Trompette, having allowed for a moment of silence to let the news sink in, resumed speaking.

"Abraham was a unique man," he said philosophically. "Not an easy man to get close to, and by no means an easy man to predict."

"I'm afraid I hardly knew him, sir," said Nora.

"Which, Miss Bergen, is precisely in keeping with his character and relates directly to what I have to tell you."

"Sir?"

"First allow me to say that Mr. Seymour was a man who kept all of his business and financial matters in fastidious order. Every decision he made was thoughtful and considered, and his records were meticulous. And one of Mr. Seymour's chief financial concerns, particularly since the untimely passing of Mrs. Seymour, was the dispensation and subsequent administration of his will and estate in the event of his own demise. Both of these tasks have fallen upon the legal firm of Trompette, Kristoff, Tinker, and Petty, of which I am the chief officer and sole executor of Mr. Seymour's estate. And while the administration of the estate is a matter of considerable complexity, the actual dispensation of this wealth is quite simple, as in his will and testament, which I drafted myself, there exists but one heir to this fortune, and one heir only."

Here again Mr. Trompette allowed a moment for this information to sink in.

"Sir?" she said.

"The sole heir to Mr. Seymour's estate, to whom in eventuality all of this shall belong, is none other than you, Miss Bergen."

"Pardon me, sir?" said Nora, ears ringing.

"You, Miss Bergen, are the sole inheritor of Mr. Seymour's holdings in totality, which I can assure you are substantial," he explained. "We shall reserve the specifics for a later time. For now, we must give everybody involved the necessary time to grieve, of course."

"Sir, I don't understand. Me? Why me?"

"To be quite frank, neither do I understand, Miss Bergen. As I said at the outset Mr. Seymour was not an easy man to predict. I am aware that while you did not inherit his name, you were his legal ward, and that alone should entitle you to something. But as per Abraham's wishes you are entitled to all of his holdings, including all properties and all business holdings."

Nora nearly fell out of her chair.

"Even the books, sir?"

"To which books are you referring, Miss Bergen?"

"These books," she said, encompassing the room with a panoramic gesture.

Hoisting an eyebrow, Mr. Trompette seemed to be caught slightly off guard by this line of inquiry.

"Yes, of course the books," he said. "In addition to the library itself, the entire house; all of it Mr. Seymour has bequeathed entirely to you."

"But . . ."

"Yes, I can imagine this might be quite a shock," he said.

"I am nothing but a laundress and a cleaner and a cook," she said. "If Mr. Seymour cared so much for me, why did he not make me his own daughter? Why did he condemn me to slave away in the basement all these years?"

Mr. Trompette shook his head.

"Again, I cannot venture to speak on Mr. Seymour's behalf," he said. "But were I to speculate — knowing what I know about Abe, his mettle, his temperament, his romanticism, and his somewhat hard-won path in life — I would guess that this circumstance was intended as an exercise in character building, and possibly employed as something of a test, which needless to say you have passed, Miss Bergen."

Nora was numb with disbelief. Mr. Trompette's voice washed right over her, though she sat attentively, nodding her head on occasion.

"With regard to this money," he said, "it is to be kept in trust until such time as you are of sufficient age. At that time we shall discuss the administration of the estate, and it is my sincere hope that you will continue to employ my firm, whose long-standing association with Mr. Seymour cannot be understated."

"What happens to me, sir? Where do I go?"

"What do you mean, young lady?" he said, seemingly amused by the question. "Why, you stay right here."

"In my quarters?"

"Good heavens, child, wherever you want. The house is yours, all of it. Yes, even the books," he added wryly.

"But, sir, I still . . . I just can't seem to believe such a thing."

"Give it time, child," he said. "I suspect you will adjust."

"What of the rest of the staff, sir? What becomes of them?"

"That is for you to decide."

Here, Mr. Trompette reached into the pocket of his frock coat and produced a small card, which he presented to Nora.

The card was emblazoned with the name of his firm — Trompette, Kristoff, Tinker, and Petty — accompanied by an address, which Nora assumed could only be downtown in some impressive stone edifice.

"Should you need me for anything at all in the meantime," he said, "alert Edmund as such, or arrange a carriage yourself with the stableman, and call on me at the address on the card."

With this Mr. Trompette stood, took a bow, and proceeded to exit the library, where Edmund met him at the door to usher him out of the house. Nora remained seated. Surely all of this was a dream. When Edmund returned a moment later Nora was still seated, numb in her haze of disbelief.

"Should I move your belongings upstairs, Miss Bergen?" he said, startling her.

"Miss Bergen?" she said. "Edmund, it's me, Nora."

"I expect, Miss Bergen, that you're about to become something else to a lot of different folks, and that includes me," said Edmund. "Now, how would you prefer I proceed?"

"Oh, Edmund," she said. "All of this defies reason! Why me? How in the world has this happened?"

"Well now, Miss Bergen," said Edmund. "I suppose if I knew the answer to that, well then, it might just as well be me that was the sole heir to Mr. Seymour's estate."

"This is impossible. Oh, I'll never get used to this, Edmund, never," said Nora. "It doesn't make any sense!"

"Miss Bergen," said Edmund, "in my experience, a body can get used to just about anything, most especially money."

FINN BERGEN

Iowa, 1857

The Vogels finally settled with the Illinois & Missouri & Iowa Railroad Corporation, relinquishing their farm to the tune of thirty-five dollars per acre despite the misgivings of the loquacious Mr. Baxter and the flinty retorts of Mr. Anderson. Weeks later the IMIRC was absorbed by the MMRR, which had recently absorbed the RIRR and IIRR in its effort to connect Davenport to Council Bluffs at the state's western border. The result was a confusion of acronyms, the slow development of a railway across Iowa, and the quick manipulation of stock by a handful of wealthy gentlemen, among them a Mr. Worthy and a Mr. Best.

With their newly acquired capital, the Vogels relocated to Davenport, where they soon purchased a large city lot two blocks off the river and commenced construction of a sprawling three-story inn to be appropriately named the River Inn.

Though his labor was no longer necessary, Finn, having no plan of his own, accompanied the Vogels to Davenport, where he worked for some time toting water for construction crews. The work was monotonous next to the varied labor of farming, and Finn found his mood growing increasingly morose and dissatisfied as the weeks wore on.

Without Nora, what was there to pursue? What purpose could his life possibly fulfill when nobody needed him? Stasis might have been the natural course of action for a man seeking nobody and nothing, a man destined for a life of solitude. He ought to have surrendered gratefully to the tedium of his livelihood, he ought to have eaten and slept and toiled to the monotonous rhythm of his inconsequential life in Iowa. But there was no denying the restlessness that simmered beneath the surface of him. One afternoon he dropped his bucket and walked off the job, never to return.

And that was the beginning of Finn's wandering ways. With his obligation to the Vogels fulfilled and nothing else to hold him in place, his only impetus was to move; to where it did not matter. Within the week, he managed to secure employment with the MMRR, where he would soon drive what would be among the first railroad spikes into the Iowa hardpan. The days were long and the labor was arduous.

In the hours before dawn, Finn and the other workers would load the wagons with ties and haul them ahead, laying them out on the roadbed on four-foot setters. Then they'd double back in crews of two and four and set the rails upon the ties, adjusting them to gauge and bolting them together. When the wagons were empty they reloaded them once more and began the process over again.

When the rails were set, they began spiking. One man would start a spike and move on to the next rail, while the next man would finish driving the spike. In this manner they laid as much as a mile of track per day until, by the end of spring, they were thirty miles outside of Davenport, living in camps.

In summer, prior to his journey further west with the railroad, Finn returned to Davenport to bid farewell to the Vogels. He shared a tearful goodbye with Hans and Katrin on the steps of the Vogels' temporary residence, the River View Hotel, an establishment that, unlike their own soon-to-be-completed River Inn, conferred no view of the river whatsoever.

"I always said you are good boy," said Hans.

"You will always be our son," said Katrin, succumbing to grief as she clutched him fiercely about the shoulders.

"I'll be back," he said.

Even as the words left his mouth, Finn knew he was lying. He could not say why he'd never be back, but he knew he would not. He would stay the course west on the whim of whatever wind blew him there.

"You promise you'll be back?" said Katrin.

"I promise," said Finn.

"This is for you," said Hans, presenting him with a thin stack of banknotes.

"I can't take this," said Finn. "After all you've done for me, I can't."

"You will, it is yours," said Hans. "It is not much, I'm sorry to say, but it is something. The construction is accounting for most of the railroad money. You earned every penny of it, and you will take it. Now, put it somewhere safe."

Clutching the notes in his fist, Finn stuffed them deep in his pocket.

"Thank you, Papa."

"Go," said Hans. "Make good."

Finn's eyes were clouded with tears as he walked away from the River View Hotel, the goodbyes of Hans and Katrin trailing in his wake.

Within three days he caught back up with his crew, forty miles west of Davenport, and resumed his employment. He stayed on with the MMRR, laying rails and setting ties and driving spikes for an additional thirty-five miles west across the prairie. There was little talk among the workers. They worked in concert like the parts of a machine, forging ever ahead across the twenty-ninth state of

530

the union, shrinking the great wide world with every mile of track they laid.

Hourly Finn and the other men paused in their labor to watch the endless wagon trains stream past in the distance, bound for the western territories, for Nebraska, and Colorado, and beyond. And each time Finn paused to regard the ragged procession of humanity over the rutty trail, it seemed to take a little bit more of his imagination along with it, as the days unfolded, each like the last: loading wagons before dawn, laying ties, bolting rails, and driving spikes through the gritty afternoon heat.

After months with the MMRR, Finn's restlessness got the best of him again, and he walked off the job at the end of a long hot day in August. With the money the Vogels had given him, and what he'd managed to save in wages, he geared up in Iowa City and picked up a wagon train headed west through Nebraska and into the Oregon country. It was a Mormon family named Cowdery who took him on, a party comprised of two grown men, six children, and four women, one of whom was in a family way. Finn quickly learned that the Cowderys were not a talkative people except for the women, who talked among themselves, which was just fine with Finn, who was content to listen. By day he guided the wagons and scouted for game, and in the evenings he collected firewood with the children along the periphery of the trail.

As generous and kind as the Cowderys proved, Finn was never made to feel he belonged to them as they moved steadily west for days on end. More than anything, Finn felt like a curiosity to the Cowderys, particularly the children, who seemed to watch his every movement surreptitiously, peering out from behind their dirty bangs.

Finn spent three weeks on the wagon train before his supplies dwindled to nothing. Not wanting to be a burden in spite of the Cowderys' insistence, Finn abandoned his westward progress in the little village of Lancaster, amid the buffalo grass and salt marshes of the eastern Nebraska territory. The village, set along the east bank of Salt Creek, wasn't much to speak of; in fact it comprised only a rather shabby mercantile, an even sadder saloon, and a handful of intrepid settlers scattered across the vast prairie. The barren landscape of the place was like a reflection of Finn's inner life. Had Lancaster offered any opportunity, Finn surely would have hocked the little blue locket, his only unnecessary possession of any value, if only to escape the place.

For six nights he slept beneath the prairie sky, gazing up at the unfathomable firmament, the stars splashed across the bowl of night. He took no solace in the night sky. The loneliness was crushing, as though he could feel the weight of the heavens pushing down on him. He tried desperately to convince himself that maybe, just maybe, Nora was not dead after all. Perhaps the lone magpie had only been superstition. Perhaps if he clutched the locket tight enough, he could connect with her; maybe somewhere under the stars, Nora was listening for him, a notion Finn clung to as his eyes grew heavy each night.

On the seventh morning Finn opened his eyes to find a young Indian man standing directly above him, a knife clutched in his hand. Despite the weapon, he was not in a threatening posture; rather, he seemed to be regarding Finn curiously. Nonetheless alarmed, Finn raised his head slowly and propped himself up on his elbows as the Indian continued to scrutinize him.

He looked roughly Finn's age, though smaller in stature. He was barefoot and scantily clad, his skin bronzed in the morning light. He wore his black hair piled atop his head, and around his neck he wore a necklace, which looked to be strung with some manner of animal teeth.

For a long moment Finn engaged the young Indian, whose dark eyes were at once impassive and intense, and seemed capable of looking straight through Finn. The effect was chilling, and Finn knew instantly that the eyes of the Indian would never leave him should he manage to survive the encounter.

When Finn moved as if to stand, the young Indian tightened his grip on the knife but did not raise his hand or so much as flinch. Finn immediately rested back on his elbows again, the implacable eyes of the young Pawnee boring holes in him.

Though Finn himself was armed with a pistol at his waist and a rifle propped atop his leather pack beside him, the thought of making a move for either one hardly occurred to him. Finally, Finn rose to his feet slowly. The Indian, his flat expression unchanged, made no move with the knife. Slowly, Finn bent down and reached for his bag and rifle, the young man's gaze stuck to his every movement. Slinging the bag and rifle over his shoulder, his heart beating like a war drum in his chest, Finn turned his back and deliberately began walking away, half-certain that it would be the end of him. But it wasn't. Finn kept right on walking, and though he never dared to look back, he could still feel the Pawnee's eyes fixed on his retreating figure.

Malik Flowers

Portland, Oregon, 2019

His mom was nervous; Malik could tell because she was already clutching the little hand-carved wooden figurine that she always clutched during games, or just about any other time she was anxious. The figurine, a female form, arms akimbo, no more than three inches in height, was ancient and crudely carved, the work of not a craftsman but an amateur. It was worn smooth from handling for who knew how many years. Her grandmother had given it to his mom when she was a child, and his mother claimed it had been old even then.

His mom insisted they arrive at Union Station forty-five minutes early, but Malik didn't mind. In his seventeen years, he'd never set foot in Union Station, though it was a landmark he knew well, with its slim clock tower and its elegant brick sprawl. Sometimes Malik thought he wanted to be an architect. Sometimes he thought he wanted to be a poet. Sometimes he thought he wanted to be an actor or a director. But always, since age three and a half, he had known he wanted to ball, every minute of every day. Because hoops had it all: architecture, poetry, drama. Hoops was a dance, and a battle, and a story all at the same time. If hoops wasn't his destiny, it was at least his ticket there.

"Okay, you were right," said his mom. "We're too early."

"Whatever," said Malik. "I'm good."

It was true there were worse places to spend forty-five minutes than amid the ornate ceilings and marble walls of Union Station, looking out the window at the falling snow. Really, it was idyllic. If only he could get his mom to stop worrying long enough to see that.

"You got your brace?" she said.

"Yeah, Ma, I got it," he said.

"What about your IcyHot?"

"I got it, I got it."

"I want you to stay hydrated. Just because it's cold out, don't mean —"

"Ma, relax, would you?"

Malik set a hand on her shoulder and gave it a squeeze. Though she was five foot ten, with an athletic build, her shoulder felt tiny in Malik's giant hand.

"Now, when we get on the train you should rest. You might have a hard time sleeping tonight. God knows I will."

"Ma, stop, would you?"

"Baby, I'm just being a mother."

"I get it, Ma. But we've been over all of this stuff like a million times. Let's just enjoy the moment."

His mom heaved a sigh. "You're right. Just too nervous, I guess," she said. "What about you, you nervous?"

"Heck no," he said. "I'm excited. It's gonna be crazy fun."

"You just take care of that rock, Malik Flowers," she said. "Some of these boys are going to be quicker than you're used to. If you get matched up with that Jamal Victor from Memphis, and I've got a feeling you will, you use that quick first step of yours. Use your eyes if you face him up. Head fake, twitch, get him to bite. You're quicker than he is."

"I will, Ma," he said.

"And he's a bully, so don't let him muscle you down low. He's got a few pounds on you, so you gotta be aggressive — but not too aggressive. Use your hips. Last thing you want to do is get in foul trouble. Folks are going to be looking at your whole makeup, remember that. They want to see how you conduct yourself on and off the court."

"I know all this already."

"Well, I'm just reminding you," she said. "That's my job."

"Well, maybe you need to take a break once in a while."

No sooner had the words left his mouth than Malik felt guilty.

As aggravating as his mom's badgering and relentless instruction could be, Malik was beholden to it in so many ways. He knew he'd be nowhere without his mom. More than anybody or anything else, she accounted for who he was. It was his mom who had shaped him, more than school, more than the neighborhood, more than his friends, and more than his dad, obviously. And yet she rarely felt it necessary to remind him, though pretty much her entire life for the past seventeen years had been focused on creating opportunities for Malik, something Malik had been given to understand at a young age. His mom worked her tail off at a job she didn't love, and she never complained, all so that Malik could thrive. Malik knew it cost a small fortune just to feed him, let alone clothe him, and send him to camps, and pay for the dentist. His mom did his laundry, she made his meals, she relearned math in order to help him with his studies and paid for Kayla Ramsey once it was beyond her facility. She grilled Malik on the playbook: Flex, shuffle, swing, zone, man-up — his mom knew the concepts almost as well as Coach M. And the way she constantly advocated for Malik, the way she held him to a high standard, the way she pushed him to be his best self, hardly ever giving so much as a thought to herself or her own needs. And then there was this: Whatever his mother couldn't give him, God had provided Malik in size and strength and agility, quickness of mind and foot.

Just as the intercom disrupted Malik's thoughts, the line began to move, and he and his mom hefted their bags and shuffled forward.

"You got your ticket?" his mom said.

"Of course I've got my ticket."

When Malik got to the podium, the ticket taker, a bald guy in a visor, with reading glasses perched on the bridge of his nose, looked up at Malik as though his size were amusing.

"Don't bump your head boarding, son," he said.

"No worries, I'm used to ducking," said Malik with a grin.

The platform was bustling with passengers and crew. Yet, for all the activity, the train yard maintained that muffled, peaceful quality that Malik liked more than anything else about snow, the way it quieted the world, and seemed to slow down time, and forced you to acknowledge its beauty.

"Wait, Ma, stop," he said, pausing on the platform and holding his forearm out to impede her progress.

He wanted to savor the moment. Tomorrow he had an opportunity to shine on the biggest stage he'd ever known, and everything felt right; he could see it all before him as sure as if it had already happened. He knew he was going to have a monster game, he knew it in his bones, in his muscles; he felt the certainty coursing through his veins. And he was so grateful for this knowledge, this certainty, so grateful for the doors opening up one by one in front of him, that it was almost embarrassing sometimes.

With his hand resting once more on his mother's tiny shoulder, Malik stood perfectly still looking up at the falling snow, his heart beating the slow, steady rhythm of a basketball on hardwood. And he thanked God, just as his mom had taught him to.

"You're gonna catch yourself a chill standing around in this, boy," she said.

No sooner did they take their seats in the second-to-last car than Malik's stomach started complaining, despite a six-egg breakfast, which had also included three pieces of toast, a grapefruit, two strips of bacon, and a glass of milk.

"I'm hungry," he said.

"What else is new?" said his mom.

"Can we go to the food car?"

"I packed hoagies," she said, reaching for her handbag.

"Righteous," said Malik.

The whistle sounded and the train pulled out of the station. Malik unwrapped his hoagie and turned his face to the window as the train left Portland through the back door, a part of the city Malik had never seen: an industrial backwater, wedged between the hillside and the river with blocks of graffiti-covered warehouses, a power station, an army of fuel tanks squatting in odd formation along the riverbank, all of it practically deserted in the snow.

The next bend offered a feast for the eyes. There, rising out the murky Willamette, at once majestic and a little sinister, was the St. Johns Bridge. Malik stopped chewing his bite of hoagie and craned his neck as the train passed under the bridge. His entire life he'd lived in Portland and he'd never crossed the St. Johns Bridge. How small his world had been up to this moment. Once again he could feel the budding possibilities of his future about to blossom.

"You gonna choke if you don't swallow that bite soon," said his mom.

Malik swallowed as instructed, then smiled.

"What are you smiling about?"

"This," he said. "All of it. It's happening. It's all coming true."

Malik watched as his mom tried but failed to suppress her own contentment, a hint of a smile playing at the corners of her mouth.

"Malik, baby, this is just one more rung in a long ladder," she said. "And the Flowerses been climbing a long time. I hope you appreciate that, how long we've been climbing."

541

"I do," he said. "I was just thinking that. I was thanking God for giving me this opportunity. I was thinking how I'm gonna make the most of every moment of it. I'm gonna own it, Ma, then I'm gonna give it all back once I got it."

"Well, you ain't got it yet," she said. "We still got a lot of work to do."

"Aw, don't you ever relax?" said Malik with a sigh.

"This is no time to relax," she said. "You gotta stay loose, sure, relaxed in your body, but focused, poised, inside yourself, Malik Flowers. So you can slow the game down like you do, so you can slow your whole life down. Make those grades, get that scholarship, get that degree."

Malik refreshed his smile and shook his head.

"I love you, Ma," he said. "But dang, you need a vacation."

"I wouldn't know what to do with a vacation," she said.

Someday, thought Malik, someday not too distant, someday so close he could smell it, feel it, taste it, he could send his mom on a real vacation — Hawaii, or Las Vegas. God, but he was impatient to get to that someday.

"I'ma buy you a big house someday, Ma."

"Hush your mouth," she said. "Don't be counting your money piles before you earned them."

"Well, some house, anyway."

"You just keep climbing that ladder one rung at a time, Malik Flowers. Maybe you ought to finish that hoagie and get some rest."

"I don't want to miss anything," he said.

"Miss what? Ain't nothing to see but more snow," she said. "You best get your rest."

Oh, but there was so much to see! How could she diminish it like that? Once they crossed the river and were finally clear of the city and its outlying sprawl, the countryside opened up, white, and still, and full of promise. Vast fields and gently rolling hills, and marshes studded with bare trees, all of it shrouded in a bracing stillness. The scene was like something out of one of the poems Miss Reko read aloud in class, plain and magical at the same time. Maybe that was the whole key to life, to celebrate the magic amid the plainness.

In spite of all her hounding about getting some rest, it was Malik's mom who fell asleep within twenty minutes of leaving Union Station. Head slumped against Malik's arm, she snored softly.

The conductor strode down the aisle in his goofy hat and vest, nodding at Malik as he passed. Malik gave a little nod in response before turning his attention back toward the window. Outside, the early-afternoon sky had darkened. The snow was beginning to hit the glass slantwise, blurring Malik's view. Malik thought about fishing his earbuds out of his backpack. He almost reached for the phone in his pocket. But in the end he decided to sit back and embrace the quietude and feel the hypnotic rhythm of the rails pulsing up through his legs to his chest.

WALTER BERGEN

Southern Washington, 2019

A frozen air compressor cost them six minutes in Portland, where the desk made the decision to bypass the device in order to avoid further delay, which was nothing too unusual; Walter couldn't count the times they'd bypassed a compressor. Still, as the Coast Starlight crossed the Willamette in the shadow of the St. Johns Bridge and hurried on its way north, Walter was doing more gauge-watching than usual, keeping a cautious eye on the main brake reservoir, where the pressure read a stable 125 psi, with the brake pipe holding steady at 110.

The snow started falling harder and the wind picked up considerably once the train cleared Vancouver and began skirting the Columbia Slough. Abrupt hills now rose to the east, hunkering around the little interstate towns of southwest Washington. Now and again the train shuddered in the wind, and though visibility was not great, the sight lines and signals were clear throughout the block. Anticipating no restrictions and determined to make up time, Walter kept running at speed through Kelso, where the Cowlitz merged with the Columbia and the big steam turbines of the power plant were still pumping their plumes into the frigid air.

Macy popped into the cab once more.

"You change your mind about smoking that cigarette in here?" said Walter.

"Nah," said Macy. "Maybe I can sneak one in Olywa."

"You should have thought of that when they were dicking with the separator back in Portland."

"Can we not talk about smoking, Wally?" said Macy. "Anything from dispatch?"

"Nothing."

"How's the pressure on the main?"

"Steady."

"Didn't see that one coming, eh?" said Macy. "Oh, and by the way, if the train feels heavier it might be because we picked up a giant in Portland — gotta be seven feet tall, I swear. Hands like this big. You should see this kid, Wally. He can hardly fit in his seat."

"Imagine what economy class on Delta would look like for a guy like that," said Walter. "No wonder he's taking the train. Can't beat it for elbow room."

"A company man to the end, Wally," said Macy, patting him on the shoulder, before ducking back out.

The end. That was how Macy must have viewed Walter's retirement, too, like a sort of death. To think some people actually looked forward to it. What on earth had Walter been thinking when he decided to pull the pin? The truth was he never would have taken the buyout if it weren't for having to pay for Wendy's wedding, though he'd never let Wendy know as much.

Walter continued to eye the gauges and monitor the main reservoir. He now had limited sight of the wayside through the windshield, as the snow had begun to freeze on the wipers and the engine was running directly into the wind. But with no restrictions, Walter maintained maximum speed, running his headlights on high against the driving snow.

Walter would have the rest of his days to contemplate what happened next. He knew the block inside and out. He could have navigated the curve south of Centralia in his sleep. Thus, it did not sneak up on Walter, despite the terrible visibility. Nor did Walter underestimate the curve, which was graded for high speed with its banked high rail. He eased back on the throttle through the turn, then started picking up speed again on the straightaway. It was at that juncture that Walter, contrary to every regulation, not to mention his better judgment, unpocketed his buzzing phone and not only dared to glance at it but began reading the most recent of the three texts he'd received since morning — the first of them from Annie.

Oh, and honey, can you pick up a bag of ice on your way home?

There it was, just as he'd suspected, the surprise party. The text was as good as an admission. Since when did they ever buy ice by the bag?

As he was about to flip to the second message, Walter glanced up to check his speed, then peered out the windshield, where, like a shock of cold water, reality crashed upon him. They were at full speed when Walter dropped the phone, threw the throttle into idle, and laid on the brakes. Even as the ear-piercing squeal shattered the calm, he knew there was no avoiding impact; the best he could hope to do was slow the train. In that terrible instant, as the train began to shudder and Walter bore down on the brakes, willing the train to stop with every fiber of his being, it was impossible to discern the riot of his thoughts from the cacophony of the screeching train as it hurtled toward the obstruction.

A half second later, the train lurched violently, throwing Walter headlong against the instrument panel.

WINSTON CHEN-MURPHY

The Coast Starlight, 2019
After an hour on the Coast Starlight, Winston's opinion of the journey had begun to soften considerably. The scenery was actually pretty epic, especially once they crossed the river into Washington and the train hugged the bank of a wide river he overheard a man behind him call the Columbia Slough. Maybe it was the snow rushing past, but eighty miles per hour actually felt faster than he expected, though he was not about to tell his dad that. It was relaxing the way the speeding train jostled him side to side, and he found the rhythmic clatter of the cars over the rails hypnotic.

For weeks, Winston had been missing his friends, particularly Evan and Hunter. Not a day went by that he didn't think of his old life in San Francisco. Just the regular stuff he took for granted, like riding the Muni or the way the skyline looked when it was all lit up at night. Or the fact that everybody wasn't white. Though his mom hadn't really warmed to their new life in Oregon yet, it was obvious to Winston that his dad was happier, and more relaxed, and Winston was glad for that. He didn't understand it, or wouldn't accept it at first, but now he understood why the move was a good idea, how it made sense in a lot of ways for the family, and his dad's being happy was one of those ways. He wished his mom would be happier. It was like she'd forgotten how. When he'd said as much to his dad last week, his dad had told him that they all needed to cut Mom some slack, and explained that she was burned out from her job and that she just needed some time to sink into what he called a more "mellow" life. Yes, his dad had said *mellow*.

And it seemed on the Coast Starlight just then that maybe it was finally starting to sink in. For, as she sat directly across from him, looking out the window, oblivious to his steady gaze, with Tyler sound asleep against her shoulder, Winston thought his mom looked prettier, and happier than she had in months. He almost didn't want to disturb her, but he really wanted to check out the dining car, and he needed money.

LAILA TULLY

The Coast Starlight, 2019

With her stomach protesting, and her buffet leftovers long exhausted, Laila finally resolved to buy something in the dining car. There was a line all the way into the next car and past the bathrooms. Laila took her place in line behind the tallest human being she'd ever encountered, a young Black man, maybe seventeen or eighteen, standing head and shoulders above anybody else in line.

"I wonder if we'll get to the front of the line before Seattle," said Laila.

"I hope so," said the giant.

"I was just joking," said Laila. "That's in like three hours."

The kid broke into a broad grin. "I gotcha," he said. "I'll already be hungry again by then. I can eat like a boss."

"You would have liked my old job," said Laila.

"Yeah?"

"All-you-can-eat buffet," she said.

"Sounds righteous," he said. "Me and my mom used to go to the buffet once in a while. Until one time she got sick. Boy, did she get sick."

"That sucks," said Laila.

"Yeah, I used to load up two plates at a time," he said. "Those cheesy potatoes were the ticket."

"You gotta eat them with ham," said Laila.

"Facts," he said.

"I'm Laila, by the way," she said, thrusting a hand upward at him, which he soon enveloped in his own giant hand as if it were a baby bird.

"I'm Malik," he said. "Malik Flowers."

"Cool name," she said.

"Yeah, it's all right, I guess," he said. "Mom won't let me use my dad's name."

"What's that?" said Laila.

"Woods."

"Hmm," said Laila, considering. "Malik Woods. Nah, personally, I like Flowers better. Malik Flowers. It sounds like somebody famous."

"You think?" said Malik.

"Yeah," said Laila. "Totally."

"You going home to Seattle?" said Malik. "Or you just visiting, or what?"

"I'm going to a place called Queets," she said. "Not very exciting, unless you're really into rain. It's supposedly really pretty, but there's nothing much there."

"So, why you going?" said Malik.

"Just for a change," said Laila.

"I feel ya," said Malik.

Laila and Malik made small talk until Malik finally reached the front of the food line. He tried ordering a sandwich or a burger, but they'd already run out. So he ordered two bags of chips and a yogurt, then retired to the only unoccupied booth, his legs not quite fitting beneath the table.

Laila almost bailed at the counter when she saw the prices, but in spite of herself, she ordered hummus and Pretzel Crisps, to the tune of four dollars and fifty cents. She almost bought a bottle of water to wash it down, but she couldn't justify the two-dollar-and-fifty-cent expenditure.

"You mind?" she said to Malik, approaching his booth.

"Nah," he said. "Go for it."

Laila sat herself opposite Malik in the booth, peeling back the plastic seal of her hummus container.

Malik was tapping his giant foot under the table.

"So, what are you doing in Seattle?" said Laila. "If I'm not being nosey."

"I gotta ball tomorrow," he said. "Invitational basketball tournament. Man, I can't wait. Been waiting forever for the opportunity to get on the court with some of these guys."

The way he said it, his urgency, and his

conviction, made Laila wish that her own life possessed any such focus or clarity. She wished she had something that she simply had to do tomorrow, something she'd been looking forward to forever, some commitment so pressing that the very idea of its not happening was inconceivable. If only she were running toward something, instead of away from something. What would that even feel like? When had Laila's life ever promised anything better than what she was born into? When had anyone expected anything remarkable from her, let alone encouraged her, or taught her how to navigate a future?

Looking across the table at Malik, Laila noted that he'd stopped chewing midbite, and had tilted his head back slightly and closed his eyes.

"Are you okay?" said Laila.

"Oh, yeah," said Malik, opening his eyes and resuming his chewing.

"What were you thinking about? Is it all right if I ask?" said Laila. "I mean, you don't have to tell me. You just looked so, I don't know, at peace or something."

"Just daydreaming tomorrow," he said with a smile. "Man, I can't wait. I'm gonna own tomorrow."

"How do you do it?" she said.

"Do what?"

"Daydream it."

"It's like you just see it in your mind," he

554

said. "You visualize what it's gonna be like."

"Does it work?" said Laila hopefully. "I mean, does it happen the way you daydream it?"

"Not exactly," he said. "Sometimes it does. But it prepares me, you know? So, when I get there, it's like I've been there before, and I know what to expect, and that allows me to be confident, and that's when I play best."

Laila couldn't help but lean into Malik's assurance, wishing that she, too, could somehow envision her own tomorrow, and that it could be as tangible as a basketball game.

Malik soon finished his second bag of chips, then, with some difficulty, extricated his enormous legs from beneath the table and rose to his full, stooping height.

"Good luck tomorrow," said Laila.

"You too," he said.

As she watched him stride down the aisle and duck out of the dining car, she said his name under her breath, so as to remember it when he was famous: Malik Flowers.

When she returned to her seat, Laila sat back, and closed her eyes, and tried to daydream tomorrow. All she could see, though, was herself in another casino kitchen, wearing another dirty apron, with another lousy truck waiting for her in the parking lot. But at least there was no Boaz.

About an hour north of Portland, the Coast Starlight was humming along, and Laila was

555

right on the edge of a much-needed sleep, when there came a terrific caterwaul from beneath the train, a hideous metal screeching. An instant later, her body was racked when she was thrown suddenly forward into the empty seat across from her, her chin hitting the padded armrest. Momentarily dazed, but otherwise unharmed, Laila gathered her bearings. Following the brief, stunned silence after impact, the train was brimming with chatter.

"Are you okay?" asked a middle-aged man across the aisle from her, himself discombobulated.

"Yeah, thanks," said Laila. "You?"

"I think so," he said.

A moment later a crewmember stumbled into the car, blood smeared on his face. He took three or four steps past Laila before a woman burst into the car at the opposite end and appealed desperately to the dazed crewmember.

Laila would not soon forget the look in the woman's eyes, the fear and helplessness she saw there.

"I need medical attention for my son immediately," she said.

Brianna Flowers

Southern Washington, 2019

A few miles north of Woodland, Brianna awoke with her head on Malik's shoulder and straightened up, feeling neither rested nor refreshed. She smoothed the lap of her work slacks and straightened her hair before sinking back into her seat, jostled ever so lightly side to side by the shuddering progress of the train. Hard as she tried to relax and enjoy the ride, it was no use. She couldn't settle her worried mind. The snow, the finances, Malik's performance tomorrow — all of these concerns cycled through her thoughts relentlessly.

Meanwhile, beside her, though the seat could barely contain his colossal frame, Malik seemed perfectly at ease, texting with giant thumbs and smiling, apparently without a care in the world.

"Who's that you texting?" said Brianna. "Is that the girl you're not telling me about?"

"Nah, no girl."

Brianna didn't buy it. There had to be somebody. No teenage boy was impervious to girls. And she knew Malik was a hero in the hallways of BFH, so it wouldn't take much effort on his part.

"You can tell me, you know," said Brianna.

"Ma, I told you, there's no girl."

"Who is it that's got you smiling like that then?"

"It's just Dad," he said, evading her eyes.

Brianna slumped inwardly. "Hmph," she said.

"What?" said Malik.

Brianna resisted the urge to comment. She usually pulled her punches when it came to Darnell, if only for Malik's sake. It wasn't a mother's place to put down a boy's father, no matter how much of a deadbeat he was.

"Nothing," said Brianna, looking across the aisle out the opposite window, where the snowy hills huddled around the sleepy town of Kalama.

No matter how many promises Darnell Woods made or how many new leaves he turned over, he always was, and always would be, short on commitment and long on charm, with his toothy smile and silver tongue, his gold filling and tattoo sleeves and contagious enthusiasm for anything that didn't require his paying a price. Darnell had left when Malik was only four years old. Not that he had been around much prior to that time. He wasn't even at the hospital the night Malik was born. He hadn't paid his child support in eight years despite any number of court orders. Brianna could probably have had him arrested for noncompliance. Occasionally Darnell showed up on weekends or holidays to visit Malik, but beyond that he couldn't be counted on for anything.

Brianna was willing to give Darnell credit for quitting drugs and alcohol and getting some counseling, but she would only give him so much. Sure, he'd gotten a steady job for once; good for him. About time he grew up. Sure, he'd managed to stay out of jail, and mostly out of trouble. He'd even managed another baby mama along the way. But for three years he hadn't even called or sent a birthday card. He hadn't shown back up in Malik's life until Malik was eleven, when the five-foot-ten prodigy started showing athletic promise in such a way that folks began taking note.

"Aw, c'mon, Ma," said Malik, pocketing his phone. "He ain't asking me for anything."

"Don't say *ain't,*" said Brianna.

"When you gonna give him a break?" said Malik.

"As soon as he gives me one," she said.

"Look at it this way: He gave you me, right?" said Malik.

Brianna arched her brow and cocked her head to one side. "Oh, did he?" she said. "Is that how that worked?"

"You know what I mean," he said.

"Why don't you go ahead and call yourself Malik Woods then?" she said.

"Knock it off, Ma."

Brianna turned her face to the window, her own weary expression reflecting back at her. He had a lot of damn nerve, Darnell. Being Malik's biggest fan sure was a convenient distinction these days, wasn't it? All that promise just waiting to happen, who knew how a dad might benefit if Malik rode out a Division I scholarship and cashed in come the draft? You could bet Darnell would be hanging around then, even if he didn't come to but one game every season, even if he hadn't called the night the Quakers won state and Malik scored thirty-eight points. But you could bet Darnell was bragging about Malik to somebody somewhere. And with Malik on his way to the big time, Darnell would be just one more hanger-on, insinuating himself into Malik's life as though he'd been there since the beginning, but really just looking to catch a ride on Malik's coattails, when it was Brianna who'd done all the work, Brianna who'd supported Malik every minute of every day, Brianna who'd nursed him through his every ailment and bitten her nails to the quick worrying about his future.

Not that Brianna wanted to profit from Malik's success, not monetarily anyway. No, this wasn't about money. She'd lived without money for so long she wouldn't even know what to do with it. Pride was at stake. As far as Brianna was concerned, Darnell didn't deserve to share the pride in or the credit for Malik, because Darnell hadn't helped build or mold what Malik had become and was becoming. Darnell had made his careless contribution eighteen years ago and moved on shortly thereafter. But you could bet he'd come back around when there was something to profit by. You could bet he'd be filling the boy's head about how much he always believed in him, and how he knew Malik was destined for the big time, and how Malik wasn't just born with that wicked crossover or that sweet midrange jumper, he'd learned them from Darnell.

"What'd he say?" said Brianna.

"Almost the exact same thing as you," said Malik. "If I get matched up with Victor, use my first step. And he said the same thing about facing guys up. That's why I was laughing. You two say the same shit all the time."

"Watch your mouth," she said.

"Well, it's true," he said. "You sound just like each other, but y'all both won't admit it."

Brianna turned her attention out across the aisle again as Malik slid his earbuds in and faced the window, looking perfectly relaxed. And why not?

Imagine dunking on doubt. Imagine throwing a crossover on guilt, powering past poverty with your shoulder down, and driving to the rack while your opposition cringed. Imagine dreaming. Malik did it almost every day of his life, in heart and mind and body. No wonder he was so relaxed, no wonder he was so confident.

Brianna had been adulting so long she couldn't remember what it looked like to have the world in front of her, what it felt like to let herself dream, what it felt like to let her joy or her confidence lead her, to throw her yearning out in front of her actions. For most of her life she'd played defense: defending against disappointment and worst-case scenarios, fighting her way around screens, navigating zones, and getting beat.

When she was nine years old Brianna wanted to be an actor. Nothing ever became of it, except that she ended up being a player in her own life, playing whatever role would benefit Malik, or her father and sisters before him. Whether it was dressing up for interviews or applying for health insurance, even if it meant sucking up to Don, or the four bosses before him, Brianna was always acting the role of responsible adult. All that she'd ever wanted for Malik was that he wouldn't have to do the same, that he could define the terms of his own life, if only on a basketball court.

With the vibration of the train wheels pulsing up through her body, Brianna let her mind wander into the realm of the unthinkable. Rarely did she allow herself to contemplate life after Malik. But something about being on that train with the open landscape speeding past and the hum of the rails rumbling up through the soles of her feet put Brianna in just such a contemplative mood. Once Malik was on his path, what then? Would she stay in the same apartment? She supposed she would, if only so Malik could have something familiar to come back to from college. She had to find something else, anything else. She'd clean houses, or wait tables, or work as a receptionist before she spent another day working for the likes of Don LoPriori, even if it paid less than what she'd made at Consolidated.

And what about meeting somebody after Malik was gone? Now, there was a possibility that Brianna had scarcely entertained since Malik was in kindergarten. At thirty-three Brianna was an island. She couldn't even remember what it felt like to be lonely. She had given the last of her adolescence and the whole of her adult life exclusively to utility, leaving her own needs in the rearview mirror. Her small pleasures did not include the touch of a man. She couldn't remember companionable silence. She couldn't remember eating off somebody else's plate or sipping someone else's beer. At this point Brianna couldn't even imagine sharing a bed with anybody.

What would become of her alone in the empty apartment? What would she do every evening after work, if not serve Malik? How would she fill her weekends without the occupation of being Malik's taxi between practices, and tutors, and friends' houses? And after all these years, what would she do on game nights? What would become of her well-worn purple foam butt pad and her customary thermos of black coffee if he played college ball in North Carolina or Kentucky? What would she keep score for, what would she tally up at the end of each night? The thought of her life alone was too depressing to contemplate.

Malik must have seen these thoughts written on her face.

"What's up, Ma?" he said, removing his earbuds. "What're you thinking about?"

"Nothing," she said.

"You nervous?" he said.

"What about you?" she said.

"Nah, just hungry."

"Again?" she said.

Malik smiled sheepishly and gave a shrug. "So, like, we got any more sandwiches?"

"Boy, you just came from the dining car ten minutes ago."

"All they had was chips."

"There's one more sandwich in the backpack," she said. "Get it yourself. I gotta use the ladies' room."

Brianna was about four strides down the aisle when suddenly there came a terrible metallic squall from the undercarriage as the train halted abruptly, throwing Brianna headlong down the aisle three rows, where she glanced off a seat back as the train came crashing to a halt. Brianna careened forward another two rows, her body twisting in midair before she landed hard upon her back in the aisle, her head ringing as the babbling of stunned passengers washed over her.

WALTER BERGEN

Southern Washington, 2019

For a moment after the impact Walter lay stunned, facedown on the floor of the cab. No sooner did he roll over onto his back than Macy burst in.

"Wally? Wally, you okay? What the hell happened? You're bleeding."

Walter sat up groggily, and immediately blood from his nose streamed down the front of his vest and he was forced to lie back down.

"Don't sugarcoat it," said Walter. "How bad is it?"

Macy couldn't even look him in the eye.

"Not good, Wally."

"How bad?"

"Not good. I don't know if we jumped the rails, but we've got problems. Look, stop the bleeding with your nose there, and call the bureau, put them on standby. I've got to run damage control."

Walter swiped at his face with a sleeve and pinched the bridge of his nose to staunch the bleeding as Macy gazed grimly out the cracked windshield of the engine, taking inventory of the jumble of branches.

"You didn't see it coming?"

"It snuck up on me," said Walter.

Macy sighed, checking his watch reflexively, then gazing back out the damaged windshield at the dense tangle of limbs.

"Look," he said. "Don't beat yourself up about this, Wally."

But before Walter could even formulate a reply, Macy had already leapt back into action.

As Walter lay on his back, he listened to the discord all about him: the muffled distress of the passengers, the hiss of the ruptured brake lines, the squawk of the radios in the distance. "Not good" was a massive understatement. This was an unmitigated disaster. For three decades Walter had managed to avoid such a fiasco, and here he was shitting the bed on his final day as an engineer.

Once his nose stopped bleeding, Walter sat up, then rose to his feet, swooning. He steadied himself against the panel and radioed the bureau, whose primary concern seemed to be the condition of the train. Walter left Cal, the brakeman, to monitor the radio. Donning his jacket and clutching his Maglite, Walter climbed down out of the engine into the frigid evening.

The snow had stopped, but the wind was

whipping around pretty good. Though a plow had apparently been through recently, there were already three or four inches of fresh snow drifting along the rails. Walter tromped around to the front of the engine, obscured by the fallen tree, a fir maybe three feet in diameter with a dense canopy, pressed and twisted against the front of the engine. Fighting his way through the limbs, Walter eventually got a decent look at the damage.

Miraculously, the engine had not derailed upon impact, though countless limbs were wedged up under the dented grille and between the drive wheels. Ducking under the downed tree, Walter fought through the limbs and around to the far side of the engine, where he found many more limbs wedged up under the drive belt. Though several of the running lights were shattered, and the windshield was cracked, and the grille was caved in a bit by the force of the impact, the engine had weathered the collision surprisingly well.

The butt of the tree was positioned at a twenty-degree angle across the track, between two and five feet off the ground. The end of the tree extended thirty feet beyond the wayside. Even if the engine were in running order, there'd be no getting around the tree moving to the north. Walter could try to charge her back south with the rear engine, but that remained to be seen. Likely they were going to need another train to get these people out of here.

Bending down as much as his sixty-three-year-old body would let him, Walter peered under the skirt, shining his flashlight beneath the chassis and surveying the length of the engine. There was quite a bit of debris, but not so much that he couldn't see past it. He frisked the drive belt with his light beam, and he could see the limbs were pretty well lodged. There were several more limbs behind the drive wheels. Walter straightened up, clicked his light off momentarily, and looked at the stars now splashed across the sky, filling his lungs with the frigid air. As long as nobody was hurt, he could endure this.

Clicking his Maglite back on, he began walking the length of the passenger cars, avoiding the inquisitive faces pressed to the windows, shining the beam of his Maglite in and around the wheels and hoses beneath the chassis. When he'd walked the length of the train, he circled the rear engine and did the same on the other side. Everything with the exception of the ruptured brake line and the hoses between ten and eleven, which had disconnected upon impact, was in order. He started trudging back toward the rear of the train past the expectant faces, his leather boots soaked on the inside. When he reached the rear engine, Walter mounted the ladder and hoisted himself aboard. Once inside the cab, he removed his coat again. The blood on his vest, though not dry, had turned to a darker shade of black. He turned on the overhead lights, fired up the panel, and charged the engine. Cupping his hands, he tried to blow some warmth back into them.

Finally, Walter eased the throttle in reverse to determine whether the train would budge. He gave it several goes, but just as he'd suspected, he was unable to break the front engine free of the entanglement. Now it was settled; they would need a train to drag them south to the nearest platform. That, or they'd be forced to offload passengers on-site and into another coach, and that would be more of a hassle by a magnitude of twenty.

Walter reached for the handset just as Macy joined him in the cab.

"What's the status?"

"We're not going anywhere under our own power," said Walter.

"I figured as much," Macy said. "I'll update dispatch and the desk, you radio the bureau."

"Anybody hurt?" said Walter.

"Yeah, uh, there's some . . . some injuries, it looks like," he said, trying to sound casual. "Look, Wally, you gotta get out there and help me."

And with that, Macy ducked out of the cab and resumed his duties, leaving Walter to make the call to the bureau. No sooner had he completed this dreaded task than Walter felt as though he might pass out. Gathering his equilibrium, he strode out of the cab to run damage control and see what his negligence had wrought.

MALIK FLOWERS

The Coast Starlight, 2019

Malik rushed to the prone figure of his mom and kneeled directly above her. She was bleeding from a cut on her forehead, and though she was conscious, she had a thousand-yard stare.

"Ma, talk to me, you okay?"

She moved her lips, but Malik was unable to register her response, her voice faint, the syllables all rolled together like she was talking in her sleep.

Malik was about to help her to her feet before a longhaired guy with facial piercings stopped him short.

"You're not supposed to move them," he said. "In case, like, they broke their neck or severed their spine or something. Go get help, bro."

Malik leapt to his feet and strode the length of the car, ducking through the tiny vestibule to the next car, calling out for help. Nobody among the bewildered passengers answered his call. Midway through the second car he practically collided with an old guy wearing a vest and tie and a black Amtrak hat. His name tag read "Walter." There was dried blood under his nose and on his chin, and what looked like more blood upon the front of his vest.

"You gotta help me," said Malik. "Come quick."

"What is it, son?"

"It's my ma, she's hurt bad, you gotta do something."

"Okay, now, stay calm," Walter said. "Where is she?"

"Two cars back," said Malik.

By the time Malik rushed Walter back to his mom, she was alert, though still flat on her back, the guy with the pierced face offering her assurances. He soon cleared out to make room for Malik and Walter.

"Ma'am," said Walter, kneeling down, "can you tell me where you're hurt? Is it your head?"

No sooner had he said it than Walter produced a handkerchief from his inside vest pocket and daubed the blood off her forehead.

"No," she said. "It's my shoulder."

"Is anybody a doctor or a nurse?" Walter called out.

"We need to get her to the hospital," said Malik.

"We will, son," said Walter.

Walter was winging it, and he was sure it was showing. Somewhere in the distant past he'd received cursory training, had been briefed on dealing with such medical emergencies, but none of it came back to him now when he needed it.

"Tell me about your shoulder, ma'am," he said. "Can you feel it?"

"Oh, I can feel it plenty."

"It hurts?"

"Yeah, it hurts all right," she said.

It was a stupid question, and Walter knew it. Even worse, he had no idea what stupid question to follow it up with. How was he to proceed, what was the medical protocol? Obviously, he shouldn't move her. Would it be okay to prop something, a coat, a pillow, under her head? Should he cover her up with a coat or a blanket? What could he possibly ascertain through questioning that might help remedy the woman's situation, or at least get things moving in the right direction?

"Can you move it?" he said.

"I sure don't feel like trying," said the woman, her face sweating profusely.

"What do we do?" said the woman's son, the giant.

Walter daubed the cut on her forehead once more and could see that it was not a deep cut, rather a glancing cut, more of a nasty scrape than a laceration. Walter had no answer for the boy. All Walter could think to say was *We wait,* but he didn't say it because he knew it wouldn't inspire confidence. Mercifully, a young woman in a purple sweatshirt with UW emblazoned upon it arrived on the scene to relieve Walter, promptly declaring herself an RN.

Walter made to stand and make room for the young woman, and found himself lightheaded as he rose. He caught himself on a seat back before anybody seemed to notice his swoon. Again, he found himself at a loss as to how to proceed. How could he possibly know? He was an engineer, not a doctor or first responder. Apparently it wasn't enough that his negligence had landed them all here; now that the crisis was in full swing, he was virtually useless. He was supposed to be in charge, and yet he could not move himself to decisive action. Finally, he resumed his progress further down the train, passing through the vestibule into the next car, where a determined young Asian woman immediately accosted him.

"I need medical attention for my son immediately," she said.

"I . . . ," said Walter, still dizzy and at a loss. "There's a nurse . . ."

"Where?" the young woman demanded. "Where's a nurse?"

When Walter was sluggish to respond, the young woman pushed past him impatiently, leaving him there bewildered. Mechanically, he resumed his dazed progress toward no particular purpose. In the next car, he came upon a crowd in the middle of the aisle who dispersed upon his arrival, exposing the prone figure of a boy about ten or eleven years old, unconscious, bleeding, his body sprawled unnaturally.

"I'm his father," said the one still squatting. "He's got a pulse, he's breathing, but . . ."

Having exhausted her line of questioning, the young nurse in the purple sweatshirt assured Malik that paramedics were likely already en route, and that his mother's condition was stable, and that her vitals were good, and there was no apparent head trauma.

"I'm not a doctor," she said. "But my guess is, without seeing an X-ray, she's fractured her scapula. The discomfort and swelling are pretty centralized."

"Is that bad?" said Malik.

"Much better a scapula than a neck," said the woman. "What's your name?"

"Malik."

"I'm Anne Marie," she said. "I need to see if anybody else needs help, Malik. You just stay here and keep your mom company until I come back or somebody else comes to help, okay? Your mom is gonna be all right."

"Thanks," said Malik, reassured.

"She was nice," said his mom, wincing

through a smile. "Still snowing out there?"

"Not right now," he said.

Indeed, outside the snow had relented, at least temporarily, and the far reaches of the basin were now visible through the darkness, shrouded in white, buttressed by the low, gradual slopes of the coastal range to the west. For all his consternation, the beauty of the scene was not lost on Malik.

"Hang in there, Ma," he said.

Within an hour aid cars and fire trucks arrived in a convoy, slipping and sliding along the snowy access road, a chaos of colored lights refracting through the train windows to disorienting effect. Soon the snarl of chain saws en masse could be heard outside the train as substantive news of their rescue began to circulate in bits and snatches via Twitter. Before long it came to Malik by way of the guy with the pierced face that the Coast Starlight was completely out of commission, and that another train was said to be coming south from Olympia.

Still on her back in the middle of the carpeted aisle, teeth gritted, sweat glistening on her forehead, Malik's mom reached for his hand and gave it a squeeze.

"Help is here now, Ma. Everything's gonna be all right. They're gonna take us to the hospital."

"Not you. You gotta get yourself to Seattle, child. The room is prepaid."

"Nah, Ma, screw Seattle. I'm going with you."

"The hell you are," she said. "You listen to me, Malik Flowers. You got too much riding on tomorrow."

"Nah, it's just a game," he said. "One game."

"And this is just a shoulder. Go, Malik, it's your future, and it's been a long time coming."

Just then an arctic blast enveloped them as two medics stormed into the car from outside and promptly kneeled down on either side of his mom, where they began questioning her as they checked her vitals.

"You related?" said the bearded one after a minute of inspection.

"Yessir," said Malik.

"We're going to stabilize that shoulder and transport her to Providence St. Pete in Olympia. Are you coming along?"

"No," said his mom.

"Yes," said Malik.

JENNY CHEN

The Coast Starlight, 2019

The instant Winston stepped out into the aisle, a terrible metallic scraping shattered the calm of the cabin as the train lurched violently. Jenny was thrown forward from her seat, her head landing hard against Todd. Tyler's sleeping figure was thrown from its place and came to rest miraculously in his brother's vacated seat. Winston was not so fortunate, would in fact prove to be the least fortunate of all passengers aboard the ill-fated Coast Starlight. Flung half the length of the car, Winston collided with such violence against the vestibule door that the terrible thud of the impact, a sound Jenny would never in all her life forget, was audible over the din of the screeching brakes.

The moment the train had pulled out of Salem a half hour earlier and begun picking up speed, Jenny had felt a slackening in her shoulders as she sank into her high-backed seat and turned her attention out the window.

Beside her, Tyler was content to do the same. Awash in the snowy landscape, Jenny found it impossible to entertain anxiety. The Coast Starlight was exactly the salve she needed — even if it was only temporary.

With the scenery hurtling past, clean and white and sprawling, and the churning steel wheels rattling rhythmically up through the soles of her shoes, the train ranging gently side to side as it sped north, Jenny listened to Todd and Winston talking in the seats directly across from her.

"I'm telling you, Dad. Eighty miles per hour is not fast."

"Why does it have to be about speed, bud?"

"Well, for one, because you get there faster."

"Get where faster?"

"Wherever you're going, duh."

"Yeah, buddy, but what I'm saying is that it's about the ride itself, the journey, the becoming."

Jenny found herself smiling, heartened by the content of their conversation, but even more so by the familiar sound of their voices washing over her.

The becoming. Jenny liked the sound of that. It was hard to imagine old Todd, San Francisco Todd, stressed-out, vaguely unsatisfied Todd, saying such a thing. But new Todd, big-yellow-bong-hiding, sawdust-in-his-hair, relaxed Todd, was full of such little gems.

"Uh, becoming what, Dad, late? The journey is all about getting where you want to go, like the actual place."

"So, just point A to point B, and that's it?" said Todd.

"Exactly," said Winston. "It's all about getting to point B."

"And what determines point B?" said Todd.

"The ticket you bought," said Winston. "Duh."

"But why'd you buy the ticket in the first place?"

"Because you want to go somewhere," said Winston.

"Why do you want to go there?"

"Dad, that's irrelevant. We're talking about getting there as quickly as possible."

"I don't know, bud," said Todd. "I guess I just don't see what the big hurry is."

Out the window, the snow was still fluttering to earth, accumulating in the fields, and blanketing the barns, and gathering in drifts at the base of grain silos. Everything seemed at once closer and more distant in the wash of white.

The wide valley spreading out to the west, the frosted hills beyond hunkered together like cattle. How trivial Jenny's problems seemed compared to the huge frozen world outside the train.

Jenny had nearly dozed off by the time the train slowed upon its approach to Portland. Cleaving the hills south of the city, the Coast

Starlight rounded a corner to reveal the panorama of downtown, the jumble of buildings huddled together beneath the low sky, the river running like a dark zipper through the otherwise snowy sprawl, and Jenny was ready to give Portland another chance. It wasn't fair to compare it to San Francisco. She vowed to explore the city more thoroughly in the coming weeks, to embrace its quaintness and quirkiness and accept it on its own terms. She vowed further that she would learn to accept a lot of things on their own terms. What a relief it would be to stop trying to dictate the terms of the entire universe and just grow a beard like Todd.

By Kalama the boys were already getting restless, and their continuous whining soon began to test Jenny's serenity. Fortunately, Tyler whined himself out and soon fell asleep with his head on Jenny's shoulder, whereupon Winston doubled down on his own whining. It wasn't long before Jenny's patience wore thin.

"Can't we walk to the dining car?" said Winston.

"Not now," said Jenny. "Look out the window. It's beautiful."

"But the window is boring."

"Only a boring person would say that."

"C'mon, Mom. I won't even spend any money."

"Fine," she conceded.

"Can I have some money?"

Jenny sighed. "Ask your father."

"Dad?"

Todd pulled out his wallet begrudgingly and fished out a five.

"Five bucks?" said Winston. "C'mon, Dad, it's not 1970."

Todd peeled off another five and, before Winston could ask for more, said: "That's it."

"What do you say, Win?" said Jenny.

"Thanks, Dad," said the boy.

The exchange was enough to break the spell of Jenny's newfound serenity and sour her mood somewhat. Her kids weren't bad people, they weren't petty or mean; she'd merely taught them to expect too much, systematically trained them to be entitled. Through lazy parenting, through always taking the path of least resistance, always giving in, never standing her ground, always half-heartedly convincing herself that she was only trying to give Winston a better quality of life. And this is what she got, an eleven-year-old who, though he was capable of sweetness and affection, and at times grace, had no idea how good he had it. These were Jenny's final ruminations before life as she knew it ceased to exist.

Immediately after the impact, Jenny and Todd untangled themselves and rushed in unison to Winston, motionless in the aisle at the front of the car. He was unconscious, his neck resting unnaturally upon his torso, blood beginning to pool beneath his head. In the chilling moments that followed he was unresponsive to the desperate entreaties of his parents.

The spectacle of her son twisted, and from all indications lifeless, seemed unreal, impossible. Jenny could not even begin to accept it as reality before she was thrown into action.

"Go," said Todd, and instantly Jenny was off to find help, stepping over the figure of her son and rushing through the vestibule toward the front of the train, her galloping thoughts singular in their focus.

In the second car, Jenny thought she'd found the help she was looking for in a middle-aged man, obviously an official of some sort with his jet-black cap and vest, someone dependable and informative, someone with a radio who could make things happen. However, after several entreaties, it was quite clear that "Walter" was going to be of little assistance. In fact, he seemed unwell himself, his face streaked with blood, and more blood soaking the front of his vest. She pushed past him and continued her desperate search for help, tears streaming down her face. In the next car she was directed to the nurse in the purple sweatshirt.

"Help me," said Jenny. "Please."

■ ■ ■ ■

Kneeling above the motionless body of the boy, Walter began to swoon once more but caught himself short of passing out.

"You've got to do something!" demanded the father. "Call somebody!"

Walter groped for his radio, unsure of whom to call. Having alerted the desk and the bureau, Macy seemed the only other option.

"Mace, we've got a . . . a situation in seven," he said.

"I've got my hands full back here," came Macy's crackling response. "What have you got?"

"We've got an injured boy . . . he's —"

The father seized the radio from Walter.

"My son is dying!" he shouted into the receiver. "We need help, now!"

"Copy that," said Macy.

Seconds later Macy's voice sounded over the PA, all but the apparent urgency of his message lost on Walter, now slumped woozily in the aisle, his head lolling to one side. Walter felt his consciousness slipping away from him and this time did not fight it. An instant after he checked out, he opened his eyes as the boy's mother returned to the scene along with the nurse in the purple sweatshirt, both crowding into the cramped space above the boy's body.

"Make room," said the mother, jostling for position.

"Sir, please make room," echoed the nurse.

Even in his disoriented state, Walter felt the shame coloring his face, for here in this dire hour, when he ought to have been in control of the situation, when he ought to have been directing traffic and setting the tone, when he ought to have been orchestrating their rescue and providing the leadership the situation so desperately needed, Walter had been reduced to an obstacle.

"Sir, please, step aside," urged the young nurse.

"Move," said the mother.

■ ■ ■ ■

III
HORIZONS

■ ■ ■ ■

III

Horizons

NORA BERGEN

Chicago, 1859

July 8, 1859

My dearest Finn,

The insufferable humidity of high summer has arrived in Northern Illinois and there is no escaping its ubiquitous presence; it sits heavily in the air, seeping into every crack and crevice, penetrating walls, and permeating clothing. Neither shade of tree nor even the breeze off the lake offers respite from it. Wherever you may be, I can only hope that it is an arid climate.

I write you with news, which of course shall not reach you. Still, as with anything that happens in my customarily uneventful life, I yearn to share it with you. Dare I say this news is as unexpected to me as it might be to you? Fate is a strange master. For, it is only by a stroke of fate that my fortunes have changed overnight, and the circumstances of my life have been forever altered by events I could have never guessed at.

I have told you of the elusive Mr. Seymour, and how the wealthy gentleman saw fit to bring me here from the prison of the Catholic Orphan Asylum, only to consign me to a life of domestic toil in the servants' quarters when it was apparent that the late Mrs. Seymour wanted nothing to do with me. Thus, you can imagine my confusion and consternation when, upon Mr. Seymour's untimely passing, I found myself, without explanation, the sole heir to his considerable fortune. For weeks after receiving this news I fully expected that some mistake had been made, and that Mr. Trompette and his associates would soon discover the oversight and remedy the situation accordingly. But after a year of assurances, I have finally come to accept the fact that, shy of my — of our — nineteenth birthday, having arrived in this country destitute and promptly orphaned, I now find myself wealthy beyond my wildest imagination.

Though my circumstances have changed, my heart remains the same. If it is difficult to fathom that I could still feel unfulfilled while virtually any purchase I might desire is now within my reach, consider that the late Mr. Seymour himself has already served as a cautionary tale that happiness as a matter of course does not follow wealth. We

cannot fulfill ourselves by worldly possessions. Wealth is but a tool that can be put
to use for better or worse, but material
wealth pales next to the bounty of human
connection. Brother, I would gladly surrender every penny of my newfound fortune
to find you. Without connection this life is
meaningless.

Oh, but listen to me, a dreary prosperous
woman, young and healthy, lamenting her
fortune. Who knows how strained your
circumstances might be? As always, I try to
imagine you thriving; I see you in a fine suit
of clothes, your hair coiffed to perfection. I
see a handsome woman at your side, and a
little boy in your spitting image, right down
to the parted ginger hair and suit of clothes.
I wonder, do you still imagine me? Though
it is a comfort to think so, it is equally
comforting to think the opposite, to think
that your life has moved forward into the
future, unlike my own life, borne forever
back into the unassailable past.

Oh, Finn, why have you not found me?
Have you tried? I dare to imagine sometimes that you have returned from Iowa in
search of me, that one day I might walk past
you on a busy street, and I should recognize
you immediately. I know I am weak to
nurture such fantasies, as I am weak to
cling to your memory as though I might put
my arms around it. That is the unflattering

truth: that I am not strong, however much the world asks me to be. What else does it say about me that I have no intention of ever being with anybody if I cannot be with you? I know it is an unhealthy aspiration, but perhaps if I knew for certain that you were okay, that you were not alone, I could take solace enough to proceed with my life as though I were a complete person.

I am ever your loyal sister,
Nora

WALTER BERGEN

Southern Washington, 2019

It was difficult to tell if Detective Barnes was in uniform beneath his knee-length black parka. He kept blowing on his hands for warmth between scratching out notes on his pad.

"I'm from West Texas, originally," he said by way of an explanation. "I'll never get used to the cold. So, you say you looked away briefly?" said Barnes.

They were standing on the perimeter in a slushy clearing, just outside the pulsing lights of the police and rescue vehicles, away from the snarling chain saws and the chatter of radios.

"Yes," Walter said. "I had just come out of the turn —"

"Pardon me," interrupted Barnes. "Bear with me, here. I want to get the details right. How fast were you going through the turn?"

"About forty."

"About?"

"Somewhere between thirty-eight and forty-one."

"That's normal?"

"Yes. The bank is graded for higher speed than that."

"But the snow, the ice, wouldn't you want to slow down more than usual under the conditions?"

"The corner wasn't the problem," said Walter. "Like I said, I was getting back up to speed after the corner, we made the turn fine. We were on the straightaway when I looked down."

"Looked down? At what?"

And that was the moment Walter faced the big decision, the one likely to define his culpability and determine the fallout. He needed to either make something up, anything — he was scratching his calf, he was checking gauges, his thermos rolled across the floor — or come clean.

"My phone buzzed," said Walter.

Walter saw the air go out of Barnes immediately, as though this was the very truth he'd feared.

"And you looked at it?" said Barnes. "Tell me you didn't look at your phone."

"Just for a split second," said Walter.

Barnes stopped scratching out his note and looked up from his pad.

"I've got a teenage daughter," he said. "Just got her license in January. I'm always on her about this."

"I thought it might be important," Walter offered weakly.

"Yeah," said Barnes. "You must have. That the first time you looked at your phone like that while you were driving?"

"As a rule, I never check it," said Walter.

"Only takes once," said Barnes. "That's what I'm always telling Tiff."

After the interview with Detective Barnes, Walter tried unsuccessfully to lie low in the shadows, ducking the medics before a cop finally corralled him and led him back into the fray. Though Walter had rejected all but the most cursory of medical examinations, insisting that he was fine and the damage to his face looked worse than it was, he had no choice but to submit to a blood draw.

Four hours and five interviews after the collision, crews finally managed to clear the engine from the wreckage and began limping the Coast Starlight the eighteen miles back to the platform at Kelso, where the 236 remaining passengers, those who were not receiving medical attention in Olympia, would be offloaded and prepared to board a replacement train northbound for Seattle once the tracks were clear.

Having balked at any further aid from the medics after the blood draw, Walter stood off to the side avoiding the scrum, both eyes blackened, nose swollen to the size of a small potato.

And that was the least of his problems.

In the coming weeks and months he'd have a lot to answer for — to the bureau, to the safety board, to the press, to his family, and to himself. There would be much further probing, a toxicology report, subpoenaed phone records. Already there was so much doubt being cast upon his competency. His once-sterling reputation would be forever sullied. All that Bergen history on the rails, all that belief, all that toil, all that romance, only to end a 160-year run in disgrace. This could cost Walter his buyout, even his pension. And he had only his own negligence to thank for all of it. That he'd allowed his own puny first-world personal concerns — his daughter's wedding, his early retirement, his unwanted surprise party — to endanger the lives of hundreds of people was a stupefying revelation indeed, and one he would have to account for.

He still had yet to call home or answer Annie's texts. She had been expecting him to walk through the door an hour ago with a bag of ice. Somehow he just couldn't muster the nerve to disappoint her presently. Walter hunched in the shadows, a hive of activity still buzzing all around him. Even after the removal of the train, there were too many competing emotions for Walter to process:

guilt, fear, dread, humiliation.

It was a relief when Macy joined him in the shadows, slyly cupping a cigarette in his palm.

"You look like cold shit," he said, sneaking a drag.

"I wish I felt that good," said Walter.

Macy clapped him on the shoulder. "Ah, now, quit beating yourself up about it, Wally."

"Sorry about your daughter's recital," said Walter. "And pizza night and all that."

Macy waved it off and snuck another drag of his cigarette, blowing the smoke slyly over his shoulder.

"No biggie," he said. "I've been to a million of the things."

"Macy," said Walter, grief welling in his throat. "I just can't get the boy out of my head. He couldn't have been ten years old. Any indication if he's . . . ?"

"No," said Macy.

With that, the two of them retreated into silence as they stood in the shadows, Macy sneaking hits off his cigarette.

"What I don't understand is," Macy said at last, "how did you not see it coming, Wally?"

Macy was referring to the tree, of course, but at the moment he may as well have been talking about Walter's whole life. Either way, Walter didn't have a good answer for him.

Luyu Tully

Mariposa Springs, California, 1851

"Right here," said John Tully, dismounting the old brown mare. "We shall make our lives here in this spot."

Indeed it was a beautiful spot: a wooded plat beside a swift-moving mountain stream in the foothills seven or so miles east of the little town of Mariposa Springs, the town that time seemed to have forgotten, the town they had spent months in and about, abandoning their wandering ways, determined to make a plan, to stake some claim for their future, until finally, their search took them further into the hills.

Luyu sank her toes in the sandy shallows of the stream and felt the chill water wash over them. Resting both her hands upon the bulge of her belly, she listened to the whispering of the stream.

"Do you hear it?" she said to the bulge.

"We'll clear a spot there where it's flat and build our cabin," said John. "And the baby shall have its own room."

"Do you hear that?" said Luyu to the bulge. "Your very own room."

"The game here will be plentiful," said John. "We can raise hogs and chickens. We can tan hides and trade them in town. We will be happy here. And the baby, she will be happy too."

"He," said Luyu.

"Better yet," said John.

And this was like music to Luyu's ears. All she wanted for her child was happiness and stability. When Luyu thought of being a child herself, she recalled above all else the constant yearning that filled her, the desperate, insatiable want that resided at the very center of her. This longing was so consuming that it had colored her every perception of the world. And yet she had no language to express it. She had scarcely any conception of her parents and had been shown little kindness by her keepers. What joy Luyu had experienced at Sutter's Mill comprised such fleeting moments of wonder as the clouds above rolling past or the giddiness of watching bear cubs tumble down the hillside in tandem. All of these moments were inseparable from the knowledge of their impermanence. Nothing good ever lasted long, nothing promising seemed to be repeatable. The only permanent thing seemed to be the deficits themselves, and the inexpressible yearning for something more.

Luyu could remember very little of the circumstances precipitating her escape, or who aided her. All she could recollect was that several days prior to her escape a Miwok child was flogged senseless by the overseer and left lying in a field in the heat of the afternoon. Nobody was permitted to aid the child. Eventually the flies swarmed, and the buzzards began circling.

What Luyu remembered, what she would never forget for the rest of her days, was running for her life, running until it seemed her lungs would burst, running until her feet were bloody, running until her legs finally gave out and she collapsed in darkness under the wheeling stars.

That was how the old Mexican Donato found her the following morning: unconscious and half-starved in a field of alfalfa. He took her up in his arms and brushed her hair from her face and wept at the sight of her. Donato, the old widower, provided Luyu with the first kindness she'd ever known. He nursed her wasted body back to health with beans and tortillas and goat's milk.

But like everything else good she'd ever known, life with Donato was also impermanent. Soon she was delivered to the Younts, with whom she came at last to know security and permanence of a sort. Yet, the wanting only grew, for the Younts and their zealous beliefs allowed for little in the way of freedom. Still, Luyu was grateful to the reverend and his wife. They most certainly showed her decency. They educated her and expressed their kindness in such ways as their one true God permitted them.

But only now, toes in the little mountain stream, with John Tully at her side and the child growing inside of her, could Luyu guess at what fulfillment might look like. Only now could she begin to see past the yearning.

The unglamorous town of Mariposa Springs was one thing, but the foothills above the town were another thing altogether, with their views of the great Central Valley where the trees would allow it, and even an occasional glimpse of the distant dome of Mount Shasta, from which they'd come.

"It will be a good home," Luyu concurred.

Finally an end to the running. A home as she had never known. And this child would know all the joy that Luyu had not known, know the love and wonder and freedom that Luyu had never tasted. This child of hers would never want.

And so they had begun clearing their little plot of forest above Mariposa Springs, felling trees, sometimes two dozen a day, limbing them and rolling them with blistered hands over the uneven ground, staging them along the wooded edge of the clearing, where they stripped them and left them to dry. Early in fall they began the careful work of notching and saddling the logs, setting them into place with the aid of ropes and spars, until the structure began to take on a shape.

Luyu worked hard in spite of her condition, or maybe because of it, lifting and hauling and digging and notching endlessly, all in a furious effort to complete their little home before fall gave way to winter. The rains came in mid-October and the little stream swelled and the ground grew soft and muddy, and the work of cabin building became a slippery, treacherous affair, slowing their progress to a crawl even as the days grew shorter.

At night they slept within the walls of their roofless cabin, huddled together to consolidate their warmth around the bulge of the boy, their hot breath warming the air beneath their heap of hides. Undaunted by the elements, Luyu and John kept working by day, hoisting and fitting and chinking to beat the pressing deadline: the coming of the boy.

"How can you be so sure it's a boy?" demanded the father on numerous occasions.

Luyu could not say how she knew the child was a boy, but she knew it for certain, her entire body knew it, no matter how many times John Tully insinuated otherwise.

"You will see," she said.

The days grew colder in November until the mornings greeted them with a blanket of frost. They warmed their blood by the fire and set to work with renewed urgency. The weak sun was slow to melt the frost, and the frigid air stiffened their joints, reddened their faces, and sapped their breath. Their chafed fingers ached at the end of each day. Despite the rigors of the work, it was the most satisfying enterprise of Luyu's life. When had her labors ever served to benefit herself and her own prosperity?

John was nearing completion of the roof when the first snows came. Even as the snow began to accumulate on the bare beams and gabled ends, he laid the final planks. And meanwhile, Luyu, swollen to full term, her stomach out in front of her like an obstacle, hurried to complete the hearth under John's direction.

When it was finished, it was a cabin twelve feet by twelve, eight logs high to the cross-beams, with a single window facing east. Its door faced south to mark the passage of time as the shadow moved along the floor. For now it was a single room, but John assured her that they would grow it in the spring so that the baby would have her own room.

"His," she said.

"If you say so," he said.

Near the dawn of December, Luyu awoke in the middle of the night to a series of crippling contractions that took her breath away. Only after the third such spasm did she awake John.

"He's coming," she said.

John Tully shot upright on his pallet and lit the lantern. Soon the room was dancing with shadows.

"What do I do?" he said.

"Nothing," she said. "Get ready to meet your son."

But the boy did not come in the night. The spasms lasted for hours and did not seem to draw any closer. The pressure on Luyu's abdomen was almost unbearable, as she could feel the child seated low, the crown of his head pushing against her pelvis, wanting out. And yet he would not come no matter how hard she pushed. Her labor lasted through the next morning and into the afternoon. John Tully sat desperately at her side, mopping the sweat from her forehead, pacing the floor and worrying aloud.

"What do I do?"

"Nothing," she said.

"How can I do nothing?"

"You're a man," she said. "There's nothing you can do."

"There must be something."

"Keep holding my hand," she said.

Eventually the contractions drew closer. With each spasm the pressure increased as Luyu pushed desperately and unsuccessfully to expel the baby until Luyu was sure he would cleave her in half.

And yet it was John Tully who struggled to

maintain his composure. When he wasn't grasping Luyu's hand he paced the cabin floor wildly, clenching his teeth each time she cried out. The only comfort he could offer Luyu was the grip of his hand, and an encouraging word, and the occasional sip of water. She could take no food. She could hardly move by the afternoon, her aching back anchored to the floor as the spasms continued to wrack her body.

As the sun faded the second day, Luyu began to grow weak from her efforts.

John kneeled beside her and gripped her hand tighter than ever, pressing his other hand firmly to the bulge.

"C'mon, boy," he said. "C'mon! What are you waiting for?"

Finally, after the moonlight had passed through the window and the lamp was burning low as John Tully paced in circles worrying his hands over each other, Luyu gritted her teeth and balled her fists, and let loose one last agonized cry.

That was when John Tully heard it: the first cries of the baby, pinched and phlegmy and desperate. He rushed to Luyu's side and kneeled between her legs in the flickering lamplight, arriving just in time to receive the boy.

"Luyu," he said. "He's here."

But Luyu, her head slumped to one side,

did not respond. Her eyes rolled back in her head as her body went limp.

When Luyu regained consciousness she opened her eyes to behold John Tully desperately pacing the floor with the wailing infant clutched to his chest. He nearly dropped the baby when he saw that Luyu was alive. He rushed to her side and kneeled down to present her with the baby.

"I thought that . . ."

"No," she said. "I must have fainted."

"You were right," he said. "It's a boy."

Sitting upright, Luyu took the baby in her arms, and the boy calmed immediately and began to root at her chest.

"What about Luwanu, for the bear? Or Istu, for the —"

"No," said John Tully. "He will need a white man's name in this world. We'll call him William."

Though Luyu consented to the decision, she secretly took to calling the boy Istu after the sugar pines that shaded their home beside the creek. He would never be a William to her.

He was a calm infant with a shock of dark hair, almond-shaped eyes, and remarkably long feet. His fingernails were impossibly tiny. To feel the rise and fall of his little chest against her own was a sensation more profound than any Luyu had ever imagined.

"You will be taller than your father," she told the boy, clutching him to her chest. "And with any luck you will be less stubborn."

In the winter when the game was scarce, John performed odd jobs and traded hides and smoked fish in Shasta City, while Luyu spent her days alone at the cabin with Istu. Though her days were routine, they were full of purpose. Just to keep the cabin warm was enough to occupy a body throughout the short winter days. In spite of the isolation and the cloistered conditions of the cabin, it was a home, the first real home Luyu had ever known. Thus she was charmed by its squeaky shutters and sticking door and uneven floorboards. She loved the way the morning light shone through the window.

On cool sunny afternoons Luyu would strap the baby to her chest and walk him about the forest telling him stories and singing him songs.

"Do you hear that? That's the whistle of the thrush," she would say. "Doesn't it sound sad?"

Often they sat in the sunlight at the edge of the little stream listening to the cool, clear water hurrying past.

"If you listen hard enough," she told him, "you can hear it whispering as it passes."

In the evenings John arrived home and ate the dinner that Luyu had invariably prepared for him. After dinner John would sit by the fire and hold the baby in his lap until little Istu began to fuss, and Luyu would take the boy, who invariably calmed at her touch.

"What's so great about Mommy, anyway?" he'd say. "What's wrong with Daddy?"

Luyu's heart swelled to see her husband pout at these perceived slights, to know how much he cared for the boy, and for Luyu. John Tully was a good man. Strong and worthy and sympathetic.

One morning after breakfast, when the baby was almost a year old, John mounted the old mare and left for town as usual, bringing with him on that occasion two elk hides and a bear hide for trade. Luyu packed him a lunch of hardboiled quail eggs and a crust of bread, and saw him out to the front stoop, where she kissed him on the cheek.

"Please, be back for dinner," she said.

"I will," he promised, then mounted Sugar and crossed the stream and took off down the trail at a canter.

Watching him go, Luyu regretted not telling John about the new life that had taken hold inside of her, another boy. The news would have to wait until dinner.

Luyu spent the remainder of the morning tending to her daily routines: soaking hides and scraping flesh and fat from them, splitting wood and feeding the fire, and laundering clothes in the frigid shallows of the stream, Istu upon his wolf hide forever at her side.

As she worked, Luyu sang an old hymn from her days with the Younts, "O for a Thousand Tongues to Sing."

In the afternoon she strapped Istu to her chest and walked him about in the cool forest filled with birdsong and sunlight, narrating their journey, as was her custom.

"And everything you see, Istu, the mountains and the trees and the rivers, was made by Silver Fox and Coyote. It was Silver Fox and Coyote who created the world and taught the people how to live in it. But there are more things than that which you can see. There are ghosts who ride upon the wind."

Luyu was telling the child about the rock giants of the foothills when she spotted a bear sow ambling along the bank upstream. She stopped in her tracks and fell silent, watching the sow as she rooted around in the brush upon the low bank. Calmly and ever so quietly, Luyu turned back toward home without further pause, lest mama's cubs were nearby.

Arriving back at the cabin, she set the baby in the crib and spent the remainder of the afternoon preparing a dinner of rabbit and dried mushrooms, and a cake of acorn meal. As afternoon waned she rocked Istu to sleep by the fire, drifting in and out of slumber herself. Only when evening arrived and John still had not returned from town did Luyu begin to worry. When she could no longer stand the hunger, she ate alone as John's supper grew cold across the table. Afterward she resumed her station by the fire, feeding the flames through the evening and into the night.

Luyu could not shake the premonition that something had happened to John. Perhaps he'd been jumped along the trail, or fallen off a cliff, or been thrown from his horse. Perhaps he was still alive at that moment and in need of help. But what could she do? The more she entertained these thoughts, the more Luyu was convinced that her husband had met a terrible fate.

And so, Luyu paced the floor deep into the night, until at last, long after midnight, when the moon had sunk below the far horizon, she heard the nicker of a horse in the darkness. Wrapping her shawl about her, Luyu stepped out onto the front stoop to greet John Tully.

LAILA TULLY

The Coast Starlight, 2019

Laila had awoken just south of Seattle as the train began to slow through the industrial sprawl of the south end toward the stadiums squatting at the edge of downtown. The skyline, all lit up, now came fully into view, massive and resplendent and impossibly vertical. The effect of it was more than a little intimidating. As much as she'd come to deplore small-town life in the valley, Laila Tully was no city girl. Before she ever set foot in metropolitan Seattle, she longed to escape it for the shelter of the rain forest and whatever might await her there.

At King Street Station, passengers — some of them, like Laila, survivors of the wreck — spilled restlessly onto the platform. The station was a chaotic scrum inside, with passengers elbow to elbow, hurrying in every direction. Laila found all the activity overwhelming. She managed to catch up with an employee on her way past, a big-armed Black woman with a formidable carriage who walked at once deliberately and purposefully through the crowd.

"Excuse me," Laila said, "but could you tell me where the bus station is?"

"You mean like the Greyhound, sweetie?"

"Yeah, I guess," said Laila.

"Royal Brougham between Fourth Avenue South and Sixth," she said. "You wanna go south toward the stadiums and up the hill. You can get yourself an Uber right over there outside that door."

"Thanks," said Laila.

"Good luck."

Even if she'd had the Uber app on her all-but-totally-dead phone, Laila wouldn't have spent the money. The possibility of hocking the old blue locket for whatever it was worth still lingered, but it was highly unlikely that the opportunity would present itself at this hour. Instead, she proceeded out the door and up the stairs and, slinging her overstuffed sausage bag over her shoulder, began the long walk through downtown Seattle. Though the snow had stopped hours ago, the sidewalks were covered in slush and the streets of downtown were largely deserted but for the homeless and destitute, who were alternately huddled in doorways and milling about for warmth.

The fact was not lost on Laila that only the small matter of a couple hundred dollars and the lone prospect of squatting at her cousin Genie's in Queets until she got on her feet stood between her and the reality of homelessness. But this was nothing new. To be Miwok, to be Indian at all, was to live always with the idea of homelessness. How many generations since the Mexicans, then the whites, came to California to cast her people out? It made little difference what reparations were made, what tax relief was offered, what tract of land was allotted to accommodate her people; the Miwok would forever be homeless in America.

Laila tromped up the hill on King Street, past bus stops where the homeless took shelter, buffered by smudged plexiglas structures.

"You got a cigarette I can buy?" said a young man, roughly her age, though pale and already halfway to toothless, his clothes hanging off him like the wind had blown them there.

"Sorry," said Laila, without stopping.

She stepped up her pace over the slushy sidewalks in spite of her exhaustion until she reached South Fourth. A half block later, Laila crossed the street to avoid a man in a baggy army jacket blocking the sidewalk, either so high or so ill that he looked to be falling asleep standing. That her own life had not sunk to such depths did little to buoy Laila's spirits as she slogged on toward the next leg of her journey.

Her shoes and socks and the cuffs of her jeans were soaked through and her shoulder ached by the time Laila finally reached the Greyhound depot. After a brief consultation with a ticketing agent, Laila was more than a little discouraged to learn that Greyhound had no bus that would take her anywhere near Queets. What she needed was the Dungeness Line, and catching the Dungeness meant trudging all the way to Seventh and Marion and waiting in the dark for a bus that would not deliver her to Forks — still forty miles shy of her destination — until after three A.M.

Such was Laila's fatigue that she defaulted to autopilot by the time she left the Greyhound station, heading north mechanically, her giant bag slung over her shoulder, her wet feet mercifully numb.

Despite the streets' being practically deserted, those intrepid souls who were still about tended not to be shy and seemed to gravitate toward Laila as though she were a light source, seemingly bereft souls, from all walks of life, some of them Laila imagined formerly teachers and electricians and carpenters, and athletes and mothers and fathers and sons and daughters who found themselves without a safety net, all of them out there in the cold looking for relief anywhere they could find it in a land that was supposed to offer them opportunity and justice. How could America be the greatest country in the world when it couldn't even take care of its own? It didn't seem to matter whether you were born here or you came here, whether you'd been here since the beginning of time or you'd just gotten here yesterday; unless you could afford to buy in, America didn't seem to give two shits about you.

In America, the great land of opportunity and justice, if you happened to be an Indian girl with no prospects running from an abusive partner with your meager life savings strapped to your person and your dirty, overstuffed bag slung over your shoulder, containing all your worldly possessions, there was a decent chance you'd be waiting at a bus stop at ten o'clock at night in a strange city, wishing you could be anywhere else.

LUYU TULLY

Mariposa Springs, California, 1853

Never before had John Tully given Luyu reason to worry. He was nothing if not conscientious. He always came home roughly when he said he would, usually in time for dinner. If he was spending the night anywhere, like the few times he'd ridden up north to hunt, or the time last fall when he went mushroom gathering in the wooded basin, he always came back when he said he would.

Until the previous night.

Thus it was with considerable relief that Luyu heard his mare nicker in the darkness. She rushed outside to the stoop to meet John Tully shortly before dawn, while Istu was sleeping in his crib. The air was frigid, and a slight breeze stirred the pines. Her breath fogged in front of her when she opened her mouth to speak.

"John?" she said, peering into the gray predawn. "Where on earth have you been? I was worried."

The horse nickered again and let out a snort, but otherwise there came no response from John.

"John?" she said once more. "John, is that you?"

Again there was no reply, but Luyu could hear the footfalls of the horse mincing down the incline across the creek until they stopped abruptly at the far edge of the creek.

There came a voice through the trees.

"I'm looking for the wife of John Tully," it called.

"Why?" she shouted back, wishing she'd thought to grab the rifle or at least a lantern to see by.

"Come again?" called the voice.

"What do you want with my husband?" she called out.

"Ma'am," the voice shouted back, "it's not exactly that I want anything with your husband. Permission to cross?"

"Hold on," she said, ducking back into the cabin and returning moments later with the rifle and the lantern. She promptly hung the lantern on the spike beneath the overhang and brandished the rifle as though she were prepared to use it.

"Okay, then," said Luyu. "Come on across."

Squinting through the darkness as the horse crossed the shallow creek, Luyu could discern that it was in fact two horses, one leading the other across the creek. As they reached the near bank, Luyu could just make them out. Upon the front horse rode a lanky man whom Luyu did not recognize at a distance. The second horse had no rider, only a dark hump, presumably a stack of hides draped across its saddle.

"Who's that?" said Luyu.

"Sheriff's deputy, ma'am."

"What do you want?"

But before the deputy could reply, before Luyu could even make out his face, she could see the answer plainly written. The second horse was none other than the old mare. And draped across her back was not a heap of hides, but the lifeless body of her husband. He was not wearing boots.

John Tully had set off for town with a full belly not long after dawn while the baby was still sleeping. Luyu walked him out to the stoop and kissed him on the cheek, and he promised to be back by dinner. Walking across the yard, the newly risen sun slanting in beneath the pines and the little creek burbling in front of him, John Tully approached the old mare, already heaping with a mound of hides.

"Sorry, old girl," he said, more for Luyu's benefit than the horse's.

Soon he was across the creek, up over the swale, and down the back side, on his way down the mountain through the pines. There had been times when the snowpack made for difficult passage and John had wished they'd settled a few miles closer to town, but this morning was not one of them. Once the sun was up over the horizon, the day was crisp and clear, and John found the trail free of windfall and mostly dry. Though he knew that wildlife skulked all about him, but for the occasional chorus of winter birdsong it felt to John Tully as though he had the forest all to himself, and the effect was one of great tranquility. His thoughts moved in step with the old mare, and they were pleasant meditations on the twenty or thirty dollars he stood to fetch for his hides, on the improvements he'd make around the cabin come spring and the things he would one day teach his boy.

Once he reached Mariposa Springs, John's first stop was Parson's mercantile. Parson had proven his most reliable buyer and always offered a decent price.

Until today.

"The best I can offer you is two apiece, John. And four for the bear."

"But last time you gave me seven."

"I don't know what to tell you, John," Parson said. "I've got more hides than I know what to do with right now."

"The bear hide is special," said John. "The quality is better than anything you've got in here."

"Like I said, I'll give you four dollars for the bear hide."

"It's worth three times that," said John.

"Well, I have to mark it up, John. And like I say, I'm not suffering from a lack of hides."

"Seven dollars," said John.

"Can't do it," said Parson.

"Six."

"I can't go a dime over four, John."

"Okay, then," said John. "I'll test my fortunes elsewhere."

Discouraged, John Tully walked out of the mercantile and sat at the edge of the boardwalk. He unwrapped the parcel of food Luyu had packed him: four quail eggs, boiled hard, and a large hunk of bread. He sat on the boardwalk, half in the sun, half in the shade, looking out over the street as he peeled his tiny eggs with big fingers, dropping the shells in the street. He took a big bite of the tough bread and worked his jaw over it again and again before swallowing. Then he stood up and snatched his water bladder off the saddle and gave old Sugar's snout a rub before sitting back down to his lunch.

After he'd eaten, John Tully solicited a number of additional merchants, including the clothier, but was unable to draw an offer better than two and a half dollars apiece for the elk hides and five for the bear. Though John knew not selling below market value had been the right decision, it was one that would leave their resources lean through the remainder of winter if he could not find a buyer.

On his way out of Mariposa Springs he came upon a group of men loitering outside the Knotty Pine. One of them, visibly drunk and partially supported by an awning post, was vaguely familiar, with a shock of gray hair under his hat and a pair of ruddy cheeks that looked like they'd seen a blast of birdshot. The man had one milky blue eye that was all clouded over. John caught the man's good eye on the way past.

"Nice-looking bear hide," he said. "You plug that bear yourself, red man?"

"Yes, I did," said John, still trying to place the man's face.

"And now you trying to sell it, is that it?"

"For the right price, I am," said John.

"And what price that might be?" said the man.

"Ten dollars," said John.

"Ha!" said the man with the milky eye. "You hear that, fellas? Indian thinks he can fetch ten dollars for his hide?"

"It's a bargain at ten," John said.

The man hopped off the boardwalk and approached the mare and began running his hands through the hide and over the bear teeth, still intact. Only once the stranger was up close did John manage to place him. It was the desk clerk from the Mariposa Inn, the same man who had tried to gouge John and Luyu by charging them the "Indian rate" the first day they arrived in Mariposa Springs.

"Tell you what," said the man, still running his fingers through the hide. "I'll give you a dollar and a quarter for it."

"It's not for sale," said John.

Indeed, he would not sell to this man at any price.

"Okay, a dollar fifty."

"Like I said, not for sale."

The milky-eyed man scratched his chin.

"Now, you just said you were asking ten dollars for it," he said. "By my reckoning that would make it for sale."

"Not to you."

The man arched a brow.

"That so? Supposing I offered you the ten dollars you're asking?"

"Still not to you," said John.

"Hmph," said the man. "And why would that be?"

"For the same reason you wouldn't rent me a room at regular price."

"Now, that just ain't true, and it's ancient history besides. As I recall, I offered you a room at the Indian rate," he said. "Indian rate is a special rate on account of an Indian means extra cleanup afterward. And besides, not all our denizens at the Mariposa Inn are partial to Indians, in fact I reckon most of them aren't, so there's that to consider. Just to show that there ain't no hard feelings, I'm gonna offer you two dollars for that hide. And that's an offer I recommend you ought to take."

As he said it the man set his hand lightly upon his pistol grip for John to take notice.

"Not for sale," said John. "Not to you. Not at any price."

The man with the one milky eye straightened up to his full six feet and looked around at his companions.

"Well now, doesn't that strike you as awful rude? Man makes a generous offer and he gets insulted — and by an Indian no less. I think he ought to get down off that horse and offer an apology, don't you?"

"Reckon so," said one of the others as yet another man nodded his assent.

John Tully dismounted his horse, his boot heels landing at once in the muddy street. He approached the man three steps without reservation until he was right in front of him, looking him dead in the eye.

"I've done nothing to offend you," he said. "It's you, sir, who have insulted me — twice. I'd no sooner sell you that hide than I'd invite you to eat at my table. In fact, I probably wouldn't piss on you if you were on fire. Now, why don't you go back to your whiskey and rile somebody else up? Sooner or later, you'll pay for your ways."

"That right?"

"That's right," said John. "A man's only

got so many insults in him until his luck runs out."

"You apologize," said the man. "Or I'll shoot you dead right here in the street. God knows ain't nobody gonna miss one more Indian."

"I owe you nothing," said John, turning his back.

SHERIFF MCCREADY

Mariposa Springs, 1853

When Sheriff McCready arrived at the scene, his deputy Conners in tow, he found four men standing out front of the Knotty Pine like nothing had happened, though there was an Indian lying in the muddy street. When McCready turned him over, he recognized the dead man as the Indian who called himself Tully. Tully had shown up in Mariposa Springs a couple years prior, settled up in the hills with his young wife, and never seemed to find any trouble until now. As far as Indians went, he wasn't a bad one. Did a considerable amount of business with Parson, and a few other merchants.

"What happened here?" said McCready.

"We was just having some friendly conversation about hides and damned if that Indian didn't go for his iron," said Russ Hicks from the inn. "So, I plugged him before he could get to it."

"Looks to me like he's shot in the back,"

said Sheriff McCready.

"Well, now, he sort of swung around as I was drawing."

"You said he was going for his gun," said McCready.

"Yessir, he was."

"While he was turning around?"

"Yessir, that's right."

"Then why was his back still turned?" said McCready.

"Like I say," said Russ. "He turned around quick-like when he seen I was gonna plug him. Or heck, it happened so fast, might have been that his back was still turned when he went for the gun. Anyway, that's what happened. Another hot-blooded Indian, what else can I tell you?"

"Didn't know the man to run hot, Russ. Not like you."

McCready shook his head and spit in the dirt. He never had liked Russ Hicks. And even if Tully was just an Indian, McCready was damn near certain he'd done nothing to deserve a shot in the back. But what could he do? If he arrested every man who shot an Indian for no good reason, or a Chinaman, or a darkie, he wouldn't have a jail big enough to house them all.

"Don't add up, Russ," he said. "A man turns his back to reach for his gun. Just don't seem right, somehow."

"Well, sir. That's just how it happened,"

said Russ. "Might have easily been me if he'd been a quicker draw."

"Looks to me like his gun is still in the holster, like he didn't even draw."

"That's what he was fixing to do, all right. Ask any man here."

"What about it?" said McCready. "Anyone see anything different? Cal? Marty? Now would be the time to say something."

"It's just like he told it, Sheriff," said Cal.

"Were the Indian that started it," added Marty.

Bitter as the taste was, McCready knew it would only be more trouble if he took Russ Hicks and the others to task. He'd have a mutiny on his hands if he started defending Indians.

"Well then, I guess that just about settles it," he said. "Conners, I'm gonna need you to put him on his horse and ride him out to his wife. She's up Patterson Creek about six miles."

"That's an awful long ride, sir, through them woods," said Conners. "Gonna be dark here before too long. Can't this wait until morning?"

"A man is dead, Conners," said McCready. "His wife might want to know about it in a timely manner."

"But he's just an Indian," said Conners.

"Yes, he is," said McCready. "But that ain't gonna make much difference to his grieving wife, now, is it?"

"Can I at least eat dinner first?" said Conners.

McCready shook his head woefully.

"I suppose so," he said. "But get him out of the street first."

"What about his boots, can I have his boots?" said Conners. "That's a fine pair of boots to bury with an Indian."

"Hell no, you can't have the man's boots," said McCready. "What the hell is wrong with you?"

JENNY CHEN

The Coast Starlight, 2019

Later, Jenny would forget most of what happened after she located the nurse, Anne Marie, in the purple sweatshirt, and all but dragged her back to Winston. Most everything after that was a blur. She would not recall with any detail the harrowing drive over snowy roads to the hospital in the back of the ambulance, though she insisted on being there, while Todd and Tyler followed in a squad car. She would scarcely remember the forty minutes in the ER waiting room, Todd pacing the sheet-vinyl floor, Jenny rigid in her chair, ears ringing, stunned stupid by the unthinkable turn of events as she gazed in the direction of the muted television. She wouldn't remember Tyler beside her, his silent bewilderment little more than an afterthought in the shadow of the all-consuming crisis. Jenny would soon forget about the Black kid sitting across from her, though he must have been seven feet tall, worrying his teeth over his bottom lip.

Looking back, Jenny would only truly recall — and so vividly that it would haunt her in the weeks, months, and years to come — the terrible instant that Todd ceased his pacing suddenly, and the doctor, gray faced, eyes rimmed with fatigue, emerged from the mouth of the corridor to inform them, his expression expertly passive though not unreadable. Jenny had been convinced before the doctor ever said a word, before she ever climbed into the ambulance with the EMTs, the instant she gazed down at her son's ravaged body, broken and bleeding and unresponsive, that he was gone from this world.

Clutching Todd violently, his sweater bunched in her fists, Jenny's grief escaped from a hold deep within her in the form of a long, ragged moan.

"I'm sorry for the wait," the doctor said to them. "Please know that we're doing everything within our power to stabilize him. He's still fighting. We'll know more in the coming hours."

Though a rage was seething just beneath the surface of Jenny, she did not shoot the messenger.

"Thank you," she said mechanically, her voice coming from somewhere outside of her body.

When the doctor turned and strode back down the corridor from whence he came,

Todd, bewildered and inconsolable himself, tried to comfort Jenny, pulling her close, but Jenny lashed out at him and began pounding savagely at his chest with both fists.

"This stupid train trip was your idea!"

Todd tried to restrain her in a hug, but she continued to rage.

"You're the one who convinced me to leave the city!" she said. "You're the one our lives weren't good enough for! You had to uproot us and drag us all to Oregon so you could have your stupid American dream, like a million-dollar home and my job wasn't enough! You had to have your stupid three acres, and your fresh air. And look what happened!"

It was an ugly thing to say, unforgivable, and Jenny regretted saying it immediately, though once she said it she knew she could never undo the damage. It was a half truth at best. For the fact was that not only had Jenny consented to the move, she'd insisted on it once the impulse seized her. And if she hadn't been so damn needy since the day they'd arrived in Oregon, so restless and perpetually dissatisfied that Todd had begun to wonder aloud whether she might be suffering from some kind of seasonal affective disorder, Todd would have never booked the trip to Seattle, and they would've been home in McMinnville at that very moment, settling into their new house.

"I'm sorry," said Jenny. "I didn't mean that."

"I know you didn't," he said.

But the terrible fact was that she did. She blamed him.

Leaving Jenny and Tyler in the waiting room in front of the muted television, Todd retreated out the glass doors, where he waited by himself at the curb outside the ER. The snow was all but invisible under the glare of the sodium lights, but just outside their reach Todd could see big flakes fluttering down from heaven like ash and settling on the empty cars, and the pavement, and in the vast darkness beyond, and this was without a doubt the most desolate scene Todd had ever beheld. How would he ever be able to find his way in that vast darkness if Winston were not to pull through? It seemed unlikely that Jenny would walk beside him in Winston's absence — in fact, it seemed as if she was already gone.

Two hours later, the ER doctor emerged once more, informing them that Winston was stable for the moment but still in critical condition. He encouraged them to go get some sleep and check back in the morning. If anything happened in the meantime, the hospital would call. Todd booked a room at the Ramada in Olympia, the first hit he got on Expedia, then retreated outside once more to wait.

When the Lyft arrived, Todd motioned to the driver, then retrieved Jenny and Tyler from the waiting room, and the three of them piled into the backseat. Sensing the gravity of the moment, the Lyft driver, a young woman whom Todd never registered beyond the back of her head, remained silent throughout the ten-minute drive. The silence in the backseat was deafening. It followed the Chen-Murphys into the hotel lobby, and up the elevator, and into room 311, where, after several minutes, Tyler, stomach growling, dared to penetrate it.

"Mom," he said softly, having ventured near her motionless figure in the club chair by the window. "Are we gonna have dinner?"

But Jenny was unreachable. Only her body occupied the space, the rest of her having floated out the window and drifted over the parking lot, beyond the glare of the lights, and into the darkness.

Todd pulled out his wallet and, flipping it open, found it empty of cash, instantly recalling the two five-dollar bills Winston had stuffed in his pocket not three seconds before impact. The thought that Todd might have fished the bills out of Winston's jean pocket after the fact was too much to bear, and he was suddenly overwhelmed with grief and worry. Dropping to the edge of the bed, he took hold of Tyler and pulled him in close, clutching his seven-year-old frame with such force against his chest that the boy had to turn his head sideways to breathe. And even as Tyler squirmed against his father's embrace, Todd had no intention of ever letting him go.

They went to bed without dinner, except for Jenny, who remained seated all night in the club chair on the edge of the darkness until weak sunlight penetrated the room around eight A.M. Immediately upon waking, Todd called the hospital for an update, and was told the attending doctor would call him back shortly.

"No news is good news, I suppose," he said.

But Jenny didn't answer. She just sat there, as if Winston were already dead.

"C'mon, babe," said Todd. "Let's get some breakfast downstairs."

But still Jenny did not budge from the chair when Todd took Tyler down to the breakfast buffet and watched him eat three bowls of Froot Loops without reproach, as Todd sat beside him in a state of exhaustion, sipping black coffee.

Wu Chen

San Francisco, 1859

Five years had passed since Ai Lu's father returned to China, and they had been kind to Wu Chen and Ai Lu. These years saw the birth of their first child, a boy named Jack, lean and big headed, with a shock of black hair and a fiery disposition. And eighteen months after Jack was born, Ai Lu gave birth to a girl, Alice, a calm beauty in her mother's image. Both children were hearty and healthy and well provided for.

These years also saw the rapid expansion of the Chens' grocery operation from a single hand-painted storefront on Clay Street to two additional stands in Chinatown, both of which soon proved to be cash cows, and in each case earned out their initial investment within six months of opening and began showing returns by the end of the first year. As a result, Wu Chen's tainted fortune not only remained all but untouched in the safety of the San Francisco Savings Bank, it grew by 30 percent.

The extent of the Chens' good financial fortune was such that Wu Chen and Ai Lu purchased not only a two-bedroom apartment on Sansome, but also an additional rental property on California Street, which they immediately leased to Wang, the young Cantonese who managed the stand on Kearny Street. Like Wu Chen, Wang hailed from Guangdong; he'd arrived fatherless on the shores of California the very same year as Wu Chen, at the age of thirteen. Wang proved himself a hard worker who was as quick with numbers as he was with a smile. After a year, the Chens trusted Wang implicitly, and Wang continued to reward this trust with excellent performance on the job.

While Wang managed the stand on Kearny, Ai Lu oversaw the original store on Clay, baby Alice forever strapped to her body as she busied herself with customers. Wu Chen meanwhile manned the stand on Washington, which was nearly twice the size of the little store on Clay. All day long Jack followed in his father's shadow. At the age of three and a half he was a quick study, delighting customers with his antics and impressing them with his ever-growing vocabulary, which already included more English than his father's.

Indeed, the Chens were thriving in America. They had much to be grateful for and much to look forward to. But all was not well in Wu

Chen's mind. Still the specter of his past refused to relinquish its grip on his tortured conscience. It seemed that the river of his undoing would never cease undoing him. How was he ever to own his future when all his good fortune only served to remind him of his troubled past? The ghosts of the Huangs, and those of the four men he'd killed, were his constant passengers, haranguing his guilty conscience, protesting his triumphs, and thwarting his every opportunity to achieve peace or contentment, no matter how fleeting. All these years on and the images still crowded his head by day and haunted his dreams at night. So unsettling at times were the night terrors that Wu Chen was unable to sleep altogether.

It might have helped Wu Chen to unburden himself to Ai Lu, and many times he considered it, but in the end he remained true to his vow never to burden his bride with such knowledge, for what good could come of it? Nor did it help his cause that his uncle Li Jun, the only person with whom Wu Chen could discuss such matters, had abandoned him in recent years in spite of countless attempts on the part of Wu Chen to summon him.

Sometimes late at night, Wu Chen would slip out from beneath the covers and quietly leave the apartment to walk the darkened streets of the city, a specter himself moving swiftly in the shadows, his restless thoughts churning as he sought to outpace them. Street after street he wandered to no purpose and with no particular destination, past the saloons and cathouses and shuttered supply stores all the way to the ragged edges of town before doubling back. Rarely did he pause in his restless travels, and only occasionally was he approached or propositioned. For the most part he was left alone to grapple with his troubled conscience.

It had long been clear to Ai Lu that something was bothering her husband, some secret anguish she could not glean. Though she knew Wu Chen to be unfailingly loyal, and honest to a fault, she was certain that he was hiding something from her. When pressed about whether something was bothering him, he was curt and dismissive in his responses, as though he resented her asking. Moreover, he was frequently taciturn, and impatient with the children, and in recent months he had been shrinking from her touch.

Late at night he often left the apartment for hours on end, and upon his return offered no explanation for his absence. Finally, one night Ai Lu forced the issue.

"Where have you been?" she said as he slipped under the covers.

"Walking," he said in the darkness.

"At this hour?"

638

"I couldn't sleep," he said.

"Is something troubling you, husband? Please tell me."

"No," he said. "I just have business on my mind."

"Business is good," she said. "You should be happy."

"I didn't say I wasn't happy. I just said I had it on my mind."

"Perhaps if you talked about it . . ."

"There's nothing to talk about," he said. "It's just figures."

"I'm good with figures," she said.

"Good night," he said.

With that, they fell silent, and Ai Lu repositioned the blanket about herself. Turning his back to her, Wu Chen settled in beneath the covers.

"You know," said Ai Lu, "you're liable to be assaulted walking the streets alone at night."

"Bah," he said. "The streets are deserted this time of night."

At other times, Wu Chen was capable of great tenderness and patience with the children, and occasionally as he ran about with them in the square or in the street outside of the apartment, smiling, Ai Lu saw flashes of the old levity she'd once known, before they were married, before they had children. But beyond those fleeting moments, nothing seemed to give Wu Chen joy.

Ai Lu continued her attempts to earn his confidence and draw him out of his shell. A different night when he returned from his nocturnal wanderings, Ai Lu set her hand suggestively upon his back, and she could feel his body tighten at her touch before he repositioned himself.

"It's me, isn't it?" she said. "I'm the problem."

"No," he said emphatically. "Never."

To her surprise he rolled over to face her in bed.

"It is you who saved me, my darling," he said. "Every day you save me again."

"From what?"

"From myself," he said.

"I don't understand," said Ai Lu.

"I don't ask you to."

"Please," she said. "Talk to me."

"There is nothing to say."

"Are you unhappy with your life? Do you want more?" she said. "Less? Tell me. What can we do?"

"There is nothing to be done, my love. It is only the dark way my mind sometimes works. You are the light that sees me through the darkness."

But his assurances felt empty to Ai Lu, for, clearly, all was not right with him.

Without anyone in whom to confide, or any thought to comfort him, Wu Chen spiraled into a morass of guilt and self-pity. He grew increasingly irascible as the weeks wore on, and nowhere were his mood swings more acute, or more unpredictable, than in his dealings with his son, Jack, whose constant presence at the store was no longer a novelty but served to tax Wu Chen's patience daily.

"Papa, a knife," the boy said, wielding a pointy parsnip one afternoon during a lull.

"Stop that!" said Wu Chen. "Don't act like a fool."

"But, Papa, it looks like a kn—"

"Silence."

Wu Chen knew it was wrong to snap at the boy. He knew he should have more to give the child in the way of patience. But he didn't. Just as he knew that he should be happier with every dollar that came in. But he wasn't. He couldn't be; his conscience would not allow it. He lived under the constant cloud of his own misgivings.

"I will never understand," said Ai Lu. "Why are you so morose when you have every reason to be happy?"

Indeed, everything this new country had ever promised Wu Chen, it had delivered — opportunity, fortune, a prosperous future — but at what price? Wu Chen had blood on his hands. Violence had been the key that unlocked his fortune. This place had made a killer of him. Gold had made a killer of him. And now, Wu Chen was stuck here, a prosperous man, the taint of his ill-gotten fortune spread all over the city of San Francisco.

One evening late in summer, as Wu Chen was closing down the stall, his uncle Li Jun appeared to him for the first time in years.

"Do not despair, Nephew. You have done well."

"For whom?" said Wu Chen, hefting a crate of limes.

"For your children, of course."

"Of course," said Wu Chen. "And at what cost?"

"At the same cost any man would pay to secure a future for his family."

"Bah," said Wu Chen. "Security is overrated. The future is overrated. For all we know this place will be the end of us."

"Perhaps," his uncle said. "We shall see."

"Only if we are lucky shall we see," said Wu Chen, stacking one crate upon another.

LAILA TULLY

Forks, Washington, 2019

Laila awoke with a sudden jolt as her bus shuddered to a stop beneath the glare of a lone sodium light. After thirty-six hours of traveling — by car, by train, by bus — she had arrived on a deserted street in Forks, Washington, at 3:12 A.M., the storefronts shuttered and the traffic signals flashing yellow in either direction. She disembarked the coach into the chill night air, where she waited on the sidewalk, at once sleepy and alert as the driver descended the steps and opened the luggage compartment. Hefting her sausage bag out of the hold, he set it at her feet and tipped his cap as he reboarded the bus.

A moment later, the bus heaved a sigh and pulled around the corner, and a sudden and unequivocal loneliness overcame Laila as she watched it disappear into the night. Above her the stars were splashed across the heavens as she shouldered her duffel and began a slow trek through the center of town, past the Native art gallery and the hardware store, past the abandoned video store and the darkened credit union, past the Shell station and the burger joint, in search of a motel.

Forks was a veritable metropolis compared to where she was going, and walking its deserted main thoroughfare, Laila could not help but wonder whether the isolation of such a remote place as Queets would drive her crazy. Perhaps it would've been better to seek refuge from Boaz in a city, after all — San Francisco or Portland or Seattle, where there were bound to be more opportunities for her. What if she didn't stick in Queets? What if there was nothing there for her and she could never get her new life off the ground? Laila attempted to allay these fears with Genie's assurances, and the promise of companionship, and the natural beauty that awaited her. But her anxiety was at an all-time high.

On the north end of town she came upon a vacancy sign at the Farwest Motel, a cloistered little motor court, which projected all the affectation of a hokey western movie set with its false façade and splintered wood siding. The office was darkened at this hour, and the front door secured. Laila rang the night buzzer and waited a half minute until light flooded the office.

Soon an old woman in a bathrobe emerged squinting from a door behind the front desk and unlocked the front entrance, stepping aside to let Laila pass into the lobby.

"Sorry to wake you," said Laila as the old woman circled back around the desk.

"It happens," she said. "What can I do for you?"

"I was wondering how much for a room."

"We start at ninety-seven," said the old woman. "All the way up to two forty for a suite."

"Oh," said Laila, her heart sinking.

She had dared to hope for a forty-nine-dollar room when such a thing hardly existed anymore.

"You by yourself?" said the old woman.

"Yes, ma'am."

"Well, one fourteen is vacant, I could put you in there."

"How much?"

"Ninety-seven and tax."

With Laila's dwindling resources, a hundred bucks was out of the question for a few hours' sleep.

"I'm sorry to have woken you," she said. "But that's out of my price range."

Once again, Laila dared to hope as the old woman looked her up and down, from her dirty jeans to her overstuffed bag to her long dark hair now hanging in greasy straggles. Perhaps she would take pity upon Laila and offer her a deal, or even a room for free, if only until sunup. But there was no pity in the old woman's appraisal.

"Well, you're not gonna find cheaper around here," she said. "The Dew Drop starts at one thirty-four."

"I see," said Laila. "Again, sorry I woke you."

"Like I said, it happens. Good luck," said the old woman as Laila turned to leave.

Laila almost offered the woman the locket in lieu of money, but what would an old lady want with the locket unless her name was Lillian or Lenora? What good was the locket at all, really? It was just some useless relic, some token, or gift, or symbol, the significance of which Laila had never even gleaned beyond the obvious fact that L was for *Laila*. One last time Laila dared to hope that the old woman might take pity on her and stop her before she walked out the door into the night. But once again Laila's expectation was unrewarded, as the old woman followed her to the door and secured it in her wake. Laila saw the office lights go dark behind her as she proceeded across the parking lot and resumed her progress north. She briefly contemplated picking the highway back up and thumbing her way to Queets, but the late hour and the lack of traffic notwithstanding, the idea seemed ill conceived on a number of levels.

A half block from the Farwest Motel, Laila arrived at a city park, its entrance marked conspicuously by a massive steam locomotive squatted beneath a wooden awning. Locomotive number ten, squat and black and solid steel, was unmistakably authentic, no doubt a survivor from another century. Laila found the machine at once elegant and slightly menacing with its girded steel frame, its colossal burner, and its huge cylinders. She might have reached out and touched it were the locomotive not fenced in to discourage just such an impulse.

Instead she dropped her duffel bag and lowered herself wearily upon it, leaning back against the chain-link fence and wishing she smoked. She tucked her knees up under her chin and wrapped her arms around them for warmth, and gazed uneasily out into the darkness, her empty stomach protesting. Beyond fatigue, Laila huddled for warmth, eyes and ears alert to danger as she waited out the night.

Laila stirred from a fitful sleep in the dismal gray before dawn, hunkered against the chain-link fence. The streets of Forks were still deserted, the traffic signals still blinking yellow — virtually the same desolate scene that had greeted her arrival at three A.M. Except now Laila was even colder, her canvas bag heavier and more unwieldy than ever. But at least it wasn't raining.

She trudged south along the broken sidewalk as the low sky began to spit rain. Perfect.

Laila was wet to the bone by the time she reached the far end of town ten minutes later under the full light of morning, dusky and drab as it was. There were a few cars on the highway now, but mostly trucks barreling past as she tramped along the shoulder of 101 with her thumb thrust out.

About a mile out of Forks an old brown van pulled to the shoulder, and Laila hurried to the passenger door and climbed in. The driver was maybe thirty-five years old, skinny and unshaven, dressed in dirty white coveralls spattered with many-colored paint, clutching a Styrofoam cup of coffee.

"Where to, pretty lady?" he said, flashing a tobacco-stained smile.

"Queets."

"Well, this is your lucky day then," he said, checking the rearview mirror and pulling back onto the highway. "I'm going all the way to Aberdeen."

"Oh," said Laila. "Cool."

"Painting the rec center down there," he observed. "Bitch of a commute but it pays decent. I'm Denny. Everybody calls me DK."

"Hey," said Laila.

"Didn't your mama ever tell you not to hitchhike?"

"No."

"Well, she ought to have. There's a lot of creeps out there."

Laila's scalp tightened at the possibility that

DK was almost certainly one of those creeps.

"You never did say your name," he said.

"Laila," she said.

"Right on. Like the song."

"Yeah, I guess. It's spelled different, though."

Everybody said that about her name — that it was like the Eric Clapton song. But the truth was Laila had never related to the song, maybe because nobody ever got down on their knees and begged her for anything — mostly they just took what they wanted.

DK set his coffee in the cup holder, reached into the breast pocket of his coveralls, and fished out a rumpled Camel soft pack.

"You mind?"

"Nah."

He sparked up a crooked Camel, inhaling deeply.

"Where you from?"

"California."

"Never been," he said.

They drove along in silence for a few miles, the rain spitting against the windshield, the tires swishing up dirty road water beneath them over the winding road. Her cotton hoodie heavy with rain, Laila leaned into the warm air of the heater.

"You can turn on the radio if you want," said DK. "Reception is mostly shit, but you're welcome to try."

"I'm good," said Laila.

Laila settled back into the silence, increasingly confident as the miles wore on that DK was not a creep, just another skinny housepainter with tobacco-stained teeth. About twenty minutes out of Forks the highway doglegged ninety degrees, and Laila caught her first glimpse of the ocean at Ruby Beach, where great windswept sea stacks rose precipitously out the Pacific, stone buttresses hammered by the surf.

"Whoa," she said.

"Not bad, right?" said DK, firing up another Camel. "Guess I'm used to it."

As the van swished south toward Queets, the cluttered shoreline opened up into a broad, flat expanse of sandy beach stretching south for miles. For the first time that day Laila dared to entertain hope. Whatever else awaited her here at the end of the continent, there was this: natural beauty, rugged and eternal, a landscape impervious to heartbreak and disappointment. More promising still, there was everything that this place did not have, and all the old things she was no longer beholden to: her old life, her old job, Boaz. In this respect the place was paradise by omission.

After ten or twelve miles 101 diverged from the shoreline, and the breathtaking vistas were replaced by wide, ugly swathes of clearcut timber on either side of the highway. More wasteland than paradise, and clearly not impervious to human influence.

"Ugly, right?" said DK. "Shit, the Indians are just as bad as us."

"What do you mean?"

"This is all Indian land from here to Quinault, least that side of the road. Everybody thinks the Indians are all at one with the land and all that, but they don't manage their forests any better than we do. Shit, looks like a bomb went off."

Laila's brief bout of optimism was on the wane. Here at last was a landscape worthy of her story, a landscape scarred and torn by bad decisions.

"Well, it'll grow back eventually, I guess," observed DK.

Shortly before eight A.M. they arrived at Queets, a small congregation of dumpy houses huddled together against the rain, fronted by a gas station dressed up like a trading post.

"You can let me off here," said Laila.

"Yes, ma'am," said DK, a flake of tobacco stuck to his lower lip. "Have fun in the big city."

"Thanks," said Laila, hopping out of the van.

She stood in place as the brown van pulled back onto the highway with a honk. It didn't take Laila long to get her bearings. Directly beyond the town there rose a two-hundred-foot barricade of rain forest, cedar and spruce and hemlock. Further east the mountains reared out of a mottled blanket of green, their tops obscured in cloud cover.

There were only a few streets through the village, each of them flanked on either side by boxy little houses in various states of disrepair. More than one roof was amended with a blue tarp, a few of the yards were cluttered with cast-off appliances, and another was heaped with white garbage bags. There were a number of chickens ranging in the street, and a skinny dog with its nose to the ground content to leave them be. The little dog was soon following upon Laila's heels.

"Get," she said.

The little dog spooked, mincing a few steps back, but as soon as Laila resumed her progress he was on her heel again.

"Go on," she said.

But the dog persisted in following her.

It didn't take but five minutes to find Genie's place among the disarray, a little gray house with lavender trim around the windows and eaves, orderly, not cute, but comparatively less ugly than the houses around it. There were a blue sedan and an old pickup truck parked in the drive. Once it became clear that Laila had arrived at her destination, the little dog moved on, nose to the ground.

Laila's heart was in her throat as she proceeded up the walkway to the front step.

She stood there for a moment, not yet poised to knock on the door, paralyzed by all that was uncertain in her future. She was wet. She had just over six hundred dollars in her pocket and a duffel bag full of clothes. No boyfriend, no truck, and no reliable prospects. Nothing left to lose.

Finally, Laila mustered the courage to knock on the door.

NORA BERGEN

Chicago, 1859

In spite of Nora's insistence that she would never acclimate to her new unforeseen wealth or the sudden influence that attended it, Edmund had been astute in his observation that a body can get used to just about anything, especially having money. But it wasn't in the way he likely expected. In the case of Nora, this transition required hardly a fortnight to achieve equilibrium. Always a fast learner, Nora quickly developed an impressive and, to Mr. Trompette's view, aggravating facility for managing and dispensing her wealth.

Within two months' time, it was as though Nora had been born into her new station as heiress to the Seymour estate. Not that she took her wealth for granted; quite the contrary. She viewed her fortune not as an end in itself, but as a vehicle to convey her to more important ends. Perhaps this uncharacteristic attitude toward abundance was owing to the ease with which Nora had accumulated her wealth, or perhaps it was owing to the fact that having never possessed or even aspired to it, the allure of wealth had no hold on her.

Though most of her financial decisions were subject to review by Mr. Trompette, and many of her business decisions subject to the approval of her numerous partnerships, it was Nora alone who held the estate's purse strings and Nora who made the decisions, with little regard to the opinions of Mr. Trompette or anyone else. In the early months of this wealth transfer, many curious changes were made around the estate.

"Edmund," she said one morning in the drawing room, where she was taking her tea, "may I ask what Mr. Seymour has been paying you?"

"Why, three dollars a week, Miss Nora. Been three dollars a week for as long as I can remember."

"And do you think this is a fair wage?"

"Well, ma'am, if I'm entitled to say so, I do believe it was a fair wage when I first started drawing it. Right around the time President Tyler left office."

"Good heavens, has it been that long?"

"Yes, ma'am," he said. "But of course there is my room and board to be considered."

"Even so, this is most unsatisfactory, Edmund. Given the breadth of your responsibilities in running this estate, what would you presently consider a fair wage?"

"I'm not rightly sure I can say, ma'am."

"Kindly take a guess, Edmund."

"Four dollars a week?"

"That seems awfully low," said Nora.

"Four fifty?"

Nora shook her head, denoting a lingering dissatisfaction.

"Your new salary shall be eight dollars per week," she announced. "And you shall have your Saturdays off along with your Sundays."

"Well now, Miss Nora, I'm not entirely sure Mr. Trompette would be agreeable to such an increase. Matter of fact, I think Mr. Trompette likely to get a right good laugh at the suggestion."

"Do not be fooled by his officious manner, Edmund. Mr. Trompette is merely an intermediary," said Nora. "A trusted one, yes, and I daresay a well-compensated one. But I should think that you, Edmund, are equally proficient in your duties, which are at least as numerous as Mr. Trompette's. It is my decision, and I propose your new salary to be eight dollars per week. That is, should you choose to accept such an offer."

"Miss Nora, I'd be a fool not to take it."

"Good," said Nora. "Consider it done. Now what of the other staff? Will you kindly invite them in one at a time?"

"Upstairs?" said Edmund.

"That's right."

"The help ain't never been permitted up the stairs, unless it was to the kitchen, or the dining room to serve."

"Today that oversight will be corrected," said Nora. "And kindly see to it there's plenty of tea, Edmund."

"Yes, ma'am," said Edmund, very nearly betraying his delight.

Indeed Mr. Trompette did not greet any of Nora's proposed changes with a hearty laugh, and he could not disguise his trepidation when confronted with them during his weekly visit to the estate, where the pair invariably convened in Nora's favorite room, the library.

"Miss Bergen, I beg you to understand that there are shared standards for such considerations regarding labor, and your numbers are, well, shall we say, out of line with these shared standards."

"Shared by whom?" said Nora.

"By other employers with similar interests."

"And what interests might those be? Their own?"

"Suffice it to say that an equitable wage scale has been agreed upon among men of means in the state of Illinois."

"So, this is official? This matter of wages has been legislated?"

"Not in any official capacity, no," said Trompette.

"Then, deemed equitable by whom?" said Nora.

"Yes, I see your point, Miss Bergen. And while I applaud your intentions, these numbers you propose are problematic."

"Then so shall the numbers be problematic," she said. "I trust you will navigate these figures without too much difficulty. According to your own estimates, this estate is not lacking in resources. And I consider the staff, who to a man and woman work hard, exhibit a loyalty which is wholly unearned from me vantage, and never issue so much as a complaint about their condition, with which I am personally well acquainted, to be among this estate's greatest resources. Thus they shall be compensated accordingly."

"If that is your wish," consented Trompette, adjusting his silk cravat. "Though I must say I deem it unwise."

"Mr. Trompette, am I to believe that every decision is to be gauged solely on its financial advantages?"

"That is business, Miss Bergen, and thus it has always been, since the time of the pharaohs."

"Hmph," said Nora. "Then it would seem that opportunity couldn't possibly be equal, and that free enterprise is in fact costly for those less-than-equal participants."

Mr. Trompette paid out a sigh and shook his head in disillusionment.

"Miss Bergen," he said, "if I may be frank, your thinking is not in line with Mr. Seymour's own on many matters."

"That may be," said Nora. "But Mr. Seymour saw fit to leave me in charge of his estate, did he not?"

"That I cannot argue."

"Good," she said. "And for the record, Mr. Trompette, I should like to negotiate an increase in your own salary by two percent."

Mr. Trompette suppressed a grin.

"If you insist," he said.

Under Nora's dominion, Mr. Trompette soon found himself busier than ever.

One sunny and unseasonably warm morning late in winter, Nora dispatched a carriage to convey her to the offices of Trompette, Kristoff, Tinker, and Petty to undertake a matter that in Nora's eyes eclipsed all others.

"Mr. Trompette," she said upon taking her seat, "it is high time we utilize our abundant resources toward the end of locating somebody very important to me."

"And who might that be?"

"Me brother, Finn."

"You have a brother?"

"Yes, sir, me twin brother. For reasons I shall never understand, Mr. Seymour saw fit not to adopt him when he took me under his roof. And I aim to find him. I suggest, Mr. Trompette, that we contract and assemble some manner of investigative team even if it requires a small army to locate me brother. If that horrid Searles of the Orphan Asylum persists in being uncooperative, then I suggest we apply some means of pressure on him, or pay him an agreeable sum if that's what it takes."

"Legally speaking, Miss Bergen, this is liable to be a prickly matter, particularly without the consent of the adoptive parents."

"Well then, we shall find some other means of locating him."

"Very well, Miss Bergen, as per your wishes. We shall do everything within our power to locate your brother, . . . ?

"Finn," she said. "Finnegan Bergen."

"I will contract the necessary parties within the week," said Trompette.

Nora was shocked at the ease with which this arrangement was contrived. This fact, perhaps more than any other, illuminated the extent of her influence as the beneficiary of wealth. That all these years of helplessness and hopelessness, countless nights of anguish and despair, half a lifetime of yearning and longing, could be negated with a simple twenty-minute consultation was almost beyond comprehension. There were no boundaries to the sphere of influence vast wealth provided its keeper.

Within a month, Mr. Trompette returned to the manor unannounced and was shown into the library by Edmund.

"I am pleased to inform you we have some news regarding your brother, Miss Bergen."

Nora nearly fell out of her chair.

"You've found him?" she said breathlessly.

"Alas, not yet," said Trompette.

"Is he alive?"

"That we have not yet ascertained."

"So you've not found him, and you can't even say whether he's alive. What news have you that could possibly be good?" she said miserably.

"We have an address for his adoptive parents," said Trompette before Nora's spirits could plummet any further.

"Where?" she said, her eagerness renewed.

"Iowa," said Trompette. "We have traced the parents, a German innkeeper and his wife named Vogel, to a rooming establishment located in Davenport called the River Inn."

Nora's eyes immediately filled with tears. Though the information was inconclusive, at long last she had something, some hint of possibility that Finn was not forever lost to her, that her faith had not been misplaced, that her prayers had been heard.

"What now?" she said.

"As of this very morning, Miss Bergen, we have contracted a man named Bolton, who is currently on his way to Davenport to pay the Vogels a visit and report back to us within the week."

"Can we not proceed to Iowa ourselves at once?" said Nora.

"I submit, Miss Bergen, that it would be

wise first to ascertain the situation," said Trompette.

"What do you mean?"

"It could be that the young man, now past the age of independence, is elsewhere, perhaps even right back here in Chicago, for all we know."

"Here?"

"We won't know until we talk to the parents. It is our hope that Mr. Bolton will find Finn in Davenport. If this proves to be the case, I assure you we shall send for him immediately."

"Is there no way to find out sooner?"

"Until such distances are linked by rail, I'm afraid not, Miss Bergen. Were we eagles, we could fly. At least the miracle of the telegraph will cut our wait in half."

A week! Even after all those years of waiting that had never seen her relinquish hope, the thought of seven more days seemed unendurable. And knowing that Mr. Bolton in Davenport would soon be in possession of the pertinent information only made the wait more dreadful. That night in her feather bed, Nora tossed for hours as her heart raced at the prospect of reuniting with her brother.

FINN BERGEN

Nebraska, 1858

The very morning of Finn's face-to-face encounter with the young Pawnee, he scoured the little outpost of Lancaster, Nebraska, for a room, and by evening had managed to secure a ramshackle outbuilding on a farm two miles south of town owned by a couple named Meeks. The farm was so hopelessly ill conceived that it made the Vogels' farm look like a paradise. To call it a farm at all was misleading. But for a handful of chickens scratching away at the scorched earth, a pair of scrawny long-horns, and a ring of stunted poplars intended as windbreaks, one could hardly distinguish the farm from the surrounding landscape. The salt in the soil, not amenable to growing much at all, likely accounted for the stunting of the surrounding trees.

It soon became apparent that Mr. Lamar Meeks was usually absent from the farm, sometimes for days on end, for reasons Finn was never fully given to understand, though he often returned smelling of liquor. Mrs. Meeks, a childless woman who looked to be in her late twenties, insisted Finn call her Caroline, though Finn persisted in calling her Mrs. Meeks. She was quite pleasant to look at in the right light, but for a feral look in her eyes that bespoke unpredictability. Also, she possessed a palpable desperation for intimacy that put Finn ill at ease in close quarters.

Wherever Finn happened to be, Mrs. Meeks seemed to be nearby. Sometimes she passed so close to Finn that she grazed him. Despite her frequent attempts to engage him, Finn invariably demurred.

"My goodness, you are a peculiar young man," she said one day. "I wonder, do you have blood running through your veins? One thing is for sure: You're not like most men."

"I reckon not," he said.

"That's okay, I like it."

"You do?"

"I'd like to know more," she said.

One afternoon after several weeks on the Meekses' farm, Mrs. Meeks invited Finn into the main house for tea, though it must have been ninety degrees and the humidity was oppressive. Finn declined at first, but Mrs. Meeks was insistent. And so Finn finally consented warily.

Once inside, he did not venture to sit down

and immediately set his mind to effecting his retreat as Mrs. Meeks made a show of busying herself, passing by uncomfortably close as she gathered drinking tins, setting them upon the rough wooden table.

"Have you a girl back home in Iowa?"

"Yes," Finn lied.

"I'll bet she's pretty."

"Yes, ma'am, she is."

"I suppose you intend to marry her?"

"Yes, ma'am."

Once again she passed by so close that she grazed him.

"You'd think Lamar was an old man," she said, setting the kettle upon the stove. "He has no interest in me in a biblical way. He hasn't known me that way in years. And here I am in the prime of my life," she said, the crow's feet around her eyes and the little frown lines on either side of her mouth deepened by the light from the lone window.

Without warning she pressed her body against Finn, forcing her mouth to his. Startled, Finn backpedaled straight into the larder with a clatter as she thrust all of her hundred pounds fast against him, her every muscle taut, her hard little breasts flattening against his chest, her breath cold and metallic like a sick person's.

With some effort, Finn managed to extricate himself and slip out from between the larder and her advance.

"Mrs. Meeks, I-I-I can't," he said.

"Please," she said breathily.

She advanced on him once again, forcing herself up against him. Even as Finn was fighting her off, the door swung open to reveal Lamar Meeks, his figure illuminated in a swath of dusty light.

"Mr. Meeks, I —"

Without pause Meeks strode straight for the carbine on the wall as Finn darted past him for the door. He cleared the threshold just as the edge of the door frame exploded in a cloud of splinters. Finn sprinted across the dusty yard, flinching as the second shot whizzed past his shoulder. The third round from Lamar Meeks's John Brown Special nearly winged Finn, passing so close that he could hear the cartridge whistle past his shoulder. In the time it took Meeks to reload on the front porch, Finn managed to scramble over the dusty rise to the south, where immediately he heard the fourth shot whiz past not two feet above his head. He sprinted over the hardpan until he felt sure he was out of Meeks's range, but even then, he did not halt his progress altogether, but pressed on at a brisk walk.

Thank God Meeks didn't take up after him, turning instead back into the little cabin, where he began berating his wife. Even after the woman had nearly cost him his life, Finn felt mostly sorry for Caroline Meeks, her hard little undernourished figure, her bulging eyes, her pointy little chin, and most troubling of all the aching, suffocating desperation that permeated her every movement. The mere thought of her desperation sent a chill slithering up his neck.

Briefly Finn considered hiding out somewhere nearby, waiting for the cover of darkness in order to retrieve his meager holdings from the shack, but soon rejected the plan as it might get him killed. He'd miss the rifle more than anything else. But it wasn't worth risking his life for. Instead he fled town immediately on foot in a westerly direction, unarmed and without a plan, his heart pounding in his ears.

He'd covered about fifteen miles on foot by evening and slept under the stars that night. The following day he woke with the dawn and trudged through the humid prairie heat for hours on end, covering twenty more miles. By afternoon he arrived parched and penniless in the little outpost of Fontanelle along the Elkhorn River. Like so many towns in the western territories, Fontanelle had the look of a place hastily constructed and wholly without pretense. It was a wonder that the prairie winds didn't blow the place clean out of existence.

After only two hours of making inquiries out in front of the mercantile, Finn managed to secure work on the ranch of a man named

Carlyle, who lived a half mile outside of town. Carlyle was a widower, a man hard and flat as the prairie itself. He did not mince his words, and he expected an awful lot for a wage that was barely livable. He worked Finn like a quarter horse, sometimes fourteen hours a day, to the tune of a half dollar and a pallet in the stable. It was by no measure the life Finn had ever envisioned for himself, and like every other chapter of his life it left him wanting. Still, it was a good deal more than what he had left Lancaster with. If nothing else, he slept soundly at the end of each day, either too exhausted or too apathetic to dream.

That Finn would eventually leave Fontanelle was owing to no master plan or guiding principle. It was simply inevitable, like the setting of the sun. Eventually opportunity or necessity or chance would come calling, and Finn would answer the call. One morning after two weeks on Carlyle's ranch, a scruffy militia numbering three dozen men from upriver descended on Fontanelle and set to recruiting. Finn was shoveling out stalls when two men arrived on horseback. Finn paused in his labor and walked out of the stable to greet them, squinting against the midmorning light.

"We going after Pawnee," said the mustachioed one.

"What for are you going after the Pawnee?"

Finn asked.

"They're on the rampage up north county. Last two days they committed numerous depredations and degradations up around DeWitt, and they done it in true Indian fashion, too — stole the finery, burnt the houses, drove off the stock. They're still wreaking havoc up there, and the military ain't here to do anything about it, so we aim to put an end to it. We're looking for as many healthy bodies as possible. What say you?"

"Got no horse, and I got no gun," said Finn.

"Why, there's no shortage of horses right here for the taking, and I'll see to it you get furbished with a revolver."

Finn had no beef with the Pawnee or any other tribe. To his way of thinking, the Indians were only protecting what was theirs to begin with from uninvited outsiders — not unlike the Irish for so many centuries. Still, it seemed that under the circumstances, given the pressure applied by his recruiters, Finn had little choice but to take up with the militia, any more than Carlyle had a choice to provide him with the horse to do so. Surely, a half dollar a day wasn't getting Finn anywhere, and a horse and a revolver were a good deal more than he could presently call his own. And so he left with the militia on their quest up the Elkhorn River, uneasy with his charge.

Finn rode side by side with a Mississippi

native named Oswald who concealed a cleft palate beneath his thick beard.

"They ought to be exterminated, that's what I think," Oswald said as they skirted the Elkhorn. "Some of them is more agreeable than others, it's true. Take the Omaha, they ain't so bad. But it's only a matter of time afore the Omaha and the Poncas join ranks with the Pawnee Nation. Then what we'll have is a lot of Christian blood on our hands. No, there ain't no way around it I can see. If the governor would put his damn head on straight, likely we could solve the problem and restore proper order inside a year or two with military intervention. The savage would soon know his place. But I wouldn't hold your breath."

In spite of a troubled conscience, Finn never offered an opinion on the matter, only listened silently from atop his mount, six dollars in his pocket and a Colt revolver at the ready as he surveyed the prairie for any sign of Pawnee, hoping beyond hope he'd never see a single solitary one of them.

By late afternoon the company reached West Point, having encountered no Indians — Pawnee, Omaha, or otherwise. The would-be regiment hunkered down and held its position, camping in West Point until the following day, whereupon they began doubling back toward Fontanelle in search of the marauders. How that many Indians made themselves so scarce, nobody could say, but the collective mood of the men as they moved southward along the river was one of wary alertness.

At midday, Finn was near the front of the company when a scout returned breathless to report a small band of Indians no more than a mile south, over the next rise.

"How many?"

"Maybe thirty."

"Pawnee?" said the man in charge.

"Can't rightly say," said the scout. "They don't seem to be in no hurry, though."

"Well, they ought to be."

With that, the man in charge straightened up in his saddle and hoisted his saber.

"H'ya!" he said.

He was off at a gallop, a cloud of dust trailing in his wake as the rest of the company fell in behind him, rumbling over the dry grass in pursuit of the would-be Pawnee. Though Finn did not recognize this urgency as his own, he could not deny the blood surging through his veins as never before, nor could he deny the sense of purpose that captivated him as he hurtled toward his objective. Perhaps action would be his savior where everything before had failed. Perhaps the lusty thrill and the heady rush of the hunt would deliver him to the place that backbreaking work and aimless wandering had not.

It was only a matter of minutes before the militia had made up the mile, and they spotted the Indians strung out along the east bank moving at a leisurely pace, but not for long. The direness of the situation soon became clear to the Natives and they began to beat a hasty retreat, splashing west across the river. The militia charged the bank at a gallop and without provocation began firing upon the Natives, though not a man among them could actually say whether they were Pawnee or Omaha, and in the moment it seemed not to matter, for just their otherness was enough.

When the Indians splashed their way across the Elkhorn to the far bank, they immediately spread out, presumably an act of self-preservation as the militia fanned out behind them in an orgy of gunfire. The Pawnee, if indeed they were Pawnee, did not return fire but continued to flee, not once turning back toward their pursuers. Several were shot dead in the back and thrown from their horses before their identity was determined.

Charging breathlessly over the trampled ground, the hot prairie wind assaulting his face, Finn found himself on the heels of a young brave hunkered atop a brown-and-white dappled colt. Jockeying for position, Finn drew his pistol as he flanked his adversary on the left until he managed to pull even with the colt. Leveling his revolver, he took aim.

Only then did he determine that his adversary was no brave at all, but a young woman, running for her life. For an instant her dark eyes met Finn's from across the dusty breadth rollicking between them. And that was all it took, a fraction of a second, for the young woman's desperate eyes to haunt Finn forever. Immediately, he lowered his revolver and pulled back on the reins, and slowed his horse to a canter, as he watched the brown-and-white dappled colt retreat into the high grass in a cloud of dust. Sitting there atop his mount, Finn could not help but wonder at the world he lived in and where it had gone wrong.

Looking back toward the river, Finn could see the rest of the militia by the numerous clouds of dust spread far and wide in the distance, the report of their gunfire echoing across the vast plain. Without further deliberation Finn took off at a gallop west toward the horizon, to where or what purpose he could not say. He only knew that he was compelled to keep moving at any cost, to keep hurtling west to the far end of the continent, where nothing could reach him.

Parched and famished, he crossed the endless prairie through the remainder of the day and past sunset. Even the dark could not deter his progress, as he rode on into the night until he fell asleep in the saddle.

Finn was rudely awakened shortly after first

light when the horse reared suddenly, nearly throwing him from the saddle as a deafening rumble rose like thunder and the earth trembled beneath him. The horse spooked, then reared once more, this time throwing Finn to the ground before lighting off irretrievably toward the east. The earth was now quaking like Jericho as a wall of dust arose before Finn, blotting out the far horizon. As the rumbling swelled to a roar, Finn stood up, backpedaling instinctively as the thunderous percussion bore down upon him.

Awestruck, he watched the bison stream past in an interminable procession. With their shaggy outsized heads thrust out before them and their broad noses to the ground, they charged south like a hundred thousand locomotives, the earth trembling beneath their assault, the dazed prairie left humming in their wake.

Their numbers were incalculable, unfathomable. God, but they were endless.

MR. BOLTON

Nebraska, 1859

Mr. Bolton could not abide the wide-open spaces of the prairie. He held no fondness for the whispering grass. A native son of Missouri, Mr. Bolton preferred a civilized life on the delta to the desolate grandeur of the Great Plains, preferred the proximity of humanity, with its myriad sounds and smells and spectacles, to the blank canvas of prairie grass. Standing tall upon the deck of the steamer *Dubuque,* his gray topcoat buffering him from the frigid wind, Mr. Bolton was glad that his stay in Iowa would presumably be short. Find the River Inn; locate the Bergen boy, who would be thrilled with his appearance; and bring him back to Chicago, where Bolton would collect his handsome fee.

Upon landing at Davenport, locating the River Inn was not difficult. The three-story edifice occupied half a city block not a quarter mile from the boat landing. No sooner had Mr. Bolton located the inn than he mounted the wide steps and proceeded to the lobby, where he inquired at the desk for Mr. or Mrs. Vogel. The young desk clerk was most obliging and wasted no time in retrieving Hans Vogel, a stout little man of German stock with a thick accent.

"Mr. Vogel," said Mr. Bolton, "I have been contracted by the Chicago firm of Trompette, Kristoff, Tinker, and Petty with regard to your adoptive son, Finn."

"Finn?" said Hans Vogel excitedly. "You have news of my boy?"

"No, sir," said Mr. Bolton. "I was hoping you could assist me in locating the young man."

The German hung his head and groaned.

"We have not seen him in two years. Every day we are hoping for news of him. But he does not write."

Now it was Mr. Bolton groaning, inwardly. "I see," he said. "And where was the last time you saw him?"

"Here in Davenport," said Hans. "Shortly before we opened the inn."

"Have you any idea where he might be?"

"West," said Hans.

"Anywhere in particular?"

"Working with the railroad."

"Ah," said Mr. Bolton, a little dispiritedly. "Do you happen to know which railroad?"

"It was the IMIRC, but then it became something else, and then something else, and now I don't know what to call it. Why are you looking for him? Our Finn is not in trouble?"

"No, sir, suffice it to say that an old acquaintance is trying to locate him."

Needless to say, Mr. Bolton was less than pleased to extend his stay in Iowa. Mr. Trompette and his client would also no doubt be disappointed that Bolton was unable to produce the boy. But at least he had a solid lead. There were only so many rails running west.

Mr. Bolton spent a day and a night at the River Inn gathering information and formulating his course of action. From the Western Union office, he promptly sent word via telegraph to Mr. Trompette in Chicago:

BERGEN LEFT DAVENPORT STOP LAST IN EMPLOY OF UNDETERMINED RAILROAD CONCERN STOP WHEREABOUTS UNKNOWN STOP PROCEEDING WEST IN PURSUIT STOP

Indeed, Mr. Bolton would extend his search west for Finn, following the rails of the newly incorporated INRR. Three weeks later he caught up with crews south of Iowa City, where he learned from interviews that Finn had walked off the job late the previous summer and had allegedly joined up with a family of Mormons on a wagon train heading west out of Iowa City. Mr. Bolton considered cutting his losses and returning to Chicago empty-handed, but Mr. Trompette and his client would not hear of it. Thus Mr. Bolton had no recourse but to contract secure transportation west himself in the form of a pair of Pinkertons named Ames and Ross, who, unlike Bolton, were fond of life on the trail.

With the guidance and protection of Ames and Ross, the ever-fastidious Bolton stopped at every settlement west of Iowa City to make inquiries, spitefully enduring the bitter cold and desolation along with the complete and utter absence of civilized culture. Never, not once during his weeks on the trail, did familiarity with frontier life breed anything but contempt in the heart and mind of Mr. Bolton. He vowed never again to eat beans, or sleep in a tent, or endure the shrill discomfort of Ames's or anyone else's fiddle around a fire once these tribulations were mercifully behind him.

Arwen Bolton missed the spectacle of industry. He missed the conceit of civil endeavor, missed the gaslight and cobblestone of city life. He even missed the chaos and filth of the city, missed the crowds and the endless distraction of urban life. Why young Bergen or anyone else would want to run wild in this untamed country in the face of bears and bandits and savages was beyond

Arwen Bolton. But he soldiered on in the face of despair, warming his hands as he breathed the stench of burning cow chips over open fires, defecating in holes and, on more than one occasion, dining on prairie dog.

It wasn't until Bolton reached the tiny outpost of Lancaster, Nebraska, that he managed to ferret out his next lead, which arrived in the person of Mr. Lamar Meeks, a self-described dirt farmer who claimed to have "run the godless rascal right out of town."

As to where Finn Bergen might have run off to, Lamar Meeks could not say.

"Pert sure I winged him, though."

"Straight to the nearest brothel is where he gone off to if you ask me," said Mrs. Meeks, a hard, thin-lipped woman of twenty, or forty; it was difficult to ascertain. "I showed that boy kindness on account of his circumstances and let him into my home, and he thanked me by forcing himself on me. If it weren't for Lamar, I'd no longer have my innocence."

Spirits flagging but still determined, Bolton located the nearest brothel two miles west of Lancaster. There, he resisted his baser instincts, keeping things strictly professional as one by one he interviewed the girls, which numbered four. Nobody recalled anyone named Finn or Bergen, nor any man who fit young Bergen's description.

"Most the men we get is from around these parts," the madam informed Bolton.

Having exhausted all avenues of inquiry, Bolton abandoned his search and returned west as far as Council Bluffs, Iowa, where he sent word to Mr. Trompette in Chicago.

TRAIL GONE COLD IN NEBRASKA STOP BERGEN A GHOST STOP PLEASE IN-STRUCT STOP

GEORGE FLOWERS

Illinois, 1853

Hunched in the rear of a crowded produce wagon piloted by a man named Eli Ross, George clutched Cora's hand, and she, in turn, clutched in her other fist the crude little figure George had carved for her, as the wagon rattled over the uneven road. For nearly a week they'd traveled under such conditions, cramped and sweltering, stowed, buried, and contorted, ten and twelve hours a day, bodies aching, stomachs twisted in knots, the clear and ever-present possibility of capture torturing their weary minds, as their fates rested in the hands of strangers.

It was a miracle Cora didn't miscarry under the circumstances. All the while the impending birth of their child hung over Cora and George like a cloud. Any day, any minute, the baby might arrive to sabotage their escape. What if complications arose? What if the birth should draw unwanted attention to their flight? And how on earth could they possibly sustain their progress under such conditions with an infant to care for?

In Galesburg, the wagon came to an abrupt stop in the gathering darkness, heaving George and Cora forward in their cramped hold.

"Friend of a friend," they heard Eli Ross announce.

"I've been expecting you," said a voice.

Ross hopped down off the wagon and, with the help of the second individual, began shuffling crates and sacks about in order to extricate his human cargo, who soon emerged gasping from the back of the wagon into the dusky light, finding themselves in a barren lot behind an old church. Here, a preacher, to their surprise a white man with a considerable beard, was there to greet them.

"Welcome, brother and sister," he said.

Without further ceremony, the preacher led them into the musty church through the back door.

"We're much obliged to you, sir," said George.

"It is God's will," said the preacher.

In a cloistered space hidden behind the altar, he directed them up a ladder to the shutterless belfry, where they were to await the next leg of their journey north. If indeed this kindness was the will of God, he could not have chosen a more fitting place for their safekeeping. Compared to their stowage in the wagon, the belfry was roomy, despite the great bronze bell dominating the space.

No sooner had they settled into the belfry than night was fully upon them, and the brilliance of the rising moon came slanting into the tiny chamber, bathing it in silver light. Perhaps the will of God really was at work. A prayer silently took shape on George's lips.

Within minutes a young woman arrived with bread and water and two goodly-sized streaks of salt pork, which George and Cora set greedily to work upon in the confines of the belfry. When they were finished eating, they lay down upon their backs as the last of the day's heat dissipated and the night air grew cool.

"This baby want out, George," Cora said softly. "I can feel it pressed right up against me."

"You got to hold it," said George.

"Hold it?" Cora tried to laugh but couldn't. "Why, that shows you how much a man knows. I'm telling you, George, this baby is going to have its way, and soon."

Not an hour later Cora bolted upright to her elbows and gasped, wide-eyed in the moonlight.

"What is it?" whispered George.

"Just what I told you before," she said.

"You aim to have that child right here in the belfry?"

"Should I climb down that ladder?" she said.

The second contraction arrived within minutes. Cora braced herself and gritted her teeth, and somehow resisted the instinct to cry out.

"What do I do?" said George.

"Pray," she said.

The third contraction came close on the heels of the second, and this time Cora was unable to silence her agony.

George fished the dirty kerchief from out of his pocket and knotted it up.

"Bite on this," he said, handing her the rag.

George prayed like he hadn't prayed since the night he ran off in Urbana. He prayed that this child would be born quickly and have the good sense to make a quiet entrance into the world. He prayed that the child would be healthy and not leave its mother any worse for wear. And last, he prayed that God would protect them and see them on through this night and beyond. George was still praying when Cora let out another muffled cry. Spitting out the rag, she began to pant heavily.

"Now what?" implored George, kneeling beside her.

"Keep praying," she said breathlessly, clutching the little figurine tightly in her fist.

But there was no time left to pray. George reached out for her hand and she squeezed it with a force that surprised him.

"Someone's in a hurry," she said.

Her forehead glistening with sweat, Cora contorted her face, clenching and pushing and straining, until the child finally crowned. Frantically, George took his place to receive it, just as the infant emerged, revealing himself to be a boy, howling into the shock of the cool air. Like an answer to George's prayer, the infant calmed instantly once cradled in his mother's arms.

George wept to see the helpless child groping for his mother's comfort. For all that was wrong with the world, this was the rightest thing he had ever witnessed. Hard to fathom that such beauty existed in a world as ugly as this one. God had some explaining to do. What world was it, what nation, that a child, an innocent, still nameless, a child who'd never asked to be born, who'd arrived in the world homeless, a refugee under cover of night in a belfry in downstate Illinois, should already be running for his life?

Malik Flowers

Washington, 2019

Forty-five minutes after Malik's mom was admitted to the ER, the attending physician confirmed the nurse's diagnosis of a broken scapula. Fortunately, there was no damage to the lung or surrounding nerves. No surgery required. No pins or bolts. She would likely resume full function within four or five months. However, she was still showing symptoms of concussion: some drowsiness, dizziness, and nausea. Continuing on to Seattle was out of the question. She would be staying at Providence St. Peter, where she'd be monitored through the night and well into the next day.

"Hand me my purse," she said from her hospital bed.

Malik fished the purse off the chair and handed it to her. She soon produced three not-so-crisp twenty-dollar bills and the credit card from her battered red billfold.

"You get a taxi to the Amtrak," she said.

"And you get on the next train for Seattle. The room is prepaid, but take the card just in case."

"Ma, I dunno, I think maybe I should just —"

"When you get back home, you get on a bus back to the house. I imagine I'll be home by then, but if not, you go about your business."

"Ma, I really think I should just —"

"Do as I say," she said. "And one more thing. Come here."

He drew closer to the bed as she fished something out of her purse and pressed it firmly into his palm.

"Take this," she said.

Malik stuffed the little wooden figurine into his pants pocket without looking at it. Leaning way down, he kissed his mom on the cheek.

"Put some ice on that wrist when you get to the hotel," she said.

"What are you talking about?"

"I've seen you clutching your wrist since the accident. Ice it. And go straight to sleep when you check in."

"Aight, Coach," he said.

According to the meter, which Malik watched anxiously as the slushy miles to Centennial Station passed, the taxi would account for close to two of the three twenty-dollar bills his mother had given him. With the light rail in Seattle and breakfast, it was going to be tight, and that wasn't even accounting for dinner after the game, or the return trip to Portland, which the credit card would hopefully cover. The fact that Malik had only eight bucks of his own shamed him. Yeah, he was a big man on campus dribbling a basketball, yeah, the kids at the rec center looked up to him, but he was just a baby in real life; he'd barely experienced anything, or navigated anything by himself, and having only twenty-eight bucks after the cab ride, knowing his mom was in the hospital, not knowing exactly where the hotel in Seattle was, or the pavilion, having only been to Seattle once, when he was eleven years old, all of these things coupled with his increasingly stiff wrist began stirring Malik in unfamiliar ways.

As he ducked out of the taxi, it began to snow again, but just barely, big flakes like ash fluttering lazily down on Malik, or maybe more like confetti. The cool air and the open space soothed his nerves immediately. As Malik stepped onto the slushy curb and the taxi pulled away, he paused to be mindful, like he taught Michael at the rec center to be mindful, and Rashard, and Rudy, and Earl, just like Mr. Thorpe had taught him to be mindful, to gather himself and double down on his beliefs, on his determination, to believe in his habits and his hard work. To be strong.

Because ain't nobody gonna give you a break. You gonna have to make your own break. That's the way it was, and that's the way it always had been, but it didn't have to be that way always. These reminders emboldened Malik somewhat as he stood there under the falling sky, his hand nervously working over the smooth little figurine nestled deep in his pocket.

An hour after he presented his voucher, Malik was boarding the Coast Starlight northbound for the second time in twelve hours. By the time he took his seat, his wrist was beginning to swell a bit; it might've even been sprained. The pain was manageable, a little tenderness, a little pinch now and again, but he wasn't sure about his mobility or strength. He would have given his last twenty-eight bucks for a basketball just then, to grip and dribble and clutch, to work his hands around. But in the absence of a ball, Malik bunched and unbunched his fist in an effort to keep his wrist limber, clutching the little talisman in his good hand. He ought to have been taking his mom's advice and icing it, but he'd played through all kinds of jams before — fingers, wrists, toes. The trick was to keep limber; the trick was to ignore the discomfort and let the adrenaline take over.

If nothing else, this preoccupation made the train ride go fast. As the Coast Starlight began to roll into Seattle from the south, Malik pressed his face to the window and looked over the industrial sprawl to the splendor of the skyline, glowing beneath the bowl of night, more sudden and three times the size of Portland's skyline, the buildings taller and more bunched together, the effect all at once more exciting and intimidating and full of possibility.

At King Street Station, Malik ducked off the train onto the platform with his wheelie bag in tow. Guided by Google, he trudged a few blocks in the snow to the Link station, where he bought a ticket at the kiosk, taking the opportunity to preserve his funds and use his mother's credit card.

Boarding the southbound train, he sat by the window at the rear of the car, watching the city lights pass in the opposite direction as the Hec Ed Pavilion, south past SoDo and Beacon Hill, past Mount Baker, Columbia City, and Othello. Some of the guys flying in were likely staying in fancier hotels downtown, while others were probably staying closer to the pavilion. No big, Malik told himself. Even if the airport was in the wrong direction, Hec Ed Pavilion was right on the Link line, so it would only be a matter of forty-five minutes or an hour getting there tomorrow, and he'd be sure to arrive early.

Malik ducked off the train at International Boulevard and trudged down the steps to street level, whereupon Google directed him south a few blocks, his wheeled suitcase mired in the snow nearly every step of the way. Arriving at the Days Inn, he passed through the double glass doors and into the garish light of the lobby. It was pretty nice to Malik's eye, with its boxy leather couches and glass coffee tables, its bulbous lamps and busy carpet. At least they had a free breakfast and cable. And the pillows were sure to be better than at home.

Like everybody else when confronted with Malik's size, the desk woman, maybe five foot four, couldn't belie a familiar awe when she looked up at Malik.

"Will you be parking?" she said.

"No, ma'am," he said.

"I'll just need a credit card for incidentals," said the clerk.

"The room is prepaid, there won't be any incidentals," said Malik. "My mom booked the room in advance."

"I still have to take your credit card for a deposit. It goes back on your card in two to five days."

"How much?" said Malik.

"Just fifty dollars."

What was he going to spend fifty dollars on? There wasn't even any room service as far as he could tell.

"Really, there won't be any incidentals," he said. "I'm checking in and going to sleep, then checking out in the morning."

"I'll still need a credit card and ID," said the clerk. "It's just standard procedure."

Malik pulled out his wallet and warily handed over the credit card and unsheathed his driver's license from the transparent slot in his wallet. A few minutes later he was wheeling his bag down the corridor and up the elevator and down another corridor to 509, where he inserted the cardkey. The room was like the lobby in miniature: earthy colors, boxy furniture, and bulbous lamps. Malik kicked off his size-nineteen sneakers and lay down on the nearest of the twin beds, fetching the remote off the nightstand. He immediately gravitated toward basketball highlights on ESPN, but they failed to hold his attention. Nervous and hungry, he walked down the hallway to the vending machines, where he pondered the possibilities, the financial repercussions playing out like story questions in third-grade math. *If Malik has twenty-eight dollars, and spends two dollars on a Snickers bar, then spends an additional four dollars on two granola bars, how many dollars does Malik have left?*

Twenty-two dollars, that's how many dollars Malik had left after one Snickers and two granola bars. And he was still hungry five minutes later as he lay atop the covers, *SportsCenter* on mute, the adjacent twin bed conspicuously empty. For a moment he flirted with anxiety but managed to shut it down before it could get any traction. Better get some rest. He set his phone alarm for six forty-five A.M. and turned off the TV, tossing the remote on the nightstand. Snapping the lamp off, Malik lay flat on his back staring into the unfamiliar darkness of the Days Inn, the quietude of the fifth floor alien.

WALTER BERGEN

Eugene, Oregon, 2019

An hour after the damaged train had backed clear of the scene, grinding and lurching, it was none other than Detective Barnes who drove Walter back to Kelso in the backseat of an unmarked squad car. The snow was falling again, big wet flakes that hit the window like bird shit. Though the access road was a slushy mess, the interstate had been recently plowed. They drove the first mile in silence, Walter peering out at the oncoming snow swirling in the headlights. The nausea was still arriving in waves, and the dizziness was intermittent. He was glad there was no mirror in back, so he didn't have to see how bad he looked.

"Saw you dodging the medics back there," said Barnes over his shoulder. "You know, you really ought to get that nose checked out. You look like you got in a fight."

"You should see the other guy," Walter said miserably.

"Look at the bright side," said Barnes. "Small miracle you didn't jump the rails, right? Hitting that sucker at forty miles per hour. You figure something would have to give. Could have been a lot worse."

"Any word about the boy?" said Walter, casting his eyes out the side window.

"No follow-ups yet from Olympia."

Far more than Walter dreaded the coming inquest, the loss of his pension, or even the possibility of prosecution, he feared for the boy's life. Something like that would haunt Walter forever. And all because he'd looked at his stupid phone when he knew better. He still hadn't mustered the nerve to call Annie, though he'd finally sent word to her by text:

Ran into trouble up near Kelso. Am OK. Will call later. Expect me late.

Short, a little cryptic, maybe, but informative enough to ease Annie's mind, Walter hoped. The world had been coming at Walter plenty fast the past five hours without having to explain it all to Annie, especially about the boy. She'd take the boy even harder than him.

"How you holding up, hoss?" said Barnes.

"I've had better days," said Walter.

"I'll bet," said Barnes. "But I have a feeling it may work out for you, assuming the toxicology comes back clean. You've got a good track record, right? And a long one. Then there's the weather conditions; all of that ought to account for something."

"I'm mostly worried about the kid," said Walter.

"Yeah, I'll bet," said Barnes, lapsing once more into silence.

Ten minutes later, Barnes pulled to the curb in front of the train station in Kelso.

"I hope it works out for you," said Barnes.

"That's it?" said Walter.

"We're finished with you on this end, for now."

"So, I just . . ."

"Go home," said Barnes. "Unless you've got something else planned. I'm sure your people at Amtrak are gonna have more questions."

"Thanks for the ride," said Walter, climbing out.

"You bet."

Walter immediately ducked his head back into the car. "How will I find out about the boy?"

"We'll let you know," said Barnes. "I'll see to it personally."

Watching the unmarked squad car pull away from the curb, Walter, a little unsteady from standing too fast, had the distinct sensation he was dreaming. After a moment, he gathered himself, turned, and proceeded up the steps, kicking the wet snow from his feet before pushing through the glass door.

A half hour later, Walter boarded the Coast Starlight, a mere passenger headed south. Thirty-one years at Amtrak, a sterling service record, the unwavering respect of his peers, and Walter could count on one hand the number of times he hadn't finished a route, and that would include the afternoon Wendy was born and the day his father died. Yet there he was, after a five-hour delay, aboard the Coast Starlight, headed for home.

Walter felt every day of his sixty-three years as he stared out the window.

The snow had relented, and the clouds began to scatter. The moon shone directly overhead now, illuminating the snow-covered valley clear to the horizon. The wistfulness that had marked the first half of Walter's last day on the job was long gone now — it seemed a lifetime ago. Regardless of Macy's numerous entreaties, Walter turned a critical eye inward and continued to berate himself. After a few miles, fatigue began to settle in, muddling Walter's thoughts until he could no longer summon the mental acuity to pursue such grim speculation. He settled into his high-backed seat, gazing fixedly out the window of the speeding train. As the thrum of its churning progress vibrated up through the floor, humming within every atom of Walter's being, the trying events of the day seemed to recede into the darkened promise of the landscape stretching out to the west.

When Walter woke up just as the Coast Starlight pulled into the old Southern Pacific station at Eugene, the dizziness and the nausea were mostly gone. Thankfully, there was no hoopla awaiting him there, no press or Amtrak official. He crossed the platform with his eyes down, lest they should meet the eyes of an associate. Likewise, through the station he moved briskly, proceeding straight to the bathroom, where he managed to clean himself up reasonably well. Walking out into the parking lot, now slushy with snowmelt, again Walter kept his eyes down.

He ditched his blood-soaked vest in the backseat of the Explorer before he climbed into the driver's seat. The chaos of the day still enveloped Walter like a dream state as he began the drive home. His senses were muddled, the world did not quite seem itself, the streets were less familiar than they ought to have been.

He arrived home shortly before midnight. The instant he pushed through the front door he was greeted by the telltale signs of the surprise party that never was: the crepe-paper bunting, red and blue; the big white hand-printed banner — "Congratulations, Wally!" The furniture was still spread out toward the corners to accommodate a large number of people.

Annie must have been waiting up for him, because she emerged from the kitchen before

Walter cleared the foyer and threw her arms around him in a fierce embrace.

"Oh, thank God you're okay, Wally. It's all over the news. I got your message and tried to call you, but —"

"I'm sorry," he said. "I had my hands full."

"Come, sit down," she said, and Walter did as he was instructed.

He seated himself on the old gray sofa, the sofa that Annie had been trying to get rid of for years, "the Barge," she called it; the embarrassment of the living room. But Walter had managed to hold Annie off all these years because he loved that sofa like an old friend. How many Ducks games had he watched from that old sofa? How many times had Wendy fallen asleep in his arms on that sofa? Just as the thought occurred to him, Wendy popped her head into the living room, and the rest of her followed, barefoot and in an old nightgown.

"Hey, Dad, we were so worried about you."

At the sound of her voice, Walter was visited by an unexpected pang of nostalgia and a welling in his chest. The way she said it, so familiar and matter-of-fact. It was like somebody had set the clock back years, like Wendy was still living there in her old room, and they were all still together under one roof, and everything was going to be all right.

Wu Chen

San Francisco, 1862

Wu Chen's life might have been ideal were it not for the legacy of the Huangs, whose violent ends still took a grim toll on his psyche eleven years after the fact. The guilt stuck to him like a shadow. Everything Wu Chen achieved, every dollar he saved, everything he experienced, including his marriage and his children, they all amounted to things that the Huangs would never have or experience because Wu Chen had not acted soon enough, because he had cowered in the dirt in fear of his own life, the sum of which he felt he owed to Jimmy and his brothers.

Though deeply ashamed of his impatience with his wife and his children, Wu Chen could not control it. He knew he was not worthy of their affection and that he ought to reward their loyalty with every kindness, yet they sometimes set him on edge, twisting the ropes of his inner conflict until his whole being burned from the friction of it. And while his rages never reached physical violence, they never failed to unsettle his children, particularly Jack, whose curious nature occasioned Wu Chen's wrath more than anything else, particularly when the boy pressed him.

Jack was of an age that found him eager to learn of his father's adventures, and Wu Chen was willing if not happy to oblige the boy when it came to his own childhood in Guangdong, wrestling with his cousins in the fields, working dawn until dusk, sleeping elbow to elbow in a thatch hut. Likewise, Wu Chen was not reticent to share his early adolescence, or his burgeoning understanding of the world and the necessity of escaping the poverty and upheaval of his village — that he had to leave everything he knew behind and try to find something better. He wanted his son to know of his sacrifice. Though Wu Chen would do everything within his power to make sure they did not present themselves, he wanted his son to be prepared for the rigors that the future might hold. He wanted to impress upon his children the possibility of hardship, along with the value of hard work and struggle. He was even willing to share with Jack his travails in the hellish confines of steerage as he crossed the Pacific. But over a decade removed from his unraveling on the bank of the Shasta, he still had limits.

One evening, as Wu Chen tucked the boy

into bed, Jack dared to broach the forbidden subject.

"Papa, tell me about your gold," he said.

"There is nothing to tell," said Wu Chen. "I dug a hole, I found gold."

"How much gold?"

"Enough."

"How deep did you have to dig, Papa?"

"I don't remember. Deep."

"Do you still have some? Can I see it?" said the boy, undaunted by the evasions.

"No," said Wu Chen. "All gone. There's nothing to see."

"Where did it go?"

"In the bank," he said irritably.

"Can we go there and see it?"

"No," he snapped.

"But, Papa, I just wanted —"

"Hush! Go to sleep, now."

Wu Chen left the boy confused in the darkness. A few minutes later, Ai Lu found Wu Chen outside on the front stoop, his head in his hands, crying.

"What is it?" she said.

"Let me be," he said.

"No," she said. "Not this time. You must tell me what is eating you. You must tell me your secret, otherwise . . ."

"Otherwise?"

"Otherwise I can no longer be with you."

Wu Chen shook his head, frowning. "You may not want to be with me when you hear the story I have to tell."

"So be it, but you must tell me if you wish to stay with me," she said. "With us."

Wu Chen cast his eyes down. "Very well," he said.

Ai Lu reached out and took his hand.

"Where to start?" he said.

"At the beginning," she said.

Wu Chen paid out a heavy sigh and tried to reclaim his hand from her grasp, but she would not allow him to remove it.

"When I first came to this country," he began, "I arrived penniless, knowing not a soul in San Francisco, or anywhere in America. I came frightened, and knowing nothing of the world beyond the delta and my little village. I had no designs for my future when I came here. My only skill was farming. The world I found here was overwhelming. I had no clue how best to navigate it, or even to begin to gather my bearings. And so I wandered the streets of the city by day, and at night I slept beneath the wharf like a rat, smoking tobacco to stay warm and curb my hunger. I was not made to feel welcome in this place, not that I ever expected to be, not exactly. But I did not expect to be treated as an outsider by people who were outsiders themselves. For, like me, they too had come here, lured by the promise of the Golden Mountain. They, too, had arrived friendless and homeless. But not a soul reached out to me. I was certain that I had made a grave mistake in coming to America."

He broke off momentarily, looking wistfully out at the darkened street, noise from the great bustling city beyond bleeding into the relative quiet of their neighborhood. Ai Lu squeezed his hand harder.

"And then," he said, "I happened upon one friendly face in the whole of this strange city. Actually, I should say that it was he who discovered me. It was as if he were sent by providence to rescue me, for why else should this man decide to stop me, an arbitrary stranger, on Grant Street, not three doors from where our grocery stands today? Of all the people in this crowded city, why me, the most beleaguered and naïve of the whole lot? Unless, of course, his plan was to exploit me somehow, for I would have been an easy target, but I was too naïve to even entertain suspicion. And this man soon proved that he was too good of heart to ever harm another.

"He was a young man, just three years older than me, but two of those years he had spent in America, learning the ways and the customs of this place, and thus he was much older than me in the way of experience. And from the first moment he engaged me, he was generous in sharing his experience. He stopped me right there in the middle of Grant Street and gently took me to task for looking like I had just walked off the boat. I explained that, indeed, I had just walked off the boat, and he told me he could see that clearly from two blocks away. 'You're an easy mark,' he told me. Instantly, he guessed that I had come from Guangdong. Like me, he had known poverty and revolution. He, too, had answered the siren call of the Golden Mountain. And it had delivered.

"He told me that he had two brothers, and that together they had staked a claim on the Shasta River. He told me that his brothers were back at the claim, and that in two days' time he would return to Shasta City to join them. They had already panned with a bit of success and had been excavating for months. The young man was certain that they would locate the vein. All of this, he told me before he ever even knew my name. When I asked him why he was willing to share the details of his soon-to-be fortune with me, a perfect stranger, he told me that he was a shrewd judge of character and that he could tell immediately that I was a good and honest man. And looking at my hands, he said, he could tell I was a good worker. I did not contradict his verdict on either count, but in the years that followed, I would have many occasions to question his wisdom concerning my goodness. But none of us could foresee the future.

"There, on Grant Street, as the man considered my miserable, hopeless personage, he offered me a stake in his claim, and in doing so he saved my life. Were it not for him, I surely would not be here today. That I was never able to return this kindness is the great regret of my life. That man's name was Jimmy Huang, and his brothers were Tommy and Johnny, and I, too, was to become as a brother to the Huangs.

"And this is where the story begins."

Luyu Tully

Mariposa Springs, California, 1855

It had been nearly a year since John Tully's murder, and Luyu had given birth to their second child, whom she had named Kiku, for the little stream that flowed past their cabin. Like his brother, Kiku was a calm baby with a strong constitution. Istu, now twenty months old and already running and climbing and scrambling, adored his baby brother, though he was unintentionally rough, abrupt, and often overzealous with his affections.

With no help to care for and provide for her children, Luyu's life was more challenging than ever. She hardly had time to grieve John. Meanwhile little Istu was convinced his father would be returning, no matter that she'd explained otherwise on a dozen occasions. Already the trees were beginning to change color, and Luyu knew that she must begin stockpiling food in earnest for winter. Hunting and fishing were not easy tasks with an infant strapped to her chest and a toddler forever tugging at her sleeve. When Istu was not spooking the game, he was usually underfoot or running off, and more than once Kiku's crying had foiled her opportunity for a clean shot.

One chilly morning late in summer, Luyu managed to bag a pair of rabbits in the underbrush. With Kiku secured to her chest and Istu on her shoulders, too tired to walk on his own, Luyu was making her way home to dress the rabbits when she was startled to meet a man in the forest, not two hundred yards from the cabin.

"Howdy," he said.

He was a white man in a hat, tall, with a pitted red face and one milky blue eye. Though he was familiar from town, Luyu could not place him.

"Looks like you got your hands full," he said without offering assistance. "Where's your man?"

"There," said Luyu, nodding toward the cabin, where a plume of blue smoke was still trailing from the chimney.

"That's funny," said the man. "Because I was just in there, and I didn't see no man or anyone else. I did put some wood on the fire, though."

"What do you want?" she said.

"Well, I was thinking you could use a man up here. In fact, I'm sure of it. And it turns out I'm that man."

"I have a man," said Luyu, the baby stirring as Istu began to shift restlessly upon her shoulders.

"Now, that's what you said," said the man with the milky blue eye. "But let's just say that I happen to know otherwise. So, we may as well dispense with the stories. I know you're alone up here, and that you need help. Protection. That's why I'm here."

"I don't want you here," said Luyu. "I don't need any help."

The man scratched his neck. "Well, now, I figured the idea might take some getting used to. I mean, admittedly, this is not much of a courtship. But I suspect you'll cotton to me eventually."

"No," said Luyu, just as the man reached out and grabbed her by the wrist, wrestling the rifle from her clutches.

The baby began howling, Istu joining him almost immediately.

"You just quit your fussing and keep still now, boy," said the man.

With Istu kicking and screaming and threatening to fall off her shoulders, the man all but dragged them to the cabin and forced them through the front door, where they were greeted by suffocating warmth. The man wrestled a kicking Istu off Luyu's shoulders and pushed him into the corner, where he landed in a heap and continued wailing.

"Now, let's get a few things straight," said

the man, raising his voice to be heard over the crying. "Like it or not, this here is my house now. And we have got to set us some ground rules. And the first one is, 'less I'm talking to you, I highly recommend keeping your mouth shut."

With that the man took hold of Istu, lifting him by the collar and clapping a firm hand over the boy's mouth to muffle his screaming.

"I'm a patient man, but I have my limits. Shut him up," he said, shoving the boy across the floor to Luyu.

She wrapped Istu up in her arms and began to comfort both him and Kiku simultaneously as the milky-eyed man watched on impatiently.

"That's more like it," he said, once the boy had left off screaming in favor of sobbing into his mother's thigh.

"Now, as I was saying. I'm the new king of the castle around here. Without me you'll all be dead by Christmas, anyway, so you ought to be grateful I'm here. The sooner you all accept the new order, the sooner we're all gonna have a nice life up here in the mountains serving each other."

Luyu glowered at the ugly man and said nothing.

The man did not object to her silence.

"Okay, that's fine," he said. "Fact is, I prefer silence. Now, why don't you make us all something to eat, and we'll sit down here like a family and eat."

Luyu had no choice but to comply. She kept the baby strapped to her as she heated the grease atop the stove, Istu clinging to her side. The milky-eyed man sat down and kicked his leg up on the table, and ran a hand over his pitted red face as he watched Luyu. It sickened her to feel his eyes upon her like that.

"Just get it over with," she said as the grease began to crackle in the skillet.

"What are you talking about?"

"I see the way you look at me. I know why you came."

A yellow-toothed smile cut across his face. "Now, that just ain't true," he said. "I'm here to save you."

In that moment Luyu nearly tossed the popping grease directly in his face and clubbed him with the skillet, but she lost her nerve. Instead, she fetched the can of batter from the larder.

"You can call me Russ," he announced. "But I'll answer to 'sir.' "

In the coming days, Luyu was essentially a captive. She was Russ's servant, cooking and cleaning for him, fetching and warming water for his bath. He scarcely let Luyu or the boys out of his sight, watching them warily from the porch each time they went to the stream for water or to the privy. Russ always kept

711

the rifle close at hand, or at least out of Luyu's reach.

Late upon the third night, Russ decided he was done being a gentleman and forced himself upon Luyu, even as Kiku was nursing. He was not rough with her, though she knew the potential was there. Thus, as the days wore on, Luyu became increasingly submissive to his demands and advances, and Russ began to let his guard down.

"See, I told you," he said after she'd lain with him for the third time, Kiku asleep in the crib at the foot of the bed. "I said you'd cotton to me, and here we are. Trust me, you're gonna be awful grateful I'm here in six weeks' time, yes, ma'am. The mountains in winter ain't no place for women and children. Not without a man."

Luyu clutched his arm, nestling closer to him, wanting to vomit. She could feel the satisfied tobacco-stained smile upon his face. An hour later, he was sleeping like iron. An earthquake likely would not have awakened him. Luyu stole out from beneath the covers and groped her way quietly to the rifle beside the dresser. Clutching the butt and the barrel, she moved back to the bed in the darkness and set the end of the barrel to Russ's forehead. He flinched awake and his good eye bulged, but not his milky one.

Quickly assessing the immediate peril facing him, Russ remained on his back and did not move a muscle, looking straight up the barrel at Luyu, his yellow smile conspicuously absent.

"Now, listen here," he said calmly. "You don't want to do this."

The baby began fussing in the crib.

"You kill me and you'll answer for it," he said. "Pull that trigger and you might as well just —"

Then came the blast, then a ringing shock of silence. The silence ended abruptly when Istu and Kiku began howling simultaneously. Luyu plucked the baby from the crib and wrapped Istu in her arms.

"Sshhhh," she said, her ears still ringing as blood began to pool on the floor of the cabin.

Istu tried to look at the bloodied figure sprawled lifeless on the straw mattress, but Luyu shielded his eyes and held him tighter as he continued to sob desperately.

"It's okay," she said softly. "We must go now."

NORA BERGEN

Chicago, 1871

Having invested a small fortune in the infrastructure of Chicago, Nora Bergen had already quietly made a name for herself in Illinois by the dawn of the 1870s, exhibiting a business acumen that was equal if not superior to that of her benefactor, Abe Seymour. All this despite the fact that she refused to prize profit over ethical considerations, defying inequitable wage scales for her workers, forbidding conditions that she viewed as inhumane, shortening hours in her factories, bestowing benefits upon her workforce, angering her peers and competitors alike at every liberty she granted the common laborer.

Her trusted ally Mr. Trompette, though at times dubious with regard to such unorthodox practices, had little choice but to consent to them, so long as they were still profitable. Still, Trompette abided in his campaign to temper in Nora what he perceived to be an unhealthy contempt for the status quo.

"You would be wise not to ruffle too many feathers," he cautioned.

"And why is that?" said Nora.

"You wouldn't want to be viewed as some kind of an agitator."

"If by *agitator* you mean one who wants to bestow upon the workers a dignity worthy of their efforts, and wages commensurate to the profits they help generate, then I have no reservations about being viewed as an agitator."

"To put it another way," said Trompette, "you wouldn't want to make enemies."

"Rather I should exploit the people who account for my wealth to appease a class of greedy profiteers, is that what you're suggesting? Exactly what are they afraid of?" said Nora.

"I'm merely suggesting that these people might one day be useful."

"I have no use for people who believe themselves superior to others, people who believe their own interests carry more weight than those of the people who serve them."

"And that is your prerogative, ma'am," Trompette conceded. "I only hope this policy serves you well."

Among her class, Nora was quite unique in her sympathies, and just as Mr. Trompette suspected, this did not enhance her popularity among certain circles of industry, who viewed her as at best an outsider and at worst a firebrand.

Nora was at once amused and disgusted by the wealthy class, particularly the manner in which they flaunted their purported generosity, forever making a display of it when it was obvious to Nora that among their concerns, self-interest was paramount. Nora loathed those society gatherings she was occasionally persuaded to attend, often retreating to the kitchen to visit with the help, who never seemed to know quite what to make of her presence there. And how could she blame them? For likely they did not see in Nora an orphan who had spent the better part of her youth as a servant, but a woman of inexhaustible means who knew little of their struggles. Perhaps they viewed her visits as an unwelcome reminder of their station. Perhaps they were suspicious of her motives.

Once, at an extravagant affair hosted by a meatpacking magnate named Crowell, Nora was accosted in the corridor by none other than the host's wife, who was mortified by Nora's fraternization with the servants.

"How is it you're so high and mighty when you align yourself with such low company?" said the hostess.

"Because I am not aligned with them," said Nora. "I'm standing on their shoulders."

It was not long before Nora's reputation preceded her. Among the working classes of

Chicago, among the Blacks, and among the Polish and German and Irish immigrants who crowded the city's central neighborhoods, among the ironworkers, and the stevedores, and the stockyard hands, Nora was viewed as a sympathizer.

Despite her expanding influence in the world, like the city of Chicago, Nora found her abilities diminished. The trouble had begun several years earlier with the gradual onset of numbness in her feet, which soon alternated between the tingling of an unreachable itch and bouts of stabbing pain. It was only a matter of six months before her legs were beset by uncharacteristic heaviness, until soon she had difficulty getting out of her chair or dismounting a carriage.

As the months wore on, a certain listlessness began to take hold of her at all hours of the day. Even her equilibrium began to fail her. Twice over the winter she had fallen climbing out of bed. The second time she had nearly required Edmund's assistance in getting to her feet before she managed on her own with considerable effort and a bedpost to brace her. There was little doubt that the privation of Nora's early life, the neglect and malnourishment and crushing insecurity of it, had extracted its toll on her body and mind. Somewhere in the far West, Finn, too, was probably growing prematurely old.

Though Nora did her best to disguise these

difficulties, she had recently begun to suspect an awareness on the part of Edmund and other members of the staff, as well as Mr. Trompette, who, somewhat compromised himself by the ruinous effects of age, still met with Nora weekly to discuss any number of business concerns, charities, and, to a lesser extent each year, the search for her long-lost brother.

Regardless of the interceding decades, Finn continued to populate Nora's dreams upon occasion, and arbitrarily occupied her waking thoughts. Mr. Bolton, Mr. Keach, Mr. Mc-Cleary, Mr. Smithson; how many men had Nora and Trompette enlisted over the past fifteen years in the search for Finn? There was no end to the resources they had committed to this quest, nor any lack of imagination, speculation, or psychic energy. And yet it had been nearly three years since they had managed to obtain so much as a lead.

Her brother was an apparition, a ghost blown upon some western wind. By now, Nora entertained little hope of ever finding him. Thus it was with great surprise that Mr. Trompette arrived at the manor unannounced to convene with Nora in the library.

"I've brought news of your brother," he said.

"Have you? Is it good?"

"See for yourself," said Trompette, reaching into his leather attaché, where he fished out a newspaper clipping and presented it to Nora.

Nora tried to still her trembling hands as she clutched the clipping. The item, already beginning to yellow, was a year-old clipping from *The Burlington Free Press*. Voraciously Nora began reading the piece, which comprised six paragraphs depicting a disastrous house fire just outside of Denver City involving the family of an Arapahoe County legislator, whose wife and child might have perished in the fire *"were it not for the heroism of one intrepid citizen who happened to witness the blaze upon that late evening. This extraordinary individual proceeded to break down the front door and rush into the inferno at his own peril, saving woman and child only moments before the roof collapsed in a fiery heap. The good Samaritan, Finnegan Bergen of Denver City, declined to comment on the incident."*

Nora clutched the clipping to her chest.

"If we know nothing else at present," said Trompette, "we can at least take comfort in the fact that your brother is presumably quite alive somewhere in the western territories, hopefully still residing in Denver City."

"We must immediately send a —"

"I've already dispatched a Mr. Trembly, who comes highly recommended. He's a retired marshal living nearby in Boulder. And smart, too, not only a tracker but a philosopher and an investigator. I daresay he's our best man yet. But we shall see."

For the briefest of moments Nora let her heart thrill at this news before she checked her optimism, recalling Davenport, and Lancaster, and Omaha before Denver City.

Though to be sure Nora lacked nothing in the way of occupation with her various business concerns, and the rebuilding of the city, and her continuing advocacy for the displaced, still, it was three agonizing months before she received a report from Mr. Trembly.

"What does it say?" said Nora when Trompette presented her the envelope in the library.

"I haven't read it," he said. "I felt it wasn't my place. I thought you should read it first."

Indeed, the report was still sealed.

Nora tore open the envelope and removed the report, which consisted of two pages. Even as she began to read, Trompette excused himself to browse the bookshelves as though out of respect for Nora's privacy.

The crux of Mr. Trembly's report ran thusly:

"In the months following his act of heroism the night of the fire, the subject, Finnegan Bergen, continued to board at the house of Miss Gladys Springer in a second-story room at 1211 Larimer Street until February of the following year. According to Miss Springer, the subject, three weeks remiss in his rent, vacated his quarters early one morning, never to return. Divining my connection to the subject's family, Miss Springer immediately requested recompense in the sum of eleven dollars, nine for the rent, and two for damages. This request was fulfilled for the sake of Miss Springer's cooperation.

"Miss Springer characterized the subject as a silent sort, polite, and generally pleasant with no apparent predilection for drinking or whoring, which Miss Springer described as 'a refreshing quality around here.' According to Miss Springer the subject was employed as a laborer, most recently with the Colorado Central Railroad, though he had terminated his employment in February of that year, accounting for his financial difficulty. Miss Springer further stated that she was less surprised by the subject's heroism than she was about his 'bilking on his rent.'

"Miss Springer referred this investigator to three additional sources, all of them boarders in her house: a Mr. Kurtis Leonhardt, a Mr. Lincoln Mackenzie, and a Mr. Francis O'Leary.

"Mr. Leonhardt described the subject as 'not much of a conversationalist' and 'a decent enough fellow.' Mr. Leonhardt had no notion of where the subject might have gone once he abandoned his room at Miss Springer's establishment, and had little more to offer beyond the fact that the subject still owed him four bits, a debt also paid by this investigator on behalf of the client in return for Mr. Leonhardt's cooperation.

"The second source, Mr. Mackenzie, informed this investigator that he played chess with the subject on occasion, and found him to be a formidable if somewhat impatient opponent. Moreover, Mr. Mackenzie added that the subject was in his opinion a restless spirit who did not seem to feel at home in Denver City or anywhere else. When asked to speculate about the subject's whereabouts, Mr. Mackenzie commented that it 'depended on which way the wind was blowing the morning he left.' When pressed, Mr. Mackenzie said the subject was wise to flee the wrath of Miss Springer, and that if he was really smart he'd clear out of Denver City altogether. Knowing what little he did about the subject, Mr. Mackenzie's best guess was that Finn Bergen headed west into the mountains, where like as not he'd make a good meal for a grizzly bear.

"The final source, Mr. O'Leary, had worked for eight months with the subject in the employ of the Colorado Central and characterized the subject as 'unknowable.' Though they spent countless hours side by side on the job, Mr. O'Leary was able to glean very little with regard to the subject's past. Though according to Mr. O'Leary, the subject referred upon occasion to numerous locales including New York, Chicago, Iowa, and Nebraska, he never lingered in his reflections on these places. As far as Mr. O'Leary could surmise, the subject had no surviving family, and on several occasions alluded to childhood tragedy without ever elucidating the specifics. This, according to Mr. O'Leary, seemed to be a pattern with the subject, an inability to settle down. In Mr. O'Leary's estimation the subject would eventually drift west, though probably not before spring if he had any sense."

In conclusion, Mr. Trembly expressed his willingness to "sniff around Denver" through the remainder of winter "collecting information" and "making inquiries" before proceeding west in the spring, provided his contract was extended, and his expenses reimbursed.

Setting the pages upon her lap, hands trembling, legs numb, Nora Bergen no more recognized herself sitting there in the library than she recognized the subject of the report. What had this place done to them, how had it reshaped them? Suddenly a chill came over Nora as she worked her hands over her aching thighs.

"Edmund," she called from her place on the chair, the ancient quilted chair that was becoming her prison.

"Yes'm?" called Edmund.

"Dear, could you kindly bring me my blanket?"

"Yes, Miss Nora."

FINN BERGEN

Colorado, 1869

Finn took his leave of Denver City early one crisp, blue morning in February with precious few dollars to his name and even fewer options. The afternoon previous, he had nearly pawned the old blue locket for ready cash but couldn't bring himself to do it. Though the locket would never reside with Nora, L still stood for his love, and loss, and longing. How could he ever part with these things when they were all that he amounted to beyond a wool coat and a good pair of boots? The shine of his heroism, along with the fleeting celebrity and goodwill that briefly attended it, had begun to wear off abruptly the moment his money ran out in late January, particularly where the landlady was concerned. Miss Gladys Springer — she of the pointed chin and suspicious gaze — was not quick to forget a debt, let alone forgive one. In fact, she was downright single-minded in her attempts to collect on said debt with her daily reminders, innuendos, and veiled threats. But to her credit, Gladys Springer never threw Finn out on his ear as he'd seen her do with a handful of other boarders, and for this reason Finn experienced a pang of guilt at skipping out on her, even as he convinced himself he'd square with her eventually — somehow, some way.

His experiment in wandering had proved a failure, another dead end. He was no vagabond. Idleness did not suit him. It led him to contemplation and mental anguish. Being temperate in the ways of alcohol and suspicious of frivolity in any guise, and immune to the drudgery of Catholicism or any other religious affiliation, Finn acknowledged what he already knew: that he needed to occupy himself. Not only occupy, but wear himself out, body and soul, lest he spiral downward into that dark place. Like food and water, the mindless toil of labor was essential, and it protected Finn from himself.

But dirt farming was no more his destiny than hod carrying or Indian fighting. It seemed that to move was his only impetus, to continue his progress and not stop until he reached the edge of the continent, the end of America. Leaving Denver City behind, Finn followed the prairie wind west into the Rocky Mountains, bound for the Utah Territory. He reasoned that the railroad stood the best chance of delivering him to the edge of

America, for the railroad had already brought him this far. He'd laid rails nearly halfway across Iowa for the MMRR, and countless more for the Colorado Central. In Omaha he had witnessed the locomotives, the great steam-chuffing colossi that were to deliver America to the future, and they were indeed a sight and a sound to behold. But they hardly seemed a match for the mighty Rockies, which were far grander and more rugged than Finn had ever imagined. What were the green hills of Ireland next to these vast and inconceivable islands of rock?

For five weeks Finn journeyed southwest, skirting the Rockies, mostly, largely dependent on the kindness of strangers, fellow travelers bound by wagon train for parts west, men and women like the Vogels braving starvation, and the elements, and brutal terrain in search of a better life. Along his journey he ventured into the cruel and precipitous highlands. Such was the cold that some nights he was afraid to fall asleep for fear he'd never wake up. Other nights in his despair he would have welcomed such an end to his western odyssey.

In late March, windburned and half-starved, Finn finally caught up with the Union Pacific at the foot of the Wasatch Mountains in Ogden.

"What is the sum of your experience?" the foreman inquired.

"Years, sir. With the MMRR and Colorado Central, mostly."

"The prairie is one thing when it comes to laying track, son. These mountains, they are an altogether different proposition. Do you understand the risk?"

"Yes, sir, I do."

"And you agree to the wage?"

"I do."

Thus, Finn joined a crew that was Irish to a man. That the Irish more than any other group had accounted for the Union Pacific's western progress was a source of pride to Finn. That a Bergen should be among the men to lay the final rails and complete the transcontinental railroad seemed a worthy climax to his American odyssey.

In spite of the perilous conditions and the total disregard for the safety of the workers, setting aside the terrible wage and the flagrant profiteering of officials, Finn's labor felt more vital and essential than ever before. The days were as long as the light would allow, and not a moment of daylight was wasted as they blasted the mountains to dust. Daily, Finn brushed up against death in many forms, but fate, and caution, and more than a little luck, saw him through.

In the tent city west of Corinne, less than a mile from Promontory Point, where the golden spike was set to be hammered, and the Central Pacific's Chinese crew already awaited their arrival, the Union Pacific ran into trouble. First, a deluge washed out a spindly trestle above the canyon, temporarily halting their progress. No sooner had they reconstructed the passage than tempers flared, and a labor dispute escalated into an outright revolt, resulting in the loss of more than half their crew. It seemed the closer the Union Pacific drew to Promontory Point, the more fate was determined to thwart its progress. But American determination was not in short supply, and Irish labor was practically disposable and could be easily replaced by more Irish labor. Within a week, Promontory Point was within reach.

Four years after the end of the Civil War, on May 10, 1869, two days late, the all-Irish crew finally arrived at Promontory Point to meet the Central Pacific's all-Chinese crew, and the final two tracks were laid. Over seven hundred people gathered for the ensuing celebration as the two locomotives, one from Sacramento, the other from Omaha, were jock-eyed into place, poised nose-to-nose, so close they were almost touching.

There were banners, and ubiquitous flags, and a white grandstand festooned with red, white, and blue bunting. There were ladies in bright dresses, little boys in knee pants, and girls in bonnets. There were laborers with dirt-streaked faces and railroad officials in tall black hats, the waistline of their pants straining against their ample midsections. Among the crowd there were Germans, and Swedes, and Chinese, and Irish in abundance. They were short, and fat, and tall, and thin. They were wealthy and impoverished, self-made and delivered. And collectively they represented the great dynamic throng of America. They pressed in on the engines from all sides, the pitch of their eagerness nosing toward chaos, until officials were forced to clear the hordes from the track.

The great men, those architects of American progress, Hewes and Stanford, delivered speeches. They spoke of overcoming the impossible and of shrinking the world one track at a time. At last, they raised their silver hammers above the golden spike, and though they both missed their mark, they pronounced the job complete.

Finn was not among the eight Irishmen who laid the ceremonial track or stood nearby as the historic spike was driven, those same eight Irishmen who rode the rails laid by their Chinese brethren to Sacramento to be cheered in a parade, their wagons showered with flowers. Instead, Finn stood three-deep in the crowd and drank in the scene. A momentous event, to be sure. Nothing less than the culmination of America's greatest undertaking. And yet, for all the pomp and circumstance, the proceedings failed to stir Finn in the way he had hoped they would.

For that great historical connection of rail, that bridging of east and west, that great abbreviation of time and space, that blossoming of the nation, still wasn't enough to redeem this place that had taken his mother and sister from him, that had cast him aside as an orphan and set him adrift in the wilderness of the frontier.

Standing there on the summit, Finn listened for yet another call to another place that might yet redeem his mother's decision to seek out this nation and forsake their long history in Ireland. Maybe in California he would finally discover that promise he had not found in New York or Chicago, or in the river valleys of Illinois and Missouri, or in the endless high grass of the Great Plains, or in the rugged grandeur of the Rocky Mountains. Maybe, just maybe, this evasive place, this promise of belonging, lay still further west. Though Finn doubted this with nearly every fiber of his body, he was compelled to keep moving.

WALTER BERGEN

Mariposa Springs, Summer 2019

Maybe it was the wine, but after dinner a wistful mood took hold of Walter, which lasted all through the wedding rehearsal. He even got a little misty during the walk-through as he ushered Wendy down the long pretend aisle to the pretend altar.

"Are you crying, Dad?"

"Of course not," he said, turning away. "It's just the damn rehearsal. I'm saving the waterworks for tomorrow."

Wendy squeezed his hand and kissed him on the cheek. She looked so lovely, so feminine in her breezy summer dress, her hair the longest he'd seen it in years, her skin radiant, her smile so natural.

"You know, I'll always be your little girl," she said. "Just like you made me promise a million times when I was little. Remember?"

"Of course I remember. Like it was this morning. I never wanted you to grow up. Almost every day I wished I could stop the clock, And yet, here we are."

Walter squeezed her hand a little tighter.

"I'm sorry if I'm not what you imagined I'd be," she said.

"Are you kidding me? You're perfect," he said. "Angel, I couldn't possibly be prouder of you. You're smart, and kind, and principled. You're beautiful inside and out. How could a father ever ask for anything more?"

"I know it hasn't always been smooth with you and Kit, but, Daddy, she really does care for you."

"Smooth is overrated," he said. "The roads to the best places are usually gravel, right? What matters more than anything to me is that you love Kit, and Kit loves you — and that much is obvious."

"Oh, Daddy, I love you," she said, threading her arm inside of his and leaning her head into his shoulder. "We were so worried when we heard about the wreck that night. Mom was sure you were dead."

"I wished I was at the time. When I saw with my own eyes what I'd done. That boy. Seeing that boy all broken up like that, I thought of you, baby. What if that had been you?"

The floodgates nearly opened right then, but somehow Walter managed to hold back the tears, just barely. How had they arrived here so fast? How had his life outrun him like this? Had he not cherished each moment

733

enough? Had he failed to reflect on the minute-winning days as they passed one after another? Even the accident, four months removed, seemed like another lifetime. Thank God, the boy, whose name was Winston Chen-Murphy, had lived. And though the inquest had dragged on for months, and the hearings had been a continuing exercise in humiliation, and it was still not clear what would become of Walter's pension, all of that amounted to nothing next to the child's life.

Shortly after the walk-through concluded, Walter excused himself from the ensuing cocktail party and set out on an aimless stroll around Kit's family's property, four acres nestled in the hills a few miles east of Mariposa Springs. In the days of the gold rush, and even before, Mariposa Springs had been a sleepy western outpost, practically the only settlement east of the valley, and the last supplies before Reno on a route few people dared to take. The setting was idyllic: rolling hills of golden grass spotted with live oak and a smattering of pines, cut through with a tiny creek running low this late in summer. Far to the northwest, at the end of the long valley, Walter could just make out the distant dome of Mount Shasta.

From the remove of the little creek, Walter turned his back to the festivities and looked east, beyond the hills to the High Sierras, a gray ridge running north to south for four hundred miles, one massive batholith embedded in the earth's crust, pushed upward by tens of millions of years of relentless but ever-so-gradual subduction. In a world moving too fast, Walter took comfort in this timeless landscape. If only the movements of his own life would assume such an unhurried pace.

"You clean up pretty good, Mr. B."

The voice startled Walter from his reverie. He turned to find Kit standing there in her blush pantsuit, her hair grown out to a bob, a slight bit of mascara applied below her blue eyes, and just enough lipstick to make her lips look a bit more generous. The cumulative effect was a softening of Kit's features.

"Sorry if I surprised you," she said. "I just need to get away from all the activity for a minute, you know?"

"Me too," he said.

"I can leave if you —"

"No, no, I'm glad you're here," said Walter.

They defaulted to silence, and Kit joined Walter in turning toward the mountains, the little creek trickling at their feet. In the distance, laughter from the party could be heard, and hearing it from such a remove only seemed to enhance the quietude of the spot, high upon the hill, the valley behind them and the mountains before them.

"So much has changed," Kit said.

"Oh?" said Walter.

"None of that development was there when

I was a kid. That whole hill there used to be woods. There was an old cabin upstream, ancient, tiny, maybe twelve feet by ten feet, that was half–caved in. The place was supposed to be haunted because somebody was murdered there. We used to smoke cigarettes up there. You'd be crazy to smoke cigarettes in these hills anymore, what with the fires." With that, Kit let out a sigh. "I hardly recognize it anymore."

"Hmph. Wait until you're my age," said Walter. "You'll have that thought daily."

"God, I hope not," she said.

"Oh, I don't know, maybe it's not a bad thing," said Walter.

They settled back into silence, the party carrying on without them in the distance, the little stream burbling as it hurried on its way west. They were facing the sunset now, swathes of pink and orange and violet illuminating the great golden valley below. It felt normal, comfortable even, to be standing there next to Kit, and that was surely a step in the right direction. On the eve of his daughter's wedding, Walter reckoned that in a world that was forever changing, we were only as sure, and only as good, as our next step.

"Shall we?" he said, taking Kit's hand.

And together they began walking down the hill to the rehearsal party.

"You nervous?" said Walter.

"Not at all," said Kit. "You?"
"A little," he said.

GEORGE AND CORA FLOWERS

Galesburg, Illinois, 1854

Though frightened and anxious, their futures unknown, George and Cora were nonetheless smitten with their big-footed baby boy, whom they named Gale, after Galesburg, the town of his birth. Ostensibly healthy, if a little underweight, with a shock of dark hair, Gale was blessed with a calm disposition that served him well under the circumstances. So long as the boy was in his mother's clutches, he was agreeable to travel, even cramped in the sweltering rear of a covered wagon, hemmed in by a bulwark of caged poultry and grain baskets. As if the stink alone were not enough, the hens never ceased clucking as the wagon rattled along. That is how the Flowerses left Galesburg.

On this occasion it was a farmer named Hobbs to whom they were indebted, a hearty, gray-haired man approaching fifty years. Hobbs was a man who liked to inform.

"Up here on the left, that all used to be

woods when I was a boy. Trees as far as the eye could see. We used to hunt squirrel and rabbit up in there. Then about thirty years ago they started clearing it for farmland. Family of Swedes, Gustavsson. Whole mess of kids. Grew corn mostly. But some soybeans too."

Hobbs also reported on the weather:

"I don't reckon we're likely to see any rain, or I'd be feeling it down deep in my joints. Don't ever rain without my joints start aching the day before."

Cloistered behind the sorghum bins and the agitated chickens, Cora found Hobbs's voice comforting as they trundled along the uneven road.

"Now, me, I won't be departing the Prairie State anytime soon, not at my age. Not that I got any particular affinity for the place — I'm just old. But if I were a young man, I reckon I'd want to venture west like everybody else. Yessir, I figure O-re-gon, that would be the place for me. All the way out west on the shores of the great Pacific Ocean. Green hills and green pastures. They say the ground out in O-re-gon is softer. They say the soil is more fertile. And I hear where they're still giving away land out there. I reckon a body could just go about his own business in O-re-gon without anybody sticking their nose in a man's affairs. Don't many people live there, for starters, and them that do are liable to be cut from a different cloth. I reckon they don't make such a fuss about a man's color out in O-re-gon, but I could be wrong. The way I see it is —"

Hobbs stopped in midsentence and pulled the wagon to an abrupt stop, startling baby Gale awake in Cora's arms.

From the back of the wagon it was impossible to see what was happening, but Cora heard voices.

"Boy, who you yapping at all day long?" said a voice most assuredly not belonging to Hobbs. "I've been glassing you for the last mile, all the way since that rise back yonder, and your lips ain't never stopped moving once. Just what are you rattling on about, boy?"

"And to whom?" came another voice, lower, gruffer.

"Why, I was just singing," said Hobbs coolly. "Ain't no law against it. And I am not your boy. I'm born a free man in these parts, eighteen hundred and two, and a landowner besides. You must not be from around here, because you wouldn't have to ask far about the name Hobbs before someone set you straight on that account. Now, if you gentlemen would kindly —"

"Why the big hurry?" said the first voice, his boots mashing the gravel as he dismounted. "You act like a man with something to hide. Makes me think I ought to have a look in the back of your wagon."

"Ain't never seen a chicken?" said Hobbs.

As if sensing the tension, the horses began to snort and shift about restlessly in the road.

"Happens I'm looking for a particular kind of chicken," said the voice. "And I have reason to suspect he might be skulking in the back of your wagon."

In the depths of the wagon, Cora stilled the baby, grateful for the ruckus of the caged hens to drown out his whimpering.

"You ain't got no cause to stop me," said Hobbs. "Let alone delay my schedule."

"Oh, we got a cause," said the gruffer voice.

In the breathless depths of the wagon, George heard their feet moving deliberately over the gravel toward the back of the wagon, and he knew he must act in that instant. He looked at Cora meaningfully, and shaking his head, he felt a single unchecked tear streak down his cheek as he held a finger in front of his lips. It was him they were after, but they might take Cora and the baby, too. Because freedom for their kind was an illusion.

Throwing aside a stack of cages, George Flowers burst from the rear of the wagon trailing feathers and began running as fast as his legs would take him. He jumped the culvert and came down hard, scrambled to his feet, and took off again through the endless furrows of corn stubble. George knew he didn't stand a chance. He was running for

Gale, and for Cora, just trying to put a safe distance between the wagon and the men on horseback, so that Hobbs might drive his wife and child on to safety. And so George ran once again, ran like always, his ragged shoes over the corn stubble, the prairie wind whistling past his ears. But this time George Flowers ran with no hope for himself.

It was not until the first horse overtook him and George heard the second horse pulling up behind him that he dared to look back at the wagon, which was moving once again along the road north, a cloud of dust in its wake. The two men on horseback now circled round George, one of them smiling, the other glowering as they closed in on him.

As the wagon resumed its progress at a brisk but not urgent pace, the baby began to howl, though Cora could scarcely hear his cries over the squawking of the outraged hens. Stunned, Cora soothed the child, holding him close and blowing gently on his forehead as the wagon jostled them side to side. If ever she needed to hear a voice, a voice of direction, a voice of reassurance, any voice at all that might hold her in place in a world that seemed determined to break her, it was then, but Hobbs, no doubt anxious at the helm, was silent for the first time in hours.

Hobbs delivered Cora to a farm in Princeton at dusk, at which point she and the baby spent two nights on a mattress in the root cellar, well fed and well cared for. On the third morning, rudely awoken by Gale's hungry protestations, Cora opened her eyes to find the sunlight penetrating the darkness through the cellar hatch, twin shafts of light swimming with dust. As she nursed the baby in the cool darkness, she conjured a vision of green hills and green pastures, ground soft and fertile: O-re-gon. And in that instant Cora resigned herself and her child to that vision, to that idea, to that faraway promise called O-re-gon, not knowing that she was not wanted there.

MALIK FLOWERS

Seattle, Washington, 2019

Malik checked out of the Days Inn at eight A.M., but not before he ate his fill of free breakfast fixings in the lounge adjacent to the lobby, a feeding frenzy that included three waffles, a cup of yogurt, fruit salad, scrambled eggs, a half dozen sausages, and three glasses of orange juice. The snow had largely melted by the time he wheeled his bag down to the Link station and bought his ticket north, arriving at Hec Edmundson Pavilion a full three hours before tip-off.

A security guard escorted Malik to the bowels of the pavilion and down a concrete corridor to the locker room, where he was greeted immediately by Coach Cook, who shook his hand and sized him up.

"You've grown, Flowers. You ready to ball?"

"I was born ready, Coach."

"All right, then, let's get after it. Dress down and loosen up," he said, clapping Malik on the shoulder.

Malik found a locker and began undressing. Sitting on the wooden bench, he methodically laced up his wet sneakers. A few of the other guys were bantering among themselves in their nervous excitement, but at least half of them, like Malik, kept silently to themselves as they prepared. To say that he had not slept well the previous night was a huge understatement. Hours after the collision and the ensuing havoc, long after he'd snapped off ESPN, Malik's adrenals were still pumping. He lay on his back for what seemed like forever worrying about his mom and the logistics of his return trip to Portland, until finally he fell asleep, only to awaken to the ringing silence of the fifth-floor hotel room hours before dawn. He never quite managed to get back to sleep.

The massive breakfast had perked him up for a while, but two hours later Malik was hungry again, and his energy was low. Moreover, something seemed to be missing; something just felt off with his pregame ritual. He thought about fishing the little idol out of his front pocket — it always worked for his mom — but he couldn't risk the embarrassment of having to explain himself. And so he slipped into his uniform, then into his warm-ups, fighting off the uneasiness.

Coach Cook soon appeared, introducing himself to those who had not met him yet, shaking hands and slapping shoulders. Stationing himself at the head of the locker room, he opened by talking about the level of competition and the unique opportunity this matchup presented. This was where the men separated themselves from the boys, he told them. Finally, he began to address the playbook. They would be operating within simple concepts for the most part, a few zone looks and a lot of man coverage, and some press depending on the situation. It became quickly apparent that among Coach Cook's mantras was "take care of the rock," along with various other platitudes about "playing clean," "executing," and not beating yourselves.

Twenty minutes before game time, the pavilion was half-empty, but the crowd was still bigger than any Malik had ever played for. Who knew how many scouts were among the four or five thousand in attendance? During warm-ups Malik's wrist was stiff and a little tender. He wasn't hitting his midrange jumper with much consistency, but it was only warm-ups. Sneaking an occasional glance toward the other end of the court, Malik was able to identify a few of the players from his research: Ramsey, the seven-foot center from Oak Hill Academy, and Kahlil Howard, the point guard from Kentucky. Malik took particular note of number thirty-two, Jamal Victor, the junior from Memphis, already anointed by many scouts the most coveted prep player in the nation, and likely the player with whom Malik would be matched up much of the night.

Though Jamal Victor was the same age as Malik, he looked five years Malik's elder. While Malik possessed the rangy adolescent leanness of a boy still growing, Victor, at seventeen, had the thick-armed, broad-shouldered build of a full-grown man. At six foot eight and two hundred and fifty pounds, Victor would be a handful for Malik, even if Malik did have an inch on him.

Three minutes before tip-off, Malik shed his warm-up bottoms and began rolling his shoulders and neck to stay loose. He stretched his quads and hammies before huddling around Coach Cook with the rest of his teammates, every one of whom besides Mixon, whom he had played against, was a complete stranger to Malik: ten of the most promising prep hoops prospects in the western United States, the least gifted among them as skilled as anybody Malik had ever played with or against. On the opposing side were the best prep ballers from east of the Mississippi, from Illinois and Ohio, New York and Kentucky.

When the horn sounded, Malik took center court with the rest of the starters, wearing number twenty-three. As the crowd settled in and readied themselves for tip-off, Malik took a deep breath and closed his eyes in a final act of mindfulness, reminding himself to execute the little things: Set the screens, take care of the rock, mind his assignments. But stay loose, have fun, don't force anything. Let the game come to him. Like Coach M always said, "We *play* basketball, we don't work basketball."

Giving the crowd a cursory scan right before the whistle, Malik could not help but feel the absence of his mom.

East won the tip, no surprise, with their seven-foot-two center from Carmel Christian. West immediately dropped back into zone coverage. The point guard, a white kid — one of the few — from Columbus named Helms, set the offense, dribbling with his left hand. Two quick passes and a questionable pick later, Malik was saddled with his first foul when Victor lowered his shoulder on the way to the rack and Malik failed to set his feet in time to take the charge.

His mom had told him so.

To make matters worse, his wrist didn't seem to want to loosen up, the adrenaline wasn't doing it, and thirty seconds after drawing the foul he left his first midrange jumper flat. And suddenly, for the first time in as long as Malik could remember, he was experiencing a crisis of confidence. The game wasn't slowing down like it usually did. He was unable to visualize his success. He could not feel the calming sureness of it. After Malik left a little floater flat at the end of a dribble drive, he picked up his second foul at the other end on a nearly identical drive from Victor, who, unlike Malik, finished.

And just like that, he was riding the pine after the whistle. He didn't resume action until the nine-minute mark of the first half. On his first touch he caught a screen and drove baseline before pulling up and sticking a crisp ten-foot jumper. After grabbing the rebound on the opposite end, he hit another baseline jumper on the following possession. Two possessions later he drew a foul on his way to the rack before hitting a pair of free throws. Finally, he was feeling the juice. The game was coming to him.

West had a three-point lead at the half, at which point Malik had accounted for twelve points and five rebounds despite his limited minutes. Thanks mostly to Malik's coverage, West had held Jamal Victor to six points on three-for-nine shooting from the field. A minute into the second half, Malik picked up his third foul, a ticky-tacky hand check, but Coach Cook left him on the floor. Malik promptly rewarded this decision on the next possession with a nifty drop step on the baseline. He rewarded Coach Cook again eighty-four feet later on the defensive end with a contested rebound in traffic and a forty-foot outlet pass that led to an easy two points in transition.

West maintained a seven-point lead with

three minutes left in the fourth, despite a monster second half from Jamal Victor, who, largely frustrated by Malik's long-armed coverage in the low post, had moved his game to the perimeter and started raining down threes to the tune of five-for-six. Following a turnover, and another three-ball from Victor, West's lead was cut to four points at just under two minutes.

Coach Cook called a time-out to regroup. In the huddle he told them to bide their time and play smart, to protect the lead and wait for their shot. Don't force anything, he told them. After the whistle, Mixon immediately botched the inbound pass and East turned it into numbers and an easy transition bucket. The lead was down to two points with a minute forty to go.

On the ensuing possession, West worked the perimeter and the clock until an open shot presented itself at a minute ten, when Calvin Kearse from Bishop Montgomery launched a three that came up short and caromed off the front of the rim. East grabbed the rebound and immediately called a time-out.

East inbounded the ball trailing by two as the clock wound down under a minute. West pressed, hoping to force a mistake, but East beat the pressure and worked the ball down-court, setting their offense at the top of the arc. Catching a pick from the big man from

Carmel Christian, Neely, the scrappy if undersized guard from Scott County, let an open jumper fly from just inside the arc that tied the game with nineteen seconds left.

Coach Cook called his final time-out, and in the huddle he drew out a play to attack their man coverage.

"C'mon, now," said Cook. "Let's do this."

When the huddle broke, Malik took a deep breath. His whole body, from the soles of his Nikes to his scalp, felt electric.

After the inbound, Mixon set the offense, letting the clock tick down to ten seconds before swinging a pass to Richardson from Rainier Beach. Malik caught the screen but East executed the switch, and though he didn't get the look he wanted, Malik received the pass anyway. He now found himself squaring up in the face of Jamal Victor near the top of the key as the waning seconds ticked off the clock. Clutching the rock, Malik looked Victor right in the eye and held his gaze for another precious second before throwing a head fake that Victor bit on. With a sudden burst, Malik blew past him and drove to the rack, where no help was waiting. About five feet from the hole he left his feet and took flight, and the world seemed to slow down. He was floating on air, defying gravity. Rearing back with a handful of leather and a clear path to the rack, Malik let loose a yawp

as he brought the hammer down a half
second before the buzzer.

Luyu Tully

Northern California, 1855

Luyu's ears were still ringing, and the blood of the stranger was pooled thickly on the cabin floor as she strapped Kiku to her chest and hoisted Istu into the saddle amid the gathering light of the new day. Sugar, the bow-backed mare, now thirty years old if she was a year, balked at the load initially, but after a gentle word from Luyu, she resolved to carry them across the little stream, and over the hump, and into the thick of the forest.

Thus Luyu set out once again for the unknown, displaced, the destiny of her people. As they wended their way through the forest in the chill of morning, the sun in its eastern aspect casting long shadows before them, Kiku began to fidget and protest in his leather sling, restless to take his nourishment. But Luyu pushed onward until the baby surrendered to sleep, while behind her in the saddle, silent Istu, still shaken from recent events, clutched her about the waist with all his might.

Within an hour, the warmth of the sun began to penetrate the forest as Luyu fought hard to suppress the grief welling up inside of her. As if reading her thoughts, Istu clutched her still tighter from behind. When they neared the bottom of the basin they arrived at the familiar crossroad two miles before town. To the south lay Coloma and the Sacramento River Valley, a place already dead to her, a place where the Miwok, living or dead, would never again rest peacefully. To the north, beyond the great dome of Mount Shasta, past the well-meaning Methodists of her later youth, to the north and to the west, lay the unknown.

And so she chose life over death, north over south.

Within a day's travel, after they had escaped their perilous crossing of the Shasta River wet but otherwise unscathed, the trail arrived at a second junction. To the north lay a sprawl of folded green mountains as far as Luyu could see, and somewhere in the thick of them began the place called Or-e-gon. Beyond the verdant hills to the west lay the Pacific Ocean, which Luyu in her twenty years had scarcely ventured to imagine, let alone intended to set eyes upon.

She chose west.

And so west they traveled through the hills

and valleys for four days, sleeping under the sky, all but exhausting their meager stores until they arrived suddenly at a muddy outpost amid a timberless wasteland of scarred hills at the edge of the Pacific. The ocean itself was a wonder equal to the sky, endless and unknowable. The ugly settlement was an affront to such grandeur. The place soon revealed itself to be the town of Eureka, which did not to Luyu's eyes suggest any of the promise its name portended.

While it was the busiest place she had ever encountered, Eureka was not a place Luyu was happy to find. The town lay at the head of a sheltered bay, choked with floating timber, all about which the land was ravaged, the surrounding hills bristling with redwood stumps, cut through with rugged access roads and railroad spurs. To the west, a bustling port brimmed with schooners moving lumber out of the bay.

Eureka: *I have found it.* Eureka, the white man's vision of God's blessed bounty: commerce and industry, splinter and mud.

Luyu never intended to stay in such a place. But with her stores depleted, she was forced to regroup. Within a day she was fortunate enough to secure board at the home of a hatchet-faced old widow named Carlsen whose manner, at least initially, was as sharp as her face.

"You're a sorry sight," she said upon greeting Luyu on the front steps. "What is it you want, a handout?"

But it was not long before Mrs. Carlsen proved herself to be Luyu's ally. Not only did she agree to take Luyu on as a boarder, within the month she allotted her a small salary for domestic chores: laundering, cleaning, and seeing to chamber pots. Mrs. Carlsen even condescended to oversee Kiku and Istu, bottle-feeding the infant while occupying the toddler as Luyu went about her duties. From there her generosity extended to the instruction of Kiku and Istu in the ways of the "civilized world." It was only a matter of weeks before she bestowed the pet names Kiki and Izzy on the boys.

As much as Luyu disliked Eureka, she was beholden to the generosity of Mrs. Carlsen. This was a state of affairs that Luyu was both grateful for and at the same time ashamed of. But Mrs. Carlsen was quick to remind Luyu of her value.

"You're a breath of fresh air in a stinking town. These children of yours are about the only thing worth hoping for around here."

As much as Luyu grew to cherish the old woman's familiarity, life in the boardinghouse was cloistered and her work far from satisfying. She yearned for quietude and wide-open spaces. She could not commune with the spirits of the land in a place that churned such spirits to sawdust. Though Luyu did her best to disguise her ennui, it was not lost on Mrs. Carlsen.

At the dawn of the spring, after five months of Luyu's service, Mrs. Carlsen approached Luyu in the backyard, where she found her hunched over the washbasin.

"You do not like this town," she observed. "And I can't say that I blame you. I'm simply used to it, all the clutter, and the activity, and the ceaseless racket of the mills, though I'm beginning to suspect that you'll never acclimate yourself to it. Am I right?"

"I fear as much," said Luyu.

"It's settled then," said Mrs. Carlsen.

"What's settled?" said Luyu, straightening up to face Mrs. Carlsen.

"The place is sure to be in need of repair, and it's quite crude, but I think you'll find it to your liking."

The place to which Mrs. Carlsen referred proved to be a small hunting cabin built by the late Mr. Carlsen, nestled in the still-redwooded hills east of town. Though it was sorely in need of repairs, Luyu was up to the task, patching the roof and floor, chinking the walls, reclaiming the corners and the larder from the rodents, until the little cabin was tidy and habitable. Once again there were wide-open spaces and quietude, that the Tullys might live peacefully.

And they did, without interruption. For eight years, Luyu remained in the employ of

Mrs. Carlsen, commuting the four miles to Eureka, where, three days a week, Mrs. Carlsen continued the boys' education and, at least to her mind, betterment, while Luyu toiled long days with the laundry and cooking. Luyu could not say what she had done to earn Mrs. Carlsen's loyalty or affection, but she suspected that Mrs. Carlsen approved of her independence and self-reliance. If not a good life in the hills above Eureka, it was a better life than Luyu had come to expect in the absence of her husband.

Then, in the winter of the eighth year, Mrs. Carlsen took ill suddenly, and within a week died of a fever. Just when it seemed Luyu was destined to be uprooted once more, Mrs. Carlsen, by way of a lawyer named Tad Lundgren, bestowed her final generosity upon Luyu, leaving her the cabin in perpetuity. There, in the hills east of Eureka, Istu and Kiku grew into young men before Luyu's eyes, hunting, and fishing, and trading in town, not unlike their lives in Mariposa Springs might have unfolded under different circumstances. Their survival was hard-won, their lives earnest but uncomplicated, and mostly uneventful with regard to outsiders.

However, one night, in the winter of 1870, returning from Eureka, the late hour owing to an untimely departure, Luyu, along with Istu and Kiku, now sixteen and thirteen, respectively, found themselves traveling the last leg of their journey under the cover of night. The travel conditions soon grew worse. About a mile from the cabin the snow began to fall, further obscuring their path. But the horses led them by memory, plodding through the gathering snow, snorting into the chill darkness, as they proceeded deliberately over the uneven terrain.

When the cabin was just out of sight, the horses pulled up abruptly, balking, then rearing at the appearance of a dark form sprawled in the middle of the trail before them. Luyu settled the horses and dismounted, unsheathing the rifle fastened to her saddlebag before cautiously approaching the motionless form impeding their progress. At first, Luyu reasoned the dark mass was carrion, perhaps the remains of a yearling mule deer left for scavengers, but when she drew within ten feet, she could see it was the figure of a man lying flat on his back, a thin dusting of snow gathering on his person. His eyes were closed and his expression passive.

Bending down, Luyu placed her hand in front of his nose until she felt the faint warmth of his breath. Checking his pulse, she found it likewise faint. The man was unarmed and unfamiliar, and in his present condition of little threat to them. There was but one thing to do.

"Come," she said to the boys. "Get him in the saddle."

FINN BERGEN

Utah, 1869

The train skirted the northern edge of the Great Salt Lake before beginning its descent through the pinewood forests. At last the great chuffing colossus plunged into the high desert of the Great Basin, a sprawling expanse as wide and unfathomable as the plains, and looking out the window, Finn thrilled at the otherworldly spectacle. Here was an arid landscape, the likes of which in all his travels he had never seen: a vast panorama of parallel mountain ranges and valleys, smelling through the partially open windows of sage, pocked by creosote bush and little else. Yet, for all its bareness and inhospitality, an evocative landscape full of mystery.

After a water stop east of Wells, the train shuddered on through Elko, and Battle Mountain, and Winnemucca, contracting time and space as it sped boldly into the future. The desert landscape remained novel through the first three water stops. The repetition of it lulled Finn into a contempla-tive state of mind as he stared out the window. But as the journey progressed, the heat began to wear on him. The bareness and the dry-ness of the Mojave, the utter lack of shade or shelter, began to put him slightly on edge.

By the fifth water stop it seemed to Finn that the insidiously patient, bone-bleaching force of the desert epitomized his life: hill after barren hill, valley after parched valley, nothing and nobody to cling to. Finn was relieved when the train began climbing precipitously into the Sierras. For, there in the thick of the Sierras, hugging the moun-tainsides along impossibly narrow cuts, a thousand feet above a peril one could only guess at, with nothing but steel and hardwood and American ingenuity to deliver them, Finn began to feel once more the thrill of achieve-ment, even if it was not his own. He counted fifteen tunnels through the Sierras, all the while marveling at the feat of the Central Pacific, more specifically the feat of the nameless Chinese laborers who had blasted their way through those mountains, faces pocked with black powder and burned by nitroglycerin, hanging in baskets above vertiginous canyons, dangling by ropes, mak-ing the impossible possible so that the world could be smaller overnight, and all for barely half the wage Finn had collected laying rails across the prairie.

The wayward descent out of the High Sierras, from Dutch Flat through Cape Horn, dipping finally into the Central Valley of California, was a more gradual transition than the leeward climb that had begun a day earlier in Reno. In that respect, Finn reasoned, the Sierras were not unlike the Rockies: a barrier that seemed kinder and more promising when viewed from the west. That was Finn's hope as he arrived in Sacramento, still not quite at the edge of the continent, his bones humming from six hundred miles of rails.

Five hours later he boarded the great side-wheel steamer *Chrysopolis* on its journey down the San Joaquin River to Suisun Bay, and onward to Alameda and San Francisco. Perhaps the Golden Gate would make good on its promise where the Golden Door had failed. Perhaps California would embody the dream that drew Finn's beleaguered tribe to this country from the bogs of Ireland.

Upon approach, the city was promising, far more dramatic than any city Finn had ever encountered from New York to Chicago to Omaha to Denver City; San Francisco was a collision of steep hills and sudden valleys, the whole of it surrounded by water, from the hammered steel of the Pacific to the flat blue sheen of the bay hugging the peninsula. Even the names of the streets were a comfort: O'Farrell, O'Shaughnessy, Geary, McAllister.

His people had been here before him and left their mark. But it was the Chinese who had put their stamp on the city more than anybody else, and having traversed the cuts and tunnels of the Central Pacific, that was not surprising to Finn. Of all the neighborhoods in the city, none was more vital and colorful than the Chinese enclave centered around Portsmouth Square, with its bustling markets and storefronts and stalls painted red, and yellow, and green.

At a produce stand on Grant Street, Finn asked directions to the wharf from a boy of twelve or thirteen. The boy told him west and pointed him in that direction. When Finn was about to leave the stand, having paid for his carrots and cabbage, the boy asked him where he came from, and Finn told him Utah, by way of Colorado, by way of Nebraska, by way of Iowa, by way of Illinois, by way of New York, by way of Ireland. The boy asked him what brought him all the way to California, and Finn told him that he had come here to find out.

"You sound like my father," he said.

"And what did your father find?"

The boy looked over his shoulder at the man who was presumably his father, busy stocking bins in the rear of the space, then leaned in conspiratorially.

"Gold," he whispered.

Indeed, Finn had arrived at last in the

Golden State, the promised land. As much as he would have liked to cling to such a promise, after three days in the city Finn soured to the charms of San Francisco. For arm in arm with those charms walked the same busy hordes, the same filth and depravity, he'd witnessed in New York and Chicago. City life would never appeal to Finn. And so, with fifteen dollars in his pocket and nobody to hold him there, he kept moving as always, securing passage on a lumber schooner bound for the northern coast of California.

Three days later, he arrived at Humboldt Bay, where he was greeted by two dozen schooners just like the one that had delivered him there, all of them crowding in on the overburdened wharf.

Eureka: splinter, and sawdust, and grime. Eureka: mud, and timber, and relentless production. Eureka: raped hills and disfigured forests, a million red giants pillaged and maimed, the raw materials to fuel insatiable American dreams. Eureka: the future.

For three weeks Finn lived in a lumber camp north of the bay, working twelve-hour days laying short-gauge rails from hill to harbor through the mutilated forests. There, he found that his labor no longer sustained him, his sweat and toil were no longer enough to quiet his restive spirit. He had reached the edge of America and it seemed that there was nowhere left to go. He was a bottomless hole never to be filled.

He left his job before the month was out with nary a plan, or even so much as a whim. Without his labor to exhaust him, his restlessness turned inward on itself and began to eat away at the mental fortifications he had spent most of his life erecting. More troubling still, he found that he could no longer take shelter in his solitude. Finn yearned for human connection; to whom, he could not say.

With no clear objective, he took a room in town, and seeking the diversion of public life, he began for the first time in his life to frequent saloons, but soon found that the succor of spirits did not soothe or comfort him as it seemed to comfort most men. Instead, the spirits agitated his moods and amplified his empty yearning. His temperament, once steady and resilient, began to run hot and cold at turns. Knowing that the spirits did not agree with him, he still could not resist them. Just as the pulling of the cork liberated the spirits from the bottle, so imbibing the spirits liberated Finn's inner turmoil, discharging a lifetime of pent-up rage and dashed hopes upon anyone within earshot. Everything he had managed to suppress in his silence — the death of his father, the death of baby Aileen, his fleeing Ireland, the death of his mother, his forced separation from Nora, the subsequent wanderings across America that had yielded nothing in the way of wisdom — all of it spewed out of Finn's drunken mouth nightly for weeks, searing anything in its path. To hear him in this bitter aspect, it was hard to believe that he had ever managed to remain silent.

Had he revisited that silence to some degree, had he exercised any control at all over his venomous verbal impulses, he might have fared better in the rowdy saloons of Eureka. Instead, he found his unsolicited opinions and angry screeds roundly unwelcome by his fellow patrons. On a number of occasions he found himself enmeshed in barroom scuffles, only to awaken upon his naked mattress in the morning the recipient of lumps and bruises, which he had no memory of acquiring.

During one such altercation with a bald-headed giant at an establishment named the Iron Door, Finn received such a beating that his assailant accused him of liking it when he kept coming back for more.

"Where do you want it this time?" said the giant.

"It doesn't matter," said Finn, still on his feet somehow.

That was the final beating. Bloodied and bruised, Finn managed to leave the saloon under his own power that night. Disconsolate, he wandered to the edge of town, reeling, his thoughts taking their darkest turn yet. It occurred to him that his life was worthless, and should he choose to end it, not a soul would mourn his passing, whereas several saloon-keepers, after knowing him only a matter of weeks, might very well sigh with relief. Troubled by these ruminations, Finn kept walking past the darkened fringes of town and into the hills as a fresh snow began to fall. Had he been in possession of a rifle, he might well have ended his life abruptly then. Instead, he kept moving into the depths of the snowy night. He must have walked two miles, dried blood crusted upon his face, ears still ringing from the barroom drubbing, before he lost consciousness and collapsed in the snow.

When he regained consciousness sometime later — how long he could not say — he found himself slumped on horseback being led through the ankle-deep snow by an Indian woman and her two grown sons. Still dizzy and insensible, he did not inquire as to their destination, nor even question their ap-pearance in his life. He barely managed to keep himself upright until they delivered him to a small cabin, which appeared tinier still in the thick of a redwood grove.

They set Finn upon an upholstered chair in the light of an oil lamp, and the woman fed him black coffee.

"I am Luyu. My sons are Kiki and Izzy. You might have froze to death out there," she said.

"The world would have been none the

poorer," he said. "Perhaps you should have left me."

"That is the drink talking," she said. "What is your name?"

"Finn," he said. "But my name is of no account. I amount to nothing."

"I will ask for nothing," she said.

"Forgive me, I've come from a very long and unsatisfying journey," he said. "I have lost everything along the way, including myself. And now I've washed up here by no design whatsoever. You were kind to save my life. You didn't know any better. How could you guess at my despair?"

"I would not guess at such a thing," she said. "Here, have some broth."

This was the manner of Finn's savior; she absorbed his dissatisfied presence like water, neither encouraging nor discouraging his forthrightness. She was effortless and disarming in her demeanor, and unconditional in her ministrations. As to why she persisted in her kindness, Finn would never understand. She had nothing to gain by it.

For two days, Luyu nursed him back to strength, feeding him broth and flat cakes made of flour and corn.

"What about you?" he said over the rim of his tin cup. "I know nothing about you."

"What is it you wish to know?"

"Anything you are willing to tell me," he said.

Luyu proceeded to tell him how both of her parents had been slain before her eyes at the hands of overseers at Sutter's Mill when she was a girl.

"Dear God, I'm so sorry," he said.

"I hardly remember it now. I was so young."

She told him how she ran for freedom, narrowly escaping with her life.

"I watched a girl not two years older than myself die in the fields. I knew I had little choice."

She told him how the Methodists had taken her in, and how she had forever felt like an outsider at the Younts', how her true self had been bottled up, and her spirit was slowly suffocating.

"And so I ran away."

Finn listened raptly as she told him of meeting John Tully in Shasta City, and of their long journey through the mountains and the valley upon the bow-backed mare, and how she had at last found happiness with John Tully, and how they had built a cabin in the hills above Mariposa Springs, and started a family.

"But as you know, nothing lasts," she said.

Finn was horrified to learn of John Tully's murder, and Luyu's subsequent capture and enslavement in her own home up until the moment of the grisly reckoning.

"My God," he said. "And here I am complaining of my own dashed hopes and promises."

"This place is the land of broken promises," she said.

By the third day of his convalescence, Finn's vision had cleared, and the dizziness had left him, though his jaw still ached when he talked or chewed. Under Luyu's care, almost in spite of himself, Finn's tireless will to abide returned, and with it his heartier spirits.

On the fourth day, which was a Sunday, Izzy and Kiki were eager to hear of Finn's adventures, and Finn obliged them. Sitting by the stove in the corner, he regaled them with descriptions of the vast cities of Chicago and New York, of their grandeur and filth and head-spinning diversity. They hung on every word as he painted for them a portrait of the endless prairie, with its merciless heat and humidity and its bitter cold. He told them of awakening at dawn to the whole world's quaking, and how he had seen with his own eyes the endless procession of buffalo.

Izzy and Kiki were entranced. They wanted to know about the great Rocky Mountains, and Finn told them of the all-but-impenetrable granite fortress they presented. They wanted to know about the transcontinental railroad, and he told them of that final, historic run at Promontory Point, and the impossible journey through the Sierra Nevada.

And the more Finn spoke of the wonders of America, the more the wide-eyed boys leaned into his every word, the less Finn felt like he was lying. Somehow, some way, in spite of his experience, the sum of which had brought him penniless to the edge of the continent, he still believed in America.

"Where will you go next?" said Izzy.

Finn cast a sidelong glance at the kitchen, where Luyu was chopping onions.

"I thought maybe I'd give Oregon a try," he said.

"Why Oregon?" said Izzy.

"I don't know, why not?" said Finn.

But despite the return of his high spirits, his devil-may-care posture, and his dogged will to endure, a wistfulness marked Finn's final days with Luyu and her sons. Not since his life with the Vogels in Iowa had he been moved to any sense of belonging. The attentiveness of Luyu and her sons had given his life a momentary sense of purpose, if only to entertain. Had Luyu asked him to stay, whatever that meant, had she so much as hinted at any such circumstance, Finn would have stayed without question. At least for a while.

But such an invitation was not forthcoming. And so, Finn found himself as ever unbound and untethered, when early on the seventh morning, Luyu saw him to the front steps of the little cabin with a sack of food for his travels: quail eggs, boiled hard, and a good-sized hunk of bread.

"Thank you," he said.

"You don't need to thank me. The bread is stale, and the eggs are from summer. They smell okay, though," she said.

"I mean for saving me."

"If you say so," she said.

Somehow Finn was determined to disarm her matter-of-factness, to break through to her vulnerability before taking his leave of her. He longed to forge some lasting connection to Luyu, even if it was fleeting.

"It's true I said I no longer wanted to live, but I've reconsidered, thanks to you."

"Let's hope the eggs don't kill you."

It was then that Finn plunged his hand into his coat pocket.

"There's something that I want you to have," he said, presenting her with the neatly folded handkerchief, which she proceeded to unwrap.

"What is this?" she said, clutching the little blue locket.

"Open it," he said.

NORA BERGEN

America, 1899

It was raining when Edmund, now stooped, his hair a tight shock of white, came to fetch Nora from her bed as he did every morning. His strength had diminished; the days of Edmund's assisting Nora from bed to wheelchair were surely numbered. Edmund was not the only thing changed on the eve of the new century. The whole world had changed. Change itself had accelerated. What had seemed impossible a half century prior was now taken for granted. Why, a body could begin their week with steak and eggs on Rush Street on Monday morning, and by the miracle of the transcontinental railroad attend church services on Columbus Avenue in San Francisco the following Sunday. Almost overnight the miraculous had become the mundane.

The active life Nora had once taken for granted was long in the past, along with other staples that had marked the prime of her life, not the least of whom was her friend and trusted confidant Mr. Trompette, who had passed away not so suddenly of heart disease nearly a decade ago, leaving Nora's affairs in the hands of a young man named Lanning, with whom Nora rarely convened. Her business affairs were stable and mostly turnkey at this point, with most of her wealth consolidated in stocks and bonds, and the rest mostly consisting of railroad concerns she no longer managed. Nora's shrewd business acumen was of little more use than her withered legs anymore.

Though she'd never officially abandoned her search for Finn, the search had become mostly a symbolic exercise, yielding next to nothing despite the miracle of modern technology and the vast resources she'd committed to his pursuit for decades. As the years had passed, Nora had come to accept the likelihood that she would never reunite with her brother. The open wound left in Finn's absence had slowly grown over, though the scar it had left was tender.

Wheelchair waiting, Edmund hefted Nora under the arms and dragged her to the edge of the bed like a sack of potatoes.

"And how are you today, Miss Nora?"

"Rested," she said. "And you?"

"Tolerable, Miss Nora, thank you. Should I take you to the library? The week's mail is waiting."

"Yes, dear, please."

Edmund wheeled her down the long hallway to the library, parking her chair directly in front of the coffee table where her old quilted chair, formerly Mr. Seymour's, had once rested. In the gloomy light of the library Nora thumbed through the stack of envelopes, which included several financial statements from young Mr. Lanning, along with a number of appeals from charitable causes.

Among the stack of letters, however, was one of particular interest. With trembling fingers, Nora separated this one from the rest and unsealed the envelope, removing the letter.

February 18, 1899

Dear Ms. Bergen,

I write to you from the tiny outpost at Farewell Bend along the Deschutes River in Central Oregon, a place so far off the beaten path that no railway has yet managed to reach it. I first came to this place two years prior in search of my father, whom I never knew, and who never knew of me before his travels took him elsewhere. I knew very little about the man beyond the fact that for many years he worked for the railroad, and that he eventually wound up here in the high desert of Central Oregon, and even that was a matter of speculation.

I am not certain what inspired me to undertake this journey for my father, which began west of the Cascade Mountains, up north in Portland, where I live with my wife, Sarah, along with my son and daughter, whose names are Sadie and Finnegan. My name is Emmet, and I'm a former brakeman of eleven years on the Central Pacific, and now the proprietor of a reputable saloon, at least so far as saloons in these parts go.

It has come to my attention, Ms. Bergen, that you are a woman of considerable means, and it is imperative to me that you understand from the very outset that your wealth or standing has nothing at all to do with my contacting you. I hope to gain nothing by this correspondence but my own peace of mind, and perhaps some sense of the fulfillment that I might achieve from knowing my history. For, as it happens, Ms. Bergen, I am your nephew.

What little I know of my father, I learned from my mother, Jane McArdle, God rest her soul. As my mother told it, my father arrived in New York by way of Ireland in approximately 1850 at the age of ten, and was orphaned shortly thereafter. He was allegedly committed to an orphanage in the state of Illinois along with yourself, where he was subsequently adopted by homesteaders named Vogel bound for Iowa, at which point he was separated from you.

When he was of sufficient age my father left his adoptive family and for a number of years worked various jobs, primarily in the employ of the Union Pacific Railroad, or a number of its concerns. From what I gather, my father was primarily a drifter who made his way west over the decades with no real plan for himself. My mother claimed that he had resided in no less than six states before arriving in Oregon, where she met him at a horse auction in the little town of McMinnville, just south of Portland. They soon settled together near Hood River, briefly, whereupon they conceived yours truly. Shortly after my arrival, my father drifted east of the mountains without, according to my mother, ever knowing that he had sired me.

Though my dear mother had every reason to begrudge the man, she never had a bad word for my father, for whom she entertained considerable sympathy until the end. She claimed that my father was haunted, and as far as she could surmise, he was haunted by the memory of you, from whom he was separated at such an early age. Without siblings, this is hard for me to imagine, and I find it heartbreaking.

Thus I cannot help but feel that it would please my father's ghost for you to know that following my extensive search I found that my father is buried here, in Farewell Bend. Unfortunately, I can offer little insight as to the cause of his untimely death, and perhaps I am presumptuous in delivering this missive at all. It is possible that the memory of my father faded long ago in your consciousness, but somehow I doubt it.

It is my sincere hope that this brief accounting, such as it is, will be of some comfort to you. If not, please accept my sincere apologies for contacting you.

Sincerely,
Emmet F. Bergen

Numbly, Nora set the letter aside, gazing across the library into the near distance. And so it was done. At last she had her answer, though it was not what she had dared to hope for most of her life. Still, in a strange way the news came as a relief.

"Edmund," she said.

"Yes, Miss Nora?"

"Kindly accompany me to the bedroom so I might pack my bags."

"You plan on going somewhere, Miss Nora?"

"Oregon," she said.

Nora sent word of her intentions to Emmet Bergen via wire that very afternoon. The following morning she boarded the Overland Limited at Union Depot, a passage she insisted upon undertaking alone in spite of her trepidation, and in opposition to Edmund, who was clearly entertaining reservations as he saw her off at the platform, watching on skeptically as two smartly uniformed porters hoisted Nora's wheelchair, Nora and all, onto the train. From the window seat of her cabin, Nora watched Edmund recede as the train pulled out of Union Depot.

The Overland Limited to Portland took eight days, during which Nora's needs — only those needs she was unable to fulfill herself — were attended to dutifully by a handful of rotating porters. After a lifetime of self-sufficiency, it embarrassed Nora to be so dependent on others. But to a man the porters objected graciously to her genorosity, and each was tipped lavishly upon the conclusion of the journey.

As Nora had never ventured west of the Mississippi River, the journey was nothing less than a revelation to her. Not until she had crossed the sprawling prairies herself could she truly fathom their breadth. Not until she was confronted firsthand by the great continental barrier of the Rocky Mountains, rearing up suddenly out the plains, could Nora conceive of their grandeur and scale. And not until, by the wonders of American ingenuity, Nora had passed miraculously through this rugged wilderness could she begin to fathom the obstacles that America presented.

Hands trembling in her lap, Nora fixed her gaze out the window of the train as it pulled into Union Station in Portland, searching the crowd on the platform for a vision of her brother. Among the expectant was a dizzying variety of humanity, male and female, short and tall, round and thin, mustachioed and bearded, shaved and coiffed. And yet by the time the train came to rest with a hiss and a great chuff of steam, Nora had already spotted Emmet at the edge of the throng.

Even at a distance of a hundred feet, she recognized the face: the high cheekbones, and the full lips, pursed in silence, and the glorious head of untamable ginger locks. And even at a distance, she could see, too, the kindness of his mother's blue eyes. Here was Finn as Nora had never been able to see him, Finn as she'd been forced to imagine him as a young man. And the sight of him caused her eyes to sting with gratitude.

Emmet was standing front and center as the porters hoisted Nora down from the train in her wheelchair. Nora felt herself blushing at her own indisposition as the porters lowered her onto the platform, but Emmet's warm smile eased her discomfort immediately.

"May I call you Auntie Nora?"

"Please do," she said.

Within two hours, Emmet presented Nora to his wife, Sarah, a sturdy young woman with a kindly face, and his children, Finnegan and Sadie, both of whom bore an unmistakable resemblance to their father, and by extension, Finn.

"Twins?" Nora said.

"No, ma'am, a year between them."

"My goodness, just look at them, they're lovely."

Nora spent two days with Emmet and his family, where she was warmly received at every turn, almost as though she belonged. In those two short days, something awakened in Nora, and the fist of her heart seemed to open like a frostbitten hand regaining its warmth.

"Tell us more about Chicago, Auntie Nora."

"What's it like in New York, Auntie Nora?"

"Why did you never marry, Auntie Nora?"

On the third day, Emmet and Nora embarked on the journey upon the rails of O & CRR, traveling south through the gold-green promise of the Willamette Valley.

"Mother says Father loved it here in Oregon," said Emmet, somewhere north of Salem.

"I can see why," said Nora.

"My father, what was he like? I mean, when he was young?"

"He was kind, and loyal, and reliable."

"Why was he such a wanderer, do you suppose? Why did he never settle down?"

"That, I can't say."

They disembarked the train in the muddy little outpost of McMinnville, where they soon chartered a wagon to take them east over the Cascades and into the high desert. Their driver was a strikingly handsome man of perhaps forty-five years, the first Negro Nora had seen since she was hoisted off the Overland Limited in Portland.

"Apologies in advance for the rough travel," he said, looking kindly down upon her in her wheelchair, even as he contemplated how best to get her in the carriage. "Name is Gale, ma'am."

"A lovely name for a man, Gale," said Nora.

"Named after the great city of Galesburg, Illinois," he said, as though it was a point of pride.

"I, too, come from Illinois," she said.

"Don't tell nobody," he whispered in mock confidence, "but really I consider myself a native son of Oregon."

Regarding their journey, Gale had not overstated the case: The travel east over the mountains proved arduous, particularly for Nora, confined to her wheelchair and tossed about like cargo.

"My apologies," he'd call out after a particularly jarring stretch of road.

As for himself, Gale seemed to take it all in stride like one born to adversity.

For all Nora's discomfort, and her aching joints, there was nowhere she would have rather been, and no company she would have rather been keeping than Emmet, whose kindness and inquisitiveness, and easy familiarity, were a revelation.

"Perhaps the West suits you, after all," Emmet observed as they wended their way down the leeward side of the Cascades.

"Perhaps you're right," said Nora.

The four-day journey finally delivered them to the little outpost at Farewell Bend, a town so small that it made the Magh Eala of Nora's youth seem like a teeming metropolis. With Gale's assistance, Emmet lifted her out of the coach and they set her in the empty street, where a few miserable hens were scratching about.

"Best of luck, ma'am," said Gale, tipping his hat.

"Thank you, Gale, and safe travels to you."

Together, Emmet and Nora remained in the street, and watched as Gale rattled away, trailing a cloud of dust. When he cleared the corner and started up the hill, Emmet pushed Nora the fifty feet to the only inn in town, the Farewell Inn.

Nora's room on the first floor was crude and unadorned. The clapboard walls were thin and the wind could be heard whistling through the cracks. There was no bureau, no mirror by which to freshen herself up, only a pitcher of water, and a chamber pot, and a high bed, which she would surely require

Emmet's assistance to get into.

A few minutes later, Emmet tapped on the door. He wheeled Nora down the narrow corridor and out into the hardpan street. He pushed her down the main street, such as it was, which took less than two minutes. At the edge of town, he pushed her halfway across a potter's field, where he stopped finally before a humble gravestone marked only by the name Bergen and no dates.

"It's not much, to be sure," said Emmet.

"It's something," said Nora.

Indeed, it was more than something. Finally, after a half century of searching, of yearning, and speculating, and mourning, Nora had located her brother. That she'd been too late in her arrival was a misfortune she could now endure, for time and distance had softened the blow. That Nora now had the sturdy presence of Emmet beside her was perhaps the greatest salve she could have asked for.

Gazing upon her brother's grave in that field not unlike the blighted fields the Bergens had left behind in County Cork a lifetime ago, Nora recalled her hired man Mr. Trembly's report from Denver City, now more than a quarter century old. Specifically, Nora recalled the observation of Finn's fellow boarder Mr. O'Leary that the subject was "unknowable." Similarly, Nora recalled a certain Mr. Mackenzie's conclusion that the subject was a "restless spirit." Restless, indeed, for what other force might have blown him clear across the continent to this barren place on the ragged edge of civilization?

It seemed to Nora that more than anything else this restlessness, this yearning for something out of reach, or something missing, this incessant, unanswerable, unconquerable call that urged him, and all of them, collectively forward like a runaway train, this was America.

Standing there at the edge of the potter's field beside her nephew, Emmet, until the previous week a complete stranger, and now the only living thing tethering her to this place so far from home, Nora Bergen gripped his hand tighter and wept for the world.

ACKNOWLEDGMENTS

When I write outside the purview of my personal experience, which is often, it is my hope to honor and acknowledge those experiences I'm trying to bring to life on the page, and I could never in a million years do that myself. As much as I'd like to think I contain multitudes, I really only contain a lot of curiosity, and a willingness to ask the questions I think will help me get these experiences right. That's the goal: Get it right. If I fail in that mission, I probably asked the wrong questions. If I succeed to any degree, I owe it to those people who let me ask them questions, seek their opinion, and mine their personal experience.

For their assistance on various matters research related, I gratefully acknowledge the King County Library, Kitsap County Library, and North Olympic Library System; the state historical societies of Illinois, Iowa, Nebraska, California, and Oregon; the Owen Lovejoy House; and Knox College in Galesburg; the

Chinese Historical Society of America in San Francisco; and, for their various areas of expertise and personal experience, Shannon Evans, David Calloway, Christina King, and John Cox.

Thanks to my early readers: Chuck Adams, Harry Kirchner, Hugh Schulze, Thomas Kohnstamm, Katrina Woolford, Zachary Cole, Davis Slater, Brock Dubbles, Kaytie Lee, Doug Pope, Kurtis Lowe, N. Frank Daniels, Aaron Talwar, Emily Shepherd, Florian Raymond, Charisse Flynn, and Nellie Waddell.

A big thank-you to everybody at Dutton: Cassidy Sachs, Aja Pollock, Alice Dalrymple, and Rick Ball. I am greatly indebted to my editor, John Parsley, for his belief and confidence in me, and for helping me bring my work to the next level. And finally, thank you to my longtime agent and champion, Mollie Glick, for her editorial stewardship, advocacy, and boxes of food.

ABOUT THE AUTHOR

Jonathan Evison is the author of the novels *All About Lulu, West of Here, The Revised Fundamentals of Caregiving, This Is Your Life, Harriet Chance!, Lawn Boy,* and *Legends of the North Cascades.* He lives with his wife and family in Washington State.

The employees of Thorndike Press hope you have enjoyed this Large Print book. All our Thorndike, Wheeler, and Kennebec Large Print titles are designed for easy reading, and all our books are made to last. Other Thorndike Press Large Print books are available at your library, through selected bookstores, or directly from us.

For information about titles, please call:
(800) 223-1244

or visit our website at:
gale.com/thorndike

To share your comments, please write:
Publisher
Thorndike Press
10 Water St., Suite 310
Waterville, ME 04901